DIVING ADVENTURE

Roger very slowly put his face between the open jaws. It was like going into a cave. There was plenty of room for half a dozen heads like his.

He brought his entire head within two rows of teeth. Now if the jaws closed on his neck he would be trapped and nothing could pull him loose. He was glad his mother couldn't see him now – she would faint.

AMAZON ADVENTURE

Gone were the arid, sandy wastes of the Pacific coast where rain almost never falls. Below stretched brilliant green forests that never lacked for water. Winding streams made silver alleys through the green.

"Look at the pink cloud," exclaimed Roger, hardly believing his own eyes.

Sure enough, a coloured cloud drifted over the forest.

"Butterflies," said Terry. "Just a few billion of them. And there's another cloud – parakeets. You get your clouds in all colours in this country – green, yellow, red and mixed. Wait till you see the parrots and toucans. You'll think you're looking at a picture in technicolour."

DIVING & AMAZON
ADVENTURES

Willard Price

Illustrated by Pat Marriott

RED FOX

DIVING & AMAZON ADVENTURES
A RED FOX BOOK 0 099 48773 X

Published in Great Britain by Red Fox,
an imprint of Random House Children's Books

Diving Adventure first published in Great Britain by Jonathan Cape Ltd, 1970
First Red Fox edition 1993
Text copyright © Willard Price, 1970
Illustrations copyright © Jonathan Cape Ltd, 1970

Amazon Adventure first published in Great Britain by Jonathan Cape Ltd, 1951
First Red Fox edition 1993
Copyright © Willard Price, 1951

This Red Fox edition 2005

3 5 7 9 10 8 6 4 2

Red Fox Books are published by Random House Children's Books,
61–63 Uxbridge Road, London W5 5SA,
a division of The Random House Group Ltd,
in Australia by Random House Australia (Pty) Ltd,
20 Alfred Street, Milsons Point, Sydney, NSW 2061, Australia,
in New Zealand by Random House New Zealand Ltd,
18 Poland Road, Glenfield, Auckland 10, New Zealand,
and in South Africa by Random House (Pty) Ltd,
Endulini, 5A Jubilee Road, Parktown 2193, South Africa

THE RANDOM HOUSE GROUP Limited Reg. No. 954009
www.**kids**at**randomhouse**.co.uk

A CIP catalogue record for this book is available from the British Library.

Typeset in Bembo by Palimpsest Book Production Limited,
Polmont, Stirlingshire

Printed and bound in Great Britain by
Bookmarque Ltd, Croydon, Surrey

DIVING
ADVENTURE

Contents

1
Undersea City

About to descend to the sea bottom, they strapped on their gear – face mask, scuba tank, weighted belt, and fins.

"Ready?" asked Dr Dick.

"Ready," Hal said.

Ready for the great adventure. Hal Hunt and his younger brother, Roger, had made many dives in the past. But never to an underwater city. They looked over the rail of the research ship, *Discovery*, but could not see to the bottom. The idea that there were streets, houses, parks, factories down below seemed utterly fantastic.

"Over we go," said Dr Dick, and they dropped from the deck into the tropical waters of the Great Barrier Reef.

They sank rapidly through shoals of brightly coloured angelfish. Deeper, the many colours merged into a rich blue. They began to see the roofs of Undersea City. They felt like aviators winging down from the sky to a busy town.

Dr Dick began to swim and signed to them to follow. He led them to a broad avenue and they slowly dropped into it, until their feet touched the ground two hundred feet below the surface of the Pacific. A sign told them that this was Main Street. They half walked, half swam, among other men who were doing the same.

All were light on their feet. In fact, it was a little difficult to stay on the sea floor. They floated rather than walked.

The weight of the lead in their belts held them down, but was nearly offset by the density of the water. The result was that the least extra pressure of a foot against the earth sent them soaring like birds.

Mischief-loving Roger could not refrain from trying out his powers of flight. With a sudden push of his foot he bounced himself upwards a dozen feet and came down like an acrobat to stand on Hal's shoulders.

Hal, surprised, unable to see straight above him because of the mask, didn't know what had struck him. It might be a dangerous fish. He reached up to push it away. His hand encountered Roger's ankle.

He closed his hand on the ankle, brought the rascal down, turned him over and stood him on his head. Dr Dick looked on with tolerant amusement as the boy got back on his feet.

At the corner of Main and Research Streets Dr Dick stopped at a house somewhat larger than the others. Like all the rest, it stood on stilts about seven feet high. There were no steps up to the front door – in fact, there was no front door. Dr Dick went beneath the building. Then, with a thrust of his fins, he sent himself up until his head went through a hole in the floor. He clambered up into the house. The boys followed.

There was no water in the house. The boys and their leader removed their masks and tanks.

Roger's eyes were wide open in disbelief. He stared at the hole in the floor.

"Why doesn't the water come up into the house?" he squeaked.

Hal laughed. "You sound like Donald Duck," he said. But so did he.

Dr Dick smiled. "You'll have to learn to keep your voices low. The reason they are so high is that the air supplied to the houses down here is not like the air you breathe up above. There, it has a lot of oxygen and nitrogen in it. At this depth so much of those gases would be poisonous. Here you are breathing mostly helium and it's the 'squeak gas' – but you'll soon learn to talk low.

"Now, you asked why doesn't the water come up into the house. It's because we keep the air pressure in the house exactly the same as the water pressure outside."

Roger looked blank.

On a side table was a pitcher of drinking water. Dr Dick took a glass, turned it over, pressed the open end down into the water.

"You see what happens," he said. "No water goes up into the glass. The air in the glass keeps out the water. Every house, office and shop in town is kept dry in the same way. So long as the air is as strong as the water, the water is kept out. There's a dressing-room yonder. You'll find towels and some dry clothes."

The boys stripped off their gear and swimming trunks, towelled themselves dry, and dressed. They come out to find the living-room empty. Dr Dick called to them from another room. They went into what appeared to be an office. Dr Dick sat behind a large desk.

Alan Dick was a kindly man, with a twinkle in his eye, but looked just what he was – a distinguished Doctor of Science, Director of the Undersea Science Foundation which had built Undersea City and was in charge of its many experiments.

"Well," he said. "How do you like it in our new world?"

"It's amazing," Hal said. "A very strange world to us. Perhaps you'd better start by briefing us on what we are supposed to do."

2
Treasures of the Sea Bottom

"Let me tell you first," said Dr Dick, "what we are trying to accomplish here. Then I'll tell you how you fit in. We're here to study the best ways to use the fabulous riches of the sea.

"The world needs these riches. The land is not producing enough. After all, only one quarter of the world is land. All the rest is sea. We have dug out of the land a large part of the valuable metals. You don't hear any more about a Gold Rush in California or Australia – the gold is gone.

"The silver mines are being exhausted. Copper mines are dying out. There is a severe shortage of magnesium. A single big aeroplane needs a ton of it. There are five million tons of magnesium in every cubic mile of sea water.

"Manganese is necessary to make steel. Much of the sea floor is covered with potato-shaped lumps of manganese.

"There's plenty of nickel and cobalt in the sea. There are great reservoirs of oil beneath the sea floor. There are vast stores of potash, platinum, titanium, sulphur, zinc, uranium, bromine, tin, and diamonds."

"Why isn't something being done about it?" Hal asked. "Why aren't the mining companies interested?"

"They are," said Dr Dick. "Deeply interested. Many British and Russian firms and more than a thousand American companies are digging the sea bottom. They want to know how to do it better. Some of the big ones are paying us to find out. That's the reason why our Undersea Science Foundation was formed."

"And now tell us what we can do to help," Hal said.

"In a way," said Dr Dick, "your job is the most important of all. There's just one thing that the world needs more than metals."

"And what is that?"

"Food. Eighty per cent of all animal life is in the sea. And ninety per cent of the vegetation. And yet only one per cent of human food comes from the sea. That's a problem for naturalists like you. How can we get more out of the sea? How can we make the sea produce the kinds of food that people like? We have something to learn from the Orientals. The Chinese have been running fish farms for centuries. The Japanese make seaweed farms – seaweed is a good food. They grow millions of oysters in their oyster beds. And the oysters produce millions of cultured pearls that bring a good price all over the world.

"Whales should be protected so they can breed freely. The meat and oil of one whale is worth thirty thousand dollars. The Lapps don't go out in the wilds when they want a reindeer. They raise their own. We don't depend upon finding a wild sheep when we want some mutton. We have our flocks. We cultivate the earth. Why not cultivate the sea?"

Hal's eyes were shining. "Now I begin to see what you want of us."

"Of course you do," Dr Dick smiled. "We've followed your career with interest. Your father is a famous collector of animals and has sent you to many parts of the world to take land animals and creatures of the sea alive for zoos and aquariums so you have had a lot of experience as a naturalist. And we need a naturalist to head up these studies."

"But why me?" Hal asked. "There are many naturalists much older and more experienced." Hal wished at that moment that he was a lot more than nineteen years of age.

"You have more experience," Dr Dick said, "out in the wilds than a naturalist twice your age gets in the laboratory with his eye glued to a microscope. Don't be ashamed of your youth. It's just what we need – work undersea is much tougher than up yonder and takes plenty of physical strength and endurance." He looked Hal over. "You look as if you could stand the gaff. And your brother too. How old are you, Roger?"

"Fourteen."

"Big for your age. You look as if you could take on a gorilla single handed. You both understand the arrangement I made with your father. Besides helping us, you will be allowed to collect rare fish for his aquariums. So your career as take-'em-alive men will not be interrupted. Of course we will provide you with food and lodging. Perhaps you would like to see now where you will live. Your cottage is just round the corner on Barracuda Street. Let's go."

Changing back into their diving gear, they dropped through the "front door" and swam round to Barracuda Street.

3

Home Beneath the Sea

Entering their cottage through the hole in the floor, the boys found themselves in a comfortable living-room that opened into a kitchen, bathroom and two bedrooms.

"How do you like it?" Dr Dick asked.

"It's groovy," Roger exclaimed.

"Wonderful," said Hal. "Who would ever imagine a place like this at the bottom of the sea! But we don't need so much space. Two bedrooms – one would be enough."

"And one will be all you will have," Dr Dick said. "You see, there isn't enough housing to go round, so it's necessary for us to double up a bit. I hope you don't object to sharing your cottage."

"Not at all," Hal said. "In fact, we'll enjoy having company."

"I think you'll find Mr Kaggs good company," said the director. "He's a well-educated man of the highest moral principles."

Hal knitted his brows. "What did you say his name was?"

"Kaggs."

Hal was trying to remember. "Is he – a preacher?"

"Why yes. How did you know? The Rev. Merlin Kaggs. He's the pastor of our church."

"Merlin Kaggs," said Hal. "Yes, we know him."

"Fine. That makes it all the better. Since you are already friends you should get along very well together."

Hal thought bitterly, I'd rather share the cottage with a snake. But something kept him from saying it.

Roger was not so discreet. "Isn't that the guy who—"

"Pipe down," said Hal sharply.

He, or Roger, could ruin Kaggs's reputation with ten words. Kaggs was no holy man. He was a criminal with two murders to his credit. He pretended to be a missionary, went about with his hands clasped in prayer, and quoted the Bible while plotting to steal and kill. He had schemed to steal a pearl farm and because the boys stood in his way he had left them to die on a desert island.* Yes, Hal remembered the "Reverend" Merlin Kaggs only too well.

But perhaps the rascal had reformed. Dr Dick thought well of him. He was honoured in this submarine community. Hal was no tattletale. He believed in giving every man the benefit of the doubt. He must keep quiet – at least until he had had a chance to talk with the fellow

* As told in *South Sea Adventure*.

12

and find out whether he was the thief and killer he had always been, or was now a new man.

Thinking these thoughts he stood by a Plexiglas window looking out into the strangest street he had ever seen — a street swarming with fish.

"What made you choose this spot for your town?" he asked Dr Dick.

The director came to the window. "There's part of your answer," he said, nodding at the fish. "Sea life is more plentiful in tropical waters than anywhere else. And coral reefs attract fish. They eat the coral animals and they love to hide in the holes in the reef. The Great Barrier is the largest coral reef in the whole world — one thousand two hundred and fifty miles long — and harbours the world's richest sea life. The sea floor is full of minerals. So it's the ideal place for a study of oceanic resources."

Roger was peering out of the window. "What's that small building behind the cottage?"

"That, my boy, should be of special interest to you. That's your garage. Your car has already been parked in it."

"My car?"

"Well, not exactly. Underwater, it's better than a car. Really, a diving boat. You're our official errand boy, you know. You will carry messages, tools, supplies from one part of the town to another. You know how to drive a car?"

"Of course."

"Then you'll have no trouble with the glass jeep."

"Glass? How could it be glass?"

"Something new," said Dr Dick. "Other diving boats are made of steel – the Diving Saucer, Deep Star, Deep Diver, Midget Sub, Cachalot, Sunfish, and the rest. This is the first to be made of glass."

"Why glass? I should think glass would break."

"On the contrary, glass will resist sea pressure better than steel. The more you compress it, the stronger it becomes. Also, it has some fibreglass and plastic in it. Naturally, it's much lighter than steel. And salt water doesn't corrode it, so it can stay under water for weeks or years without damage. And the most wonderful thing about it is that you can see through it – ahead, behind, up, down, everywhere."

"Great," Hal said. "Who was smart enough to invent that?"

"The first was built by a physicist named McLean – the same man who invented the air-to-air missile. Director of the Naval Ordnance Test Station. He was awarded the Rockefeller Public Service Award of ten thousand dollars

14

for his invention. Ours is not like the original. We have improved it a lot for our own use. But it's still glass."

"Will it actually go deep without breaking?" Hal wanted to know.

"We think it can go to the deepest trenches of the ocean, thirty-six thousand feet down – nearly seven miles. That seems hard to believe, doesn't it? It hasn't been tested yet at such depths. Anybody who wants to take his life in his hands can go down with it that deep and see what happens. I wouldn't care to be the one. Here's a manual that tells you how to operate it." He handed Roger a small booklet. "And now if you will excuse me I must get back to the office."

Roger studied the manual, then popped out to the garage to examine the glass jeep.

Hal, left alone, thought sourly about Kaggs, though happily about the work that lay ahead of him.

Roger came back full of enthusiasm. "Greatest thing you ever saw. Want to take a spin?"

Hal was a little apprehensive. "Sure you can manage it?"

"It doesn't look too difficult. Let's try it out."

4
The Glass Jeep

It was the strangest garage they had ever seen. It was open to the sea and full of water. A large window in the roof let in light.

At first Hal could see no glass boat. Then he realized that he was looking straight through it. It had just enough positive buoyancy to hold it against the roof of the garage.

It was like the house – the front door was a hole in the bottom.

The glass diving boat resembled a large egg, about six feet long. The small end was the bow. There was a low seat in the rear for the two occupants. The boat looked rather like a large shiny bug because the four short jet pipes projecting from it were like legs, and a jointed arm stretched out ahead with jaws at the end ready to bite. This was the "grab" that could be used to seize objects, animals or fish.

They swam up and crawled in through the hole. The inside was dry and full of air. Roger closed the hatch.

"How do you get it out of the garage?" Hal asked. "I don't see any propeller."

"It works by jets – something like a jet plane." Roger was in his element. He enjoyed teaching his elder brother. "Each of those pipes is a jet, but they spout water instead of air. So they're called hydrojets. Hydro means water."

"Yes, I know," said Hal impatiently. "Get on with it."

"The rear jets push the thing forward. The left forward jet turns the bow to the right. The right jet turns the bow to the left. You can go up by pointing both forward jets down. You go down by pointing them up. You can even back up – by turning the back jets off and pointing the front jets straight forward."

"Yes, but how do you operate these jets?"

"Simple. See this lever? Push it up and you go up. Down, and you go down. Left, you go left, and right you go right. Over here into reverse and you go back."

"And that button?"

"That works the grab. Pull it out and the jaws open. Push in, and the jaws close."

"Sounds pretty simple," admitted Hal. "I wonder if it's as simple as you think. Let's go."

Roger started the motor. The glass jeep slid out of the garage and headed straight for the next house.

"Look out, we're going to crash."

17

Roger seized the steering lever. In his excitement, he pushed it the wrong way. The boat plunged towards the downstairs window.

In a panic, he jammed the lever to the right. The jeep turned smartly right, and threatened to take off the heads of some of the men passing along the street. Roger pushed the lever up and the jeep climbed like a scared cat.

It taught Roger two things. One, be sure you know what you're doing. Two, this jeep was like something alive. It could turn on a sixpence, shoot up like a meteor, drop like a falling star.

"It beats a car forty ways," he said.

Now they were passing over the roofs of Undersea City. All the roofs were flat – they did not need to be gabled since they never had to shed rain or snow. Both the roofs and the walls were covered by seaweed and molluscs, food for the thousands of fish. Clouds of fish parted before the bow of the glass jeep.

Columns of bubbles rose from the buildings and from the aqualungs of swimmers and pedestrians. A building marked AIR was evidently the point from which pressurized helium breathing gas was distributed by underground conduit.

There, with a small spire, was the church of which the

rascally Rev. Merlin Kaggs was pastor. Roger could hardly resist the temptation to nip off the spire. He high-jumped over it.

The jeep skimmed over what appeared to be a power plant turning out electricity to supply the town with light and heat.

There was a building that Hal guessed might be a desalting plant to turn salt water into fresh and distribute it round the town.

There were streets of residences, green with tropical growth. The houses were set in pleasant gardens with the most fantastic and beautiful plants – and animals that looked like plants – sea fans, coral trees, sea anemones, gorgeous gorgonias, waxy little animal flowers like tulips.

The principal shopping street appeared to be Main where shops had windows but no doors. Stilts anchored them to the ground and the entrances were underneath. People floated up into them and came out with plastic bags of groceries and household articles.

There was a dairy that advertised whale's milk, a book store announcing "Books on the Underworld", a restaurant, barber's shop, a shop that offered "Deep-down Souvenirs", a hospital, a pharmacy, a bank and a shop where one could buy "Jewels from the Sea-bed".

A man came out of a hardware store with a piece of iron machinery as big as himself.

"Golly," exclaimed Roger. "That thing must weigh half a ton."

"Up above, it would," Hal said. "Down here, he can carry it easily because the dense water helps hold it up."

There was even a pet shop – but the pets were not dogs, cats and canaries. They were dolphins, porpoises and ornamental fish.

And there were several shops specializing in diving gear, scuba tanks patterned after Cousteau's aqualung, fins, masks, snorkels and everything else the well-dressed underwater man would wear.

Now the scene changed. Here was a lovely underwater park with paths winding between the "trees", brain coral, corals like minarets, starfish, wonderful shells, giant clams and other strange and beautiful sights of the sea-bed.

On the edge of town was the industrial district where experiments in mining were going on. The sea floor was being explored by men with magnetometers that would detect any metals below the surface. Ore containing gold, silver, uranium, magnesium and other buried treasure was being lifted to the ship above by electromagnets.

Roger throttled down the motor and drifted slowly

over a great iron see-saw rocking back and forth like a teeter-board. "What's that?"

"A pump bringing up oil," Hal said. "You've seen them in the Gulf of Mexico."

"But there they were up on platforms over the sea."

"Yes, but that's a very poor way to bring up oil from the sea floor. It's terribly expensive to reach down so far to get at the well. Besides, it's extremely dangerous – the platform may be torn down by a typhoon or rammed by a ship. Great waves may destroy it. It's far better to get right down where the well is and escape all the things that can happen up on the surface. Watch out – there's something dead ahead."

Roger turned the glass jeep just in time to escape crashing into a towering cliff.

"It's the reef," exclaimed Hal, "the Great Barrier Reef itself."

The precipice rose as straight as the wall of a skyscraper. This was the greatest structure ever built by living creatures. It was greater than the pyramids of Egypt, greater than the Aswan Dam. It was one thousand two hundred and fifty miles long, stretching from one end to the other of the Coral Sea, walling in the north-east coast of Australia. And this colossal structure had been built by one

21

of the smallest of builders, the coral animal – so small that it was hard to see it without a microscope.

This part of the great Pacific had been quite properly named the Coral Sea because it afforded the finest display of coral to be found in all the world.

The coral cliff was the home of millions of fish. Some with hard-as-rock snouts battered off chunks and ate them. Countless small fish of every colour shot into caves and crevices in its surface to escape big fish-eating fish determined to devour them. Sharks were so numerous that the boys were glad to be protected, although they felt terribly exposed with nothing between them and these predators but a plate of glass. Moray eels and octopuses made their homes in holes. A writhing sea snake coiled around one of the jets. Sea anemones, clinging to the wall, stretched out their tentacles to sting any hand that might touch them or paralyse any small fish that might come within reach. Barracuda with open jaws rushed in to get a closer look at the boys and appeared much surprised when they banged into something they could not see.

Altogether, it was a bit terrifying. But suddenly a more friendly creature appeared. It was a dolphin, and the boys knew that the dolphin is the friend and protector of man.

The dolphin had a pointed, bottle-shaped nose. In that

way it differed from the porpoise, which has a blunt, rounded nose. Both are like man in one respect. They must come to the surface to breathe. But unlike man, who cannot hold his breath for more than three minutes, they could stay down some thirty minutes at a time.

They were like man in another way. They were intelligent. Along with their air-breathing cousins such as whales, they were the most intelligent creatures of the sea except man – who also must be reckoned now as a creature of the sea.

The dolphin, peering into the glass jeep, seemed to be smiling. The smile might be just the natural turn-up of the corners of the mouth, but it gave the boys confidence that here was someone who would never do them harm and just might become a good and faithful companion.

If anyone could win him over, Roger could. He had a way with animals. So had Hal. But Hal was so big and powerful that animals were a little afraid of him. They seemed to feel that they had nothing to fear from his young brother.

Roger turned off the motor and drifted. He tapped on the glass.

"Hi there, Mr Bottle. Come over and say Howdy-do. You're the finest gentleman in the sea. Come and get acquainted."

He kept on talking quietly and the dolphin seemed to be listening. "I don't suppose he can really hear me," Roger said.

"He can hear you."

"I don't see any ears."

"He has ears, but they are very small. He does most of his hearing without ears."

"How can you hear without ears?"

"You can't," Hal said. "But the dolphin can. Sound makes vibrations in the air or water. Delicate nerves in the skin of the dolphin feel these vibrations. Different sounds make different kinds of vibrations, and the dolphin can tell one from another. The sound doesn't have to be strong. Scientific tests have shown that even the splash of a falling drop of water causes a dolphin to turn his head in that direction and look. He knows pretty well what is going on around him at all times."

The dolphin was talking back. His speech was a sort of whistle and sounded friendly. It came not from his mouth, but from the blowhole in the top of his head.

"The dolphin has no vocal cords," Hal said. "But he has a big vocabulary just the same. They've made tape recordings of the dolphin's whistles and they find he has thirty-two different kinds of whistle. Each one means something different. Friendliness, fear, anger, weariness, pleasure, distress, a cry for help, and so on."

"Well," Roger said, "that's one way the dolphin is not like us. No human beings talk in whistles."

"That's where you're wrong," his brother said. "The bushmen of Africa talk in whistles. So do certain tribes in the Amazon jungle. Some Mexican Indians use whistle language, but can't express as many different ideas and feelings with it as the dolphin can. In the Pyrenees there is a whistling speech. Canary Island shepherds on mountain peaks three miles apart talk with each other in a whistling language.

"And the dolphin has another language – a language of clicks. It's not every human being that knows two languages. But the dolphin does. Dolphins that have been around human beings develop a third language – an imitation of the speech of the humans. In an oceanarium they get to understand what their trainer tells them to do, and they try to repeat what he says. They don't do too well with it because of the lack of vocal cords. But they understand it well enough to follow instructions. They even learn to answer in a low enough voice so that they can be heard."

"What do you mean, low enough voice? Can't you hear a high voice?"

"Not if it's too high for our ears. Sound is measured in kilocycles. A man can't hear any sound above twenty kilocycles. A dog can hear up to forty kilocycles. A bottlenose dolphin can hear sounds above a hundred and twenty kilocycles. He can make sounds that high, but it doesn't take him long to notice that his human friend doesn't hear them. Most of his talk to his fellow dolphins is up in that range, but he learns that he must get his voice down if he wants to talk with us. He must think us pretty stupid."

"I wish we had some fish to feed him," Roger said. "Then perhaps he'd stick around."

"That would help," said Hal. "But it isn't really necessary. You have to feed a cat or dog if you want to keep it. But a dolphin may stay with you just because he likes humans. You've seen them gambolling along beside a ship. They're not looking for food, but just want to play and enjoy the admiration of those creatures up on deck that they seem to think are very much like them.

"And so we are. They breathe air and so do we. They don't wear scales as the fish do, but have skins as smooth as ours. They have very highly developed brains and we think we have too. We are built more or less alike. We are mammals and so are they. We lived on land for ages and so did they. They once walked. They took to the sea again, but if you take a dolphin apart you find that what are now fins were once legs and all the joints are still there including five complete fingers. We don't know why they decided to go back to the sea, but today man also is going back to the sea – at least you and I are and thousands or millions will in the future."

"Look – a moray," Roger said, pointing at a greenish black tail projecting from a hole in the precipice.

The dolphin saw it too and at once undertook to capture the vicious moray eel, a choice meal for a dolphin.

Mr Bottle's jaws closed on the tail, then he paddled strongly backwards, trying to dislodge the snakelike creature from its retreat.

Roger thought Mr Bottle would win easily, for he appeared to weigh about four hundred pounds and the moray would not tip the scales at a hundred.

But the more the dolphin pulled, the tighter the eel wound itself into the rock crevice. Its muscles expanded and gripped the walls of the crack so firmly that it could not be pulled loose.

Mr Bottle had to give up and go to the surface for a breath of air. Then he came down and lay contemplating the moray, tilting his head to one side as if thinking things over.

A scorpionfish swam lazily out of the next hole. The scorpionfish is one of the most venomous inhabitants of the sea. The dolphin eyed it thoughtfully.

Then he chased it, swept down below it, and came up like a thunderbolt to plunge his hard bottlenose into the fish's belly. One blow was enough to kill the fish.

Then the dolphin seized the scorpionfish by the belly and jammed the poisoned spines into the moray's tail.

The moray relaxed like a punctured balloon and was easily pulled out of its hole. It was six feet long – six feet of good eating.

The performance gave a good idea of the almost manlike brain of the dolphin. He knew the scorpionfish had poisonous spines. He also knew he needed a tool to dislodge the eel. He didn't seize the fish by the back where the spines were but on the underside where there were no spines. He used this deadly tool to kill the moray eel.

"I can't believe my eyes," Roger said.

"You can believe them," said Hal. "Exactly the same thing happened in the fish tank of Marineland of the Pacific near Los Angeles. Spectators looking in through the glass windows on the side of the tank saw the whole act."

The glass jeep now floated lazily, without movement, near the coral cliff. The dolphin returned from his meal to rub his nose against the glass just where Roger's fingers were tapping it.

"It looks as if he'd like to get closer," Roger said. "Would it be all right to open the hatch?"

"Why not? Go ahead."

Roger dropped the hatch. Immediately the dolphin swam beneath, poked his nose up into the jeep, and whistled a friendly greeting. The jaws were open and the teeth looked sharp. Roger, a little timidly, reached down and stroked the creature's neck much as he would have petted the neck of a dog or cat. The dolphin made a series of soft clicks almost like a purr.

5
Mr Bottle and the Tiger

This happy scene was interrupted by a savage visitor. A huge tiger shark that had been swimming around idly at some distance, minding its own business, suddenly became interested in that open hatch. It came over at full speed, pushed Mr Bottle out of the way and thrust its whole head up into the jeep. Its jaws also were open, but how different they were from those of the dolphin. They were armed not with one row but with five rows of deadly teeth, the largest and most terrible being in front, the others getting smaller, the last row far back in the jaw not more than a half inch long and sharp enough to tear a man to pieces.

The shark is believed to be the only animal with five semicircles of teeth. They all tilt backwards so that once they grip their prey it cannot pull loose. The teeth are so keen-edged that they are used by primitive tribes as razors for shaving. They have been known to cut a man in two at a single bite.

The shark is believed to have been the first creature to grow teeth. Later they were adopted by the bony fishes, amphibians, reptiles, mammals and humans. Even the great tusks of the elephant go back to the shark's invention of teeth.

The shark liked teeth so well that it was not satisfied to have them just in its mouth. It grew them all over its body. The scales of the shark are really teeth. Every scale is pointed and sharp like a tooth, made of the same material, covered by dentine, and has a central pulp canal containing a nerve.

These denticles gave the tough hides of most sharks a roughness like that of sandpaper that can scratch or tear a swimmer's flesh. In fact, before sandpaper was invented shark hide called shagreen was used by carpenters to smooth hard wood. The teeth are so large and close to each other that it is difficult to drive a harpoon into the hide. Even bullets bounce off.

But the best, or worst, of the teeth are in the mouth. Why five rows? The shark is a tremendous eater — it may use its teeth a hundred times in a day. As the front teeth wear out the row just behind moves up to the front and another row begins to form far back in the mouth. The result is that the shark always has good teeth no matter how long it may live.

"I never saw such teeth," Roger said. "The front ones must be four inches long."

"Shark's teeth are the largest in the fish world," said Hal. "After all, they've taken a long time to evolve. Fossil shark teeth are found in rock a hundred and thirty million years old. And they are very much like those of today. So it must have been many millions of years before that when the earliest sharks began to be equipped with teeth."

"I don't see any molars," Roger said. "All the teeth appear to be cutters."

"You're right," said Hal. "They don't grind. They slice like a knife. The lion has terrible teeth but they can't compare with a shark's. The lion has to chew and worry at a carcass to get a mouthful – but a blue shark or tiger or mako can slide up to a victim in the sea and spoon off ten pounds without slowing down. Its teeth go through hide and flesh and muscle as if they were soft ice cream."

"Shark bite must hurt like the dickens."

"Strangely enough," Hal said, "it may not hurt a bit. It happens so quickly and is so clean that it may not be felt until later. The nerves don't have time to talk back. A Malay pearl diver swam up to his boat and said to his friends, 'I don't know whether a shark bit me or not.' They pulled him in and saw that he had been bitten in half just below the heart."

Roger, shrinking against the side of the jeep, felt himself all over.

"Just want to make sure that I haven't been bitten in half," he said. "Why, that monster must have enough teeth for a dozen men."

"Enough for twenty-two men," Hal said. "A tiger shark has about seven hundred and twenty teeth – man has only thirty-two. Of course I don't need to tell you that not all sharks are the same. Some have blunt teeth and seldom use them in fighting. The thresher shark fights with its tail and its bill, not its teeth. The whale shark has no teeth – it can't bite you, but it inhales you. The basking shark is one of the biggest of all, about forty feet, but is quite harmless. It feeds on tiny things no bigger than mosquitoes."

"I wish this thing would go away," Roger complained. "I'm getting tired of its company."

The tiger had no intention of going away. Instead, it gave a strong thrust of its tail and sent itself farther up into the glass shell. Now it might be able to reach either of the boys although they had plastered themselves up as tightly as possible against the glass.

The shark twisted itself within reach of Roger. Its jaws were about to close on his shoulder when it gave a violent start and dropped out of the hole.

34

"What happened?" gasped Roger.

"Your dolphin came to the rescue. He rammed his hard head into the shark's tummy."

"Would a shark feel that?"

"Not if it struck his armour plate. But his underside is soft, and the dolphin knows it. Dolphins have often killed a shark by one blow where it hurts most."

But this shark was by no means dead even though its small enemy had struck it harder than a mule can kick.

It wheeled about and went straight for Mr Bottle. The terrific size of the creature made the boys fear for the dolphin's life. Nearly all marine animals of the Great Barrier Reef are larger than their cousins elsewhere. The tiger was a good thirty feet long. It must have weighed at least seven tons, and the four-hundred-pound dolphin looked like a toy beside it.

The shark came on with amazing speed, maintaining its reputation as the fastest of all fish. In short bursts it could do fifty miles an hour.

The shark was not only the fastest and largest of fish, but the most dangerous. In that flashing moment Hal remembered what they had been told by one of the leading surgeons in Sydney. He had treated hundreds of cases of shark bite.

"It is possible," Dr Coppleson had said, "that sharks in

35

some other parts of the world are harmless, but in our waters they are certainly not. Here is a collection of over a hundred reports concerning men who have been attacked by sharks. As you can see, eighty per cent of these cases were fatal. We have here in Australia five sorts of shark that attack men: white sharks, tiger sharks, hammerheads, grey nurse sharks and makos. As Australians, we are ashamed to have to say that Australia leads the world in shark attacks and deaths."

The boys would never forget the tiger's eyes as they looked at that moment. They were blacker than onyx, and powerful, calm and cruel. No wonder that the English sea captain who in the sixteenth century had first placed one of these monsters on display in London named it from the German word *Schurke*, meaning villain. *Shurke* became shark. It was still the villain of the sea.

The boys were astounded by the gape of those open jaws. Now they understood the Australian report that a great white had been cut open and the remains of a whole horse found inside. This was possible only because of the elastic muscles between the upper and lower jaws – they stretch like rubber bands so that the villain can take in food larger than its own head.

Before their eyes, they saw this happen. The cavern with its seven hundred and twenty teeth took in Mr Bottle's head and shoulders before he could get out a single whistle or click and proceeded to swallow him whole.

It was more than Roger could bear. Mr Bottle had saved him, now he must save Mr Bottle. Forgetting his own danger, deaf to the shout of warning from his brother, he plunged out of the glass jeep and made straight for the villain of the sea.

He had no idea yet what he would do. He had a knife in his belt, but he had sense enough to realize that he might as well attack this monster with a tooth pick. He wished he had a spear gun – but that too would probably have been useless. He had no weapons but his bare hands.

He would try the dolphin's favourite trick. He swam beneath the shark, then came up with all the speed he could muster and rammed his hard head into the villain's tummy. The flesh went in like rubber but bounced out again like rubber. The shark didn't seem to mind in the least.

How about the gills? They were supposed to be very sensitive. Roger swam to the right gill and beat upon it with all the force of his fists.

The shark did not seem to feel it. It was too fully occupied in getting down its four-hundred-pound mouthful of food. This was a slow process, but very steady, and another inch of Roger's friend had now disappeared.

Roger could at least be glad that the shark had not bitten Mr Bottle in two. There was no need to bite it if it could be swallowed whole. If the shark changed its mind and closed its teeth that would be the end of Roger's dolphin. He must act fast, but what could he do?

He remembered that no fish liked to have anything on its back, whether it was octopus, giant squid, conger eel or sea snake. Or man.

He swam up and came down straddling the back just behind the head.

This bothered him much more than it bothered the shark. Roger was not protected by a rubber suit but wore only swimming trunks since these tropical waters were very warm. The teeth that covered the tiger's back pierced his legs. Trickles of blood began to turn the water pink.

The tiger switched violently. It had caught the smell of blood and that made it all the more determined to get this meal down as quickly as possible.

Through the pink mist Roger saw Hal coming to the rescue. Roger wanted to win this battle all by himself. What could his brother do? Nothing more than he could.

There was one thing he had not tried. He had battered the belly and punched the gill and tried to distract the creature by straddling its back.

But those great black eyes. They were more tender than stomach, gills or back. Roger leaned forward and sank his thumbs into the two black pools.

The shark took notice of him for the first time. It thrashed about violently, churning up the water, frightening away the reef fish. It took to swimming around in a circle, its tail beating violently while the tortured dolphin's tail beat as violently in front. Here was something new in natural history – a monster with a tail at each end.

Roger was nearly unhorsed by the frenzied creature's leaps and surges. He must not lose his grip and fall off. He pressed his bare legs more tightly against the cruel teeth, regardless of the pain, and dug his thumbs deeper into the eyes. His mount was now circling at such speed that Hal was left hopelessly behind.

Roger could see that his strategy was having some effect. The shark was loosening its hold on the dolphin. Roger had spoiled its appetite. Now it could only think of escaping those cruel thumbs.

Mr Bottle evidently thought that at last there was some hope of escape, and wriggled vigorously. The teeth no longer held him, but still he could not pull loose. The muscles of the great fish's throat held him fast. How could

Roger help free him from those great rubbery pincers that gripped his head?

The boy decided it was time for the last act. He leaned forward with the idea of helping the dolphin to prise himself loose, but could not reach him. He saw that he did not need to put his thumbs back into the shark's eyes; the pain he had already inflicted was enough. Enough to make the shark forget its meal, but not enough to rescue the dolphin.

If he could only get hold of the dolphin's tail and pull him free. Suddenly it occurred to him – there was a way to do that.

He slid off the shark's back, scraping himself more badly in the process. He turned about and got ready to meet the shark as it came round again. He saw that Hal had done the same thing. Between them they might be able to lay hold of that squirming black tail that projected from the shark's mouth like the tongue of a great snake.

Here it came, the weird double animal. The shark's bleary eyes did not see the two obstacles that lay ahead until within a dozen feet of them. One obstacle was big and the other only half its size. With a strong thrust of its tail the shark avoided the big thing and came within reach of the smaller one.

Roger grabbed the waving tail of the dolphin.

It was then that the shark made a serious mistake. It wrenched to one side to avoid the strange object that it dimly saw blocking its path. Thus it did what Roger could not have done by himself. With Roger holding firmly to the tail, the sidelong twist was enough to jerk the dolphin loose from the grip of those powerful throat muscles.

Out came Mr Bottle, so dazed by his experience that he lay without movement like a dead thing. For a moment Roger feared that he really was dead. Trapped in the shark's throat, he had been unable to get to the surface to breathe. Perhaps he had suffocated.

Roger must get that blowhole into the air at once. The air mixture inside the glass jeep would do. Hal came to help. One on each side, locking their arms around their helpless friend, they propelled him towards the jeep. The effort to move this inert dead weight of four hundred pounds made them breathe heavily from their scuba tanks, but at last they crawled up into the jeep and drew the animal's head above water.

Hal put his hand close to the blowhole. His face became very grave.

"Well," said Roger anxiously, "is he breathing or not?"

"He is not," Hal said. "I'll try artificial respiration."

But how do you practise mouth-to-mouth resuscitation with a dolphin? In this case it must be mouth-to-blowhole.

Hal placed his mouth over the blowhole and exhaled, inhaled, exhaled, inhaled.

He kept this up until he was blue in the face. It takes a lot of air to fill and empty the lungs of a dolphin.

Roger pushed him aside and took his place.

Hal put his ear to the dolphin's chest. "His heart is still beating. Keep it up – I think he'll come round."

Roger kept it up until he was completely winded.

He stopped to rest, while keeping his face close to the blowhole. He felt a breeze fanning his cheek. It came and went. He suddenly realized it was no breeze.

"He's breathing!" he exclaimed.

The dolphin's soft brown eyes were fixed upon him. A weak smile curved the animal's lips. Mr Bottle seemed to know to whom he owed his new lease of life. He clicked a little. It was a very faint click, more like the chirp of a small bird.

Roger and Hal still supported him. Roger stroked his neck. The animal's strength rapidly came back. Soon he was whistling and clicking like mad, saying a hundred thank-yous in his own two languages.

He began to struggle a little, and the boys let him go. He dropped out of the hatch and swam happily about.

A voice came over the radiotelephone. "Captain Murphy calling Hal Hunt."

Hal replied, "This is Hunt. Where are you, captain?"

"Over your head," replied the captain.

"It must be the *Flying Cloud,*" cried Roger.

This was to be their own ship for a while. They had chartered it in Sydney and had left it in the shipyard to be fitted with tanks to hold the fish and other sea animals they hoped to capture to send home to their father's aquarium in Long Island. It would carry their prizes to Sydney where they would be transshipped on cargo vessels to America.

They had named it *Flying Cloud* because of its glorious white cloud of sails.

6
The Good Ship, Flying Cloud

"Let's go aboard the *Flying Cloud*," Roger said excitedly. "I'll start the motor."

"No, wait," said Hal. "First we'd better talk about this a bit. We can't go aboard."

"Why not?"

"We might get the bends."

Roger objected, "You're off your head. You get the bends when you've been breathing ordinary air. We've been breathing helium."

"You're right – and wrong," said Hal. "It's true that you have more trouble if you've been breathing air, because air is eighty per cent nitrogen. If you don't come up very slowly and give your lungs time to get rid of the nitrogen it makes bubbles in your blood that cause cramps in your muscles and joints, and that's what they call the bends. The helium mixture that you've been breathing has only a small amount of oxygen and nitrogen, so you're not so likely to get a bad case of the bends. But still you have to be careful. I'll tell you what we can do. We can go up until the top of the jeep is just above the surface. Then we can get a good look at our ship. But we'll stay there only a minute and come right down. Now you can start the motor."

Roger looked at the dolphin, swimming round and round the jeep. "I just had a better idea. Let's go without the motor."

"How can you do that?"

"Let Bottle take us. He can be a big help to us if we train him right. Now's a good chance to begin."

He slipped out of the jeep and stopped the circling dolphin, who clicked and clattered affectionately and rubbed against him much as a cat rubs itself against the legs of a friendly human.

Roger took the end of the tow rope attached to the nose of the jeep and placed it in the dolphin's mouth. Then, with his hand still on the rope, he started to swim towards the *Flying Cloud*, gently drawing the dolphin along with him.

Once the dolphin separated his jaws and the line dropped out. Roger replaced it and pinched the jaws together to give his friend the idea that he must hold the line tight. The boy guided the dolphin close to the ship, where a rope ladder dangled to the water.

A sailor who had seen the operation came down and took the end of the line.

The dolphin had learned his first lesson. Hal understood

45

what Roger was trying to do. He wanted to make Bottle a good messenger between Undersea City and the *Flying Cloud*. The boys themselves could not go up and down without some danger of getting the bends, but the dolphin had no such difficulty. Dolphins could and did swim up and down between the surface and depths of a thousand feet or more without the least trouble. They were ideal delivery boys. A famous dolphin, Tuffy, made a name for himself as an expert messenger carrying mail, tools and supplies between the surface ship and Sealab II, two hundred feet down.

With the top of the glass jeep above water, the boys could plainly see their ship and the captain looking over the rail. They had met him before in Sydney, where they had chartered the ship along with Ted Murphy and his two-man crew.

Captain Ted was a genial man with a leathery face, tanned by the tropic sun and wrinkled by smiles and rough weather.

The *Flying Cloud* was Captain Ted's own ship, but it belonged to the boys as long as they held their charter. And they were very proud of it. From bow-sprit to rudder it measured eighty feet and had a beam of thirty. It was equipped with an auxiliary engine but depended chiefly

upon its magnificent spread of sail. Its engine served only to get it in and out between the reefs. Given a fair wind, its sails would carry it along at seventeen knots. Indeed it had formerly been used as a racing yacht and had won several of the annual cup races.

Hal had ordered the construction of specimen tanks, and the captain now assured him that they had been built – two large tanks for the large fish, and several small ones so that creatures who were inclined to eat each other could be kept apart. All the tanks had lids that could be left off in fair weather but clamped shut in rough weather so that fish and water could not splash out.

Hal congratulated the captain on a good job, then powered the jeep down. Roger was feeling his right shoulder.

"What's the matter, kid?" Hal asked.

"Nothing," Roger said.

"When you say nothing, it's something. Your shoulder hurts – right? We'll go deeper."

When the depth gauge registered nearly two hundred feet Roger showed relief. "Pain's gone," he said.

"Good," said Hal. "That was a near one. It just shows that we can't risk running up and down."

"Then how'll we ever get out?"

"When we get ready to come out permanently we will

have to come up very, very slowly to allow plenty of time to get rid of the nitrogen. A real case of the bends could paralyse a man for life. Remember that poor old fellow we saw in a wheelchair in the Hawaiian Islands? He had been diving off the coast of Lahaina to get black coral which grows only at great depths. That was forty years ago. He's been in a wheelchair ever since. He was lucky. Other black coral divers have died as soon as they got to the surface."

The dolphin faithfully followed them down. They parked the glass bug in the garage and crawled up into their cottage. Bottle stuck his head up through the hole and started a conversation.

"It's nice to get down again," said Roger. "Boy, wasn't it hot up there? Must have been over a hundred degrees." He looked at a thermometer on the wall. "Here it's only seventy-five."

"Yes," Hal said. "There's a lot to be said for undersea climate. It's really better than the climate topside. People who live beneath the sea will not be bothered by typhoons, cyclones, tornadoes and hurricanes, thunder and lightning. There will be no snowstorms or hailstorms, no sand- and dust-storms like those that plague the American West. No smog. No flood will wash away an underwater town, no fire can burn homes that are insulated by water. No noise except the croaks of croaker fish, grunts of groupers, and other small sounds. It's been called "the silent world". It's not silent, but its sounds are nothing compared with the roar of cars, trucks, trains and planes.

"There are plenty of difficulties and dangers down here but bad weather and noise are not among them. The temperature which goes popping up and down on land is not so wobbly beneath the sea. It stays about the same, day and night, week after week, year after year.

"You do have to watch out for sea animals that bite, scratch or sting – but wounds generally heal almost overnight. Cousteau found that out in his village under the Red Sea. On the ship up above, in the burning heat, ordinary cuts took as much as three weeks to heal. Below, the same wounds disappeared in two days. Something to do with the difference in bacteria. The men up above steadily lost weight. The men below stayed rosy and plump. There's a chance that in the future people who live out their lives beneath the sea will live longer, perhaps to well over a hundred."

Bottle was bouncing up and down, eager to play, work, do something.

"I'll give you something to do," Roger said.

He wrote on a piece of paper, *Just to see if it works*.

He put it in a plastic bag, tied the bag shut with cord

and put the end of the cord between the dolphin's teeth.

Would the dolphin remember the last time a rope was put in his mouth?

At once Bottle dropped out of the hole, swam swiftly upwards and out of sight.

In only two or three minutes he was back, the bag still hanging from his mouth. Roger was disappointed. "There hasn't been time for him to get up to the ship and back. I guess he's not as bright as I thought."

He took the bag and opened it. "Yes, my note is still there. You dumb dolphin! A fine messenger boy you are."

Idly, he unfolded the paper. Then he gave an excited yelp. Under his note the captain had written, *It works*.

Roger stroked the wet head of the dolphin. "I beg your pardon for saying you were dumb. You're as smart as they come. And how speedy!"

Swift delivery between sea bottom and ship was now possible. It was no small victory, and Hal was as pleased as Roger. But the most pleased seemed to be the dolphin. He whistled with pride and pleasure. But at this moment something or someone gave him a violent jab and he disappeared.

A face by no means so pleasant as the dolphin's came up through the hole.

7
Rascal or Saint?

Kaggs stared at the boys.

"Well, I'll be a donkey's uncle," he growled. "They told me somebody would be coming in but I didn't know it would be you."

"Nice of you to remember us," Hal said.

"I thought you were dead," Kaggs grumbled.

"You did your best to make sure we'd be dead," said Hal. "Last time we saw you was when you sailed away and left us to die on a desert island."

Kaggs smiled an evil smile. "Well now, that was just a little fun. Anyhow that's all past and gone." He tried to be a little more agreeable. "I'm sure you're not the sort to hold a grudge against anybody. There's no reason we can't be friends."

He climbed in and went to his room to take off his gear and get into dry clothes.

He came back and sat down. "Now, boys, I think we should have a little talk. Did the boss tell you I was here?"

"He did."

"Did you say you had met me before?"

52

"Yes."

"Are you going to tell him anything about – about what went on?"

"We can't promise," Hal said.

Kaggs's face darkened. "So, you can't promise. Well, you'd better promise. I belong here. You know I used to be a pearl trader in these islands."

"Or a pearl stealer," Hal said. "And now you think you have a good thing going here. The stealing should be good where men will be digging up gold and silver and perhaps diamonds and pearls and treasure from wrecks and rare specimens of animal life that will be worth thousands of dollars . . ."

"Now, now," Kaggs interrupted. "You have me all wrong. I know I didn't behave myself very well when you knew me. But all that is changed. I pretended to be a man of the Bible. Now I really am. I saw the error of my ways. I was a crook – you see I own up to it frankly. I went around under an assumed name, the Reverend Archibald Jones. I didn't tell anybody I had done two murders and spent a spell in prison. All that is behind me. I am here under my own name, Merlin Kaggs. That ought to be enough to convince you that I have changed. Now I think only of others – not of myself. Don't you think I deserve another chance? If you peach on me I am ruined. I want you to promise to keep mum."

"Don't you think you are asking too much? We should tell all we know about you so as to protect Dr Dick and people here against any more of your dirty work."

"But I tell you I've changed," protested Kaggs. "I've returned to my mother's knee. In memory of my saintly father – he was a clergyman, you know – I only want to do good from now on."

"Horsefeathers!" Roger exploded.

Kaggs looked at him severely. "Young fellow, that's no way to speak to a man of the Lord. I shall pray for you both."

He went to his room.

"I vote we tell Dr Dick all about him," Roger said.

His older brother shook his head. "I don't like to do that. There's just one chance in a thousand that he means what he says. Perhaps it's only one chance in a million – I don't know. Anyhow, there's no rush. Let's wait and see how things go."

"I'm afraid they'll go from bad to worse," his brother said. "Oh, I know how you feel – you've got the crazy idea that there's some good in everybody. That's because you've had too much to do with animals. There's some good in any animal, but I'm not so sure about people.

Especially Kaggs. I'm afraid of him. If we don't promise to be quiet, he'll try to do us in."

"That's a bridge we'll cross when we come to it," Hal said.

Hal was soon much too busy to worry about Kaggs. He had a hundred ideas. He boiled with ambition to put them into practice.

"First," he told Dr Dick, "I'd like to go fishing."

Dr Dick's eyebrows went up. This young naturalist had been engaged to do some very serious work. And right at the start he wanted to play hookey and go fishing.

Hal grinned. "I know what you're thinking. But I'm not really a playboy. In fact I think fishing is about the most important thing I can do. Millions of people are on the edge of starvation. But there are billions upon billions of good foodfish in the sea. Our fishermen don't get them. Oh, they let down a hook and pull up one fish, or a net and pull up a few dozen. Our ancestors did the same thing a thousand years ago. Fishing methods haven't kept up with the times."

"I agree with you," Dr Dick said. "Do you think you can spark a revolution in fishing?"

"I don't know. But I'd surely like to try. I've been thinking about it a lot. In New York before we came I bought modern equipment that should make it possible to bring up thousands of fish at a time instead of one or a hundred."

"What sort of equipment?"

"Slurp guns, stiletto lights, machines for fishing by electric shock, ultrasonic beam instruments, anaesthetics, milking machines to milk whales, laser beam units, and an airlift like a vacuum cleaner to pump whole schools of fish up into a ship."

Dr Dick was looking at Hal as if he had never seen him before. "I think we got more than we bargained for when we got you. Most of those things are new to me. Some of them I have heard of, but never dreamed they could be used for fishing."

"Perhaps they can't," admitted Hal. "That's what we will find out."

"They sound expensive," said Dr Dick. "I think the Foundation should pay for them. If you give me a bill I will see that it is paid."

"There will be no bill," Hal said. "Let's say they are the contribution of John Hunt and Sons to your project. After all, we don't know whether they will work or not."

"One question," Dr Dick said. "Many fish are no good as food. How are you going to find great schools of good foodfish that you can bring up by the thousand?"

"One way," said Hal, "will be to let our friend help us."

"Who is that? Kaggs?"

"No, not Kaggs. Our new friend is the gentleman who is looking in through the window. Dr Dick, meet Mr Bottle."

The scientist stared at the dolphin. "Why, that's just a dolphin – how can it help you?"

"Sonar," Hal said.

Dr Dick shook his head. "I don't understand you. But I have a lot of faith in you. Go ahead with your experiments, and good luck to you."

Hal and Roger took off again in the jeep and Bottle followed. This time Roger handled the stick expertly and he gave the windows of the next house a wide berth and ran no danger of nipping off the heads of walkers and swimmers in Barracuda Street.

"What are we looking for?" Roger asked.

"A big school of fish."

"But there are fish all around us."

"Yes, but most of them aren't good to eat. Just now we're interested only in fish that would make good food."

It was a long search before they found what they were after – a large school of fat fish all close together and pointing in the same direction like birds on migration.

"Just the thing," Hal said. "Tuna – fine eating. It has taken us more than an hour to find them. But it takes a surface ship days to locate a school of tuna. And then each fisherman pulls out one at a time on hook and line. All that makes tuna in the stores cost ten times what it would cost if the schools could be found quickly and easily and the fish could be drawn up by thousands instead of by ones. A lot of people around the world who can't afford to buy tuna or any other flesh could then buy it. I'll leave you for a little while."

He dropped out of the jeep, swam to the dolphin, petted him, then put his arm round his neck and swam with him to the school of tuna.

The tuna, as curious as most fish, gathered round the man and the dolphin. Bottle tried to grab one of them but Hal restrained him. He must not be allowed to frighten the fish by attacking them. He stayed for many minutes to give Bottle plenty of time to get it through his head that these fish were something special, something more important to his human friend than most fish.

When Hal thought there had been time for this lesson to sink in, he took Bottle back to the jeep.

He stayed a few minutes, then turned his companion round and set off again towards the school. Since the tuna had been swimming slowly they were not exactly where they had been before. This time Hal let Bottle act as the guide. The dolphin immediately set off towards the new location of the school. He didn't wait to be led – he towed his friend along so fast that Hal needed to do no swimming but simply to hang on. Again they visited the school, and again returned to the jeep. They all went back to the house but did not park the jeep in the garage.

After ten minutes in the house, Hal said, "Now we will see what he has learned. You get into the jeep ready to go. I'll be with you in a minute."

He slipped out and again put his arm round Bottle's neck. He began to take Bottle where the school was – or had been.

But Bottle would have none of it. He struck off in a different direction. Hal let him go, climbed into the jeep and followed him.

"It's no good," Roger said. "He's going in the wrong direction. He doesn't know what you want him to do."

"We'll see," Hal said. "Perhaps he knows what he's doing. Put on more power. He's shooting along like a torpedo."

The dolphin constantly clicked as he swam. "What's all the clicking for?" Roger wondered.

"Sonar," Hal said. Before he could explain, they sighted the school of tuna.

Before, it had taken them one hour to find the school. Now they had reached it in two minutes.

Roger was puzzled. "Why didn't he go where the school had been? Instead he took an entirely new direction."

"Sonar is the answer," Hal said. "Sonar is a way to use echoes. You know how a bat can fly around in complete darkness and avoid bumping into rocks, trees or anything else. It keeps making little noises that bounce back from anything they strike. The bat steers itself by these echoes. It can tell just how near it is to the object by the strength of the echo. The dolphin can do the same thing. That's why he keeps clicking – so he can guide himself by the echoes. And that's why he took a new direction. The school had been swimming and wasn't where it had been."

Roger objected, "But there must have been thousands of echoes coming from all around. How could he tell which echo came from the school of tuna?"

Hal shook his head. "Now you've asked the million-dollar question. Nobody knows – yet. The American Navy is spending a million dollars a year trying to find out."

"Why is it so important?"

"Because if we knew just how the dolphin's echo system works, we could make a machine to do the same thing. That may take many years. In the meantime they have learned some amazing things about the dolphin. One of their researchers, Dr Winthrop Kellogg, has found that the dolphin doesn't even need to see to find what he is after. Dr Kellogg blindfolded a dolphin and then threw a fish into the water. The dolphin went straight for the fish and swallowed it."

"That's hard to believe," Roger said.

"So it is. But here's something harder to believe. Kellogg proved that a blindfolded dolphin can tell the difference between one kind of fish and another. A certain dolphin liked mullet but hated sprats. He was blindfolded and put in a tank with both. He promptly went around the sprats and gobbled down the mullets.

"The dolphin, with his eyes still covered, was put in a tank with one mullet and one imitation mullet made of plastic. It was exactly the same size and shape as the real mullet. The dolphin gave it the cold shoulder and went straight for the real fish.

"Another dolphin was taught to play a sort of game of ball. The dolphin was shown a steel ball and at the same time he was given a fish. Then he was introduced to another steel ball just a tiny bit smaller and he got no fish. Then he was blindfolded and both balls were thrown into the water. He immediately shot down and brought up the larger ball and was given a fish. He repeated this performance twenty times without a single mistake. And there was so little difference in the size of the balls that the trainer couldn't tell them apart and had to use calipers to find out which was larger. But the dolphin's sonar took him to the right ball every time."

Roger looked at his dolphin with pride. "Golly, he's smarter than we are."

Hal agreed. "In some ways – much smarter."

"But there's one thing I don't understand," said Roger. "You've proved that a dolphin can find in a few seconds a school of fish that it might take a fishing smack many hours or even days to locate. But after you've found your fish, how do you get them up into the boat?"

"Good question," Hal said. "We'll try to find an answer right now. Hand me that radiophone."

He took the instrument and called, "*Flying Cloud*, Captain Ted Murphy, are you there? Captain Ted, glass jeep calling."

After a moment came the reply, "Murphy speaking. Is this Hal Hunt?"

"Right. Ted, we're going to send up some fish. Fill the big tank. We'll come near you and let up a signal buoy at the end of a line. Follow the flag and we'll guide you to the fish. Make ready to drop the vac."

"Got it," replied Captain Ted. "Okay and out."

"What's the vac?" Roger asked.

"The vacuum cleaner. You know – the big suction hose we bought in New York."

Roger looked puzzled. But he asked no more questions. He would just wait and see.

The jeep, aided by Bottle, led the ship to a point directly above the great school of tuna.

"All right, Ted. Let 'er down, and turn on the pump."

The great black hose snaked down. "Turn on the searchlight," Hal said. For centuries fishermen had known that a bright light attracts fish. Roger switched on the light. The tuna at once gathered near it.

Hal slipped out of the jeep and took the end of the hose. It was trembling with the powerful pull of the pump. Hal was careful not to put his arm near the nozzle. That was a good way to lose an arm. The suction was so great that it had been known to draw the blood out through a man's skin.

The vac was nothing new. It had been used for years by treasure hunters to suck up the sand that covered old wrecks. But no one had thought to use it for fishing. That was Hal's idea, and he had no notion whether it would work or not.

Fish shot into the hose faster than he could count them. He directed the nozzle wherever the fish were thickest.

Up they streamed, and into the tank above. Dozens, scores, hundreds made the climb within minutes. Their place was taken by other fish, crowding in towards the light, curious about this great black snake. They were swallowed by it before they could flip a tail. Within ten minutes the entire school numbering several thousand fish had gone aboard the *Flying Cloud*. A fishing smack would require days, perhaps even weeks, to equal this record.

Hal returned to the jeep and took up the phone. "That's it, Ted."

"Heavens to Betsy," came back the voice of the astonished captain. "The fish in that tank are packed together like sardines."

"Good," Hal said. "Take them in to Cairns and deliver them to the fishing co-op. And tell them how we got them."

Hal went to report to Dr Dick. Dick listened with wide-eyed astonishment.

"Never heard anything like it in my life," he said. "Do you know, young man, that you've just started a revolution in fishing? Fishing by dolphin and vacuum cleaner! I'm going to send the story in to the scientific journals and the Associated Press. The A.P. will syndicate it to newspapers all over the world. There'll come a day when every fisherman will begin to think in terms of dolphin and vac instead of hook and net. But will the supply of tuna hold out?"

"It's not limited to tuna," Hal said. "There are lots of other good foodfish that travel in schools – albacore, mullet, bass, cod, menhaden, barracuda, cobia, kingfish, wahoo, dorado and a hundred others. Of course my scheme falls flat when it comes to fish that don't school and are too big to go up a vac – swordfish, sawfish, shark, Pacific sea bass and so on. I'm thinking about other ways to get them."

"You have a good think-machine," Dr Dick said. "I'm sure you will solve that problem too."

8
Killer Whale

"We have visitors," Roger said when Hal returned to the cottage. "There they are, just outside."

Two other dolphins had joined Bottle. Now they came and thrust their heads up through the "front door" in the floor. All three sent up fountains of spray from their blowholes as dolphins and porpoises commonly do when they thrust their heads into air.

Kaggs happened to be sitting near by and got the full benefit of the shower. He leaped up, wiped his face, and said angrily, "That's the limit. I object to sharing this cottage with three wild beasts." He kicked at the nearest one, and all three dropped out of the hole.

Roger was annoyed. "That's no way to treat guests."

Kaggs growled, "They're no guests of mine. If you want to associate with animals, that's your lookout. Perhaps you're half animal yourselves. I'm above that sort of thing."

"I'm sorry they frightened you," Roger said.

"Frightened nothing," Kaggs retorted. "It would take more than that to scare me."

He promptly got more than that. He got the shock of his life.

Up through the hole came two terrific jaws. They towered up into the room five feet high. Both upper and lower jaw bristled with savage teeth. There were half a hundred teeth and each was as long as man's hand and sharp as a spear. The great mouth looked like that of a huge crocodile.

The monster gnashed these great teeth together with a sound like that of a machine gun. The terrified Kaggs shrank into the farthest corner of the room.

"It's a killer whale," Hal said.

That was enough for Kaggs. He slid along the wall to the door of his own room, got inside and slammed the door.

Here was a creature that had often been described as the "most fearful animal on land or sea". There were many stories of killers having bitten holes in small boats, upset the occupants, and swallowed them whole. And yet, whenever these stories had been carefully investigated, it was found that the attacks had been made by great sharks and not by killer whales.

"What do you suppose made him come around?" said Roger.

Hal said, "I suppose he saw the dolphins visiting us and he wanted to take a look too. He belongs to the dolphin family, you know – he's the biggest of all the dolphins. He's the fastest of them all and the most dangerous to other animals. Those jaws can bite a sea lion in two with one snap. He is not afraid of the largest whale. He will attack it, tear at its lips, get inside its mouth and devour its tongue – that's the bit of food he likes best.

"He has a stomach six feet long. In the stomach of one dead killer men found fourteen seals and thirteen dolphins. They had all been swallowed whole."

"But why would he attack dolphins? You said he belongs to the family."

"He does. But men attack men, don't they, and why shouldn't a great dolphin attack smaller ones?"

"But he didn't do anything to those three dolphins who had their heads in the hole. He just pushed them out of the way."

"I don't know why," Hal said. "Perhaps he thought they were going to attack us."

"What would he care if they did?"

"He's like the other dolphins," Hal said. "He's the friend of man. Oh I know there have been plenty of tales about him attacking men, but it's my personal opinion that they

68

are all nonsense. And I don't believe he has any desire to bite holes in boats. It's not that he couldn't do it. He could very easily. His teeth could go through a hull two inches thick. The thinnest hulls on all the oceans are the hulls of the Eskimo kayaks. They're made of sealskins less than a quarter inch thick, but there isn't a single reliable record of a skin boat being attacked by a killer whale."

"Do you think I could make a pet of him?" Roger wondered.

Hal laughed. "A pretty big pet. He must be thirty feet long and weighs as much as an elephant. But I believe you could do it. It has been done. At that oceanarium near San Diego called Sea World they have a pet killer whale named Shamu. He comes whenever you call him, carries articles here and there, draws a canoe by a loop over his head, tows a man hanging on to a fin, rings a bell, walks on his tail, leaps clear up out of the water, and even sings a song – though I wouldn't say he is a very good opera star. He lets men ride on his back round and round the pool at a terrific pace. He opens his mouth to have his great razor-sharp teeth brushed by a giant toothbrush. He actually lets his trainer put his head into his mouth."

"Do you think this one would let me do that?" Roger asked.

"I don't know. I wouldn't like to see you try it."

The killer whale was talking. "I think he's asking me to come and do it," Roger said.

Hal objected, "You're letting your imagination run away with you. I don't want a brother without any head."

Roger moved closer to the great mouth. The sight of it gave him a chilly feeling down his backbone. The jaws were as tall as he was.

Roger talked as quietly as he would have spoken to a kitten. He kept this up for many minutes, moving a little closer all the time. The great jaws stood open as if waiting for something juicy to fall into them.

Roger wished he hadn't begun this experiment. Hot and cold waves seemed to be running over his body. But he couldn't stop now. He wouldn't let his brother see that he was scared out of his wits. Nor could he let the animal know that he was frightened. That would only make him more likely to attack. If he really wanted to make the monster his pal he must go through with this.

Finally he stood close enough to touch the visitor. He did a little more soft talking, then gingerly reached out and stroked the smooth hide just under the chin. Cats, dogs, and dolphins liked this, perhaps killer whales did too.

"That's enough for now," Hal said. "Wait till later to do the rest."

"I think he's in the mood right now," Roger said.

He brought his hand up and stroked the lip. Then, still speaking quietly, he put his hand up over the sharp teeth.

Down came the upper jaw. The hand was lightly gripped between the upper and lower teeth.

It was a test, and Roger knew it. He had enough knowledge of animals to know that if he snatched away his hand now, his chance to become friend and trainer of this animal was gone. The points of the sharp teeth were not too comfortable. Those teeth could go through his hand like a knife through butter.

The teeth relaxed their hold. Now Roger could withdraw his hand. Instead, he reached farther in until his arm was in up to the elbow. Hal held his breath.

The killer was talking back and although Roger did not understand his language he felt that the tone was friendly. He slowly took out his hand and scratched the whale again under the chin. Then he brought his face close and looked down the monster's throat. It was big enough to swallow him at one gulp.

Roger rather expected to feel the hot breath of the creature on his face. But no air was stirring. Then he remembered that the breathing was done through the blowhole, not through the mouth. There was no smell from the mouth. A crocodile's mouth stank, because bits of the meat it had eaten remained between the teeth. But the killer whale did not chew his food – he swallowed everything whole. The teeth were for hanging on to wriggling fish, not chewing them. The teeth were all canines for gripping, no molars for grinding.

Roger very slowly put his face between the open jaws. It was like going into a cave. There was plenty of room for half a dozen heads like his.

He brought his entire head within the two rows of teeth. Now if the jaws closed on his neck he would be trapped and nothing could pull him loose. He was glad his mother couldn't see him now – she would faint.

9
Brave and Almost Brainy

Roger slowly withdrew his head from the jaws of death. He couldn't help heaving a deep sigh of relief.

His brother also was very happy to have the experiment over with. "Thank goodness," he said, "he could tell the difference between your head and a fish. He must be very intelligent."

"How about that?" Roger asked. "Is he really very intelligent? I always thought the elephant was about the most brainy of the animals."

"The killer whale's brain is about seven times as large as the elephant's," Hal said. "People who know the land but don't know the sea imagine that the elephant and the chimpanzee are the most intelligent of the non-humans. But experiments with the dolphins, including the killer, show that they have a higher I.Q. than any other animal we know about in the sea or on the land.

"A great trainer named Frohn who used to put on animal shows said about the dolphins: 'Of all the animals I've worked with, these are the ones who catch on quickest to what you want them to do.' You've seen the dolphin Flipper on TV. His trainer is O. Feldman, and he says, 'As soon as I can get him to understand some new trick I want him to do, he does it, and he'll never forget. Six months later I can give him the same signal, maybe no more than a click of my fingers, and he'll do exactly the same thing.'

"The famous scientist, Dr Lilly, who has made the study of dolphins his life work, goes even further. He says dolphins learn as fast as humans. The killer whale knows the difference between a steamer and a sailing ship. If he is chased by a steamer he goes deep to escape it. If he is chased by a ship under sail he knows that all he has to do is to go straight into the wind and the ship can't follow him.

"And killers have their own language. If one is attacked he can warn other members of the herd. The alarm can be sent instantly as far as six or seven miles away. If one is wounded by a harpoon-gun, the kind that a whaling ship carries on its bow, he warns others to look out for harpoon-guns, and to make them understand he must be able to describe the weapon so that they will recognize it when they see it."

"If he's so smart he should be able to help us a lot," Roger said. "But what can he do that a dolphin can't do?"

"Well, for one thing, he can pull heavier loads than any dolphin. He can easily tow a ton. He has the strength of a team of elephants. The dolphins can run many of our errands up to the ship and back carrying tools and loads of fish, but when it's something very heavy it will be a good job for the killer whale. The only question is whether we can get him to stick around."

"I think he'll stay with us," said Roger.

"I don't know," Hal said. "He's gone already."

Sure enough, the "front door" was empty. Roger anxiously looked out of the window. There he saw his new friend swimming about close by. Up and down Barracuda Street swam the killer whale and terrified people rushed to get into their houses. They knew a killer whale when they saw one by its dorsal fin six feet high, its black back and white belly, and terrible jaws, and they had read the wild stories of this evil creature, said to be the most fearful animal on land or sea.

But Hal and Roger and the other experimenters knew better. If everybody knew, perhaps the senseless murder of killer whales would stop.

Hal called up Dr Dick and reported what had happened.

"You've made an important contribution to science," Dr Dick said. "Your brother had a lot of courage — and brains."

"Yes," agreed Hal, "I think he's brave and even a bit brainy."

He saw that Roger was listening, so he added mischievously, "Almost as brainy as a killer whale."

The door of Kaggs's room slowly opened and Kaggs peered out. When he saw that the great jaws were gone he threw out his chest like a pouter pigeon and came in.

"Why didn't you stay to see the show?" Hal asked. "Were you afraid of our visitor?"

"Well – I – no, of course not – but I have more important things to do than to watch a stupid animal."

Roger resented the remark. He said, "If you think that killer whale is stupid you are pretty stupid yourself."

Kaggs glared at the boy as if he could shrivel him with a look. He opened his mouth to make an angry reply – then seemed to think better of it. After a moment he replied softly:

"There was a time when I would have flayed you alive for that. But now that I have made my peace with the Lord, all I want is peace on earth. And under the sea. As I said in my sermon last Sunday, much of man's destiny in the future will be lived out in this world beneath the waves – a world four times as great as the dry world above. Until now this has been a world of peace. But the troubles that infest that old world begin to threaten the new. The great powers are rivals for possession of the ocean floor. Russia's underocean fleet is twice the size of Britain's and

America's combined. America is arming her Polaris subs to be ready in case of war. We must avoid wars in the depths. And the way to ensure brotherhood between nations is to begin with brotherhood between man and man, between ourselves right here in Undersea City, in every home. And that means between you and me."

He enveloped both boys in a gentle smile that seemed strange on the cruel face they had known in the past.

"A very good sermon," Hal said.

Even Roger was touched. "I'm sorry I said what I did."

Kaggs's smile broadened. "That's all right, my boy. In this quiet undersea world I am sure we'll all find it easy to forgive and forget." He retired to his room.

Hal and Roger were silent for a few moments. Then Hal said, "Maybe he was sincere. What do you think?"

"I don't know what to think," said Roger. The three young naturalists, Hal, Roger and Bottle, had solved the problem of taking up a whole school of hundreds of thousands of fish and pouring them into a ship, thus doing in a few minutes what would have taken many days to accomplish by the old methods.

That would work well with small and even medium-sized fish. But how about the great ones, too large to go up a vacuum hose? The saw of the sawfish would not fit in any hose, the marlin's spear would puncture the vac. The wahoo was a whopper, the grouper and the giant barracuda grew to immense size, and some sharks were as big as telephone booths. Yes, and how about the whale?

"To get the big fish," Hal said, "there are a couple of experiments I'd like to make."

He went to the phone and called up Captain Ted.

"Ted, I'm going to send up Bottle. Give him the electro fishing outfit and the laser machine. I'm going to see if I can use them to hunt down the big ones."

"Very well," replied Captain Ted. "But I don't see how you can fish with those things. And I've spent fifty years at sea."

"You spent the last fifty years," Hal said. "The next fifty years may be different. Of course these things may not work – but I'd like to try them out. Oh yes, another thing I'd like to have – one of those packages of balloons and a bottle of compressed air."

Captain Ted laughed. "Now that's one for the book. Fishing by balloon! You're sure the helium hasn't gone to your head?"

"Perhaps it has," Hal admitted. "Anyhow, watch for Bottle."

"Will do," Ted replied, and Hal could hear him chuckling again as he rang off.

Bottle, as usual, was waiting and ready with his head poked up through the front door. Hal put a short length of rope into the dolphin's mouth. Bottle had learned by this time that this meant a trip up to the *Flying Cloud*. But Hal didn't want to do this rope trick every time Bottle was sent on an errand. So he pointed up, and at the same time looked up, and said very distinctly, "Ship – ship – ship." Other trainers had taught dolphins to obey spoken commands. Perhaps he could do the same. Again he repeated several times the word ship.

From the dolphin's blowhole came an answer. This time it was not a click or a whistle but an imitation of Hal's voice. It was not a very good imitation, but certainly the animal was trying to say, "Ship." He ducked out of the hole and shot upwards. Immediately the other two dolphins and the killer whale followed him.

"Good," exclaimed Hal, much pleased. "I was *hoping* that Big Boy would go along. That will teach him where to go when we send him on an errand."

In less than five minutes Bottle was back. Captain Ted had put a loop around his neck and to the loop was attached a net containing the articles Hal had ordered.

That was not all Bottle had brought with him. In addition to Big Boy and the two dolphins there were now half a dozen more dolphins. Dolphins love company, and they are very curious. These new recruits had evidently been interested in Bottle and his friends, the ship above, and Bottle's load of instruments, and now they were fascinated by the humans in the house below. They swam round and round the house, looking in at the windows, poking their heads up the front door, keeping up a continuous whistling and clicking. Hal was delighted.

"This is too good to be true," he said. "The more who join the gang, the better."

"Why do you want so many?"

"They'll come in handy later on. They'll make good cowboys for our cattle ranches."

"Cattle ranches?"

"Well, not cattle, but fish farms, lobster farms, oyster farms, crops of special seaweed that is good to eat."

"Who would eat seaweed?"

"The Japanese eat it all the time. They wrap it around rice, dip it in soy sauce, and love it. It's wholesome and nutritious. And there are a hundred million Japanese – that's a big market right there. And there's no reason why millions of people the world around shouldn't come to like this new food. But that's all in the future – let's get on with this job of catching big fish."

81

10
Shocking Way to Fish

The glass jeep carried the two fishermen near the coral cliff. Here they turned off the motor and waited.

There were thousands of fish poking about in the cracks, crevices, caves and grottoes of the coral precipice and they were a gorgeous sight in their costumes of red, gold, blue, lavender and dozens of tints and hues for which there are no names because they are never seen in the world above.

Some of these little beauties were very rare, possibly unknown to science. Aquariums would be glad to get them and pay well for them. But they were not what Hal wanted just now.

They were all small. Surely a big visitor would be coming along pretty soon. To avoid exhausting their aqualungs, the boys breathed the jeep's helium.

A half hour passed, an hour, an hour and a half. Finally a large swordfish appeared. Hal took up the electro-gun and slipped out of the jeep. He waited for the swordfish to come within range.

But the swordfish was not interested in him or the jeep. It swam idly here and there. It grazed on the plants sprouting from the cliff. It pushed its sword into a hole and brought out an octopus and looked very odd swimming about with eight tentacles wriggling from its beak.

"How can it get it back to its mouth?" Roger wondered.

The swordfish answered by scraping the octopus off against the cliff and caught the squirming thing in its teeth before it could retreat into another hole.

"What kind of a gun is that?" Roger enquired. "Like the dart guns we used in Africa?"

"Not quite," Hal said. "Those darts carried tranquillizer to put the animal to sleep. This carries electricity."

"How can you fish with electricity? You have the craziest ideas."

"Not so crazy," Hal said. "And it's not really my idea. The Swedes started it. They fish for tuna by electricity. The Norwegians use it for killing whales."

"Oh, I know," said Roger. "You shoot a bomb into the whale, it explodes and blows him to bits."

"No. That was the old way. It destroyed too much of the carcass. Besides, it was very cruel. Sometimes it didn't kill the whale instantly and it swam away before they could fire another charge. Of course a whale is a mammal, like ourselves, and its nerves are as sensitive as ours. So the whale would suffer terribly, for hours, perhaps for weeks. The new way is to shoot a harpoon charged with electricity. It is very sharp and penetrates the hide like a hypodermic without causing pain. And the electric shock kills instantly."

Hal had his head up through the hole so that he could carry on this conversation with his brother. Suddenly he dropped down as he saw the swordfish coming straight for the jeep. He raised the electro-gun and was about to fire when the swordfish, with a powerful flick of its tail, shot again out of range.

They had already waited two hours; now they waited another hour before Hal could deliver the final blow. The sharp hypodermic did its work and the swordfish lay still.

"But it seems cruel just the same," Roger said.

"Any killing is cruel," said Hal. "You and I prefer to take animals alive. But remember, just now we are not trying to get animals for a zoo. We are trying to find better ways to get food for people. And you can't get meat without killing. This way of doing it didn't hurt the fish one bit. Don't you think it was a lot better than stabbing the fish with a big hook in its mouth and torturing it for several hours before you can pull it aboard?"

He slipped out with a net which he threw over the swordfish and looped the rope around Bottle's neck. The eager dolphin shot up towards the ship, easily towing the big fish. Hal phoned Captain Ted to stand ready to haul the fish aboard.

But the young naturalist was disappointed with his experiment. He considered that it was a failure. It had taken three hours to get one fish. Such a slow procedure would never feed the world's hungry millions.

But there was the laser. It was something quite new. He had never used it before. He examined the instrument. It was about the size of a cine-camera.

Roger said, "Is this all there is to it? I don't see any harpoon or gun or anything."

"Yes," Hal said. "This is all there is to it. But it's a pretty wonderful thing. That electro-gun isn't much good unless what you're shooting at is not more than thirty feet away. This will reach a hundred thousand miles."

Roger was incredulous. "You're putting me on."

"No, I'm not. Astronauts half-way to the moon could use it to talk to the earth. It sends out a beam of light and a voice can go along on the beam."

"I'll bet anything that could do that will be terribly expensive."

"The first ones were. But an I.B.M. research man, Dr Peter Sorokin, has invented this cheap model. I bought this for only fifty dollars."

"But what use is it to you? Do you want to talk to the fish?"

"No, but I want to find them. This should help me find them. It works like an echo sounder, only better. It will not only find a big fish, but tell me how far away it is."

"You mean, it talks?"

"Not exactly. It clicks. Listen." He turned on the machine and a ray of light shot forth. At the same time the thing began to click. There was quite a long pause after every click.

"That click goes out along the beam," Hal said, "and if it strikes a large object like a big fish, the echo will come back. And the length of time it takes the echo to come will give us an idea of how far away the fish is. Now, let's go hunting."

He slowly turned the eye of the machine and the beam began to travel to the right. The clicking continued but for a while there was no answer.

Then suddenly there was an echoing click.

"There's our fish," said Hal excitedly. "Must be a big one, because it's a strong echo. The larger the fish the better the echo. According to this dial it must be about two miles away."

"But what good is that?" Roger objected. "By the time we get there it will be gone."

"We don't go to it," Hal said. "It will come to us."

Roger stared at him. "What would make it come to us?"

Hal turned a dial and the clicks became very rapid and strong. "A hundred clicks a second," Hal said. "And carried along by the beam, they strike the fish very hard. Fish have a lot of curiosity. When they hear an unusual sound they come to see what is making it."

"I know that," Roger said. "When we went shark-hunting in the islands we rapped on the side of the boat to attract the shark. It came to see what was making all the noise and when it got within a few feet of the boat we would give it the harpoon."

"Yes," Hal said, "and this big fellow is coming fast. The dial shows he has covered a mile in the last few minutes. I'm going to get out with the electro-gun and be ready to give him a warm reception when he arrives. Do you think you can operate this thing? Wait until I get this fish – then immediately turn the beam until you get another echo."

"Sure, I can do that," Roger said, proud to have a part in this strange experiment.

Hal dropped into the sea, gun in hand. In an amazingly short time something that looked like a zebra but was twice as large came charging down the light beam. It was more colourful than the zebra. Its stripes were lavender against a silver background, its fins were deep blue, its back was green and belly white. Hal recognized the famous striped marlin. A record specimen that had been taken by Zane Grey off Tahiti weighed one thousand and forty pounds. But nearly all fish of the Great Barrier Reef were larger than those of Tahiti waters and this one was a true monster.

It did not act like the swordfish, which had dilly-dallied around for an hour before it came close enough to be shot. This fellow could not wait to investigate that clicking sound. It came straight to the jeep and did not stop until its bill touched the glass. Hal fired. The electric shock acted instantly and painlessly.

The end of the coil of rope that Hal carried over his shoulder was slipped into the open mouth and out through the gill, then made fast to one of the jet pipes of the jeep.

Roger had already turned the beam and located another echo. This time the distance was much less and it was not two minutes before another big visitor appeared, this time a silver marlin of somewhat smaller size, no heavier than a horse, about five hundred pounds.

Hal easily bagged it, slipped the same rope through mouth and gills and left it beside its cousin.

He had hardly finished before another marlin hove in sight – evidently this was to be marlin day. This one was the famous Pacific black marlin. The record catch of black marlin weighed one thousand two hundred and twenty-six pounds and was caught in these same waters by a sportsman who struggled most of the day to haul it in.

Any fisherman with rod and line would be very lucky to get one marlin in a day, and it would more likely take a week. And laser had brought in three in ten minutes.

The next was also a black marlin that looked as big as an elephant. It was followed almost at once by a huge grouper with goggle eyes and heavy jaws, an astonished look, and mouth opening and closing that seemed to be saying, "Oh, brother!"

The laser was working well. It picked up only fish that sent back a strong echo, and that meant a big fish every time.

After six more takes, Hal signalled Roger to turn off the beam.

He slipped the rope off the jet and noosed it around the neck of Big Boy in spite of eager whistles from the dolphins who wanted to get in on the game. But this was no job for a dolphin. It took a monster to haul these monsters to the surface.

It was hard work even for the powerful killer whale. He knew where he was supposed to go but found the load almost beyond his strength. Slowly he swam upwards. Hal returned to the jeep. He phoned Captain Ted and told him what to expect.

But even with this warning the captain was not prepared for what he saw when Big Boy broke the surface beside the ship with his cargo of monsters. Captain Ted phoned Hal.

"What sort of a joke is this? How do you think I'm going to get these elephants aboard?"

"Use your crane," Hal suggested. "Take up one at a time."

"But where will I put them? The tanks aren't big enough."

"Stow them in the hold," Hal said. "And be ready to take on a lot more."

Hal could hear a deep sigh from the other end of the line. "Fifty years at sea," moaned Captain Ted, "and I've never seen anything like this."

But he was to see a lot more. Within an hour a distress call came down from above. "Let up, will you? The hold is chock full and every inch of the deck is taken. We're walking around on fish. We're going to sink if we take on any more of these brutes."

Hal laughed. "Okay. Take them to Cairns and deliver them. Use both sails and engine and make a quick trip of it. We'll wait, and have a lot more for you when you get back."

Captain Ted groaned and rang off.

"What do you mean, more?" Roger complained. "Don't you think we've done enough for today?"

Hal smiled. "We've done enough to prove that the laser and electric gun work well together. Any fishing smack can afford to buy a laser. But perhaps it won't be equipped with the electric shock apparatus. I want to see if the laser alone will do the trick."

Roger looked puzzled. "The laser pulls them in all right. But it doesn't kill them."

"I think perhaps it will if we turn up the power," Hal said. "In medicine, laser is used to cure some diseases. For instance, there's a very bad tumour, something like cancer. It's called melanoma. At the Pasadena Tumor Institute they use laser to kill melanoma. It takes only a very weak beam and only a thousandth of a second."

"What does curing that thingamajig have to do with killing fish?"

"The reason for using a weak beam is that a strong one would kill both the tumour and the patient. We've been using a very weak beam to bring in these fish. But suppose when the fish arrives we suddenly turn on the strong beam. Of course these big chaps are much more powerful than a human and they may be able to stand the shock. I don't know — that's what we'll find out."

They soon found out. The low-power beam brought in the fish. At the last moment when the inquisitive fish nosed the jeep the laser was switched to high-power and the fish, without knowing what had struck it, passed out.

Long before Captain Ted telephoned that he had come back from the twenty-mile trip to Cairns, there was another big load waiting to go aboard.

This time neither the dolphins nor the killer whale were to have the fun of towing the catch to the surface.

"Break out the balloons," Hal said. "I think we'll need three."

"What are the balloons for?"

"To do the same job that the dolphins and Big Boy were doing."

"But if they can do it, why use balloons?"

"We have to think of all the possibilities," Hal said. "Let's suppose you are the captain of a fishing smack. You may be able to train dolphins to help you, or you may not. Or perhaps there are no dolphins in the seas where you are working. Your divers round up the fish by laser, but how are you going to get them up to the ship?"

"I see," said Roger. "But you can't use balloons for that. They work only in the air."

"What makes you think so?"

"Because I've seen them in the air, but never underwater."

"But why won't they work underwater? They work in the air because we fill them with gas that is lighter than air. They should work underwater if we fill them with gas that is lighter than water."

"What gas?"

"Any gas. Air itself is a gas, and it's a lot lighter than water."

He took up the bottle of compressed air that Captain Ted had sent down. "This is air under great pressure and it will expand enough to fill three balloons. I'll go out, and you can hand me the balloons one at a time."

Hal went under and Roger passed him the first balloon.

Hal roped together about a dozen of the big fish and made fast the rope to the balloon. Then he latched the air bottle to the balloon nozzle and turned on the valve.

The balloon filled at once and lifted so powerfully that Hal could no longer hold it. Up it went, towing the heavy load.

Hal returned to the jeep. "Phone the captain," he said. "And pass me another balloon."

Another haul of fish went up with the second balloon, and the final lot with the third. Altogether, the boys had taken several hundred groupers, barracudas, wahoos, cobias, giant mullets, dorados and albacores — all good foodfish.

The distressed voice of Captain Ted came over the radiophone. "You're driving us wild. What do we do with all these?"

"Take them in to the packing plant," Hal said. "They'll know what to do with them."

What the city of Cairns could not use could be shipped by train to the towns of the Australian coast all the way from Cape York at the northern tip to Melbourne in the south. Or they could be canned to go to India or any other part of the hungry world.

The important thing was not this great haul of fishes, but the fact that ways had been opened up for the fishing industry everywhere to increase its output perhaps a hundredfold. But only if fishing captains everywhere knew of the success of these experiments. Hal knew that Dr Dick would eagerly take care of that by his reports to scientific journals and journals of the fishing industry.

That was up to Dr Dick. The boys were already impatient to get on to something else.

"What'll we do now?" demanded Roger.

"Well," said Hal, looking out at several writhing, twisting, evil-looking things close to the jeep, "if you don't mind doing something a bit more dangerous, let's go play with snakes."

11
Sea Snakes

Roger was not bubbling with enthusiasm over the idea of playing with snakes.

"They don't look like good playmates," he said. "But I suppose they can't really do any harm."

"I don't know why you suppose that," said Hal. "Of course there are many kinds of sea snakes and some of them just swim away. But the ones along the Great Barrier Reef are not so meek and mild. They are big – those outside seem to be about ten feet long. And they would as soon bite you as not. They are supposed to have the same ancestor as the cobra and krait. The venom of one species is fifty times as strong as the king cobra's."

"Then why do you want to fool with them?"

"Because one of the most important things we have to do is to collect poisonous animals for laboratories."

"What can they do with them?"

"Extract the poison. You know how they milk a snake to get the venom. Then they use the venom to make anti-venin to cure snakebite. But they also use all sorts of poisons from snakes, fish, jellyfish, sea wasps and many other sea creatures to make medicines good for all sorts of diseases. So far as I know, no such collection of venomous animals has been made in the waters of the Great Barrier Reef."

Roger understood. "I get you," he said. "Let's go. How do we kill them?"

"We don't kill them. We take them alive. If we kill them the poison would spoil before we could get them to the labs."

Roger looked closely at the sea snakes. "You say their grand-daddies were cobras. They don't look much like cobras to me. See how broad and flat their tails are. Besides, how could they be descended from cobras? The cobra is a land snake."

"So were these – once. They used to live on land. Then, for some reason they took a fancy to go to sea."

"How do you know that?"

"We know it because they have lungs, not gills. They breathe air. They can stay down for a long time, even for hours, but then they must come up to breathe."

"But," objected Roger, "no land snakes have broad tails like those. How do you explain that?"

"Well," Hal said, "think of the dolphins. They once walked around on land. But when they came to the sea their feet gradually changed into fins and their tails became wide and flat so they could push themselves through the water. The tails of those snakes are now powerful paddles that can shoot them through the water at tremendous speed."

Now there were more snakes than ever. Some were darting at the jeep as if trying to get at the luscious morsels inside. Their fangs thudded against the glass.

"Come to think of it," Hal said, "I believe you had better stay inside."

Roger screwed up his courage enough to say, "Not on your life. If you can take it, so can I." He was done with being considered the baby of the family. He was big for his age and almost as strong as his brother.

"All right," Hal said reluctantly, "but you know how to take a snake?"

"Sure. You grab it behind the head."

"And hang on," Hal added. "They're strong. They'll twist away from you and bite if they can."

"Enough instructions," Roger said. "Let's get going."

They slid out through the hatch. The snakes scattered. Probably they had never known sea monsters like these and were a little afraid of them. But they were very curious. Or hungry. They would attack other sea animals of all sizes, so why not these?

They swam about with their jaws open. Their hollow, poison-filled fangs did not lie down like the fangs of some snakes, but stood erect like those of the cobra. Their forked tongues darted in and out.

They were really a gorgeous sight, evidently of several different varieties. Some were yellow-bellied, some a dazzling blue, some brown with yellow bands or yellow with black bands. Both boys had seen enough snakes in their father's zoo to appreciate their beauty and they had taken snakes alive in Africa, but never before beneath the sea. These creatures were so much at home underwater and glided about with such ease that the boys, who had not spent millions of years beneath the waves, felt clumsy and out of place. These were their air-breathing cousins – but cousins far removed.

They swarmed around the boys, staring at them with big beady eyes. Why was their stare so menacing? Roger decided it was because they never blinked their eyelids. Then he saw that there was good reason why they never blinked – they had no eyelids. And they had no ear openings. They heard (or rather felt) with their tongues. Those darting tongues looked dangerous. But Roger knew that even the tongue of a poisonous snake is quite harmless. The tongue is used to detect sounds, just as the nerves in the lateral line down the side of a fish are sensitive to any sound.

One big snake, after due inspection of these strange creatures, resolved to try its luck. It shot in and closed its fangs on the seat of Hal's swimming trunks. It squirted some of its poison into the cloth, then waited for this big animal to die. Its teeth had certainly penetrated what it supposed to be the skin of this beast, and by all the rules of snakedom the poison should spread through the body, causing terrible convulsions, and death.

It was doubtless quite surprised when things didn't work out as it had planned. Instead, it suddenly felt a choking grip around its throat just behind the head.

Hal jerked it loose from the cloth and stuffed it, wriggling violently, into a plastic sack he had brought with him.

Three more snakes charged in and joined the others in the sack. Roger had not yet had a visitor.

But now he found himself unable to move his right leg. Perhaps he had been bitten and had not felt it. Hal had told him that the fang of a sea snake is so sharp that the bite is not felt. Roger went cold with fear. He tried again to move his leg. Surely he had been bitten and the leg was numb. The numbness would spread and soon he would not be able to move a muscle. Then the terrible pains would start.

He could still swim with his left leg but the right one was no good. Soon the left also would go back on him. He was sorry now that he had been so cocky. He should have stayed in the jeep as his brother advised.

He put his hand down and gripped his right leg. Much to his surprise, he felt the pressure of his fingers. The leg was not numb after all. Then what was the trouble? Had he caught his foot in a tangle of seaweed?

It is not easy to see in all directions through a face mask. But he managed to look down and saw the answer to the mystery of the wooden leg.

A snake nine feet long had buried its fangs in the rubber of his flipper.

Roger tried to kick it off but the weight of the big snake was enough to hold the leg rigid. He swatted the unwelcome visitor with his other fin. With the fin he tried to scrape it off, but it hung on like grim death.

Then he reached down, took it by the neck, and pulled. It came loose, taking a piece of the fin with it.

It began whipping about and Roger could hardly hold it. Hal saw what had happened and came with the sack. Before he could get to his brother, the snake had wound itself tightly around Roger's arm. Luckily it was not a constrictor like a boa or python and was not in the habit of squeezing its victims to death. It trusted its poison fangs to do this deadly work.

Roger tried to tear it off with his other hand. Hal had joined him now and both boys exerted all their strength to pull away the black and yellow coils. Finally it came loose and Roger stuffed it into the bag.

But as he let go of the neck the snake twisted its head and one fang brushed against his hand.

It was just a scrape and Roger thought nothing of it. He was greatly relieved to get this pest safe in the sack.

Hal put his hand on Roger's arm and drew him back to the jeep. They climbed in.

"Let me see that," Hal said.

"It's nothing," said Roger.

"Let me see it anyway."

"It's only a scratch. Look."

A drop of blood was welling from the scratch.

Hal brushed away the blood. He put his mouth to the slight abrasion, sucked hard, then spat. He sucked again and again until he was blue in the face.

"A lot of monkey business about nothing," Roger said.

"I'm not so sure of that," said Hal. "You didn't get

much. It won't be enough to finish you off. But it may be enough to make you mighty uncomfortable. Wish we had some antiserum. But it hasn't been invented yet."

"I thought you had some."

"For land-snake bite – not sea snake. If you had just waited until we could get these snakes to a lab and get some antiserum back . . . But you were in too much of a hurry."

In spite of his joking manner, Hal was worried. He had tied a tourniquet of rope around the wrist above the scratch. He must release it every thirty minutes. He continued the mouth-to-hand treatment.

"I don't feel a thing," Roger said, "except a little stiffness."

Hal looked at him anxiously. "That's the first sign of trouble," he said.

"But it isn't my hand that is stiff. It's my legs."

"That's the way it starts," Hal said. "Funny, how a bit of poison in your hand can make your legs stiff. Then the stiffness slowly goes up through your body."

"Perhaps I'd better exercise my legs to keep them limber."

"No. Lie still. I'd better get you back to the house and into bed."

"Bed nothing. You're making a big thing out of nothing."

But Hal was already at the controls. He put on full

power and the jeep sped to town. Arriving home, he helped Roger out of his clothes and into bed.

By this time the stiffness had risen to the neck. It climbed farther to the jaws. It might cause lockjaw. Roger could speak only with difficulty and complained that he could hardly swallow. But he wanted to swallow because there was a burning or dryness in his throat and he was uncommonly thirsty.

Hal took his pulse. It was not fast, but it was weak and irregular.

The poison had reached the eyes. The pupils were dilated and the eyelids drooped.

Then the pains began. The muscles of Roger's arms and legs jumped and twitched. It seemed to Roger that every nerve in his body was hopping. Spasms of pain ran through him from head to toe. Hal found that the patient's skin was cold and clammy. He covered him with another blanket.

The next hour was pure torture. Convulsions racked the poisoned body. Roger had never known such suffering. He wanted to scream. But men did not scream. Trying to control himself, he bit his lip until it bled. He could hardly breathe. He felt as if an elephant were sitting on his chest.

The convulsions suddenly ended when he became

unconscious. Hal anxiously put his fingers on the boy's pulse. He could feel nothing.

After a few moments there was a slight throb, then a very feeble beat. It was come and go. It would stop for as much as ten seconds and begin again.

Finally the boy passed from unconsciousness into normal sleep. The heartbeat became stronger. This lad was a tough customer – he wouldn't die easily. Hal sat by his bed all night.

He was ready to give up his search for poisons to be turned into medicines. The idea had seemed good, but now he hated it. It was a thing that ought to be done, but why not let others do it?

Roger slept late the next morning. When he opened his eyes the pupils were back to normal and there was no droop in the eyelids. He lay quietly without any sign of pain.

"You poor boob," he said. "How long have you been sitting there?"

"A while," said Hal. "How do you feel?"

"Just fine. Rarin' to go."

He threw off the covers, got up, and began to dress.

"Hadn't you better stay quiet?"

"I don't know why," Roger said. "'Fraid I've been

wasting a lot of time, lying there half the day when there's
so much to do."

"There's nothing to do," Hal said.

"But your poisons?" said Roger.

Hal said, "We're quitting all that. We'll find something
else to do."

Roger scolded, "Listen, big brother, you don't need to
baby me. Don't tell me you're quitting. You're no quitter,
and neither am I. I tell you I'm all right. I bet you haven't
had breakfast yet, and I'm hungry too. Let's have a snack,
then get back to our nice little poisons."

12
The Floating Death

So they went out again, looking for trouble.

There was no lack of that under the sea. Plenty of beauty, plenty of trouble. Thousands of harmless and lovely angels such as the angelfish and moorish idols. Hundreds of ugly creatures that looked and acted like the devil.

Some were both beautiful and devilish.

The first the boys saw was one of the handsomest creatures of the sea. It had as many gorgeous plumes as an Indian chief's headdress.

"It looks like a bird of paradise," Roger said.

"Yes," said his brother. "Or a peacock. But those fine feathers conceal stingers full of poison. Especially at the back end of the fish."

"What good do they do back there? I should think he'd have them up at the business end."

"The back end *is* the business end. And it's really a very clever arrangement. Any fish would expect the danger to be up front. This rascal takes them by surprise. When he sees some creature he wants to eat, he passes and goes ahead of it. The fish he is after thinks it is safe and pays no more attention. Then suddenly the lionfish shoots backwards and stabs it with his rear spines. The poison promptly kills the fish, and the lionfish can feast upon it at leisure."

"Why do they call it the lionfish?"

"Because some people think its plumes look like the mane of a lion. I'll go and get it."

"Let me," Roger said.

Before his brother could object he grabbed his sack and slid out of the jeep.

The lionfish took an interest in him at once. It came close and studied him with big eyes. Then it pretended to have other business, and passed him. It stopped and drifted. Then it came back like a bolt of lightning going the wrong way.

Roger slid out of its path at the last instant and held the sack with its mouth wide open. The lionfish shot into it tail first and Roger flipped the bag shut. He tied it to one of the legs of the jeep and got back inside. The whole operation had not taken two minutes.

Hal congratulated him. "Pretty neat," he said. "There's a sea wasp. This time it's my turn."

"But that's only a jellyfish. Does it have any poison?"

"I'll say it has. The sea wasp has killed a lot of people

along the Australian coast. Some scientists say it's the most venomous marine animal known. A boy twelve years old up near Darwin was swimming when one of these things showed up just ahead of him. He thought it was harmless and brushed it away. He died in seven minutes. Another swimmer was finished in three minutes. He was pulled out with the sea wasp still clinging to his dead body. When they pulled it off the skin came with it. Always look out for jellyfish. Most of them won't do you a bit of harm except perhaps give you an itchy skin, but there are a few that are downright murder. And when you can't tell which are the bad ones, it's best to avoid them all."

The sea wasp wasn't going anywhere. It didn't need to. All it had to do was to wait until something brushed through its tentacles.

It happened very soon. A fish as large as the sea wasp itself wandered into the stingers and lay dead. Then the sea wasp performed a miracle. It protruded its stomach, wrapped the fish in its folds, and drew it inside. It expanded to accommodate this meal and was twice as big as before. As it digested the fish it would shrink to its former size.

When Hal came out it made no effort to move away. The mushy body was scooped up without difficulty and another bag was tied to the jeep.

"Be nice if everything were as easy as that," Hal said when he returned.

Roger spied a pretty shell on a ledge of the reef. He instantly dropped out and was astonished when he was grabbed by the hair and pulled back into the jeep.

"What did you do that for?" he demanded.

"Before you grab that shell, I want to tell you something about it. That's a cone shell."

"You don't need to tell me about cone shells. I've picked up lots of them."

"But not that kind. There are more than four hundred species of cone shells, but only six of them are very poisonous. This is one of them."

"But it's so small, it can't really be bad."

"It is bad – one of the worst. It's called a marbled cone because it looks like patterned marble. Go ahead and get it but take it by the large end. The small end is open and just inside there is a little black animal with a stinger like a harpoon that it is ready to jab into anything that comes along."

"It must be a very tiny stinger," said Roger. "How could that hurt you?"

"It's connected with a sac of deadly poison. One little squirt of that, and you would be dead."

"Aren't you exaggerating?"

"Not a bit. An Australian boy walking on top of the reef when it is bare at low tide picked up one of these and held it in his closed hand. The thing stung him on his finger. The poison acted so fast that he was dead in three minutes. Now, go ahead, but take it by the large end."

Roger left the jeep and swam close to the ledge. The shell looked so harmless. It was only about an inch and a half long. The large end was closed, the small end was the front door. It was a tiny opening, no bigger than the head of a pin. Roger could not see inside the hole.

He took out his knife and tapped on the shell. Instantly what looked like a black needle came out of the hole. Finding nothing to murder, it drew back into the shell.

Roger picked up the shell by the large end and held it gingerly as he swam back to the jeep.

"Wish I had a toothpick," Hal said.

"What do you want with a toothpick?"

"To plug up that hole. Of course out of water the thing will die – but that will take some hours. In the meantime it's a dangerous thing to have lying around. You might put your hand or foot on it and then good night. When we get home we'll plug the hole shut with a toothpick or chewing gum or whatever else we have handy. A lab will be glad to get this. Its poison is more powerful, drop for drop, than the poison of a big land snake. And it can be converted into a number of different medicines."

"I still can't understand," Roger said, "how something that can kill you can be made into something that can cure you."

Hal agreed. "We don't pretend to understand it. Even the lab men don't. But it works. Just as the bad-smelling stuff a civet cat shoots out can be made into perfume, or garbage can be made into soap. Perhaps there's nothing in the world that is altogether bad."

The search for bad-good fish continued. It was not hard to find them. Possibly nowhere else in the world was there so great a gathering of sea creatures as along the face of the Great Barrier Reef.

The sea scorpion was added to the collection.

"Boy, is it ugly," said Roger. "Like something out of a nightmare."

"Ugly and edible," said Hal. "The French consider it very good to eat. They make one of their famous soups out of it."

"Where is the stinger?" Roger asked, examining the specimen they had captured.

"He carries it in a very strange place. It's underneath.

Instead of killing its victims by shooting forwards or backwards it surprises them by dropping down on them."

"The sea is full of surprises," said Roger.

"I'll say it is," agreed Hal.

The stonefish, so ugly that it is called the 'horrida', was added to the collection. It is also called 'the waiting one' because it doesn't move from morning to night. It simply lies on the ground waiting for someone to make a mistake. It is about the colour of the sea bottom and is usually half concealed by mud or sand. A man wading or swimming is very likely to step on it and the poisonous spines that stand up from its warty back stab his foot. Fish grazing along the bottom for food suddenly become food for the stonefish when they are stabbed by the spines which then bend to push them over into the great mouth.

The boys did not make the mistake of stepping on it. That was the mistake of a crab which crawled over the waiting one only to be caught on the spines and promptly eaten.

Although it did not move, catching it was a delicate matter. You could not grab it by the spiny back. When Hal tried to pick it up by the tail it clung to the rock beneath.

Roger brought the jeep into position so that its iron

claw could close on the stonefish. Then he backed the jeep and pulled the thing loose. Hal held a sack open below the victim, Roger opened the iron jaws, and the horrida was bagged.

Both boys breathed a sigh of relief. "I'm glad that's over," Hal said. "Just one little jab from those spines and if you didn't die you might go insane and spend the rest of your life wandering around as crazy as a loon. It's the chief cause of insanity among the islanders of the South Seas."

The jeep was now within two feet of the reef and through its glass wall they could see the reef builders at work. Some people suppose that you have to have a microscope to see these tiny coral animals, called polyps. This is not always true. The polyps are different sizes. Some are no larger than pinheads. Some are half an inch wide and can be plainly seen with their flowerlike tentacles extended, each polyp sitting in a cup of limestone secreted from its own body.

The word polyp sounds as if the thing might be a bit of pulp or plant growth, not the well-constructed and efficient animal that it is. It gathers food, builds a house for itself, poisons unwelcome visitors, and erects a monument far greater than the Washington Monument or the Taj Mahal.

All about the boys was an underwater paradise. They looked down on a dream forest. Imagine a twenty-foot tree bearing only one leaf twenty feet broad. It and a hundred like it had been built by the small coral animal. Under the shadow of the great leaf hundreds of brilliant little fish flitted like butterflies.

And there was something that looked like the banyan, a tree with a hundred trunks like the columns in a cathedral. It was densely covered with coral leaves, and under them a scuba diver might easily get lost exploring the submarine labyrinth.

This part of the ocean floor did not look like a floor, but like the top of a fantastic woodland seen from an aeroplane – a jungle of trees of all sizes. What a thrill to look down between the weird branches into these blue and purple canyons, where tiny flecks of colour shot in and out among the twigs while bigger and more solemn fish swam slowly near the bottom.

The colours looked delicate and the stone leaves fragile, and it was an odd sensation when the jeep bumped against one and found it as hard as rock.

It was not all so lovely. On one of the stone branches lay a horrible-looking creature which Hal identified as a sea centipede. It looked as unpleasant as the land centipede, so unpleasant that even an animal lover could not like it. It had perhaps a hundred legs — the boys didn't attempt to count them. The most frightening thing about it was its size. The centipede one sees on land may be only two or three inches long. This watery cousin was a good two feet. Another one crawled along near by.

"I think we want both of those," Hal said, "one to send to a lab and the other to eat."

Roger's face crinkled in disgust. "Who could ever eat that thing?"

"You and I could," said Hal. "And will. You'll like it. It's even better than lobster. It is called a varo and the Polynesians like it so much that they frequently name a son Varo. Then every time they look at him they think of the delicious sea centipede."

"What good is one to a lab?"

"Every one of those feet is full of poison. The centipede will tackle even a large fish, dig its claws into it, paralyse it with poison and then eat it."

Here again the iron claw was useful. It clutched one of the centipedes, tore it loose from its hundred-foot grip on the coral branch, and dropped it into the bag that was this time held by Roger. In the same way, the other joined its mate in the bag.

"We'll have to be careful when we cook it," Hal said. "Those claws cut like scissors and the poison makes wounds that will fester and swell for weeks."

"How nice," Roger said. "I think I'll leave the cooking to you, and the eating too."

"How generous you are," said Hal.

Roger dismissed it with a wave of his hand. "Don't mention it. Just call it brotherly love."

The climax of the poison hunt was "the floating death", as it is called by some Australians. Elsewhere it is known as the Portuguese man-of-war.

The boys noticed first that the water had turned light blue. Then they saw that the colour came from dozens of tentacles trailing down from the surface. They were attached to what looked like a bright blue boat. The tentacles were at least thirty feet long.

"There's the best prize of the day," said Hal, "if we can just get it. Those tentacles carry a lot of poison and, believe it or not, electric batteries. The thing up there that looks like a boat is really a big blue bag filled with gas."

"It seems to be moving away," Roger said.

"Put on low power and follow it. It has a sail on top of the bag and the wind moves it slowly along."

"Those tentacles can't be so bad," said Roger. "I see some little blue-black fish swimming in among them."

Hal said, "Those little fish are the man-of-war's buddies. It leaves them alone. Other fish see them there and are fooled into thinking the tentacles are harmless. They plunge in after the little fellows, get tangled up in the tentacles and get both electric shock and poison. Then they are gathered up to the hungry mouth of the man-of-war."

Roger was puzzled. "I don't see how you're going to take it. If it were near the ship the captain might snare it and pull it aboard. But the wind has carried it a good distance and we've gone with it. Besides, it's such a sprawly thing, and all those long tentacles! I think we can find something that will be easier to get."

"We're going to get this," Hal said. "But it's a job for two men — one to hold a coil of rope and the other to pass the end of the rope around the bunch of tentacles. Then Bottle can tow it to the ship."

"I'll bet it won't be as simple as it sounds," said Roger. But he took up a coil of rope and both adventurers left the jeep and swam close to the dangerous dangle of blue tentacles. Roger held the coil while Hal looped the end around the stringy mass and tied it.

So far, so good. The faithful Bottle, as usual, was close

119

at hand. Hal gave the free end of the rope to Bottle, who at once understood what he was supposed to do.

He swam off towards the ship. But even a dolphin can make mistakes. In his eagerness to carry out his errand he drew the twitching ends of the tentacles straight over Hal's body.

The tentacles at once wrapped themselves around the naturalist's back and chest. Hal felt a series of quick electric jolts. He knew that thousands of tiny darts were pouring poison into him. He struggled to get away but was firmly held.

Roger ventured close and at the risk of getting stung himself seized Hal's foot and tried to pull him loose. It didn't work.

What to do now? As fast as he could he swam back to the jeep, powered it up, and brought it near enough so that the iron claw could grip Hal's arm. Then he backed away.

With the dolphin pulling in one direction and the iron claw in the opposite direction, Hal felt as if he were about to be pulled apart. But the powerful engine succeeded in pulling him free of the strings of death. In doing so, the ends of the tentacles were broken and stuck to the boy's body with their darts penetrating the skin and administering more poison.

At first there had been terrifying pains. Now the pains were dying down. This was a bad sign. Hal knew it meant that he was being paralysed. The paralysis was numbing his nerves so that he could no longer feel.

He could hardly make it back to the jeep. Roger hauled him in. Hal muttered, "Phone the captain to watch for Bottle."

Roger did so. "Now," Hal said, "get these things off me."

Roger slipped on a pair of rubber gloves and tried to strip off the blue strings of poison. They stuck so tightly to the flesh that he could not get them loose. "Can't do it," he said.

"You've got to. If they don't come off, I'm dead. Dig them off with your knife."

This was not a job to Roger's liking, but he went to work. With the sharp end of his knife he cut into the flesh below a tentacle and managed to prise it loose, pulling out of the skin the hundreds of little barbed hooks. Of course the flesh came with them and as each tentacle was dug away it left a track of blood.

Hal was hopelessly dizzy and nauseated. His mind began fogging over. His eyes were glazed and his teeth clenched. His chest tightened up until it was as hard as a board. That meant his lungs were being paralysed. His breath came in gasps.

"What else can I do?" Roger said in despair.

"Nothing. Get me back to the house."

Returning home, Roger somehow got him out of the jeep, up into the house, where he lay on the floor while Roger sponged away the blood trails and applied some antiseptic. He wrapped a towel around his brother and helped him struggle into bed.

The patient was still conscious, but it was so hard to breathe that he feared he would suffocate.

"Be ready," he managed to mumble, "to give me artificial respiration."

Dr Roger Hunt was at his wits' end. His medical knowledge was too slight and he was painfully aware of his own ignorance. His brother was feverish, so he laid a wet rag over the hot forehead.

What would he do if his brother died? He knew that death was possible. He remembered the news report of the Australian boy who had been attacked, managed to pull himself loose, swam fifty yards to shore, then collapsed and died. A fourteen-year-old girl at Kissing Point Baths, Australia, made it to the hospital but died a day later. Just the electric shock alone was serious, without counting the poison. It was like being wrapped in high-powered electric lines.

The phone rang. It was the captain. He said, "Bottle is alongside with the man-of-war. What will I do with it?"

"Hoist it aboard with the derrick," Roger said. "Give it a tank all to itself."

"But its tentacles hang down thirty feet," objected the captain. "And our tanks are only ten feet deep."

"Can't help that," Roger said. "It will just have to spread its tentacles out over the floor of the tank."

"But that's not natural for a man-of-war. It will be mighty uncomfortable."

"I don't give a hoot if it's uncomfortable," exclaimed Roger. "It nearly killed my brother." And he told the captain what had happened.

"That's bad," said Captain Ted. "Did you put on the shaving cream?"

"Shaving cream!" exploded Roger. "I don't think that's funny."

"I didn't intend it to be. Shaving cream is the old remedy for man-of-war stings."

"Well, I'll do it," said Roger doubtfully. "But do you think I'd better get him to the hospital?"

"No. He shouldn't be moved. You've done everything they could do – except the shaving cream. In fact I think you're a pretty good doctor. But get the cream on right away. Then keep him quiet. He'll come out of it."

Roger got the tube of shaving cream and rubbed in a streak of it along every cut.

He could only hope that the captain knew what he was talking about. He should know – for he had spent his life along this coast where the man-of-war was a well-known pest.

Kaggs came in. "What's the matter with your brother?"

"Tangled with a man-of-war," Roger said.

"Oh, now, isn't that just too bad?" But somehow Kaggs didn't look too sorry. In fact there was something that seemed like a gleam of satisfaction in his eyes. "Suppose I take over. What he needs is some exercise."

Hal's eyes were closed. He was either unconscious or asleep. The captain had said to keep him still.

Kaggs started towards the bed. "Leave him alone," Roger said.

Kaggs looked astonished. "Now my boy, don't tell me what to do. Remember. I'm a bit older than you, and perhaps a little wiser. We should wake him up and give him a workout."

"Don't touch him," said Roger angrily. "If you do I'll knock your head off."

Kaggs stared. "Well, of all the impudence!" Then he

adopted his most oily manner. "I'll have to excuse you for your impertinence. I understand how disturbed you must be." He started again towards the bed.

Suddenly Hal's eyes opened and he sat up. Except for a little stiffness, his paralysis was gone. He almost sang, he was so happy to be alive. He ached all over his chest and back as if he had had a first-degree burn. But he could breathe and he could move. Seeing Kaggs, he said, "Thanks for all you did. Whatever it was, it was the right thing. I feel fine."

Kaggs smiled. "I'm glad I got here just in time. I'm sure you'll be all right now." He went to his room.

"Well, of all the nerve!" said Roger. But he was so grateful for his brother's recovery that he didn't bother to tell him Kaggs had done nothing.

13
How to Make an Enemy

Hal was reporting to Dr Dick.

"Some of my experiments worked out," he said. "Some didn't. We tried underwater fishing. Our bottlenose dolphin – we called him Bottle – learned very quickly to run errands for us to our ship, *Flying Cloud*. My brother made friends with a killer whale and he hauls up loads that would be too heavy for the dolphin. Other dolphins have joined in, so now we have a team of twenty of them and I believe they can be trained to serve as cowboys to guard the animal farms, fish farms, oyster beds, lobster fields and this and that that we're planning."

"If you can do that," Dr Dick said, "it will be a long step ahead. Single dolphins have been used before this – but I don't recall any experiment with a team of dolphins."

"Well," Hal said, "we may fail – just as we failed with the electric shock."

"Electric shock? What was that?"

"Not an original idea," Hal replied. "As you know, for some years whalers have been using the electric harpoon to kill whales painlessly. Of course they do that from a

127

surface ship. Whales come to the surface to breathe, but big fish don't usually come up; so they were safe from the electric harpoon. But if you could go down where they are, the electric harpoon could be used. We tried it, and it failed. I'm sorry we wasted so much time on an experiment that we should have known wouldn't work."

"Why didn't it work?"

"It worked if a big fish came around. But we might wait for half an hour or an hour before a big fellow happened to come by. That was no better than a fishing boat could do with a hook and line or a net. So we tried laser."

Dr Dick looked worried. "But a laser machine costs five or ten thousand dollars. I'm not sure that we could afford such an expense."

"A new one has been invented," Hal said. "It cost only fifty dollars. And John Hunt and Sons paid for it, because we can use it in our own work."

"But how can you use laser for fishing?"

"The laser beam carries a clicking sound along with it and when it strikes a big object such as a large fish the fish comes out of curiosity to see what is making the noise. When the fish came close we finished him off with the electric shock. We got more fish that way in half an hour than fishermen up on top would be apt to get in a day or perhaps even a week."

"Great," smiled Dr Dick. "Any fishing smack could afford to buy a laser at that price. But suppose it didn't have the electric harpoon apparatus and no trained dolphin or killer whale to bring up the fish?"

Hal admired Dr Dick's quick mind. "You're quite right. So we tried laser alone – no electric business and no finny errand boys. We brought in the fish by low-power laser and when they came close we finished them off by turning on high-power. Then we sent them up by balloon instead of by dolphin or whale."

Dr Dick grinned. "Very ingenious!" he said. "What other magic have you been practising?"

"Nothing really magical," Hal said modestly. "We've been picking up some poisons to send to laboratories that use them in making medicines."

"You mean poisonous fish?"

"Yes – like the sea snake, lionfish, sea scorpion, cone shell, sea wasp, stonefish, sea centipede and man-of-war."

"But isn't that pretty dangerous work?"

"Not too bad," Hal said, thinking it unnecessary to relate how both he and Roger had nearly lost their lives.

★ ★ ★

A head bobbed up through a hole in the other room. It was followed by the body of a young man who stood dripping while he gazed around until his eyes rested upon the two men in the study.

He removed the scuba mouthpiece from his mouth and said, "Is Dr Dick here?"

"I'm Dr Dick," said the director.

"May I speak to you for a few moments?"

"Come right in."

Hal disliked the face. The eyes were shifty and too close together, the chin was weak and flabby, the mouth had a mean twist at the corners.

"My name is Oscar Roach," he said. "I came to see about getting a job."

"In what capacity?"

"Naturalist," said Roach.

Dr Dick rose and shook hands. "Meet our present naturalist, Hal Hunt," he said.

Hal shook hands. "Glad to know you," he said.

Roach did not reply. Instead, he seemed highly displeased.

"If you'll excuse me, gentlemen," Hal said, "I must be running along."

After he had gone, Roach said, "So – you already have a naturalist. Guess I'm here on a wild goose chase."

"Sorry," said Dr Dick, "but the job is filled. Pretty well filled." And he went on to tell Roach of some of Hal's experiments.

"Then I suppose you have no opening for me?"

"Not as naturalist. But I might find some other assignment for you. Do you have any references?"

Roach looked flustered by the question. His face went red. "I don't have any with me," he admitted.

"But you have had other jobs?"

"Lots of them."

That didn't sound too good to Dr Dick. If a man has had lots of jobs it means that he wasn't able to hold one very long.

"I can fit you in," he said. "But it would be a minor job."

"Doing what?"

"They need a dishwasher over at the hotel."

Roach looked angry but he said nothing. "Of course," Dr Dick went on, "it would be just temporary. If Hunt should drop out for any reason, you would be considered next in line to take his place."

If Hunt should drop out. If Hunt should drop out. Dr Dick should have been able to see it going round and round in Roach's mind.

"I'll take the dishwashing job," he said.

If Hunt should drop out. Perhaps there would be a way to help him drop out.

14
Roger's Little Joke

They had never seen a shark as big as this one.

First it passed over the jeep like a black cloud. Then circled and came down to study this strange glass thing more closely. It was a good fifty feet long. Its open mouth was six feet wide.

"That's a whale shark," said Hal excitedly. "Greatest of all the sharks. You can tell it by the white spots on its hide. And by the croaks – hear it?"

The croaking sounds of the monster were quite audible. "It's the only talking shark," Hal said.

"There don't seem to be any teeth in that mouth," said Roger.

"No, it doesn't bite or chew its food. It just inhales it. It goes along with its mouth open and anything in the way goes down the hatch. Mainly it lives on plankton – those tiny bits of animal life in the sea. It's not supposed to be vicious like most sharks. It even allows a man to ride on its back. Or so they say – I wouldn't like to chance it."

"I would," said the venturesome Roger, and before Hal

could stop him he slipped out of the jeep. The monster lay still, evidently much interested in this big glass bubble. Roger swam up beside it.

What a whale of a shark! No wonder they called it the whale shark. Paste three elephants together and they would not be as big as this brute.

Roger touched its rough flank but it did not seem to notice him. He mustered up the courage to tickle it under the chin. It seemed to like it.

He swam up to the top of the back, like the roof of a house. He sat down. You couldn't straddle this thing – you had to sit Turkish fashion. It was like sitting on the deck of a ship.

The ship began to move – very slowly. It circled the jeep, looking at it from every angle. It seemed to be undecided whether to swallow it or not. But it apparently gave up the idea. Glass bubbles were not its favourite dish. Again it came to a halt and just lay, looking.

A stream of small sea bits kept flowing into the creature's mouth. Evidently there was quite a lot of suction there – like the suction of a vacuum cleaner.

Roger swam around to examine this cavernous mouth. It was quite as big as a telephone booth. Since there were no teeth. Roger felt safe. And since the monster appeared

to have a habit of keeping its mouth open, why shouldn't he explore this cave more completely?

He felt the suction and allowed it to carry him in. This was a new sensation – sitting on the inside of a fish. That story about Jonah inside the great fish, possibly it was true after all. Though how Jonah stayed alive without breathing was a mystery. Roger, inhaling from his aqualung, had no such difficulty. He was quite comfortable; and he could leave the great open mouth whenever he chose. It was like being in a submarine with an open hatch.

He could see Hal madly gesturing him to come out. But why should he come out just yet? He was enjoying this strange experience.

He was considerably surprised when the mouth began to close. The monster had evidently come to the conclusion that it had a big enough mouthful. Roger tried to get out before the jaws came shut but it was impossible.

With the mouth closed, the cave was as dark as a pocket. Still Roger was not frightened. Hal had said that the whale shark was not vicious like other sharks.

But someone was frightened, and that was Hal. He swam to the shark's head and began to beat on its mouth with the handle of his knife. He might as well have beaten a stone wall. To the shark, his blows were like love pats. It did not even flick its tail, which stood out behind like the rudder of a great ship.

Suppose the monster swam away with Roger still imprisoned? After he had used up the last air in his scuba tank, he would die.

Hal inserted the blade of his knife between the shark's lips and tried to prise them open. They did not budge.

In the meantime, Roger's eyes had grown accustomed to the darkness of his prison. The place was not as dark as a pocket after all. There was a very faint glimmer of light, possibly a phosphorescence from the tissues of the monster's mouth. No, it was not quite like that. It was more like daylight, but very faint. The boy told himself it was probably just his imagination. There couldn't be any daylight inside a fish's mouth.

Roger grinned when he thought how worried his brother must be. Why should he worry? There was nothing to worry about. He, Roger, was sitting there as snug as a bug in a rug. He hadn't a care in the world.

He thought differently when his air suddenly gave out. He sucked hard but got nothing. But there was a reserve supply. He flipped a switch and turned it on. It was a relief to be able to breathe again, but he knew the reserve was timed to last only five minutes.

So he had better open the door and get out. He tried, but the door was locked. He put his shoulders against the upper jaw and his feet against the lower and strained to force them apart. The only result was that he breathed faster and at this rate would exhaust his air supply in less than five minutes.

He sat down again to think things over. There was still that faint light even though the lips were firmly closed. He tried to find its source. It didn't come from the roof of the mouth nor from the floor. It seemed to come from the sides. And there it appeared to be in ridges, like the bars in a jail window. What could make these vertical streaks of light?

He ran his hand along the side of the mouth.

He found strips like the strings of a harp – or perhaps they were more like rubber bands, for they stretched. Each one when pressed aside let in more light, then closed again as his fingers left it. There seemed to be about five of them.

Gills! They must be gills. Every fish had them – must have them or quit breathing. They were part of the mechanism that enabled the fish to extract oxygen from the water. Scientists were already working on the problem of supplying man with artificial gills so that he could breathe like a fish below the sea. Perhaps ten, a hundred, a thousand years from now man could live and breathe underwater without an aqualung.

The question suddenly occurred to the boy, why hadn't the big fish swallowed him? There was probably room for half a dozen like him in that big stomach. Perhaps the fish was already full of food and was holding him in reserve until it was hungry. Or perhaps he tasted bad. Possibly the whale shark preferred shrimp and those other even smaller animal and plant organisms that floated everywhere. Anyhow he was glad he was unpopular.

He thought again about the gills. He remembered a report written by James Dugan, a famous diver who had worked for years with Cousteau. Dugan knew a fifty-year-old native of the Palau Islands who had been engulfed by a grouper. He made his escape through the gills.

A grouper, though a large fish, was small compared with the whale shark, and if a man could get out through a grouper's gills it should be possible through the gills of this monster. He would try it. Otherwise he was sure to die within a few minutes.

He pressed the elastic gills apart and stuck his head out. He saw his brother's foot; the rest of him was on the other side of the fish trying to open the mouth.

Even with death so close, Roger's mischievous mind suggested that he play a trick on his brother. He might as well have some fun during his last three minutes.

He squeezed out between the rubbery gills. Keeping the fish between him and Hal, he swam to the jeep and crawled inside. He didn't need the scuba tank now. He took out the mouthpiece, removed the mask, and breathed deeply. He grinned with satisfaction, and settled himself comfortably to watch his brother.

Hal had brought out a hammer and was beating the closed lips. The big fish seemed to enjoy it. It appeared to wag its tail like a dog. Hal got a piece of stone-hard coral from a ledge and vigorously scratched the hide near the mouth. The only result was that the coral suffered more than the hide. The sandpaper armour of the fish pulverized the rock and a shower of coral fragments drifted down through the water.

He resorted to gentler tactics. He stroked the monster under the chin as he had seen Roger do. The big dog accepted this petting without opening its mouth one crack.

A cloud of little nothings drifted past the shark's nose. The monster opened its great mouth wide and the cloud was sucked in. Hal could see clear to the back of the cavern and there was nothing there. The fish must have swallowed Roger, tank and all.

Hal swam below and attacked the living submarine with his knife. His brother was probably dead, Hal thought, but perhaps he could at least get his body and give it decent burial. Otherwise, the gastric juices would soon digest the flesh and nothing would be left but the skeleton to ride the seas in this living tomb.

Hal had thought of the laser to kill the fish. But a beam of sufficient power to kill such a monster would certainly kill Roger too – if he were still alive. And he was probably as dead as a doornail already.

The skin on the belly was softer than any other part of the hide but the knife, used with all the power of Hal's strong arm, did not even scratch it. He knew that he was only dulling his knife.

The big shark had had about enough of this tomfoolery. With a sweep of its great tail it swam away.

Hal swam back to the jeep, determined to turn on all power and pursue that shark to the ends of the Pacific if necessary. He crawled up into the jeep. He turned and saw Roger, sitting at ease and chewing a sea biscuit.

"How did you get here?" Hal demanded.

"Oh, I got tired of it out there so I came in. Where were you?"

"Never mind where I was. But wait until we get back to the house and I'll spank you within an inch of your life."

15
The Avalanche

The strangest job yet for the young naturalists was to hunt for water underwater.

Dr Dick called them to his office. "We've had an accident," he said. "The desalting plant that turns salt water into fresh for drinking has broken down. We can't possibly bring in enough water by ship to supply the town. We're appealing to you to do something about it."

"Why us?" Hal asked. "What can we do?"

"We picked on you because you are the food men. You have been very successful in showing how the sea can supply more food than it ever has in the past. We believe you can make the sea produce fresh drinking water."

Hal laughed. "Do you think we are magicians? We found ways to get more food from the sea because it was right there waiting to be taken. But there's no fresh water in the ocean."

"That's where you're wrong," Dr Dick said. "There are places where springs of fresh water come up through the sea floor. In the Hawaiian Islands divers discovered water twelve degrees colder than the water around it. They tasted it and found it was fresh. They drank it, and there was no taste of salt. It was pouring up through the sea bottom. In the Mediterranean the town of Cassis near Marseilles ran short of water. Scientists discovered good water welling up from the sea bottom at the base of a cliff. Rain water that fell on the top of the cliff was soaking down to the bottom where it struck a layer of hard rock and was forced to come up into the sea. The water was piped to the town and Cassis never again suffered a water shortage. We have a cliff right here, the precipice of the Great Barrier Reef. It is made of porous coral, and rain that falls on top of it must sink far down. Possibly it comes up again somewhere near the foot of the cliff. I suggest you explore a bit and see if you can find it."

Hal's eyes glowed with excitement. "It's a marvellous idea," he said. "Not just for this town, but all over the world."

"You catch on quickly," said Dr Dick. "You can see what it would do for many dry parts of the world if they could get a constant flow of sweet water pouring in from the sea. Right here, Australia is a good example. Much of the land is desert. Crops won't grow. The soil is all right, but too dry. It needs water. Not salt water — that would ruin the soil. Salt water turned into fresh would be too expensive to use for irrigation. But fresh water piped from the sea could turn bare wastes into rich gardens and farms. There would be no cost except for the pipe. No pumps would be necessary, no costly desalting plants. Think what could happen in the Sahara, the Kalahari Desert, the Gobi, the American deserts. Of course all that is a long way off, but you would be one of the pioneers in something that could be mighty important in the future."

With their glass jeep anchored near the precipice, Hal and Roger went out on this fantastic search for fresh water in salt water. Foot by foot they explored the sea bottom at the base of the cliff. They stopped now and then, removed their mouthpieces, and tasted the water. It was bitter with salt.

They were about to go home for lunch when they heard a rumbling sound above. They looked up to see a great avalanche of rocks and coral blocks pouring down the face of the cliff. It was heading straight for them and there was very little time to get out of the way. You cannot move rapidly underwater, especially at such a depth where the water is thick and heavy and makes going slow.

For a moment they froze with surprise and fright. Then Hal seized Roger's arm and pulled him into a cave in the cliff.

The landslide thundered down in front of the cave. It could do them no harm now – so they thought. The cave entrance was only four feet high and protected them perfectly.

But the rocks piled up until the opening was completely closed. Their place of refuge suddenly became a prison. The rumbling stopped. Now they could dig their way out.

But they had nothing to dig with. With their bare hands they tried to push away the great chunks of coral, some as big as their glass jeep. The sharp coral edges cut into their hands and they could feel the sticky blood that oozed out. They hoped the coral was dead – living coral could be very poisonous.

They shivered with cold. Why was this water so much colder than the water outside?

They must get out soon; their air was running low.

Ten or fifteen minutes more and they would suffocate like drowned kittens. They went at the rocks again with new vigour. The harder they worked the faster they used up their air.

It was like battling against a stone wall. Except that a wall wouldn't have all these knives to bloody the hands.

They stopped to rest for a moment. But when they were not working they got colder. Here they were in the tropical coral sea and the chill of this water was a mystery.

It was Roger this time who guessed the answer to the mystery. He remembered what Dr Dick had said about the low temperature of spring water.

He took out his mouthpiece and tasted the water. It was fresh.

In the pitch dark cave he searched for and found his brother's arm. He gave it a tug. Hal brushed his hand away. Roger felt for Hal's mouthpiece and yanked it out of his mouth.

Hal could not help gulping water and one gulp was enough to tell him that they had found what they had been looking for. Now he was conscious of an upward pressure under his feet. That must be the fresh water welling up from beneath. The pressure was powerful, like the force of water from a fire hydrant.

He felt as if he were going down from a two-hundred-foot level to three hundred or perhaps four hundred feet. This must be because the water pouring in was unable to get out and pressed harder against the body just as it would at a hundred or more feet lower down.

This couldn't go on. Either the incoming flood would

be choked to a standstill or, if it were stronger than the dam, the dam must break.

He let the pressure build up a little further. Then he fished around for Roger's hands, found them, and placed them against one of the biggest chunks of coral that blocked the opening.

Roger got the idea. Both boys pressed with all their strength. Their push combined with the pressure of the incoming spring water was enough to move the block about half an inch. A crack was opened and a little light filtered in.

Again they pushed and the big mass suddenly fell out, leaving a large enough gap so that they could crawl through to freedom.

What had caused the avalanche? They peered up the face of the cliff. They could not quite see the top because it was above the surface. But there was a moving shadow up there that might be the shadow of a man. There was no way to guess who it could be.

They returned to the jeep and drove at once to the office of Dr Dick.

"We found a spring," Hal reported. "It's good and strong and perfectly fresh. It's in a cave at the base of the reef."

"Wonderful," exclaimed Dr Dick. He turned to the

telephone. "I'll get the chief engineer and you can guide him to the spot. He and his crew will pipe the water into town and connect it up with our water system so every house will be supplied. I don't know whether you realize what a big thing this is. It means that from now on we won't need the desalting plant and that will save a lot of money. But it means a lot more than that. The Great Barrier Reef is one thousand two hundred and fifty miles long and if there is a good spring here there must be hundreds more, enough to bring millions of acres of the wastelands of Australia into cultivation – and the same thing can be done elsewhere in the world. Did you have any difficulty in finding it?"

"Well, yes. We had a little brush with an avalanche. But without the avalanche we probably wouldn't have discovered the spring. We crawled into this cave to escape the landslide. Then Roger discovered that the water was fresh."

Dr Dick looked puzzled. "Landslide? Coral formations aren't in the habit of sliding. It must have come down from the top. There's a lot of loose stuff on top of the reef, but I don't see how it could fall – unless someone pushed it over the edge. But who could possibly have done that? Surely there isn't anybody in Undersea City who'd want to bury you."

Now was the chance to tattle to Dr Dick about two men who might like very much to bury them. But suppose neither of those men was guilty. To cast suspicion on Oscar Roach would not be fair. It might lose him his job. And if they mentioned Kaggs, they would have to tell why he had it in for them – because they knew too much about his prison record and his murders. If it was true that he had reformed he deserved a chance to make good.

The chief engineer arrived. They jeeped him to the cave.

When he came back to the jeep, he said, "You must have had a rough time of it. Bad luck to be caught in there – you could have died like rats in a trap. The spring is great. Enough water to supply half a dozen towns the size of Undersea City. You were lucky to find it."

"You used the right word," Hal said. "Lucky. And if we hadn't had the bad luck we wouldn't have had the good luck."

They returned to town and let the chief out at his office. Jeeping down Main Street, they caught sight of Oscar Roach just entering the hotel where he had his dishwashing job. Arriving home, they found Kaggs sitting in the living-room reading his Bible. He looked up, and seemed surprised. "Didn't expect you back so soon," he said.

16
Bottom of the World

The telephone rang. Dr Dick's voice was excited.

"We're planning something pretty special," he said. "Thought you might be interested. Can you come over?"

They swam down Barracuda and round the corner into Research Street to Dick's office.

"We want to do some exploring for minerals farther down," he said. "Would you like to go clear to the bottom of the deepest hole on earth?"

The proposition was so startling that the boys could only look at him with popping eyes.

"We've hired *Deepboat*," Dr Dick explained. "You know, the bathyscaph something like the *Trieste* that carried Jacques Piccard and Lt Don Walsh to the deepest hole in the deepest ocean."

"You mean the Challenger Deep?" asked Hal.

Dr Dick smiled. "I see you've heard of it."

"I read Piccard's story about it in his book *Seven Miles Down*. But that dive was made back in 1960. Hasn't anybody made it since then?"

"No one, up to now. The challenge still waits for

somebody else. The Challenger Deep is a terrific canyon at the south end of the Mariana Trench in the Mariana Islands. You'll find Mariana Trench on the *National Geographic* map. It's a gorge seven times as deep as the Grand Canyon. Looking for minerals is not your job. But we thought you might like to go down to see what animal life, if any, there is down there. Some scientists say there can't be because the tremendous pressure would squeeze any fish to death. Others say it may be the home of monsters – creatures bigger than man has ever seen. Would you like to find out?"

"We certainly would," Hal said. "When do we start?"

"Our ship will leave tomorrow morning."

"But if we go up to the *Discovery* we will get the bends," Hal said.

"That's not the ship," said Dr Dick. "You'll go by hoversub."

"Now you've got me. What's a hoversub?" Hal asked.

"You know the hovercraft – the craft that floats on a cushion of air seven feet above the water. The British already have four whooshing back and forth across the Channel from England to France at seventy miles an hour. More craft are being built. The United States is designing some. It's called a hovercraft because it can hover or float in the air like a helicopter. And it can shoot along so fast because it doesn't have to fight the waves – just rides above them."

"But," said Hal, "if we go up to board the hovercraft we get the bends just the same."

"That's where the hoversub comes in. It's so new it hasn't made the dictionary yet. The hoversub is a combination of hovercraft and submarine. It can travel underwater – not very fast because the drag of the water holds it back; it can go much faster through the air. You can board it down here two hundred feet below. The air in it will be exactly the same as what you are breathing now – mostly helium. The cabin will be sealed tight so the air won't change. The hoversub will rise above the waves and make the two-thousand-mile trip to the Marianas. Then it will sink again and meet *Deepboat* two hundred feet down. *Deepboat* will be charged with the same air, and will take you to the bottom and back without any change in pressure."

"Wonderful," Hal said, "if it works."

"Well," said Dr Dick cheerfully, "if it doesn't work you won't know it – because you'll be dead."

The boys laughed, but they thought it was pretty grim humour.

The next morning, there was the hoversub waiting at the corner of Research Street and Main. At the back it had jets like those of an aeroplane. On its belly was a great superjet from which air could be expelled with enough force to lift the vessel above the surface of the sea.

The boys crawled in through the open hatch. Already aboard were two geologists and the pilot. The geologists shook hands. They were young men, perhaps in their twenties, and seemed as highly excited as the two naturalists.

The hatch was sealed tight and the jets turned on. The hoversub climbed the two hundred feet to the surface and then burst through into the air as if it belonged there. It scudded along twelve feet above the waves.

"This thing must weigh a ton," Hal said. "Must be a pretty powerful motor to lift it this high."

"They say it's three thousand five hundred horsepower," said one of the geologists. "How smoothly it rides! No pitching, no rolling. I like that. I get mighty seasick in an ordinary boat."

The sea was very choppy – but the crests of the waves never touched the flying submarine. They snarled and spit as if they were angry not to be able to toss this thing around as they could a surface craft of the same size. A fishing boat going in the same direction had a hard time bucking the strong wind and contrary waves. It was not making more than five miles an hour. The hoversub shot by it at seventy and there was scarcely time for the fishermen to wave before it was gone.

Even at this speed it would take thirty hours to get to the Marianas. So everybody settled down to sleep, or eat, or talk. The pilot put the controls on automatic and came back to join the others.

"This is a slowcoach compared with what they are planning," he said. "Ships that will weigh forty thousand tons and scoot just above the surface of the Atlantic and Pacific Oceans at speeds of several hundred miles an hour."

He sighted a coral reef lying dead ahead. It was about half a mile wide and three miles long. The pilot didn't even go back to the controls.

"Aren't you going to go round it?" Hal said anxiously.

"Don't need to," the pilot said. "Nothing to stop us there. No trees. Watch this bucking bronco get over it."

Hal and Roger watched nervously. The beach slanted up in a sloping bank. Surely the hoversub would strike the bank.

Instead, it rose as the bank rose and flew twelve feet above the land just as it had above the water. It sped across like a scared cat and slid down as the other shore sloped to sea level. And the pilot had not touched the controls.

One bare coral island after another was crossed in the

same way. Only where there were coconut palms growing did the pilot have to go forward and guide the ship through the trees.

"It will go over swamps, bogs, marshes or rivers in the same way," he said. "It will even climb a hill and go down the other side."

"Like riding a magic carpet," Roger said.

Magic carpet. It sounded good. So the men named the flying sub *Magic Carpet*.

"We'll be over an open stretch now," said the pilot. "So I think I'll take a nap. I'll have to be at the controls all night."

"But don't you need somebody up there while you're napping?" Hal asked.

"No, I don't think so. There are no more islands. Still, a ship might get in our way. Then the automatic wouldn't know what to do. I'll show you the controls so that you can take over in case of emergency."

It was very simple. Just one lever steered the craft right or left, up or down.

The pilot went back and was soon sound asleep. Hal took his seat behind the controls. He did not dare go off and leave everything to the automatic.

He studied the chart. They were over the open northern waters of the Coral Sea. He measured the distance against the speed of the craft. It would take about eight hours before the *Magic Carpet* could reach the island world of the Solomons and New Guinea. Then he would wake the pilot.

It was well along in the afternoon before he sighted the islands. The pilot was still asleep. Why rouse him? The tip of New Guinea pointed at him like a warning finger on the left. It would be easy enough to steer past it. Then there was a large gap between New Ireland and Bougainville. Anyone who couldn't find his way through here would be pretty stupid. And if any ship appeared he could certainly go round it.

But he didn't reckon on two ships, popping out from behind two islands at the same time and about to pass each other directly ahead of him. He couldn't steer either to port or to starboard without hitting one of them. He could have stopped this contraption if he knew how, but the pilot had not shown him the position of the throttle. There was no time to call the pilot. Both islands were heavily forested and the *Magic Carpet* was not designed to go over forests.

A gap suddenly appeared between the trees on the starboard point. Perhaps he could hop the island there.

As he neared the shore he saw that the hopping was not going to be easy. The beach was not a gentle slope as it had been on the coral islands. In fact there was no beach.

The surf boiled against an overhanging bank. How high it was he couldn't be sure but he was afraid it would be too high for the flying sub. If he plunged into the rocky wall below the overhang at seventy miles an hour there would be no more *Magic Carpet* and no life left in its passengers.

Perhaps he could rise above it. He threw the steering lever into the up position. The hoversub did not rise. He had forgotten that this was not an aeroplane. It would go up through water because its jets kept pushing against the water. It could ride a cushion of air over land because the big jet blowing against the ground held it up. But twelve feet up was the limit.

Hal held his breath. He wanted to close his eyes so that he couldn't see what happened. He thought of leaving the controls and rushing back to the rear of the cabin so that he wouldn't get the full force of the crash. But he kept his eyes open and held on.

He expected to hear some cries of alarm behind him. He glanced back. All the others were sound asleep.

The hoversub struck the bank. It shuddered, but kept going. It ploughed through the top layer of stones and dirt. It was crawling on its stomach. Would it make it or not? If it could just get its big jet over the ground it would be pushed up into the air.

Then suddenly he knew it was all right. The powerful jet got its mouth over the edge of the bank and at once bounced the flying sub twelve feet up. The jolt made the pilot grunt and turn over in his sleep. The others seemed dead and did not know how near they had come to being really dead. Hal breathed a deep sigh of relief. He felt as if all his troubles were over. Nothing as bad as that could happen again.

Then he saw something else as bad as that straight ahead. A house was in his way and there was no time to go round it. The hoversub tore into the thatched roof, ripped a big hole in it, and passed through. Bits of thatch flew in every direction. The people in the house must have thought the end of the world had come. They burst out of the doors and windows, screaming.

One of them had a gun and took a pot shot at the flying devil. He missed. Hal's passengers did not hear the shot over the roar of the flying sub's own engine.

But other natives heard it and ran out of their houses with guns, assuming that some enemy tribe was making war on them.

They fired at the hoversub and the bullets rattled on the fuselage. This could be serious. If they managed to make holes through the metal shell or smash a window the high-pressure helium would pour out, low-pressure air would pour in, and everybody on board would die of the bends.

Luckily the shell, built to resist great water pressure, resisted the bullets while the Plexiglas bent like rubber but did not break.

A crowd of natives directly in the way scattered with shrieks of terror to both sides, not realizing that even those six feet tall would still be six feet below the flying monster. Some threw themselves flat on the ground and gave themselves up for dead. They were doubtless surprised to be still alive after the thing had passed.

Here was something they would remember the rest of their lives. The story would grow and grow. And some day the old men would take their grandchildren on their knees and tell them about the frightful dragon as big as the island spouting flame from its great red eyes and burning wind from a hole in its stomach, sweeping the land like a typhoon, killing thousands upon thousands of men, women and children.

As a matter of fact, not a soul was hurt except perhaps a few who got bullets in their legs because the gunmen were too excited to shoot straight.

17
Seven Miles Deep

Another thrill waited for Hal at the other side of the island.

The sea here was very rough. Great billows dashed against the rocks, sending up fountains of spray. But what bothered Hal the most was that this bank was about twenty feet high. What would happen when the flying sub went over the edge?

The boat shot out into space. Now it was where it didn't belong, twenty feet above sea level. Its jet blast could not support it at this level. It dropped so heavily that it did not stop at twelve feet but went on down and ploughed into the sea. A big fish lying in its path got out of the way with a powerful flick of its tail. The sub came out into the trough of a wave and was almost at once buried in another billow.

Then it began to gain altitude and in the next trough managed to climb to its proper height of a dozen feet.

Its driver had had enough. He put the controls on automatic and went back to give the pilot a good poke. That gentleman woke, blinking.

"Oh, it's you. I thought you were going to let me snooze until we got to the islands."

"We're past the islands," Hal said. He led the sleepy pilot forward and put his finger on the chart. "We're here, just beyond the Solomons."

"How did it go?" the pilot asked.

"Fine."

"No trouble?"

"No trouble."

"You were lucky."

"We're all lucky," Hal said. "Lucky to be alive."

The little ship flew on, day and night, past wonderful Truk embracing three hundred islets inside its coral reef, on to the south end of the Mariana Trench. There the pilot located *Deepboat* by radiotelephone and dived down two hundred feet to meet it. The two boats rubbed elbows.

The pilot of *Deepboat* dropped out of the open hatch and the hatch of *Magic Carpet* was opened to receive him.

After introductions, he explained, "There isn't room in *Deepboat* for more than two men. I suppose you two naturalists will want to go down together, and you two geologists will wish to go down together. So that leaves me out. But you won't need me. *Deepboat* is not

163

hard to operate. If one of you will go over with me now I'll show him how to work it."

Hal insisted that the geologists have the first dive. One went with the pilot who showed him the controls. Then the pilot returned to *Magic Carpet* and the other geologist joined the first. They closed the hatch and *Deepboat* began to descend into the depths. Hal and Roger waited as patiently as they could for its return.

"By the way," Hal said. "Why is it called *Deepboat*?"

The pilot replied, "Auguste Piccard, the man who invented the deep-diving boat, called it a bathyscaph. *Bathy* is Greek for deep and *scaph* is Greek for boat. But the builder of this one didn't see why English-speaking people should talk Greek. So he just turned these words into English, and you have *Deepboat*."

"Was it right here that Piccard's boat made its dive?"

"Right here. You are directly above the deepest hole that has ever been found in any ocean. It's called Challenger Deep and, believe me, it's deep. Seven miles straight down."

"Did Piccard's boat go down all the way?"

"Clear to the bottom."

"Was his boat the same as *Deepboat*?"

"No. Not quite. His boat, called the *Trieste*, was much larger than *Deepboat* and heavier."

"Has *Deepboat* been down?"

"Only about a mile."

This was a surprise to Hal. He looked worried. "So if we four go deeper we'll be testing it out for the first time."

"That's right," grinned the pilot. "Whatever you do will be at your own risk. The boat is designed to stand great pressure. But, who knows, it may cave in like an egg. And you'll come up as flat as pancakes."

This seemed to amuse him but it didn't amuse Hal and Roger. "It doesn't seem to worry you," Hal said.

"Why should I worry?" the pilot answered. "It's none of my business. I was just told to bring it here and have it ready. It's ready. Of course if the geologists never come back you won't need to go down. That's a happy thought."

This fellow, Hal reflected, is just too happy for any good use.

He breathed easier when, after an hour, *Deepboat* returned. It was still in good shape. The two geologists came back to *Magic Carpet*.

"How did it go?" Hal asked.

"Very well. We studied the rock strata all the way down the face of the canyon."

"All the way? You went to the bottom?"

165

"Oh no. That wasn't necessary. We went down about two miles. We learned all we needed to so there was no reason for going farther."

"Now it's your turn," said the happy pilot of *Deepboat*, and took Hal over to show him the controls. The pilot returned in a few moments and Roger went over to join Hal. They made the hatch tight, then turned on the top jets that would push the craft down into the depths of the sea.

There was still some daylight but it faded rapidly as they went deeper. Soon it was as dark as night.

The pilot had been right, the thing was too small for more than two men. Even for two it was a tight fit. It seemed to be a perfectly round steel ball. Through its Plexiglas windows they could see the stars of this underwater night. But these stars were all racing about madly.

The stars were of all colours, red, yellow, green, blue, lavender . . . They were the lights carried by the phosphorescent fish.

A lantern fish went by, a row of lights down each side like the portholes of a ship. Shrimp threw out bright flames. Jellyfish glowed softly. Venus' girdles were outlined as with neon tubes.

The hatchetfish was equipped with indirect lighting.

The "deepsea dragon" was conspicuous with its rows of green and blue lamps. The greybeard sported illuminated whiskers.

Squid peered out of eyes rimmed with lights, and more lights dotted their tentacles. Toadfish showed no lights when their huge mouths were shut; but when open, a string of lights like a necklace of pearls appeared along the base of the teeth.

All these creatures lived far down beyond the reach of daylight, hence their need of lights. Why some of the lights were white, some yellow, some red, some blue, some green, science had not explained.

One carried what looked like a small electric bulb suspended from a sort of fishing pole in front of its face. This attracted smaller fish – then the light was jerked out of the way and the little fish found themselves between the jaws of the fisherman.

The moon rose. At least it looked like the moon, but Hal said it was a moonfish. It was perfectly round, a full ten feet in diameter, flat and thin, and glowed like the moon.

It is also called the headfish since it appears to be nothing but head. When young it has a tail, but drops it as a tadpole does. What looks like only a head actually contains the stomach and other organs. On the edge of the big moon are two small eyes. Tiny, almost invisible fins along the moon's edge propel the ton weight of the huge fish slowly through the water.

A curious thing about the phosphorescent fish was that they left trails of phosphorescence behind them, like the tails of meteors.

A fairly large fish was sprinkled all over with lights. "They call it the stareater," Hal said. Even its fins were illuminated. From its chin dangled brilliantly lighted whiskers.

"But there's one without any lights," Roger said. "Why is that?"

"It's called the blindfish," Hal said. "It's perfectly blind, so it couldn't use lights to see where it is going. It just moves along slowly like a blind man walking down the street tapping his cane ahead of him. Only in this case there are about twenty canes – those long feelers that spread out in every direction. With these the fish can feel its way along and find its food."

"How deep are we now?" Roger asked.

Hal looked at the illuminated depth gauge. "Eighteen hundred fathoms. Let's see – a fathom is six feet. So we're down about two miles."

"That's as far as the geologists went," Roger said. "Do we go up now?"

"Not a chance," Hal said. "They had good reason for going up – they had seen all they wanted to. But we haven't begun to see what we came here to see. We want to find out what there is at the bottom – monsters, or no life at all?"

"Didn't Piccard and his pal find out?"

"They thought they saw a flatfish and some shrimp. Other scientists say they must have been mistaken – that no fish could stand the terrific pressure. Perhaps we'll find out who was right."

"But we'll be the first to go down that far in *Deepboat*," Roger said. "Aren't you afraid?"

"Of course I am," Hal admitted. "But someone has to test out this thing and we may as well be the ones. Until it begins to buckle in on us we'll keep going down."

Deepboat bumped hard and stopped.

"We must be at the bottom already," said Roger. "Or else we struck a big fish."

"No," Hal said. "We bumped into a thermocline."

"What's a thermocline?"

"Look out of the window," said Hal. "See what looks like a floor?"

The thousands of small illuminated sea creatures lying on it did make it look like a floor. "That's a thermocline," Hal said. "The ocean isn't the same all the way down. It comes in layers like a layer cake. The top layer is warm water. The thermocline divides the warm water above from the colder water below. You noticed how we bounced up when we hit it. It's a sort of heavy elastic sheet like the one a circus performer bounces on when he falls from a trapeze."

"Can we get through it?"

"Sure." Hal turned on a little more power. *Deepboat* struck the thermocline again, broke through, and continued down.

Twice more they struck thermoclines, bounced up a few yards, put on more power and got through.

Suddenly everything in the sea began to rush upwards at a great rate. Hal turned on the searchlight. The canyon wall beside them was flying up at great speed.

"What's going on now?" Roger worried. "I didn't know so many things could happen on a deep dive."

Hal looked at the tachometer. It measured their diving rate. "We're going down twice as fast as we should. We've been caught in a current going down this cliff. It's a sort of river in the ocean – but a strange river because it goes straight down rather than on the level." He turned off the engine. "We don't need any power now," he said. "We get a free ride."

The free ride did not last long. The swift drop ended in a sickening crash. There was no bounce this time. They had really struck something hard. *Deepboat* stopped dead.

"I hope that didn't crack open a seam somewhere," said Hal, inspecting the inside wall of their little prison. "I don't see any water coming in."

"What happened?"

"Struck a ledge sticking out from the cliff. If we can't get off it, our trip ends right here. I'll try going up a little."

Deepboat did not budge. The force of the torrent coming from above held it firmly to the ledge.

This was a pretty pass. They couldn't go either up or down.

"We'll try going sideways," Hal said. He diverted the power to the side jets. The boat began to roll towards the edge. The boys found themselves upside down. With a great deal of scraping and grinding, *Deepboat* reached the edge and dropped off. It righted itself, much to the relief of its passengers, and then continued its swift descent.

This went on for another thousand feet. Then the torrent

mysteriously faded away like a river in the desert sinking into the sand.

No sooner had the trippers to the bottom of the world begun to breathe easily than their craft struck again. But this strike was quite different. It was not a hard jolt, but soft and squashy.

"Another thermocline?" said Roger.

"Perhaps," Hal said. He put on more power. If this were another thermocline he could break through it. But *Deepboat* did not move.

"Perhaps we've reached the bottom," Roger said.

Hal looked at the depth gauge. "Nowhere near it yet," he answered.

"Then what can be holding us up?"

"I don't know," Hal confessed.

"Look!" cried Roger. Something had come up where the searchlight could shine upon it. What looked like two enormous eyes were visible through the window.

"They can't be eyes," Hal said. "Nothing has eyes as big as those. They look as big as a ship's portholes."

The great eyes looked like pools of angry green, lit from the inside.

"Perhaps it's a giant octopus," Roger guessed.

"No," Hal said. "Even the biggest octopus has small

eyes. And they don't glow like these. These seem to be phosphorescent."

Something like a huge snake passed across the window.

Hal exclaimed, "Now I know what it is. The cousin of the giant octopus. The supergiant squid. It's ten times the size of a big octopus."

"How large do you suppose this one is?" Roger asked.

"Judging by the size of those eyes," Hal said, "and the size of that tentacle we just saw, I'd guess it might be fifty or sixty feet long."

Roger whistled. "What a monster! It's a good thing it's not dangerous."

"Not dangerous!" exclaimed Hal. "Guess again. People over here call it the nightmare of the Pacific. Another common name for it is devil-fish. Luckily it's very seldom seen because it prefers to stay far down. There's that tentacle again. Look at the big cups in it."

"Like the cups of an octopus," said Roger.

"Yes, but quite different. The cups on the tentacle of an octopus are for hanging on. They are suction cups. The squid's cups are for killing." He directed the searchlight into one of the cups. It was lined with big sharp teeth. "Anything or anybody that gets caught by those cups is dead before it gets to the squid's mouth. And the mouth is even more dangerous. Let's see if we can find it." He moved the searchlight down from the big eyes until it rested upon the animal's enormous beak.

"It looks as hard as iron," Roger said. "How could any animal with such a soft mushy body have such terrific jaws?"

"It could crush a shark with those jaws," Hal said. "Or split open your head as easily as you could crack a walnut."

Roger was impatient. "We can't stay here for ever. Why doesn't it move along?"

"It's too much interested in us. It's probably wondering if it can crack this nut and get at us."

"Let's get out of here," Roger suggested. "If you can't push it down out of the way, why not lose it by going up a bit?"

"I'll try," said Hal. He turned on the lower jets. That should send the boat up. But *Deepboat* did not move.

"The beast must have one of its tentacles wrapped around over the top of the ball."

With its prey trying to escape, the animal became infuriated and threw other arms around *Deepboat*. Some of them almost covered the Plexiglas windows.

Roger was worried. "I think it's gripping us with all eight arms."

"All ten," Hal said. "Your old friend the octopus has

eight arms – the squid has two more." Hal turned on every ounce of power.

The ball did not move. They could hear the great jaws grinding on the steel hull. The monster was fighting mad now. The sharp teeth in its tentacles were scraping over the hull.

Hal turned off the engine. "It's no use," he said. "We'll just have to wait."

The devil-fish kept on biting and scratching. It had never encountered an enemy as tough as this one. The ball was too big to be swallowed whole and it didn't crack easily. The giant was becoming more and more irritated.

"It's getting on my nerves," Roger said.

"Don't worry. It can't get through solid steel."

But there was real cause for worry when the squid attacked one of the windows. Plexiglas was very tough, yet it was not steel. It could resist tremendous pressure. But it could be cut by something very sharp and the beak that was now pounding against it was very sharp.

Hal tried to estimate the size of the creature. It was about twelve feet around and must weigh at least a thousand pounds.

"There's one good thing," he said. "Even if he breaks that little window he can't get in. He's much too big."

"I'm not afraid of his getting in," Roger said. "But if he makes just a little hole, the sea can get in and what happens then?"

Hal didn't like to terrify his young brother, but he must tell the truth. "In that case, I'm afraid it would be curtains for both of us. The water pressure must be at least a hundred times the air pressure in this ball. So the water would pour in at a tremendous rate and we would drown in a few minutes."

The squid's operations had attracted an audience. Fish of all sizes and shapes came up to watch what was going on. They were a rainbow of many colours in the glow of the searchlight.

Farther back there was something like a cloud passing through the water.

"What do you suppose it is?" wondered Roger. "It's too big to be a fish. Perhaps it's just a shadow."

The thing that looked like a great grey shadow came closer.

"I hope . . ." began Hal, but he didn't say what he hoped. He was disappointed when the shadow passed and was gone.

Presently it came back. Now it was squarely in the beam of the searchlight. It had an enormous block of a head as big as a bus. Its mouth was open and its huge teeth shone white.

"A sperm whale!" Hal exclaimed. "Perhaps it will help us out."

"What can it do?" Roger asked.

"It can save us from a watery death," said Hal, "if it takes a notion to do it. One of the sperm whale's favourite foods is squid. Not the little squid a foot or two long that swim near the surface, but the juicy giants that live far down. I only hope it's hungry."

The whale appeared again. It came within a few yards of the squid, then swam away.

"I'll bet it's afraid," Roger said.

"It has good reason to be. Many whales have been killed by squid."

"I should think it would always win," Roger said. "It's a lot bigger than the squid."

"Yes, but it doesn't have ten tentacles thirty feet long armed with thousands of teeth."

The whale drifted back and lay for a while watching its enemy with tiny eyes that contrasted oddly with the enormous hub caps of the squid.

Then with a mighty thrust of its tail, it shot forward. Its mouth, as big as a door, opened to take in its favourite food. It would have this meal all to itself because no other creature would dare attack the giant squid. The whale's teeth looked as sharp as razors. They were no good for chewing, but could inflict a terrible bite.

The squid detached one arm from the steel ball and thrashed out against the approaching enemy. The whale snapped at the great snakelike tentacle and got it firmly between its teeth. Now it was teeth against teeth. When it came to teeth the squid was a match for the whale. The hundreds of sharp points on the great arm must sink deep into the whale's enormous tongue, the most sensitive part of its entire body.

At once the whale spun about and made off, opening its mouth to get rid of this torture. But the squid did not let go. The result was a dizzy ride for the two passengers in *Deepboat*. They were being towed across the gorge with amazing speed. It was not a smooth ride. With every convulsive move of the whale in its effort to get free of the torturing arm, the ball bounced or rolled violently from one side to the other, tossing the boys against the walls until they were bruised and bloody.

Now they were getting near the other wall of the canyon. Their wobbling searchlight caught flashes of it, a straight up-and-down precipice of solid rock.

At the last moment the whale swung away from the cliff and the ball struck it with terrific force. The whirlabout had turned *Deepboat* upside down and the shock of striking the cliff while standing on their heads was so sharp that they almost passed out. Their big towboat now pulled them across towards the other cliff, where they would probably get the same rough treatment.

But the whale, finding it could not shake the toothy arm loose from its tongue, closed its teeth upon it and bit it off. The sudden pain caused the squid to change colour to an angry red. Now it took away its nine remaining arms from *Deepboat* and wrapped them around the head and over the eyes of the whale. All the sharp knives on the great arms sank into the whale's flesh and blood turned the water pink.

But the whale was by no means beaten. Its head was tied up but its mighty tail was still free. It could not reach its own head with its tail. With the intelligence of its cousin, the dolphin, it struck *Deepboat* a terrific blow and threw the hard steel ball up against the soft pulpy body of the squid.

The result was that the squid was turned into a pancake. It would soon round out again if left to itself, but the blow had also driven it up against the open jaws of the whale, which promptly bit off a chunk of squid as big as a donkey.

That was too much for the giant of the deep. The whale dined on the remains of the dead squid at leisure, while the boys felt their bruises and collected their wits.

They were not only badly beaten up but very cold. The thermometer told them that the temperature was only two degrees above freezing.

"I suppose it will get colder and colder the farther down we go," Roger lamented.

It did seem to do just that until they finally broke through another thermocline.

"Now we're within a mile of the bottom," Hal said.

He studied the thermometer. "Seems to me it's getting a bit warmer," he said.

"How could that be?"

"I don't know. But I can guess. There may be volcanic fires under the bottom. You know, the farther down you go in some mines the hotter it gets. The subterranean heat beneath the floor of this trench may be warming up the bottom layer of water. Anyhow, there's no doubt about it – the mercury is climbing a bit."

Here was something new for Roger to worry about. Would they boil when they got to the bottom? Perhaps they would drop into an underwater volcano. He said as much to Hal.

"I don't think it will be that bad," Hal said. "Anyhow we'll soon know." He watched the depth gauge. "Only thirty fathoms yet to go. Now only twenty. Now eighteen – fifteen – ten. Brace yourself – we may bump hard."

But there was no jolt. *Deepboat* settled down into something as soft as a feather bed. They were in mud almost up to the windows.

They had expected it to be icy cold down here. But the mercury had actually risen a little. It had climbed two degrees. That was not much, but enough to indicate that there was heat under this mud.

The mud that had clouded the water when they struck was settling now.

They peered out of the windows. Here they were at the deepest known spot in all the oceans. The Grand Canyon was a mile deep. They had gone six miles deeper. They had gone down farther than Mount Everest goes up. Everest was the highest mountain on the planet. Sir Edmund Hillary had climbed it. He reached the very top, 29,028 feet above sea level. Everybody thought that was a great accomplishment – and so it was. But two boys had now gone down 36,198 feet below sea level. In a few minutes they would climb again, 7,170 feet more than Hillary had climbed – but it would be much easier with the help of *Deepboat*. They had proved that this craft could stand the terrific pressure of the deep. It was as tough as Piccard's bathyscaph.

Deepboat was more like a submarine than a bathyscaph. No submarine had ever gone so far down. Perhaps builders of submarines would take advantage of what had been learned from this experiment and build subs that could go far deeper than a few hundred feet below the surface.

There was another thing they had not proved yet. Could life exist at this tremendous depth? Jacques Piccard had claimed that he saw animals on the bottom. He had taken photographs of them but because of the cloudiness of the water the photographs when developed didn't show a thing. So nobody took his report very seriously. It was almost impossible to believe that any living thing could stand such enormous pressures.

"Look," cried Hal. "Isn't that thing moving?"

It was not just a cloud of mud. It was something alive. It rose from the bottom and swam slowly away. In a few minutes it returned, bringing three others with it.

It was a flatfish, like a sole. It was about a foot long and half that across.

"See – it has two eyes on top of its head."

"I think there's something the matter with *your* head," said Roger. "You're dreaming – like Piccard."

"Look for yourself," said Hal.

Roger had to believe it. There were two wide-open eyes and they were on top of the head.

"All flatfish like sole and skate have both eyes on top," Hal reminded him.

"But why does it have eyes?" Roger objected. "If it weren't for that searchlight, it would be pitch black down here. Animals that live where they don't need eyes lose their sight."

"That's what we've always thought," Hal agreed. "But you can see for yourself it's not true. Or at least, not always. I've got to take a picture of this."

He turned the full beam of the searchlight on the flat fish, carefully read the exposure meter, and took several shots. His camera was of the instant developing sort and he could see his results within a few minutes. The flatfish showed up plainly.

"And what are those small things?" Roger said. "They look like red shrimp."

"That's exactly what they are," Hal said, and he took more pictures.

Little wriggly tracks showed that there must be more small animals beneath the mud.

"And there's a fish I've never seen before in all my life," said Hal.

It looked like a bad dream. It had a great savage mouth a foot wide armed with teeth that could easily grind hard-shelled crabs and lobsters to bits and could nip off a human arm at one bite. The mouth seemed to be about all there was to it. The rest of the body tapered down to a thin tail and was covered with what looked like feathers but must be an unusual form of scales. Hal took a photograph of it. Then he caught it between the jaws of the steel grab.

"What do you want it for?" Roger asked.

"I'll bet it's new to science," Hal said. "Of course it will die before we get it back to Undersea City. But then I'll put it in a jar of preservative and send it to a museum to be classified and named."

"What makes you think the scientists don't know about it already?" Roger asked.

"Of course I'm not sure," said Hal. "But I haven't seen the like of it in any manual. I think we've discovered a new species."

Roger was not easily convinced. "But almost everything

has already been discovered. We can't expect to find anything new."

"Why not?" said Hal. "New animals are being discovered every year. Recently the Smithsonian Institution collected fish in the Marshall Islands. They got four hundred and eighty-one species. Seventy-nine of them were new. That's one out of every six. Actually, human beings are only beginning to learn the mysteries of the ocean, and the very deep waters like these are practically unknown."

"Well," Roger said, "I have a name for this one already. *Nightmare Huntii.*"

Hal laughed. "*Nightmare* is good. But I'm sure they won't give it our name. That's too much to expect. Let's go up."

At first they climbed very slowly. The thick, heavy water held them back. They did not mind – it gave them time to see what went on about them. Many times they were happy that they were protected by the steel ball.

A huge manta or sea bat as big as a barn door peered in one of the windows. It must have been twenty feet across from the tip of one wing to the tip of the other. And almost as long as it was wide.

The sea bat was not a man-eater. But still it could cause trouble. It could come up under a small boat and upset it. It could leap ten feet into the air and if there happened to be a boat under it when it came down its two-ton weight could smash the boat and kill the passengers. But, though it had a mouth five feet wide, it had no taste for steel balls and could not have swallowed *Deepboat* if it had tried. It loved to play. It cavorted around the ball, gave it a push or two, then swam away.

"Look – a dragon!" exclaimed Roger. It certainly looked like one, and was quite terrifying as it came billowing into the beam of the searchlight. It was a full thirty feet long, not round, like a snake, but flattened and silver-sided, with a small mouth and deep-set, terrible eyes. But its most amazing feature was a flaming red mane like the mane of a horse that stood straight up from its head and neck. This waving mane did a sort of dance of fire in the unearthly submarine light. Two long spikes that looked as sharp as daggers projected from the back of the head.

Hal said, "Sailors who have spotted it swimming along the surface with its head out of the water have thought that they were looking at a sea serpent. Its real name is oarfish, because it is flattened like an oar. It rises to the surface at sunset, but spends the day at great depths like these."

The next passer-by was an eighteen-foot stingaree. It was a bad-tempered fish, would attack anything that came in its way, and did promptly attack the steel ball. It covered it like a blanket and tried to sting it to death. It was disappointed. *Deepboat* continued to rise, but more slowly because of the weight of the monster.

"Wish we could get rid of this thing," Hal complained.

"Turn on your top jets," Roger suggested.

"Good idea," said Hal, and the stingaree found itself pushed up and away from the ball by the powerful jets.

It was a parade of monsters. The terror of the western Pacific, the great white shark, sometimes called White Death, most murderous of all sharks, a good forty feet long and equipped with many rows of saw-edged, razor-keen teeth, swam slowly by.

"See the barracuda," Hal said.

Roger examined the creature. "That's no barracuda," he said. "The barracuda never gets that big."

"There are many species of barracuda." Hal said. "This one is called the great barracuda. People out here have another name for it, tiger of the sea. Most barracuda don't make trouble. But this one is always asking for it. Swimmers who have had their feet bitten off and don't know what struck them imagine it must have been a shark, but more often the villain is the tiger.

"Now there's something really exciting," Hal exclaimed. "I must get a picture of that."

"Why it's just a shark," said Roger.

"Yes, but it's a shark that has been 'dead' for seventy million years."

"Then how come it's alive now?"

"It's the goblin shark," Hal said. "Its fossil remains have been found in many parts of the world. But no one has reported seeing a live one, so the scientists put it down as extinct. But there it is, alive and well. It's only one of many creatures that naturalists have dismissed as being dead and gone, but are alive in some parts of the world, hidden away in the forests or in the deep waters of the ocean."

He took the creature's picture. That picture would make the authors of books on sea life add one more to the list of living creatures thought to have died out millions of years ago.

Arriving within two hundred feet of the surface, they used their phone to locate the *Magic Carpet*. They were glad to climb into the hoversub, which was so much larger and more comfortable than the steel ball.

"How far down did you go?" one of the geologists asked.

"All the way," Hal said.

"Why all the way?"

"We were under orders. Dr Dick wanted us to see what went on at the bottom."

"But we already know what goes on at the bottom," said the young geologist. "Nothing. Nothing could live under that pressure. Piccard took photographs down there. They didn't show a thing."

"Look at these pictures," Hal said.

The four flatfish could be plainly seen. Also the red shrimp. And the feather-scaled creature, new to science, that Roger had named Hunt Nightmare.

"Never would have believed it," said the pilot.

"But these are small things," said one of the geologists. "It looks as if the scientists who say that there may be monsters deep down are talking through their hats."

"Not quite," Hal said. "We saw a fight between a whale and a giant squid. We were visited by the dragon oarfish and a giant manta and the great white shark."

"And don't forget the stingaree," said Roger.

"And the goblin shark," Hal said. One of the geologists stared.

"You must have made a mistake," he said. "I've seen pictures of the fossils of the goblin shark. It died out millions of years ago."

"So we all thought," Hal agreed. "But look at this picture."

The three others studied the photograph with interest. "Well it seems to me," admitted one of the geologists, "you have a pretty good report to make to Dr Dick."

18
St George and the Dragon

Back in Undersea City, the boys went at their work with new energy.

They started fish farms where the best foodfish could be grown, protected from sharks by those "undersea cowboys", the dolphins. They had lobsters from Maine flown in and started a lobster farm. The best oysters from New England were planted and would grow to full size in half the time it would take in the colder waters of the American coast or Japan. By placing tiny grains of sand within the shells in the Japanese fashion they could produce cultured pearls. They discovered a place where whales gathered and conducted experiments in milking them, for whale milk is a rich, nutritious food. Milking machines drew off the milk. One whale could produce a ton of milk a day. The milk was too rich to drink but it was valuable in cooking and processing other foods.

The new fish they had found was sent in a bottle of preservative to the American Museum of Natural History by Dr Dick, who insisted upon sending along Roger's name for it, *Nightmare huntii*. The museum accepted the name and the young naturalists were more pleased to have a fish named after them than they would have been to have a monument erected in their honour.

Dr Dick called them in. "I have only one fault to find with you," he said.

"What is that?" Hal asked.

"You have neglected one of your two jobs."

"What two jobs?"

"One was to work for us. You've done that very well indeed. The other was to work for yourselves. You seem to have forgotten that. The understanding at the start was that besides serving the Undersea Science Foundation you were to be allowed to carry on your own work of collecting specimens for the aquariums of John Hunt and Sons. You'd better get on with that, or your father will be suing us for using up all of your time."

"But who will take our place?" Hal asked. "Oscar Roach?"

"If you think he can do it."

"I think so," Hal said. "I've been showing him the ropes, whenever I could get him away from his dishwashing. He'll make you a good naturalist."

At first Hal had mistrusted Roach and trusted Kaggs. Now he had grown to trust Roach, but was beginning to have his doubts about the "missionary".

193

Roach was delighted with his promotion from dishwasher to naturalist.

The boys turned to their second job. They collected rare specimens alive and transferred them to the tanks of the *Flying Cloud*. That ship would take them to Brisbane, where they would be put aboard cargo vessels that would carry them to the Hunt Animal Farm on Long Island.

Their father would sell them to oceanariums such as Sea World near San Diego, Marineland near Los Angeles, the Marineland of Florida, the aquarium at Honolulu, Hawaii's Sea Life Park and dozens of similar institutions all over the world.

Three gorgeously coloured trigger fish would be worth twelve hundred dollars. A very rare shark was caught. Australians had an odd name for it – the wobbegong. Elsewhere it is known as the carpet shark. When hauled up suddenly out of the sea it bursts with a sound like a rifle shot. The first one the boys got exploded before Captain Ted could get it into a tank. Another was eased up more slowly so as not to excite it and was successfully tanked.

The hammerhead shark was a prize worth five hundred dollars because its head, shaped like a hammer, was the most unusual in the shark world.

When the tanks were full Hal estimated the total value of the collection as coming very close to a hundred thousand dollars.

Dr Dick came round to the Hunt home with bad news.

"I'm sorry to have to call on you for a little more help," he said. "A shark has been killing some of our people. It has done away with eight men during the last seven days. We have tried to frighten it away, but it seems to prefer to make its home in Undersea City. It swims up and down the streets and when people see it coming they rush to take refuge in their houses. People are afraid to go to the stores to get food, workmen are afraid to go to work. The shark has things all its own way. It goes right on picking off one person after another and there seems to be nothing we can do about it."

"Where do we come into it?" Hal asked.

"You know sharks. We don't. Our miners know mining, the merchants know selling, our police know ordinary police duties, your good friend the Rev. Mr Kaggs knows the Bible, Roach is new to his job, nobody has expert knowledge of sharks – except you two. We want you to get rid of this unwelcome visitor before it kills any more of our people."

"What kind of shark is it?" Hal asked.

"I don't know. It's blue above and white below. Its body is slim and pointed. It has long gill slits. It's about twenty-five feet long and must weigh a ton. Most sharks hesitate to attack people but this one doesn't. It rushes in like a bolt of lightning. Sometimes it knocks a man down with its tail and then bites. Its teeth are very large and sharp. It takes off a leg or arm at one bite."

Roger looked at his brother. "It must be the mako," he said.

"Right," said Hal. "You've given us a very good description of it. It's the mako, and no mistake. Along this coast they call it the man-eater. It has terrible teeth. Weren't the teeth of your shark four inches long?"

Dr Dick nodded.

"It's a meanie," Hal said. "Even when it's full of food it will attack – just because it's vicious by nature. I wish you had given us any other member of the shark family to deal with. We don't dare guarantee results, but we'll do what we can."

"That's all we can ask," said Dr Dick. He seemed well satisfied that the boys would find some way to get rid of this killer.

After he had gone Roger said, "Let me do it."

Hal was surprised. "Of course, you can help me."

196

"No," Roger said. "You have other things to do. We can't stop all of our regular work just to fool around with a shark. I can do that alone."

"But this is no ordinary shark," Hal reminded him. "The mako is the toughest and meanest brute in the Coral Sea. A boy would be no match for it. It's a man's job."

Roger bristled. "And you think you're a man," he said. "Don't forget, you're only five years older than I am."

Hal suddenly understood what his young brother was thinking. Roger wanted to do this thing to prove that he was not just a kid.

Reluctantly, Hal said, "All right. Go ahead and try."

"You don't think I can do it."

"I didn't say that. But if you find you need help, let me know."

Roger took the foot-long knife from his belt and began to sharpen the blade on a whetstone.

Hal looked on with amazement. "You're not going to tackle that shark with a knife!"

"Why not?"

"It would never get through the shark's hide."

"His underside is soft," Roger said.

"But you tried that once and it didn't work."

"I didn't try hard enough. If I have a good sharp knife

and put some real power behind it I think I can make him feel it."

Hal saw it was useless to argue.

Roger slipped on his aqualung, mask and flippers, and slid out through the hole in the floor. Where would he be most likely to find the mako? Where there were the most people. That would be on Main Street. He went down Barracuda, turned into Research Street, and stopped at the corner of Research and Main.

There were some people but no shark. The more venturesome miners were going to work, a few housewives were going to stores, young fellows who had no work were hanging around street corners just as they did in the world above. They couldn't whistle at the girls who went by, but attracted their attention by striking their scuba tanks with a stone or stick.

Small, brightly-coloured reef fish swam around the heads of pedestrians, and there were a few larger fish, tuna, mackerel, and sea bass. Some people tried to grab them with their bare hands. One man succeeded and his family would have tuna for dinner.

Some sharks appeared but they were small and timid and certainly not man-eaters.

Then Roger saw the mako idling down the street. There

was no mistaking it – it was blue above, white below, and its teeth were four inches long. It stared about through big eyes like lamps.

People vanished from the street as if by magic. They plunged into the nearest shops, houses, public buildings. Roger felt like doing the same. People peered out through glass windows. They signalled to him to take refuge. Roger thought it was a very good idea – but there was something within him that forced him to swim up towards the oncoming enemy.

He had read about shark hunters who frightened the shark by swimming straight at it. Roger tried it. He was almost paralysed with fear. Those great lamp-eyes seemed to grow larger and more menacing the closer they came. The mako did not show the slightest inclination to back down or turn away. Instead, it opened its jaws ready to receive this tasty breakfast. Its hundreds of teeth, five rows in the lower jaw and five in the upper, made the dental apparatus of a lion or tiger look like nothing at all.

A shark that had never before met a human might be timid. But this one had met and killed eight humans within a week and had found them easy picking. Roger saw almost too late that he was not going to bluff this monster. When he was two feet away from the terrible reception committee of bared teeth, he dived and slid along the shark's underside. He turned on his back and with all his strength drove the knife upwards against the smooth white skin.

The knife slightly dented the hide but that was all. Then the shark was gone.

Roger thrust his knife into the holster and swam back to the house.

"How did you make out?" Hal asked.

"No luck. I jabbed him hard but the hide was too tough. I'm going to try a spear. After all, that's what St George used against the dragon and dragons are tougher than sharks."

He had always been fascinated by that old story. The dragon had been devouring humans and now was after the king's daughter. St George had a soft spot in his heart for the princess and undertook to kill the dragon. He drove it through with his spear and he and the princess lived happily ever after.

Now it was the same thing over again except that the killer was a shark instead of a dragon and there was no princess.

Armed with a spear of the finest steel with a point as sharp as a needle, Roger sallied forth. But just in case the

spear should fail, he carried an extra weapon – an underwater revolver.

People had left their shelters and were once more walking or swimming along Main Street. They panicked again when the great shark cast its shadow on the street. One pretty girl who did not move quickly enough was caught between the huge jaws and held, to be eaten at leisure. She took the place of the princess in the old legend, and St George Roger Hunt was here to save her.

This time he had no fear. His concern for the girl's life made him brave. He put all the power he could muster into the thrust of his sharp spear.

He did not even see a dent. He had done nothing but bend the point of his spear.

Disgusted, he dropped the spear and drew his revolver. He had read accounts of hunters who had fired at a shark only to have their bullets bounce back from the beast's armourplate. He didn't believe such stories. How could the toughest skin resist a bullet?

He fired. The bullet bounced back as if it had struck a steel spring. It struck Roger in the leaden weight belt. If it had landed an inch higher or an inch lower it would have finished him off.

However, the bullet had disturbed the shark more than

either the knife or the spear. It opened its jaws and dropped its prey. She lay crumpled up on the street. The mouthpiece of her aqualung had fallen from her lips and she must die within a few minutes for lack of air. Roger tried to replace the mouthpiece but the unconscious girl could not hold it.

He looked wildly about for help. The shark was coming back. The nearest place of escape was the hatch of the hotel. Roger dragged her up through the opening on to the floor. Here she could breathe without the aqualung. She gradually revived, and was taken to another room to rest after her harrowing ordeal.

A baffled and humbled St George looked out of the hotel window at his victorious enemy, which was nosing the glass on the other side. Roger didn't feel like St George any more. This was a tougher job than he had bargained for.

Then another idea came to him. He knew that the mako was an expert jumper. Makos have been known to leap out of the water ten or fifteen feet high. With their hatred of humans, they would sometimes make this tremendous jump just in order to fall down on a small boat, break it in two and drown the passengers.

Sometimes the leap killed the mako. If it leaped near

a beach it was apt to fall on the beach and be unable to get back into the water. After wriggling about in vain it would die.

If he could make this mako jump – but there was no beach to land on. How about the hotel lobby? The "front door" in the floor was much larger than that in any house. The ceiling was the highest in town. If the mako could be persuaded to leap up into the air-filled room, fall on the floor, and be unable to get out again, it would die.

The hotel manager might not like the idea but Roger wasn't going to ask the hotel manager.

How could he draw the shark inside? He himself must be the bait. He dropped through the great door into the water and swam out where the shark could see him. It immediately stopped trying to nose its way in through the window and swam under the hotel after the boy. Roger was only a few feet ahead of it when he clambered up into the lobby.

The shark soared up like a rocket and collapsed on the floor. Any guests left in the lobby lost no time in making themselves scarce. The big room was left to Roger and the shark.

Roger felt the flush of victory. This was the end of the

killer of Undersea City. Now people could come and go in peace – or would be able to as soon as the beast died. That would not take long. Roger made himself comfortable in an easy chair and waited for it to happen.

It didn't happen. The shark began to squirm and twist, and its tail, still down in the water, thrashed about violently, drawing the body inch by inch back through the hole. As Roger watched helplessly, the mako dropped through into the sea and swam away.

The disappointed hunter went home.

"Did you get it?" said Hal.

"No luck," Roger said. "I'm going to try laser. Why didn't we think of that before?"

"Because it's not worth thinking about," Hal said. "Our laser is a small outfit. It will kill fish as big as marlin or grouper or sailfish, but it wouldn't have any effect on a twenty-five-foot shark. I think you've done about all you can in this little contest and you'll have to admit that the mako is the winner."

"And I suppose you'll say, 'I told you so,'" Roger said bitterly.

"I'll say no such thing. I think you've put up a good fight and you shouldn't be ashamed because a twenty-five-foot beast was too much for a five-foot boy."

But Roger was not ready to give up. He racked his brain. There must be a way to get the better of that rascal. Then a spark of fire came into his eyes.

"I'm going to try one more thing," he said, and dropped through the door.

He went again into Main Street and entered a shop advertising 'Miner's Supplies'. The walls were covered with the tools of mining – picks, pans, shovels, drills, instruments for measuring gravity and electrical discharges, magnet-ometers, gravimeters and spectro-scopes. But Roger didn't see what he wanted.

"Don't you have explosives?"

"Of course," said the shop assistant. "We keep them locked up. But we don't sell them to boys. What is it you want an explosive for?"

"To explode."

"To explode what? Copper ore, lead, tin – what?"

"A shark," Roger said.

The shop assistant stared. "A shark?"

"The one that is killing people in this town."

The shop assistant hesitated. "It all sounds very irregular," he said. "Have you any authority?"

"Call up Dr Dick," Roger suggested.

The shop assistant went to the phone. He got Dr Dick

on the line. "There's a boy here who wants explosive to blow up a shark."

"Who is it?" Dr Dick asked.

The shop assistant turned to Roger. "What's your name?"

"Roger Hunt."

"His name is Roger Hunt," said the shop assistant over the phone.

"Let him have anything he wants," said Dr Dick.

The shop assistant hung up and turned to Roger. "Why didn't you tell me your name was Hunt? Everybody here knows what you and your brother have been doing." He opened his safe. It was full of deadly-looking contraptions. He took out what appeared to be a steel ball with a clock in its side.

"I suppose your shark won't stay still and wait to be exploded. So you won't have a chance to plug in at any electrical outlet. You'll need something automatic – like this. Set the clock ahead and you'll have time to get out of the way before it goes off."

"Just the thing," Roger said. "What do I owe you?"

"Not a red cent. That shark killed two friends of mine. If we can help you get rid of it we're only too glad to do so." He put the ball into a waterproof sack and handed it to his young customer.

Roger went next to a butcher's shop. "I want a chunk of meat big enough to put this inside."

The butcher was bewildered. He had never had an order like this before. "Well, I don't know. Let me see. It would fall out of almost anything you could put it into. Except – how about a suckling pig? You could jam that thing down its throat and it would stay in."

"Fine," Roger said.

The butcher brought out the carcass of a small pig from the freezer. Roger went out with the ball under one arm and the pig under the other.

The butcher looked after him and shook his head. "Crazy as a loon," he said.

Roger had to wait half an hour before he saw the shark slowly approaching down Main Street. He acted fast. He laid the pig in the middle of the street where the shark could not fail to notice it. He did not need to remove the watertight bag from the ball because it was transparent and he could see the control for setting the clock. He moved it to a five-minute delay. Then he jammed it, bag and all, down the small throat of the pig into the large stomach.

Other people had already scurried to safety and Roger now did the same. He watched from a shop window.

The man-eater lazed down the street looking for a victim. It saw the pig, swooped down and swallowed it at one gulp.

Roger looked at the watertight watch on his wrist. Two minutes of the five had already gone by. He hoped the shark would wander on down the middle of the street where the explosion could not injure any person or damage a building.

But the big fish was not moving away. It nosed about, evidently hunting for another juicy bit like the one it had just enjoyed. Only three minutes were left before that thing would go off.

If the shark had stayed out in the open Roger would not have been worried. He became nervous when he saw the beast edging over towards the buildings. Only two minutes now. The creature explored the ground under the butcher's shop. Only one minute was left.

The shark moved next door under the shop where Roger and others had taken refuge. Roger was sorry he had ever started this thing. If people were killed it would be his fault. He would never forgive himself, nor would anybody else forgive him. He could feel the cold sweat running down his back.

Only fifty seconds now, then forty, then thirty. How

strong was that explosive? Would it blow up the building and kill all the occupants? Twenty seconds.

Failing to find any more pigs, the shark idly swam out again into the street. With a dull thud the charge went off. The effect was immediate. The man-eater of Undersea City turned upside down and slowly sank to the bottom. A hole as big as a barrel was torn in the white hide that had been too tough for knives, spears or bullets.

Men began to grope through the hole for the valuable parts that may make a big shark worth seven thousand dollars.

Out came the great liver, eight feet long and weighing well up towards a hundred pounds. From it would come a valuable oil and vitamins A and D.

The hide would make excellent leather. The teeth would be used for razors, weapons and surgical instruments. They would also be fashioned into costume jewellery. The fins could be sent to China to make the famous shark's-fin soup. The cartilage (the shark has no true bones) would become a high-protein food. The air bladders could be made into isinglass for gelatine or glue. The great jaws were taken by the proprietor of the Undersea City curio store. Indeed, as was once said of the hog, everything about the shark is usable but his breath.

The heart was pulled out, and it lay, still beating, in the hands of the man who had found it. That is one of the amazing things about this amazing animal – the heart keeps on going after the fish is dead. A. Hyatt Verrill, noted sailor and author, reported that the heart removed from a fifteen-foot tiger shark captured at Silver Shoals throbbed steadily as it was passed from man to man. Even after it was tossed on the deck, it continued to beat for more than an hour until the blazing sun dried and shrivelled its surface.

It is really not so astonishing, after all, when we remember that a snake may wriggle long after it is dead, and the piranha of the Amazon after its head has been cut off will continue to snap its murderous jaws.

One thing about the shark remained really alive. This was a remora, or sucker fish, which is in the habit of clamping its vacuum mouth on the hide of a large fish and taking a free ride. But what made it more extraordinary in this case was that the remora was inside the shark's mouth, glued to the tongue. It was pulled away and given to a small boys who took it home to have it cooked for supper.

What about the eight people who had been killed by this villain? No trace of them was found. Even the bones were gone. The shark's powerful stomach acids can dissolve bones in a few hours.

However, there was plenty of proof of the monster's guilt. Among the shark's stomach contents were not only bottles, cans, chunks of wood and scrap iron, but bracelets, necklaces, long hair, a pair of spectacles and many other articles that had been worn by the shark's victims.

A woman recognized a large hunting knife that had belonged to her husband. She seized it, then hastily dropped it, as if she had been burned. The hydrochloric acid in the shark's digestive juices is so powerful that it will promptly scorch human flesh that happens to touch it. The woman wrapped the knife in a piece of seaweed, then sadly took it home.

The flesh of the shark was cut into chunks which the mayor distributed to workmen from the South Sea islands who did not share the Americans' distaste for shark meat.

One of the hotel's lady guests who had been watching all this bloody business seemed to be very weak in the knees. She turned to go back to the hotel. The mayor of Undersea City noticed that she alone was leaving with empty hands. He must give her something. He pressed into her hands the big heart, still palpitating.

The lady looked as if she were about to faint. She could not offend the mayor by refusing the gift. She gingerly carried it through the crowd, a painful smile on her face.

An island woman looked at the heart as if she would like to have it. The nervous visitor was only too glad to get rid of it. She gave it to the woman, who happily carried it home. It would probably beat until it was time to cook it for dinner. It was hard to get fresh meat in Undersea City, and what could be fresher than this?

19
Gold!

Hal sat alone in the glass jeep, superintending his "cowboys" – the dolphins who were guarding the lobster farm.

They circled the field, keeping off marauders, large fish that considered lobsters a very dainty meal. Even sharks feared the swift attacks and sharp teeth of the dolphins.

Hal saw a bumpfish at work. This was a rare specimen. He must get it. The bumpfish has a very hard head like the bumper of an automobile. The bumpfish dives swiftly at a coral block and hits it so powerfully that a piece of the coral is broken off. It then chews up the coral, not because it likes coral, but because the small living polyps in the coral are its favourite food.

This bumpfish was breaking off pieces of coral as big as a fist and chewing them up to get at the tiny animals inside.

Hal slipped out of the jeep, swam down very quietly so that the fish would not notice him, grabbed it and popped it into a plastic bag full of sea water. He returned to the jeep and settled down to examine his prize.

The fish swam about madly. It was so excited that it spilled the ground-up coral from its mouth. Hal was startled to see among the grains of coral other sparkling grains that looked very much like gold.

He looked again at the hump of coral on the sea floor where the fish had been feasting. Why had the little coral animals chosen this place to build their homes? It was mostly covered with sand. The fish must have pushed some of the sand aside to get at the coral. What had made this little hill? Was there a rock under the coral? Or just a heap of sand?

He turned on the laser and directed the beam at the curious hump. Immediately the dial on the machine showed that there was really something very hard down there.

With his laser beam he explored the edge of the hard thing for about a hundred feet. Then there was no more of it. He came back on the other side until he reached the other end.

The thing had the shape of a ship. It must be a ship. That was not strange. These were dangerous waters. Many ships had been lost in the Coral Sea off the Great Barrier Reef.

But why the gold?

Then he remembered Australia's great Gold Rush of a

century ago. Ships had flocked to Australia from all over the world. In a single year nearly a hundred million dollars' worth of gold had been taken in ships bound for Europe or America. Some of the vessels never finished the trip. They sank in the storms off the Great Barrier Reef. They could not be salvaged. In those days divers could not descend to such depths.

Almost breathless with excitement, Hal went down with a hammer and knocked off pieces of coral. Every piece showed those golden glints. This was gold dust. The sacks in which it had been stored had long since rotted away and the dust was scattered in the sand and had become part of the growing coral.

He struck deeper and came upon a solid bar of gold about a foot long. Then he found another, and another. This was too much. He felt dizzy. He took an armful of bars and swam up to the jeep. At this depth the bars were no heavier than sticks of wood. But when he tried to lift them into the jeep they showed their real weight.

He phoned Captain Ted in the *Flying Cloud* above.

"Let down the vac. I've found something pretty wonderful."

He impatiently waited until the big vacuum tube sank down.

"Turn on the power," he telephoned.

"What's coming up?" enquired Captain Ted.

"Sand."

"And you call that wonderful?"

"No. But we have to get rid of the sand before we can get at what's beneath."

"And what's beneath?"

"Gold."

"Thundering fishhooks," exclaimed the captain.

When the sand was cleared away what was left of the wreck was plainly visible. During the century since it had gone to the bottom much of it had rotted and disappeared. The strongly built bulwarks and keel were still there. The sacks that had contained the gold dust had melted away during the century underwater and so had the chests or boxes in which the gold bars had been packed. But all that didn't matter. The important thing was that the bars were still there.

Hal wondered what he should do. Should he go at once and report to Dr Dick? Why should he? He was not working for Dr Dick now, he was on his own. The wreck did not lie within the limits of Undersea City. It was a good two miles out of town.

These were Australian waters. Of any treasure found

there half belonged to the man who discovered it and half to the Australian government.

Should he notify Australian officials and have them send an inspector to examine this fortune on the bottom of the sea and make arrangements to take away the share belonging to the government?

He knew that governments work slowly. It might be days or even weeks before an inspector would arrive, then more days or weeks before a vessel would be sent for the gold.

But during all that time the gold would be exposed to view and thieves might steal it. He was still pondering this problem when he saw one of Undersea City's small subs approaching. He recognized it as the runabout used by the Rev. Merlin Kaggs. It passed close. Kaggs waved to him, then went on.

Hal breathed more easily. Kaggs hadn't noticed what lay on the sea floor, Hal thought. But he was mistaken.

Kaggs had seen just enough to make him curious. The little sub returned. It went down and circled around the wreck. Then it rose and passed out of sight.

Hal knew what he must do. Since he didn't trust Kaggs, he must put this gold where it would not be a temptation to Kaggs or anyone else. He must load it on the *Flying*

Cloud. There Captain Ted and his crew would guard it until the arrival of a government inspector.

How would he get the bars up to the ship? A dolphin could tow them, but only a few at a time. It was really a job for Big Boy, the killer whale. The whale was usually to be found near the house.

Hal drove back to the house and told Roger what he had seen. The boy's eyes popped.

"Gee – I want to see it. I'm going back with you."

"Fine," Hal said. "You can help me."

"Have you told Dr Dick about it?"

"I don't need to," Hal said. "But I think I will anyhow."

He got Dr Dick on the phone and described the wreck and its cargo.

"Where is it?" Dick asked.

"About two miles out."

"Well – thank you for telling me about it. But it's really none of my business. That's outside our territory. And remember, you're working for yourself now, not for us. Good luck." And he rang off.

Hal said, "That man is as honest as the day is long."

Hal and Roger returned to the wreck, followed by the whale.

As they neared the wreck they saw that somebody else

was there. A one-man sub hovered over the place and Kaggs himself stood on a bulwark of the old ship looking at the gold. A few sharks, held off from the lobster farm by the dolphins, passed over his head. He was so occupied in gloating over the treasure that he did not notice them.

Suddenly one of the sharks, perhaps bad-tempered because it could not get at the lobsters, dropped and closed its jaws on his shoulder.

"Come on!" said Hal. He and Roger dropped out of the jeep and swam to the rescue of the unfortunate missionary. Blood from his shoulder was turning the water pink. His mouthpiece had dropped from his mouth and if the shark did not kill him he would die by drowning.

Roger had already learned that he had little chance of puncturing a shark with a knife or spear or even a bullet. But he knew that the most tender spot on a shark is the end of the nose. The beast couldn't be killed by poking its nose, but many a diver had driven off a shark by swatting it with a club on the end of the snout.

Roger had no club. He picked up a gold bar and with all his strength hit the creature on its most tender spot.

The shark dropped Kaggs and swam away. The missionary sagged to the ground, unconscious. A few moments more without air and he would drown. Hal took

him by the head and Roger by the feet and between them they got him up to the jeep and inside. Hal pumped the water out of him and gave him first aid. He began to breathe. Slowly he came alive. He opened his eyes. He looked dully at Hal and Roger. He still did not realize what had happened.

Then he noticed his own bloody shoulder, and remembered.

"That beast almost did for me. Guess I owe my life to you."

He closed his eyes for a time, then opened them and said, "Why did you do it? After what I did to you on the desert island, why did you stop that shark from making a meal of me?"

Hall was dressing the injured shoulder with antiseptic and salve.

"I don't know," he said. "We must have thought you were worth saving."

"That was generous of you," said Kaggs. He took Hal's hand in one of his and Roger's in the other. "Now we are friends, yes? All the past is forgotten, yes?"

"Yes," Hal said.

Roger did not say either yes or no.

"I see you found some treasure," Kaggs said. "What are you going to do with it?"

"Take it upstairs," said Hal.

"To your ship?"

"That's right."

"I'll help you," Kaggs said. "That's the best way I know to show you how I feel about you."

"You'd better rest a while longer . . ."

"No, no. I'm all right now. Let's get going."

The boys would have been just as glad not to have Kaggs's help. But the fellow seemed so anxious to prove that he was their friend, they could not refuse him.

Hal phoned Captain Ted. "Keep an eye out for the whale. He'll be bringing up the bars. Hoist them aboard and stow them in the hold."

Then Hal, Roger and Kaggs descended to the wreck. Hal carried a stout rope. Big Boy, seeing the rope, guessed that this was going to be a job for him and came close.

One end of the rope was looped around his neck and the other end was tied around a half ton of bars. The load was easily pulled to the surface by the powerful whale and the crane of the *Flying Cloud* lifted it aboard.

The job was repeated time and time again until every bar that could be found had been transferred to the ship.

Kaggs returned to his sub and, with a final friendly wave to the boys, sped away.

Hal and Roger returned to the glass jeep. Hal phoned the captain. "That's all of it, Ted. Next thing is to get an inspector. This phone won't reach Cairns but yours will. Phone the chief of police in Cairns and ask him to telegraph Brisbane for an inspector."

"And I hope he comes soon," the captain complained. "Do you realize this ship is almost awash, that stuff is so heavy. If we had a spell of bad weather right now we might go to the bottom."

20
Murder Will Out

The next morning Dr Dick had a caller. He was a young man, brown-skinned, evidently a Polynesian.

"Sit down," said Dr Dick cordially. "What can I do for you?"

"My name is Taro," said the young stranger. "I'm from an island up north. It's called Ponape."

"I know the island," said Dr Dick. "What brought you here?"

"Looking for a job. I came about a week ago. I was hired by the mining engineer. Yesterday I went to church. I recognized the preacher."

"Ah, the Rev. Mr Kaggs. Had you seen him before?"

"Yes, on Ponape. I was wondering if you knew about him."

"What is there to know?"

"What sort of man he really is."

"Well, I know only what he told me. He's been a missionary in the South Sea islands for years."

"He's no missionary," Taro said. "He's a murderer and a pearl thief. He was in prison for a long spell after he

225

committed two murders. Then he pretended that he had reformed. He changed his name and called himself the Reverend Archibald Jones. He went about quoting passages from the Bible and stealing everything he could lay his hands on. He shot a friend of mine. He went with two boys to a desert island, then sailed away and left them there to die. They barely escaped with their lives. I thought you ought to know about these things. I didn't believe you would have hired him if you had known."

Dr Dick studied Taro's face. He looked honest, but how could you tell? The Polynesians were very imaginative people. Perhaps none of this had really happened. Taro might be making up the whole story.

He said to Taro, "I hope you are aware that you have been making some very serious charges. I will investigate your story. If it is true, you are to be thanked for telling me. If it is not true, you will be discharged."

"Fair enough," Taro said.

After he had gone Dr Dick phoned Kaggs. "If you aren't busy could you drop over to see me for a few moments?"

"Certainly," said Kaggs. "It happens to be my hour for prayer and meditation and I have a sermon to prepare for next Sunday. But I shall be able to give you a few minutes."

When he came, Dr Dick said, "Sorry to interrupt your

spiritual duties. When you came to us did you tell us all about yourself?"

Kaggs was startled. "I don't know what you mean. Of course I told you everything that I thought would interest you."

"You told me about your long missionary service in the islands. You told me how you had brought the Gospel to the ignorant heathen of the South Seas. By the way, did you ever meet the Reverend Archibald Jones?"

Kaggs stared. "Wh-wh-why," he stuttered, "the name is not familiar. I don't think I've ever had the pleasure of meeting the gentleman."

"Well, you may have the pleasure now. I will tell you about him. He looks very much like you. But he had an unfortunate past. He committed two murders, and spent many years in prison. When he was released he changed his name, came to the islands, and went about like a missionary preaching to the people. Since you were also a missionary in the islands I should think you would have met him – especially when you looked in the mirror."

An angry flush spread over Kaggs's face. "Who told you this?" he demanded.

"That's not important. The important question is just this: Is it true?"

Kaggs saw that it was hopeless to deny it. Dr Dick had the facts.

"It's true," Kaggs admitted. "And what of it? It's not the first time that a man has made mistakes and gone to prison. It's not the first time that a man has come out of prison determined to make a better life. Such a man should be given a chance. He has paid for the wrongs he has done. Prison has given him time to think. It has given him time to read his Bible and resolve to pattern his life according to the teachings in that book. I came out of prison a changed man. I wanted only to do good. My only desire was to be a blessing to the poor and needy natives of the South Seas. I became a missionary and have been doing good ever since."

Dr Dick smiled. "That all sounds very fine. Certainly a man who has paid for his wrongdoing deserves another chance. But if you had become such a holy man, how did it happen that you went about stealing from the very natives you preached to? Had you really changed? How about the new crimes you committed?"

"What crimes?"

"You planned the murder of two young men. You left them on an uninhabited island where you thought they would die of hunger and thirst. You shot a Ponapean. I have no doubt it was you who made the landslide down the face

228

of the Great Barrier Reef that almost killed our two naturalists. Are all these acts the acts of a man who has changed?"

Kaggs rose from his chair, shaking his fist. "You tell me who put you wise to all this or I'll push your face in."

"Try it," said Dr Dick. "You will leave this house quietly. Your services as the pastor of the church of Undersea City are no longer required. You will get out of town and never come back."

"Who told you?" shouted Kaggs.

"That's none of your business."

"It is my business. Never mind – I know who it was. And he'll pay for it." He stormed out.

He started towards the house he shared with Hal and Roger. Hal must be the one who had blabbed to Dr Dick. Probably his brother was in it too. Kaggs would kill both of them.

But before he got round the corner into Barracuda Street he had cooled down a bit. He had seen the strength and courage of both of these young men. He was no match for the two of them. Even if Hal were there alone he dared not fight him. He would have to think of another way to get back at these two tattle-tales.

Then he thought of the *Flying Cloud*, loaded to the

gunwales with rare fish worth a hundred thousand dollars, and gold bars of untold value, perhaps millions.

So when he entered the house he was all sweetness and light. He cheerily greeted the boys.

"What did Dr Dick want?" Hal asked.

"He just wanted to thank me for yesterday's sermon. He said it gave him great spiritual comfort. He wanted to increase my salary. I declined to accept more. I am here not for money, but for the good I can do."

He went into his room. He came out in a few minutes carrying a bag.

"You look as if you were about to travel," Hal said.

"No, no. Just going to the church."

"Why the bag?" Roger asked.

"Bibles," responded Kaggs. "Bibles for my people. Would you believe it – many of my parishioners have no Bible."

He smiled his way out.

"Not such a bad guy after all," Hal said.

Roger shook his head. "I think he has something up his sleeve."

Kaggs with his bag of personal belongings – and no Bibles – boarded his little sub. He knew that going up would be slow. Any sudden climb would bring on the bends.

He went up fifty feet and stopped. The open hatch allowed some of the helium air to escape and his body slowly adapted itself to less pressure. For a long time he waited, impatient to get on before his trick was discovered.

At last he climbed another fifty feet and stopped again.

The third time he was only fifty feet from the surface. When he had finally fretted through another long delay he rose to the surface, sighted the *Flying Cloud*, and steered for the rope ladder that hung from its rail. He came out of the sub, abandoning it to float wherever it chose, and climbed to the deck.

There was no one to be seen.

He went down the companionway to the captain's cabin and knocked on the door. He heard a gruff "Come in." He took a revolver from his bag, opened the door, and went in.

The captain, seeing the gun, reached for his own. A blast of Kaggs's gun stopped him. Kaggs had taken care to miss. He would need the captain to navigate the ship.

Captain Ted recognized the fellow: Hal had described him. "You're Merlin Kaggs. What do you want?"

"Just behave," said Kaggs, "unless you think you'd look good without a head. Up on deck with you and get under way."

231

"Can't do that," said Captain Ted. "My men aren't here."

"Where are they?"

"Went fishing up the reef."

"All the better," said Kaggs. "That makes two less that I'll have to shoot."

"You think I can run this ship all by myself?"

"Don't worry, I'll help you. I was mate once on a tub like this. Move."

The captain climbed to the deck, Kaggs close behind.

"Where to?" said Captain Ted.

"Some quiet cove north of Cairns. Where I can get this stuff ashore without disturbing the police. But near the railway."

The captain looked up at the idly flapping sails. "No use," he said. "The wind is wrong."

"Don't give me that," growled Kaggs. "The wind's okay. Besides, you have an auxiliary engine."

The captain looked Kaggs up and down. "You really expect to get away with this? You evidently know what we have aboard. Don't you realize that half of it belongs to the Australian government? You could be slapped in jail for the rest of your life for making off with government property. Unless you are killed first by the Hunts."

232

Kaggs laughed. "I'm not afraid of either the government or the Hunts. How can two boys stop me? I've killed before, I can kill again. But I won't need to. They'll know nothing about this until it's too late. We've gabbled too long – now get busy."

"First," said Captain Ted, "you'll have to go forward and get up the anchor."

Kaggs went forward. The captain sidled towards the phone on the bulkhead. The Hunts were going to know right now what had happened. Before he could reach the instrument Kaggs wheeled about and fired. The phone lay in fragments on the deck.

"I hope you understand now that I know how to handle this," said Kaggs, tapping his gun. "Last time I shot at you I missed – on purpose. Next time I may not miss. I can run this scow alone if I have to. Any more monkey business, and I'll do just that. Remember, I'm the boss – you're only the captain."

With the anchor up and the sails set the little ship began to move.

"Not fast enough," Kaggs said. "Turn on the engine."

"It's not safe to go too fast," the captain warned. "There are a lot of reefs ahead."

"I'm giving the orders," roared Kaggs. "Get going."

233

Ted dropped down into the engine-room and did as he was told. There was a passage leading from the engine-room to his cabin. He went to the cabin and sat down before the logbook. He would put a report of this affair into the log so that if anything happened to him there would be written evidence to show who had stolen the ship and murdered him.

The door opened and Kaggs came in.

"What are you up to?" he demanded. He looked over the captain's shoulder and saw his own name. "Still playing tricks," he said. "Get up on deck – quick."

Kaggs grabbed the log and followed the captain to the deck. He went to the rail, opened the book, tore the first sheet into two parts and threw them into the sea. He went on, tearing up and tossing away every leaf. The captain suffered in silence. Nothing is so sacred to the master of a vessel as his log.

When the two missing men returned from their fishing trip their ship was not where it had been moored. Had it sunk because of the great weight of its cargo? They saw the scraps of paper on the sea. They picked up one of them and examined it. It was a piece of the ship's log. The row of scraps led north-west. It was plain that

234

the ship had sailed away in that direction.

"Tom, whatever do you think could have happened?"

"It's clear enough," said Tom. "All that treasure aboard was too much of a temptation for him. He's made off with the ship."

"Who? You don't mean the captain."

"Who else?" said Tom. "He was the only one aboard."

"I never would have believed he'd do a thing like that."

"I know. But what else can you believe?"

"Well, I believe we've got to get word to Hal Hunt right away."

"How can we do that? Do you think we have a phone in this dinghy? Hunt is two hundred feet down. We have no aqualungs. I can't swim that deep without a tank and neither can you."

The other scanned the horizon. "There she is." About three miles off lay the ship of the Undersea Science Foundation, the *Discovery.* "They have a phone. We're lucky that the ship is down wind."

He jibed the sail and let out the sheet to get the full benefit of the breeze. The little boat sped towards the *Discovery.* On board, they found the captain.

"We're from the *Flying Cloud,*" Tom said.

"Nice to have you, boys. Make yourselves at home."

"No, this is not a social call. Our ship is gone. Did you see her leave?"

"No. We were busy below decks." He raised his binoculars and searched the sea where the ship had been.

"We want to phone Hal Hunt," Tom said.

"Yes, you'd better do that. Phone's right over there."

Hal was stunned by the news. "Can't understand it," he said. "Why did the captain sail off without telling me?"

"Perhaps something happened to the phone," suggested Roger, never dreaming how close he was to the truth. "All that gold and stuff. You don't suppose Captain Ted . . ."

"Don't be ridiculous. I'd stake my life on that man."

"Where's Kaggs?" said Roger. "He was just going to the church. He should have been back long ago."

Hal thought of the bag that was supposed to be full of Bibles. And he thought of the *Flying Cloud*'s hull, full of gold. It didn't take any great feat of arithmetic to put the two together.

"Kaggs! That rascal!"

He phoned Dr Dick. "Our ship is gone. We think it must have been stolen."

"Stolen! Who could have . . ." Then he thought of the murderer and thief he had fired that morning. "I can guess," he said. "What can I do for you?"

236

"We want to go after it. May we borrow the hover-sub?"

"Right away. It will be in front of your house in five minutes."

21
The Chase

It was there in less than five. The same pilot who had taken them to the Mariana Trench was at the controls.

It was not necessary to stop on the way up for decompression since the sub was charged with the same helium they had been breathing below, and at the same pressure. The hatch was closed and they shot upwards.

Reaching the surface, the hoversub leaped into the air like an acrobatic whale and skimmed along twelve feet above the sea, supported by its column of down-rushing air.

"It was just about here that she lay," Hal said. He noticed the scraps of paper.

"Look," he said to the pilot. "Follow those. He wasn't heading for Brisbane or Sydney. This line would take him to one of the deserted bays north of Cairns. Smugglers use them to get their stolen goods ashore. If we find the ship we'll be landing on the surface. Ease the pressure out of this thing very slowly so that by the time we get there it will be the same as the air pressure."

When there was no more paper to be seen the pilot looked at his compass and held the hoversub to exactly the same direction. The *Magic Carpet* sped over water, reefs, sand spits and coral islands with equal ease. The ship, of course, had been compelled to go round these bits of land, so by now it might be a little to one side or the other of the compass course. The pilot kept watch ahead, Hal out of the right window, and Roger out of the left.

Things were not going too well on board the *Flying Cloud*. Captain Ted made another brave effort to take back his ship from the pirate Kaggs.

When Kaggs was not looking, the captain picked up a belaying pin. This was like the heavy club used by the police. He stepped up quietly behind Kaggs and brought the weapon down with terrific force.

Kaggs moved his head just in time and the belaying pin did nothing but graze his right temple and cheek, bringing the blood.

He wheeled about and struck out with both fists, one landing under Ted's jaw and the other in his solar plexus. The stunned captain fell to the deck, unconscious. Before he could come to Kaggs seized a coil of rope and tied him up, hand and foot.

"There," he said triumphantly, "now he'll give me no more trouble."

He had no sooner spoken the words than there was a grinding sound beneath his feet and the vessel shuddered to a stop. It had run up on to a reef.

He had thought that he knew how to handle a ship. But he had never had this experience before. How do you get a ship off a reef?

He shook the captain. "Wake up, you son of a gun. Wake up and do something."

It was no use. He must do something himself. The wind pressing on the sails was pushing the ship inch by inch farther up on the jagged coral. The razor-sharp edges of coral were sawing into the hull. A bubbling sound beneath told him that one of the strakes had been broken and sea water was coming in.

He kicked the unconscious captain. He wished he had not punched him quite so hard. Well, the first thing to do was to get down the sails. He did this, then went down and turned off the engine. Now he hoped the ship would slide back into deep water. It did not. He turned on the engine, and put it in reverse. That should pull her off. But she did not move. The water was sloshing round Kaggs's feet.

The water ought to be pumped out. Did the ship have a pump, and if so where was it?

He went up and gave the captain a rousing kick. Ted opened his eyes.

"Get up, you lazy beggar. We're stuck on a reef."

A faint smile came over the captain's face.

"Don't forget," he said. "You're the boss. Get it off." He closed his eyes and seemed to go to sleep.

Kaggs realized that the captain could not help him so long as his hands and feet were bound. He got down and began to untie the knots. Then he tied them tighter than before. So long as this fellow was tied up he couldn't get into mischief.

Kaggs had another idea. The gold. The hull was full of it. It was very heavy. If it were thrown overboard . . .

The idea made him sick. Had he gone through all this just to lose the treasure after all? But he could think of nothing else to do.

He was so occupied that he hardly noticed something leap out of the sea, perhaps a whale or a marlin. He went down into the hold. He looked sadly at the tremendous store of gold bars. He could live beautifully the rest of his life on this fortune. It would all have been his if he hadn't been so careless as to let the ship run aground.

Oh well, there was nothing to do but get rid of it. He gathered as many as he could carry and staggered up the companionway. There seemed to be a shadow above him. He looked up and saw Hal and Roger waiting for him.

So that thing leaping out of the sea – it had not been a whale or a fish. Kaggs dropped the gold bars and they clattered down the steps. He began to reach for his gun. He was stopped by a sharp command, "Hold it!" It came from the captain, freed by the boys, and now standing with a ready gun in his hands.

Kaggs knew when to be tough and when to be sweet. He smiled pleasantly. "I was just trying to save your ship," he said. He came up on deck.

"So that's your idea of how to save it," Hal said. "Steal it and then run it on a reef. What will we do with him, captain?"

"Put him in the brig. It's in the fo'c's'le."

The brig was an iron cage in which trouble-making sailors could be locked up. Kaggs was introduced to his new quarters and the key turned in the lock.

"That will take care of him for a while," Hal said, "until we get the police. Where's the phone?"

"There it is," said Captain Ted, pointing to the broken pieces on the deck. "I'm afraid we'll have to forget the police for a while. The first thing to do is to get the ship off. The tide is rising. As soon as it's high, perhaps she'll float. In the meantime I'll turn on the pump and get rid of some of this water."

But at high tide the schooner was still fast on the coral.

"We need an anchor astern," the captain said, "but we have no dinghy to carry it out."

"*Magic Carpet* can do that," Hal suggested. He looked for the hoversub. It was gone. The pilot was already speeding it back to Undersea City.

"Roger and I will take it out," Hal suggested. They stripped and swam aft about a hundred feet with the anchor. There they dropped it and swam back to the ship.

Ted already had the electric capstan turning, tightening the line on the anchor. That should gradually drag the ship back off the reef.

The line to the anchor tightened more and more until it was as taut as a bowstring. The ship gritted its teeth on the coral, which cut a larger hole in the bottom. Suddenly the line to the anchor snapped in two.

All they had done was to lose an anchor.

The ship had been dragged back just far enough to make the situation worse. Now the hole was not half choked by the reef, but in deeper water so that the hold was filling faster than ever. More water came in than the pump could take out. If this went on the ship would slide off the reef, only to sink stern first.

Roger's thoughts were far away. He was thinking about Captain Cook. Captain Cook, the great navigator who had discovered Australia, had his ship run aground in exactly the same way very close to this very same place. He had saved his ship. Roger remembered how he had done it.

"Let's fother it," he said suddenly.

Captain Ted had not read much history. He smiled indulgently. What was this nonsense?

"What do you mean – fother?"

"Captain Cook did it. Why can't we? Have you got an old sail around the place?"

"Over there – in the locker."

Roger got it and spread it out on the deck.

"How about some tar?" Roger asked.

Captain Ted was getting annoyed. "What is all this nonsense?"

But Hal now remembered what Captain Cook had done. "The kid's on the right track. Let him have the tar."

He helped Roger smear the tar thickly over the canvas.

Then they carried it aft and let it down over the stern. They drew it up under the hull so that it covered the hole.

The pressure of the sea pushed the tarred sail up against the hole so firmly that the inflow of water was shut off.

"Well, I'll be hornswoggled," said Captain Ted. "I've sailed these seas for fifty years but I'm learning something new every day."

22
Safe Harbour

Now the pump could really do its work. Within an hour it had sucked up all the water in the hull and poured it overboard. With this load removed, the ship was several tons lighter than before.

The line from the capstan back to the anchor was repaired. At the next high tide the power was turned on in the electric capstan, the line tightened, the ship groaned and creaked over the coral and was drawn back over the reef into deep water.

Captain Ted went down into the hold. He came back, beaming.

"It works. Not a drop of water coming in. That Cook fellow was pretty smart. Now, where do you want to go? On to Smuggler's Bay?"

"No," Hal said. "What's the nearest port with inspectors, a good bank, and a dry dock where we can get the hull repaired?"

"That would be Brisbane," said Captain Ted. "Perhaps you can help me get these sails up."

The breeze was good and the ship sped away on its new

course. Roger clambered up the ratlines to the crow's nest. His keen eyes searched the sea for reefs. The ones above the surface were easy to see. But there were many others under water. They might be far enough down so that the ship could pass over them, or they might be only two or three feet below the surface. These he could not see, but he could spot them by the colour of the water. Deep water was a deep blue, shallow water was a light blue or tan or coral-pink. When he saw one of these danger tints ahead he would shout down to Captain Ted at the wheel and the course would be altered to go round the reef.

These waters were much too perilous to be crossed at night. So when darkness came on, the ship was moored in the lee of a small island and the sails furled.

In the morning the first light found the *Flying Cloud* on its way again to Brisbane. The ship finally circled the last island and entered Moreton Bay.

"Here we are," Captain Ted announced.

Roger scanned the shore. He had expected to see a large city. He saw nothing but subtropical jungle – palms, flame trees, papaya, frangipani, orchid trees and monster trees two hundred feet high that the captain called bunya-bunyas.

"But where is Brisbane?" Roger wanted to know.

"Oh, we're not quite there yet. It's twenty-five miles up the Brisbane River. It's a twisty river, and dangerous. We'd better get down the sails and crawl up to town by engine."

The city, when they got to it, seemed very fine indeed.

"You'd never think it was founded by murderers and thieves," said Captain Ted. "That was more than a century ago. Britain had so many criminals she didn't have prisons big enough to take them all. So she shipped thousands of them out here. This was a very tough town in the beginning. But the sons and grandsons of the criminals grew up to be fine citizens and now this is one of the best cities in Australia. That's Kangaroo Point ahead. We can dock on the other side of it."

They had no sooner docked than Australian customs officials came aboard. They saw the tanks of fish. "What is this, a floating aquarium?"

"Some specimens we took off the Great Barrier Reef," Hal said.

"Do you expect to sell them here?"

"No. They will be trans-shipped to the United States. Will there be any duty on them?"

"No. We're not interested in fish. Do you have any other cargo?"

"Well," Hal said, "there are a few little items down below."

The men went below. They came back with their eyes fairly popping out of their heads.

"Do you realize you have a fortune down there?"

"Yes, we realize it," said Hal.

"What do you propose to do with it?"

"Give half of it to you — I mean the Australian government. It's from a wreck. The wreck was in Australian waters — so Australia gets half of the gold. Can you appraise it?"

"No. That's taken care of by another department. We'll phone Government House for an inspector."

Hal was worried. He knew how slowly some governments act. "I hope it won't take too long," he said. "We don't want to stay here more than a week or two."

Hal did not have to wait a week or two. The inspector arrived in fifteen minutes. Australia was not so slow after all. With the inspector were three police officers.

The inspector and police went below and saw the stacks upon stacks of gold bars.

The police noticed the man in the brig. One of the officers asked, "Who are you?"

"Just an unfortunate seaman."

"Why are you in here?"

"The captain put me here. He's a brute. You really ought to arrest him."

"What's your name?"

"John Smith."

The officers came up and one of them said, "Who's the captain of this ship?"

"I am," said Captain Ted.

"What has this John Smith done?"

"John Smith? Who's that?"

"The man in the brig. He says his name is John Smith."

Captain Ted laughed. "John Smith, says he? His name is Merlin Kaggs."

"Kaggs? Did you say Merlin Kaggs?"

"That's correct."

"We've been looking for a man by that name for the last eight months. He killed a pearl diver on Thursday Island. Then he disappeared. Where has he been all this time?"

"Meet Hal Hunt," said Captain Ted. "He can tell you all about him."

"He's been underwater," Hal said.

"What do you mean? What's he been doing?"

"He's been pastor of a church at the bottom of the sea."

"Look here," said one of the officers sternly. "This is serious business. Don't try to be funny."

"I'm not," said Hal. "Have you heard of Undersea City?"

"Seems to me I've read something about it. Is that where he's been hiding?"

"You've got it," Hal said.

"Did you know him well?"

"We lived in the same house with him."

"It's lucky he didn't try to kill you."

Hal smiled but said nothing.

"He *did* try to kill Hunt and his brother," said the captain, "by dumping a landslide on them from the Great Barrier Reef."

"Forget it," Hal said. "He's a little unbalanced up here." He tapped his head.

"All the more reason why he should be put away," said the officer. "But there's another thing and I'm afraid it involves you, Captain. We may have to book you on suspicion of attempted grand theft."

Captain Ted's jaw dropped. "What have you got against me?"

"We have a plane that watches for any ships heading for Smuggler's Bay. Now that we see what valuable cargo you were carrying, we have good reason to suppose that you were planning to land it there."

Hal spoke up. "You have it all wrong, officer. Kaggs

stole the ship and tied up the captain. Kaggs hoped to unload the gold at Smuggler's Bay. But he wasn't too good a sailor. He ran the ship on a reef and punched a hole in the bottom. We caught up with him, untied the captain, and Kaggs was clapped into the brig. If your plane came around again the pilot must have noticed that after we got under way we no longer headed for Smuggler's Bay but straight for Brisbane. And here we are — prepared to hand over half of the treasure to the Australian government. Doesn't that prove we weren't interested in any smuggling?"

The officer smiled. "You talk sense, young man." He shook hands with Hal, Roger and the captain.

In the meantime the inspector had been making a careful examination of the treasure. He came up to say, "I can't make any estimate down there. You'll have to get these bars up and spread them out on the deck so I can make a count."

One of the police said, "I don't see why your friend Kaggs can't help you. Do you have the key to the brig?"

Captain Ted gave it to him. The three came up in a moment with the wriggling, ranting Kaggs, loudly protesting his innocence. He was told that he had to knuckle down and help bring up the bars.

"You don't know what you're asking," he said. "I'm no labourer. I'm a minister of the Gospel. I don't work with my hands."

"You don't work with your head either," said one of the officers, "or you wouldn't be in this mess. You're going to do hard labour in prison the rest of your life so you may as well get in a little practice now."

The two boys and the captain went to work bringing up bars. The inspector and police officers helped. Only Kaggs was sulky and unwilling. He refused to take part. An officer gave him a prod with his gun, and Kaggs changed his mind. As he went up and down an officer kept close to him, ready to use his gun if the criminal tried to escape.

When all the bars lay on the deck like a pavement of gold, the inspector made his count. Then he spoke to Hal.

"Forty-four hundred bars. That's twenty-two hundred for the government and the rest for you. This will have to be handled through a bank. What bank do you prefer?"

Hal said, "You know the Brisbane banks, I don't."

"I suggest the Queensland National," said the inspector. "It's the biggest, and it's close by. I'll telephone and see if they can send over a man."

What he said over the telephone must have been impressive, for the person who came was none other than the manager himself. He gasped when he saw the golden pavement.

"Verify my count, please," the inspector said. "Then will you cart this stuff away, have it appraised, divide the value in half and give us two cheques — one for the government and one made out to Hal Hunt."

"Not exactly," Hal said. "Don't make out a cheque to me. Kindly divide our half in two and write one cheque to the Undersea Science Foundation and the other to John Hunt and Sons."

"What's the big idea?" objected Captain Ted. "You found the treasure. Undersea City has no claim to any of it."

"That's the way I want it," Hal said. "I know my father would want it that way too. They are doing a great work down there. They could do a lot more if they had more funds. My father is doing a wonderful job too, protecting wild animals that might otherwise become as extinct as the dinosaur and the dodo. He can do even better with this help."

"Have it your own way," the banker said. "The bank's armoured car will be here in a few minutes to pick this up."

One of the officers telephoned police headquarters for a patrol car. When it arrived, Kaggs was bundled into it and had a free ride to the jail. His last words to Hal were, "When I get out I'll have a score to settle with you."

There remained the job of transferring all the tanks of fishy treasures to a cargo vessel that would take them to the Hunt Animal Farm on Long Island. Then the *Flying Cloud* went into dry dock to get the hole in her hull patched up.

Hal cabled his father:

SPECIMENS COMING TO YOU BY MOTOR SHIP "KANGAROO". LOOK ALSO FOR SLIP OF PAPER FROM QUEENSLAND NATIONAL BANK. WHAT DO YOU WANT US TO DO NOW? CABLE LENNON'S HOTEL BRISBANE.

It would take two or three days to get an answer, and about that long for repairs on the *Flying Cloud*.

The hotel seemed pretty luxurious after the simple quarters they had occupied at the bottom of the sea.

"And the food is better too," Roger said, as they sat at table in the Rainbow Room listening to the orchestra and absorbing kangaroo tail soup, rock oysters on the half shell, and baked Alaska.

Three days later they received John Hunt's answer:

DON'T KNOW EXACTLY WHAT YOU'VE BEEN UP TO BUT AM PROUD OF YOU ANYHOW. WHAT DO YOU MEAN, SLIP OF PAPER? I SUGGEST YOU EXPLORE WORLD'S WILDEST ISLAND, NEW GUINEA. BUT LOOK OUT FOR CANNIBALS. KEEP YOUR SHIP. WE NEED CROCODILES, SEA COWS, TIGER SHARKS, KOMODO DRAGONS, BIRDS OF PARADISE, CASSOWARIES, KANGAROOS, BANDICOOTS, CUSCUS, FLYING FOXES, PHALANGERS, GIANT SCORPIONS, DINOSAUR LIZARDS, DEATH ADDERS, TAIPANS, KOALA BEARS, CANNIBAL SKULLS FOR MUSEUMS.

23
Cannibal Adventure

Hal stared at his brother.

"That's the biggest job we've had yet," he said. "Wonder why he chose New Guinea."

"Because it's close by," Roger guessed. "Isn't it up at the end of the Great Barrier Reef?"

"Yes. Just off the north tip of Australia. But as different from Australia as a tiger is different from a lamb. I suppose it's the most dangerous place on earth for a kid like you to go roaming about. He expects me to take care of you. What does he think I am, a baby-sitter?"

Roger flushed. "I could poke you in the nose for that. What makes you think I can't take care of myself?"

Hal said, "You have a talent for getting into mischief."

"Well, don't I get myself out again?"

Hal thought about this. "Yes, I guess you do. But you've never had to face a pack of cannibals."

"Cannibals, my eye! Dad was just kidding about that. There aren't any cannibals any more – anywhere. Don't Australians run New Guinea? They wouldn't allow head-hunting there."

"They wouldn't if they could stop it," Hal agreed. "But it's not easy. Think what they're up against. New Guinea is the largest island on earth, except Greenland. And New Guinea is practically all mountains. High mountains, up to sixteen thousand feet. In most of the country there are no roads. Wild tribes are shut away in the mountain valleys. Many of these people have never seen a white man. How do you expect Australian patrols to police tribes they can't even reach?"

Roger objected, "But Dad wouldn't be sending us there if it weren't safe."

"He told us it wasn't safe," Hal retorted. "He said look out for cannibals. Well, I can't look out for cannibals and look out for you too. You can take a plane home and I'll go alone."

Roger was in a towering rage. "You send me home? Just try it. Don't forget – the name of our outfit is John Hunt and Sons. Sons, mind you, not Son. I'm part of the firm. I have the same rights as you. Besides you may need me to help you. Perhaps it'll be you, not me, who'll get into trouble."

Hal smiled. He realized that there was a man in this boy. "All right, I surrender," he said. "We'll stick together." He cabled his father.

ON OUR WAY TO NEW GUINEA.

AMAZON ADVENTURE

**For
Jonathan**

Contents

1
The Mysterious Cablegram

Hal sat on the head of a stuffed crocodile in the lobby of the Quito Hotel and cleaned his gun. He listened to the hotel proprietor, Don Pedro.

"Yes, you're going to see the greatest river on earth . . . the greatest unexplored jungle on earth . . . greatest storehouse of natural resources on earth. Some day the Amazon will feed the world."

"But are there really crocs down there as big as this one?" asked Hal, who was more interested in hunting than in feeding the world.

"Bigger. You've come to the right place if you want to get animals for the zoos. Why, I've heard say there are more varieties of wild animals in the Amazon country than in the rest of the world put together. But you'd know better about that." He turned to Hal's father.

People had a habit of turning to John Hunt when they wanted to learn about animals. He had studied and collected animals for twenty years. When Mollie the lion died at the Bronx Zoo, the curator phoned John Hunt to pick up another the next time he went to Africa. When the boa constrictor in the Ringling Circus made a slight tactical error and swallowed a valuable monkey, a message was sent to the private Hunt zoo on Long Island; if there was no such monkey in stock, would Hunt kindly get one on his next visit to Borneo? When that rare antelope called the bongo – so rare that it is worth nearly £1,000 – went down with the colic in the London Zoo, this radiogram reached John Hunt:

BONGO COLIC WHAT TREATMENT

He was supposed to know.

This was his fifth trip to South America, but it was the

first for his two sons, Hal and Roger. And yet they were not quite new to the animal game. Hal had hunted mountain lions in Colorado and Mexico, and both he and his younger brother had tended the collections in their father's Long Island supply zoo, where animals brought back from exploration trips were kept until they were bought by zoos, circuses or museums.

"Nobody knows," said John Hunt cautiously, "how many animals there are in the Amazon valley because so much of the country has not yet been explored. We're going to explore a new part of it on this trip, if all goes well. The Pastaza River."

"The Pastaza!" exclaimed Don Pedro. "That's known only as far as Andoas. Below that no white man has ever gone in and come out alive. Two tried last year. They were never heard of again. Why, the Indians down there are headhunters. Look up yonder. That's what they'll do to you."

He pointed to a strange object on the mantelpiece. It was a human head, but shrunken to the size of an orange.

Roger went over to get a close look at it. He hardly dared touch it.

"It must have been a baby's head."

"No, it was a man," said his father, "but the Jivaro Indians have a way of reducing them. You'll see when we get down there."

Roger looked doubtful. "But how about us?"

"I think we'll be in no danger. They do that to the heads of enemies, or the heads of relatives — and we're neither one."

The hotelman shook his head. "I wouldn't trust them as far as I could throw the cathedral," he said.

"What wouldn't the museums give to have specimens like that!" Hal exclaimed. "How about this one — would you sell it?"

The proprietor looked about nervously. Hal's father hastened to curb his son's enthusiasm.

"The police here would clap you in jail for making an offer like that," he said. "There's a law now against buying or selling heads. You can get imitations made out of goatskin or horsehide. But for the real article, you'll have to wait till we visit the Jivaros."

Roger was still uncomfortable.

"What do we want to go there for anyhow?" he asked. "I thought we were going down the Amazon."

"The Pastaza River is one of the headwaters of the Amazon. The Amazon doesn't start out by being the

Amazon, you know. It begins with a lot of little rivers flowing down from the snows of the Andes. The Pastaza is one of them. And a very interesting one because much of its course hasn't been charted."

"And because it goes through headhunter country," added Hal, amused to see his brother squirm. "We wouldn't want to miss that!"

Roger said nothing. He sauntered around behind Hal, quietly took hold of the crocodile's tail and, with a sudden jerk, landed his brother on the floor.

"Wait till I get you down in the Jivaro country," he said. "I'll help them do your head. Let's see, I think I'll have it fried and pickled. Only trouble is, no museum would want the ugly thing."

He got no further for Hal had grabbed him and was making a determined effort to insert him between the crocodile's jaws.

The hotel proprietor prudently removed the furniture from the vicinity of the struggling boys. He eyed their noisy antics with disapproval.

But John Hunt looked with some pride at his two sons. No man could want better pals on a jungle journey. Hal, finished with school and about to go to college, was as tall and strong as his father. Roger did not run to length, but he was alert and wiry, and brave enough, though he had admitted a natural uneasiness about associating with headhunters. Four years younger than his brother, he had jumped at the chance to spend his school holidays on an animal hunt. Their father had promised that if the boys made good on this adventure, their reward should be a trip to the South Seas.

A clerk handed John Hunt a cablegram. Hunt tore open the envelope and unfolded the message. The boys loosened their stranglehold upon each other and watched their father.

John Hunt read the cable. Then he read it again. As if not believing what he saw, he went over it a third time. The explorer's bronzed face did not grow pale, but there was a tenseness about the mouth and the fingers tightened on the paper. The boys impatiently waited.

"Well, Dad, tell us about it. What have you got there?"

Hunt laughed. "Somebody's trying to kid us," he said, and passed the cablegram to his sons. They read:

JOHN HUNT QUITO HOTEL QUITO ECUADOR THE AMAZON IS A BAD PLACE BETTER KEEP OUT OF IT

IF YOU WANT TO STAY HEALTHY AFFAIRS AT HOME WILL
REQUIRE YOUR ATTENTION

The cable was from New York. There was no signature.

2

The Following Shoes

"Who could have sent it?" wondered Hal.

"Perhaps one of the fellows up at the Explorers' Club trying to have a little fun with us," said Hunt, but his sons could see that he was not entirely satisfied with this explanation.

"Do you think there's any trouble at home?" Hal ventured.

"Of course not. If there were your mother would cable us."

Hal's forehead kinked the way it always did when he was puzzled.

"Looks to me as if we have a real mystery here," he said. "Now who could have a grudge against us? Who could want to stop us from going down the Amazon?"

"I don't know," his father said. "But I don't think we should pay too much attention to an anonymous message. If the fellow who sent this doesn't have the nerve to sign his name, perhaps he doesn't have the nerve to hurt us."

"Couldn't we trace it back? Doesn't anybody who sends

a cable have to give his name and address at the cable office?"

"Yes, but if he didn't want his identity known, he wouldn't give his real name and address."

Roger wasn't saying anything, but his eyes were growing larger every minute under the thrill of this strange situation. His father noticed the boy's excitement and said, "It's probably the work of some harmless crank. Suppose we just forget about it. We have to get up pretty early tomorrow morning so let's turn in. We get off at dawn — if that crazy flying Irishman has his plane ready."

"Perhaps I'd better drop round and see him right now," suggested Hal.

"Good idea. I'll go too," put in Roger.

"No," said his father, "you'd better get your beauty sleep."

Hal went out into the Plaza Independencia. A band concert was going on. The music echoed back from the great front of the cathedral and the archbishop's palace. The plaza was full of people, well-dressed citizens of Spanish blood, and Indians in flat hats and blanketlike ponchos.

What a city of beauty and mystery, thought Hal. It lay in a great bowl made by mountains, their snow-capped peaks gleaming in the moonlight. No wonder the people of Quito loved it. "From Quito to Heaven" they have always said.

As he slowed down, panting because of the 9,500-foot altitude, he reflected that this capital city of Ecuador was certainly next door to heaven. It was one of the highest capital cities in the world. But the air was not bitterly cold, for just outside of the city ran the equator. Still, it was chilly enough to make it hard to imagine that the equator was so near, and Hal buttoned his coat as he strolled out of the brightly lighted plaza into the dark, narrow streets of the old city.

It was necessary to walk with care over the rough cobblestones. The ancient adobe brick houses with their roofs of red tile covered with patches of green moss nearly closed overhead. It was like going through a tunnel.

Muffled shadows slid past in barefoot silence.

But Hal was conscious that one pair of feet somewhere behind him wore shoes. He thought nothing of it until, after he had turned right from Venezuela onto Sucre, he could still hear the shoes. He turned left on Pichincha. The shoes followed. Just for the fun of it, Hal went around the block. So did the owner of the shoes, always drawing closer. This was no longer very amusing. Hal quickened his pace.

He trod as lightly as possible, got well ahead, and then stepped into the intense shadow of the doorway of Terry O'Neill's house. He drew his flashlight from his pocket and waited.

Along came the persistent stranger. His footsteps were a bit uncertain now. He paused at one doorway after another and came at last to Hal's retreat.

Hal turned on the flashlight and threw the beam straight into the face of the man with shoes.

He was no Ecuadorean. He was too big and burly. Latin men are somewhat small and delicate, and the Indians are small and indelicate. This fellow could have passed as a prizefighter or a Chicago gangster. His face, twisted up by the sharp light, was inexpressibly cruel and sinister. His eyes gleamed like a surprised tiger's. No headhunter in the jungle could have looked more savage.

Hal could hardly refrain from beating on the door of his friend's house. He conquered this desire and said, "You were following me."

The man blinked. "Hey? You're crazy. I was just taking a walk."

"Funny you had to take the same walk that I did."

"What makes you think that?"

"I spotted you by your shoes."

"Shoes? Are you balmy? Lots of people in Quito wear shoes."

"Yes, but yours have a little tune of their own, and they went everywhere I did, even around the block." The stranger moved in threateningly, but Hal was a step above him and in a position to make things tough for him. A disturbance would bring out the whole neighbourhood.

The man's face broke into a sheepish grin.

"You're right, pal. I was following you. But I didn't mean nothing by it. I saw you were a Yank, and could speak my lingo, and I — well, I just wanted to ask the way to the Santo Domingo church. This being Sunday, I just thought I'd like to make a prayer and burn a few candles." And he raised his bloodshot eyes towards heaven.

"Straight down this street to the corner of Flores," said Hal.

"Thanks so much," said the stranger civilly enough, but as he turned out of the light there was a last flash of hate in his eyes that made Hal's spine creep. "I'll be seeing you."

"Don't make it too soon," was Hal's heartfelt reply and he turned to knock at Terry's door.

In the warm, comforting glow of Terry O'Neill's living room Hal related what had just happened in the street, and also the incident of the cablegram.

Terry was not the sort to take anything very seriously. He was a devil-may-care young aviator with a love for adventure that made him congratulate Hal on his success in finding some excitement.

"Looks as if you were going to have anything but a dull time," he said. "Do you suppose there is any connection between these two things? Have you an enemy in New York who might have sent an agent here to do you down?"

"We're rather short on enemies," said Hal. "Of course we have competitors. One very big competitor." He stopped suddenly and his forehead wrinkled. "I wonder—" he said. "Terry, perhaps you've given me an idea."

"Good. Do you still want to fly tomorrow morning?"

"Of course. How about the plane? Did you get those brakes fixed?"

"Well, not exactly," said Terry in his easy, Irish way. "But they'll probably do all right."

Lady Luck must play a pretty large part in Terry's affairs, Hal thought.

"Well," he said, "we'll be out at the field at dawn," and he rose to go.

"Do you want a bodyguard to escort you back to the hotel?"

"I'll make it," laughed Hal. But he did not go back as he had come. He took a roundabout route and walked in the middle of the street, eyes and ears alert. He got back to the hotel without incident and found his father and Roger asleep. He turned in, though he felt sure that he would lie awake all night, thinking. But it had been an active day. It takes plenty of rest to keep going in the thin air of sky-high Quito. In five minutes Hal, too, was asleep.

3

Dawn Flight

"All aboard for Green Hell!" cried Terry, revving up the motor of his tricky little four-seater Bonanza plane.

The Hunts climbed in with him. Their equipment and guns were stored in the baggage compartment. The Bonanza ambled bumpily down the grass airfield, gradually gaining speed.

When she was rolling at about seventy-five miles per hour a cross wind caught the ship and turned her directly towards a fire engine.

Terry could have angled her to one side or the other of the engine if his brakes had been good. They weren't. And without brakes, he couldn't stop. The airfield's crash sirens began to wail. The boys in the fire engine spilled out like popcorn.

But Terry, with a crazy Irishman's nerve, did the right thing, the desperate thing. He gave her the full gun. The plane roared across the field with the fire engine full ahead.

Would she rise enough to clear the great, red, metal monster that barred her path?

The nose wheel began to lift. The other two wheels bounded softly a few times, then rose. The plane was in the air. She cleared the fire engine by inches.

It's the people who know little about flying who don't realize its dangers. Hal and his father had both piloted planes but Roger was air green.

He looked up from the map he had been studying and, seeing the white faces of his brother and father, asked calmly, "Something wrong?"

Hal could have flayed him alive. And he could have administered a little flaying to the carefree pilot as well. Lady Luck must love this man!

The plane climbed a bit sluggishly. That was the fault not of the sturdy little Bonanza but of the altitude.

"What's your rate of climb?" asked Hal.

"About nine hundred feet a minute at sea level," Terry said. "But up here it's less than five hundred feet a minute."

"What's your service ceiling?" Hal was looking apprehensively at the towering, icy wall of mountains that they must cross before they could descend.

"This little tub," said Terry proudly, "will go up to seventeen thousand feet."

"But that will never get you over those peaks." Hal was looking at his map. Ecuador bristled with thirty tremendous volcanoes. Around Quito was a ring of giants. He looked out the window. There was Cotopaxi, the world's highest active volcano, cutting the sky at more than nineteen thousand feet. Cayambe and Antisana were almost as high.

"We'll slip through a pass," Terry assured Hal.

"But why are you going north now?"

"Just thought you'd like to have a look at the equator. And there it is. See that monument? It was put there in 1936 by a French survey mission to mark the exact equatorial line so that they could figure out the precise dimensions of this old planet. And now we're in the northern hemisphere." He banked the plane and sped back over the monument. At one instant they were in the northern hemisphere, at the next in the southern.

Roger was blowing on his chilled hands. "Pretty frosty equator," he commented.

"Is that road beneath us the Pan-American Highway?" asked John Hunt.

"Right," said Terry.

There it was, the wonder road that had now been practically completed all the way from Alaska to Patagonia.

"I'm going to make that trip sometime," vowed Roger.

"A good many people are making it right now," Terry said. "Yesterday I met a Scotsman who has a sheep ranch away down near Cape Horn. He had driven up all the way to Chicago, and was on his way back."

"But how about those breaks in the road?"

"There are three breaks in Central America. But you can put your car on a train or ship and get around them."

"The world's longest road," said John Hunt, looking down at the magic ribbon. "It will do a lot to tie the Americas together."

"But not so much as the aeroplane," said Terry, fondling the controls. For five years the flying Irishman had had his own plane. He had paid for it twice over by carrying passengers between Quito and Guayaquil on the coast, and Quito over the Andes to the jungle posts where rubber and quinine were gathered.

Hal wondered that he had never had an accident – and, as they raced towards the forbidding wall of rock and snow, hoped that he would not break his record now.

Presently the rampart ahead seemed to dissolve and a pass was visible. But what a pass! Great precipices frowned on either side of it. Couldn't the plane go higher and clear all this danger? Hal looked at the altimeter. It registered almost seventeen thousand feet. That meant that they were jammed up against the ceiling.

Suddenly even the ceiling failed them. The needle on the altimeter began to spin.

"Hey! That won't do," exclaimed Terry, trying to nose up the dropping plane.

They got out of the dangerous downdraught, but it left them only six hundred feet above the rocky bottom of the pass. In vain Terry tried to bring the plane up. So much banking and wheeling was necessary to avoid the cliffs that the little plane had no energy left for climbing. There was nothing to do but to follow all the twists and turns of the canyon and trust to luck that there would not be another downdraught. S turns and angles continually appeared ahead. Nobody was studying a map now. Roger's eyes popped as crag after crag rushed up to the windows and skimmed by with little to spare.

But a polo player would have been proud to manage his horse as Terry rode his plane. Hal thought of Ben Hur and his chariot race. Terry did not look like Ben Hur and he was not standing on a careering chariot but sitting quietly in the pilot's seat. But there was something of the heroic of all ages in the way he steered his irresistible motor around immovable objects. They melted away at his command. The impossible became possible.

Now, thank heaven, the floor of the canyon was falling a little. The savage walls were dropping back, beaten. With a final triumphant burst of speed the Bonanza swept out into a new world.

Gone were the arid, sandy wastes of the Pacific coast where rain almost never falls. Below stretched brilliant green forests that never lacked for water. Winding streams made silver alleys through the green.

"Look at the pink cloud," exclaimed Roger, hardly believing his own eyes.

Sure enough, a coloured cloud drifted over the forest.

"Butterflies," said Terry. "Just a few billion of them. And there's another cloud – parakeets. You get your clouds in all colours in this country – green, yellow, red, and mixed. Wait till you see the parrots and toucans. You'll think you're looking at a picture in technicolor."

"What's this stream beneath us?"

"That, my dear sir, is the Amazon. Or at least it's the Patate which becomes the Pastaza which becomes the Marañon which becomes the Amazon."

"And to think," said John Hunt, "that here within a hundred miles or so of the Pacific Ocean, the water turns its back on the Pacific and starts on a three-thousand-mile hike to the Atlantic."

"And we're starting on the same hike," said Hal. There was a thrill in that thought but a certain amount of fear too. The mystery of the unknown lay ahead. No other region on earth had so many secrets locked in its heart.

Presently the Patate joined hands with the Chambo to form the Pastaza, river of the Jivaro headhunters. A little frontier post called Topo passed beneath, then Mera, then Terry prepared to come down at the end of civilization, a jungle village called Puyo.

Hal was referring to his guidebook: "Here the known

288

world ends and the Amazonian wilderness begins. Penetration beyond Puyo is not possible even on horseback . . ."

It would have been possible by plane, but the plane was going back to Quito. The only other way was by boat. White men had never gone down the Pastaza, and on John Hunt's American Geographical Society map it was marked with a dotted line, meaning unexplored.

If this expedition were successful, that dotted line would be made solid. More than that, the animal life of a new region would be revealed. That was what most interested the three wild-animal collectors. A waterfall appeared below, a hanging bridge across the river, then a clearing. Terry was nosing down into it.

"What's your stalling speed?" asked Hal.

"Sixty-five."

It seemed a very small field to strike at a speed of more than a mile a minute. And no brakes!

At the far end of the field were a number of thatched huts. The plane plunged across the field, crushed the straw wall of a large hut, and came to a halt in the living-room-dining-room-bedroom among the members of a very startled household.

That was the introduction of the Hunts to the headhunters. Luckily none of the Indians was hurt, or four white heads might have been added speedily to the brown ones on the shelves.

4

Headhunters

Even so, for a moment it looked like rough going. The Indians snatched up spears and knives. Others came running into the hut and everyone was armed. The place resounded with the screams of women, the cries of children, and the menacing shouts of the warriors.

Then the smiling Irishman stuck his head out of the cockpit door. He called a merry greeting to an old man who turned out to be the chief. The angry chatter turned into a noisy welcome. These people knew Terry. This had been an outpost for the gatherers of cinchona, source of quinine, and Terry had been there many times.

Terry introduced his friends. The Indians conducted their guests in a triumphant procession through the village to the chief's house. The Hunts were astonished at the fine appearance of the village.

"Lucky we struck a straw hut instead of one of these," said Hal. Most of the houses in the village were well-built of solid timbers. One would never believe the place to be the home of savage headhunters. There were plots of corn, beans and bananas. Inside the houses could be seen looms on which cotton cloth was woven. On the shore of the swift Pastaza River were boats skilfully hollowed out of logs.

"They're really a very clever people," said Terry, noting the surprise of his guests. "And very brave. The Incas never conquered them. The Spaniards ruled them for only a short time – then the Indians rebelled and threw the Spaniards out. The government of Ecuador gets along with them by leaving them alone."

"Where do they get these shirts and shorts they are wearing?" asked Hal.

"They make them. But when they go to war they strip off their clothes and paint their bodies in bright colours."

Even in shirts and shorts, some of the men looked a bit wild. "They need haircuts," remarked Roger. Their hair was black, long and flowing, and decorated with toucan feathers.

"In every Jivaro there are two persons," said Terry, "one civilized and the other a savage. And you never know which one you are going to meet. That's what makes them interesting."

In the chief's house, the walls of which were hung with blowguns, spears, bows and arrows, and the skins of magnificent *tigres* and panthers, they were served a strange lunch.

"I never saw such large eggs," said Roger. "The chickens here must be giants."

"The chicken that laid those eggs," Terry told him, "was ten feet long and had teeth like a sausage grinder. You're eating alligator's eggs. How do you like them?"

Roger made a wry face. "I liked them until you told me that."

"And what's this steak?" asked Hal. "Surely they don't have cattle down here."

"That's from the tail of an iguana. It's an enormous lizard, five or six feet long, that is plentiful in these woods. You'll probably want one of them for your collection. And that other meat that tastes like veal – it's a slice of mountain lion. But never mind, you'll eat stranger things than these before you get done with the Amazon."

"You're right," said John Hunt, who knew from former trips to the lower river what experiences the boys were in for. He ate heartily, but the boys were very easily satisfied. It would take them a little time to get used to Amazonian cookery. Their appetites were not improved by a glance at a grim row of heads on a high shelf. One head was perched alone over the door.

"That one seems to have the place of honour," said John Hunt.

293

The old chief did not understand the English words but he saw that his guest was talking about the head over the door. He spoke to Terry and Terry translated.

"He says that's his grandfather. You see, this preservation of heads isn't quite as barbarous as most people suppose. Didn't the Egyptians keep not only the heads but the entire bodies of their kings mummified so that they would last? This is more or less the same idea. The chief says he was very fond of his grandfather and wants to keep him nearby always. It's the Jivaro way of showing respect."

Hal objected, "That's all right for friends and relatives, but why do they preserve the heads of enemies? Surely that's not to show respect."

"Yes it is," Terry insisted. "They believe that by keeping the head of a strong man they get his strength. They don't bother to shrink the heads of weaklings – it's a long, hard job and they don't consider it worth while."

"Unless they are making them for sale as curiosities to tourists," put in John Hunt.

"Yes. But if they are making them to keep in their own huts, they preserve only the heads of fine warriors."

"Then we ought to feel honoured if they decide to tan and pickle us," said Roger.

"That's right," laughed Terry. "And I may as well warn you that they believe there's some special magic in white heads. They think that the white man is especially wise and powerful and that anyone who gets his head will be wise and powerful too."

Roger made a mock show of holding his head tightly to his shoulders.

"Don't worry," said Hal. "They won't mistake your bean for something wise and powerful."

"Oh, is that so?" fumed Roger. "I bet they'll take mine first."

"Have it that way if you prefer," said Hal.

"I wonder if the chief would explain how they shrink these heads," John Hunt suggested. "It must be quite an art."

Terry passed on the question to the chief, who nodded gravely and began to explain, Terry translating.

"Everything must be done according to ceremony," said the chief, "otherwise the virtue of the hero is lost. The medicine man performs certain religious rites. That is to comfort the spirit of the dead man so that it will not be disturbed by what follows. We sew the lips together so that the spirit may not escape. Then we make a slit in the back of the scalp and take out the skull. Of course we could not shrink the head if the skull remained in it. The shrinking is done by filling the head with hot sand. When it cools it is taken out and more hot sand put in. Night and day for three days – sometimes for a week if we wish the head to be very small. That is all. It is simple."

"He is modest," smiled John Hunt. "But the truth is that no other tribes on earth have been able to do it as well. A good many have tried it."

"And it's a lot more complicated than he says," Terry added. "There's a tanning process in a secret liquid made of herbs and spices, and a boiling process, and smoking, and night and day all during the hot-sand process the face must be stroked with a smooth stone. They model it just as a sculptor would model clay or wax. It takes a real artist to do it so as to keep the natural appearance of the features."

John Hunt was examining the heads on the shelf. "The American Museum of Natural History wants one for its anthropology collection. Will you ask him if we may buy one?"

At first the chief shook his head. But Terry was eloquent. He explained about the museum. It was one of the greatest in the world. Thousands of people came to it daily. When they saw this exhibit they would respect the skill of the Jivaros. Was there not some great hero he would like to honour? There was no better way he could honour him than by placing him in this great museum.

The chief looked up at his grandfather. But no, he could not part with him. He took down another fine head.

"This was one of our noblest warriors, and a wise and good man. He will go to your country."

"What was his name?"

The chief gave a name that sounded something like Charlie. And so on all the rest of their journey the Hunts' silent little travelling companion was called Charlie.

Terry negotiated. The chief fixed the price at twenty-five dollars. John Hunt paid fifty dollars.

"Why pay him more than he asks?" said Terry.

"It's only fair. After all, the museum will pay several hundred dollars for this specimen."

And so Charlie was launched on his adventures.

"And now will you tell him of our plan to go down the Pastaza?" Terry did so, but the chief protested strongly.

Terry looked serious. "You'd better give up this scheme. He says you'd be killed. He and his people are friendly.

But he can't speak for the people down river. They are very savage and they have never made peace with the white man."

But Hunt was not to be swerved from his purpose. "They have no guns," he said.

"No, but they have blowpipes with poison darts, and spears and poison-tipped arrows. And they know how to use them."

"Yes, but I'm hoping we can make friends with them."

"Perhaps they'll shoot before you can make friends."

"We'll have to take that chance. It's important. I've promised the American Geographical that I'd make a try at exploring the lower Pastaza. And there's the chance that we'll come upon some new varieties of animals. Ask the chief if he can supply us with a boat."

The chief gloomily agreed. But he insisted that his guests should stay with him overnight.

"Where would we sleep?" asked Hal.

"On those wooden platforms."

"They look a bit hard."

"You'll be too tired to notice."

Roger was not too keen about staying. "More alligator's eggs," he moaned.

"Boys," their father said, "you wanted to come on this

299

trip. If you've changed your minds you can fly back with Terry."

The words had effect. The very idea of giving up their great adventure reconciled the boys to platform beds and alligator's eggs.

But there were no alligator's eggs for supper. Instead there was a very delicious slab of tender white meat that tasted a little like fish and a little like chicken. Roger ate it with great relish and never thought to ask what it was until he had finished.

The chief explained that it was a slice of a large boa constrictor that had recently invaded the village. Roger turned green. "You mean they eat snakes?"

"Why not?" said Terry. "Wasn't it good?"

"Yes, but nobody eats snakes."

His father smiled. "By 'nobody' I suppose you mean none of your neighbours on Long Island. But you're going to learn that other people have other ways, and they are often quite as good as ours. If Frenchmen can eat snails, and Chinese can eat birds' nests, and Japanese can eat seaweed, and hill tribes in India can eat grasshoppers, and Long Islanders can eat slimy living oysters, why shouldn't the Amazon people eat the foods that nature has provided for them?"

"I know," said Roger, determined to show as much stamina as his father. "If you can eat it, I can. Pass the snake, please."

He helped himself to another generous slice and manfully ate it. "Good stuff!" he said, smacking his lips. But he was still a little green around the gills.

That night, tossing on his wooden bed, he dreamed that he had turned into a boa constrictor and a human giant was swallowing him. He thrashed his tail vigorously, but the giant got him all down and then smacked his lips and said, "Snakes are very good to eat."

Terry had flown back to Quito in the afternoon. They were sorry to see him go. He and his plane seemed like the last links with civilization. Hal woke towards dawn and lay listening to the unearthly howls, screams, and coughs that rose from the surrounding forest. Yes, they had come to the right place for animals! He was glad that they were sleeping inside four walls. But how about tomorrow night, and many nights to come?

But Hal did not think much about the dangers that lay ahead – he had camped in the wilds before. His thoughts went back to a face in Quito, a face illuminated in the glow of his flashlight and now stamped upon his memory.

But why worry? They had left that face far behind. The following shoes could hardly follow into the Amazonian jungle. Or could they?

5
The Condor's Shadow

At dawn he was out at the river's edge, loading the boat. It was an Indian-made canoe, hollowed out of a single log. Hal reckoned the length of it to be about twenty feet, and its beam was a little better than two feet. It was just the right size for three or four men and their kit.

The interior of the log had been chipped and burned out with great skill so that all that was left was a shell about an inch thick. Hal admired the Indians' handiwork. It must have taken pretty nice judgement to make that wall just thick enough and not to cut through it at any point.

The boat would slide over the water like rain over a duck's back. The only trouble was that it would slide sidewise as well as lengthwise, for it had no keel. Of course it would clear the bottom more easily without a keel.

"But we'll have to part our hair in the middle," Hal reflected. The utmost care would be necessary to keep the craft from rolling over.

The first job was to pack the kit evenly, distributing its weight so that the balance would be perfect. Working room must be left for the paddlers. The surface of the baggage must be flat so that it would be easy to crawl or jump over it in case it was necessary to change places. Guns must be where they could be reached quickly. But both the guns and other objects too heavy to float must be secured under a thwart or tied so that they would not sink in the event of an upset.

Hal went to work. When the others came out he had everything stowed to his own satisfaction.

His father looked over the job critically.

"You haven't forgotten Canada," was his way of commending Hal. They had canoed together on many northern rivers. But Roger was without experience. This would be his initiation into river travel.

Hal and his father went back to the house but had no sooner reached it than they were startled by a yell from the river. They looked back to see the newly packed boat already upside down in the middle of the stream and Roger's head bobbing beside it. They were not worried about Roger. He could swim. But the boat was being carried swiftly downstream. Soon it would be in the rapids, and farther down were falls.

They ran to the river and plunged in. In this swift current there were not likely to be crocodiles, stingrays, or anacondas. They joined Roger, who was already manfully trying to push the boat towards shore. In a few moments they had it beached. Roger crawled up onto the bank, dripping and crestfallen.

"I just wanted to try her out."

Hunt eyed his younger son with disapproval but could not help grinning at his sorry appearance.

"Your middle name is Mischief," he remarked.

"Everything stayed in the boat," Hal said, inspecting his packing. Most of the bundles were fairly waterproof, but all the kit was put out on the bank to dry in the hot sun and was then repacked.

Roger was very quiet for a while but as his clothes dried out his spirits revived.

"We're off!" he whooped an hour later as they left the shore. The chief and his warriors stood on the bank making gestures of farewell. One of their number was in the boat. He would accompany the explorers to the edge of hostile country. More than that he would not promise. But John Hunt hoped that he could be persuaded to go on down the unknown part of the Pastaza, the river of the dotted line.

There was nothing to suggest any danger ahead. The sun shone gloriously, the monkeys chattered in the treetops, parrots and macaws made waves of brilliant colour, and far off to the west over the green forest loomed the snowy head of twenty-thousand-foot Chimborazo, looking down towards the Pacific on one side and, on the other side, to the travellers on their way to the Atlantic.

A bend in the stream, and the friendly Jivaro village disappeared. Dense jungle closed in on both sides. The river was about a hundred feet wide. The water was glassy smooth but was hurrying forward as if eager to get to an appointment. The four paddles had little to do except to keep the boat straight.

"Look at the birds," cried Hal.

Roger looked up.

"No, look down. Down in the water."

Sure enough, at the bottom of the clear, shallow stream small dark birds were fluttering about, seeking food.

There was no time to watch them, for the boat sped on.

"Water ouzels," Hunt said.

"But they were flying under water."

"You might call it flying. They beat their wings to help them move through the water. They're hunting for snails and water insects. They can stay down two or three minutes."

A shadow as of a small black cloud seemed to pass over the water. They looked up to see a wonder above as great as the wonder they had just seen below.

"A condor," exclaimed Hunt. It easily measured ten feet from tip to tip.

The Indian was much excited. "Very bad," he said out of his little store of English acquired from serving American cinchona men. He made passes over his head as if to put a protective charm over himself.

"The Indians are very superstitious about the condor," Hunt said. "I'm afraid he thinks it's a bad omen for our trip. You see, the condor hangs around where anything is dead, or where he thinks something is going to be."

"Here he comes back. We'll see who's dead." And Roger grabbed his .22.

"Save your ammunition. The bird isn't doing any harm and it's no good to eat. Besides, you couldn't hurt it with that popgun."

"He's immense," murmured Hal as the bird made another circle.

"The world's largest flying bird," said Hunt. "And although it is so heavy, it can fly higher than any other bird. It can get along without eating for forty days if necessary, but when a condor does get a chance to eat, he can put away eighteen pounds of meat at a sitting."

"I know," Roger said. "They carry away lambs and babies."

"Not exactly. They're not afraid to attack anything large, even a horse, if he looks weak or sick. But they never fly away with their food. Their talons are too weak to lift a heavy load."

The condor sailed away, discouraged, but he left behind him a very much disturbed Indian.

"No good, no good," he insisted, backwatering vigorously with his paddle. "We go back, we go back."

But it was impossible to go back at the moment, for a powerful current had seized the boat, making argument quite unnecessary.

From around the bend came the hollow roar of rapids. Whirling, boiling eddies burst up around the boat, as if sticks of dynamite were being set off at the bottom of the stream. Choppy waves began to bob up.

They swept around the curve, and the full roar of angry waters struck their ears. Ahead, the river was full of dancing white figures. Sharp rocks sent fountains of spray into the air. Over rounded rocks the water rolled in big humps.

Napo, the Indian, was in the bow, John Hunt in the

stern. Napo pointed to a chute between two big rocks. All the paddles joined forces to speed the boat like an arrow through the narrow passage. The faster the better. In water like this it was necessary to have plenty of steerage way. The boat must go faster than the current if it was to be successfully steered around rocks.

The water humped itself into a ridge as it shot through between the rocks. The canoe rode the hump like a cowboy on horseback. The spray thrown up by the rocks soused everybody on board.

No one noticed the wetting. The paddles were going like mad. The boat rolled and darted, dodged and plunged. A rollercoaster was tame compared with this.

Roger let out a whoop and the others joined him, regardless of age. This was the sort of thing that would make boys out of greybeards. The blood coursed swiftly and the spine tingled. Rocks fled past.

The boat plunged into a hollow and Napo disappeared. The bow seemed to be pointed straight towards the bottom. John Hunt and Hal backwatered powerfully to bring the bow up, and there was Napo no worse for wear. But his next yell had a watery gurgle in it.

The dugout was performing acrobatic feats. It seemed miraculous that a boat cut out of a single log could be so nimble. It almost seemed to snake through between rocks or to draw in its stomach when it went over them. Like its passengers, it would shout with joy if it could.

Now it shot downhill in a last victorious sweep and then ran out under its own momentum, paddles idle, into a smooth, broad basin.

It was pleasant to relax and to look back at the boiling staircase down which they had come.

"There's a lot of that sort of thing in these Amazon rivers," Hunt said. "I suppose you know the origin of the word Amazon?"

"Doesn't it have something to do with a tribe of warrior women that the first explorers discovered?" Hal said.

"That's one theory. The other is that the river is named after the Indian word Amassona, meaning boat destroyer. It's not just the rapids that make it deserve this name. Some of the rivers are full of dangerous logs floating just below the surface. And where the main stream of the Amazon becomes as wide as a sea there are pretty bad storms. And then there's the bore."

"What's a bore?" asked Roger.

"A moving wall of water something like a tidal wave. It rushes up the river from the ocean. It may be ten or twelve feet high."

"I'd like to see that," Roger said.

His father smiled grimly. "You will. But I hope we're in a bigger boat than this when it comes."

"How soon do we get a boat big enough so we can collect some animals?"

"As soon as we get out of this river. Nothing bigger than this would get us down the Pastaza. But we don't need to wait to collect little animals — and sometimes they're just as important as the big ones."

A sullen roar ahead warned that collecting would have to be postponed a little while longer. This roar was not like the last. It was a deeper thunder. The source of the thunder could not be seen. The river simply dropped out of sight, and where it disappeared vapour rose into the air.

"Falls!" exclaimed Hal. "We'd better stop and look this one over."

At the right was a little bay in which an eddy circled. They pulled in to the shore, beached the boat, and then picked their way through the jungle to the river's edge where they could inspect the falls.

At one point the water made a sheer drop of twelve feet into a mass of jagged rocks.

"That's where we *don't* want to go," remarked John

Hunt. "But see that slide over yonder? We can't shoot it, but perhaps we could ease the boat down by the painter."

This project proved fully as exciting as shooting the rapids. The boat was paddled to a position near the head of the chute but close to the shore where the current was not too strong. Everybody was tense with anticipation. Napo seemed to have forgotten the shadow of the condor.

They stepped out into the swift but shallow stream. The water came about chest high. What a good way to escape the tropical sun! The hunters did not wear the heavy hunting clothes common in northern climes. Thin shirt and thin trousers and a pair of South American sandals called *alpargatas* completed their costume. There was nothing that could be spoiled by a wetting – unless you were to count the tobacco in John Hunt's pipe.

The contents of the canoe were fairly well protected. Even the guns were in waterproof cases. Ammunition was packed in an aluminium box as waterproof as a bottle, and camera, films, medicines, and valuable papers in another.

But Charlie, the Jivaro head, was merely tied by his hair to a thwart. He had weathered sun, rain and wave while alive and was just as capable of doing so now.

Hal and Napo held the painter. This rope attached to the bow of the boat was made of plaited vines and was as strong as hemp. They braced themselves against the rocks and let the painter out a few inches at a time, letting the boat into the chutes stern first.

Roger and his father hung onto the stern, one on each side. It was their job to guide the canoe down through the rocks.

"If the water sweeps you off your feet, Roger, hang onto the gunwale."

The boat was in a slide of water that slanted down like the roof of a house. The bottom was very uneven. Now Roger would be perched on a rock where the water was only ankle deep, and then he would drop into a hole up to his neck. He grimly hung onto the gunwale. The boat helped him as much as he helped the boat.

"Not too fast," John Hunt yelled to the two who were paying out the painter. He could hardly make himself heard above the roar.

He spoke just too late. The advancing stern pushed him from his slippery foothold and he went over like a ninepin into a foaming whirlpool.

This could be serious. Whirled around beneath the surface, he might easily be badly bruised against the rocks. He might be knocked unconscious and be unable to come up.

The three looked anxiously for some sign of him. When they were about to abandon the boat to its fate and go to the rescue, his head emerged from under the stern. It came up slowly and Hal laughed with relief when he saw that his father's pipe was still stuck in his teeth. The dripping face wore a surprised and rather offended expression. Dad was not used to being man-handled in this fashion by the forces of nature.

A little later it was Dad who laughed. They were all aboard once more and slipping down a fast but not dangerous stretch under some overhanging trees. Hal was bent over, groping for something in the bottom of the boat. A dead snag on one of the branches slipped under his belt, and before he could make any remark on the situation, he was suspended in air and the boat was going on without him. He tried to grab the boat but got only a sack of potatoes.

There he was left, in a very undignified position, tail up and head down, hanging grimly to a bag of spuds. The snag broke and he and his potatoes took a bath.

The canoe had been beached on a sand spit and Hal was greeted hilariously as he staggered out, still holding his burden.

Lunch was served on the sand spit. During the afternoon

there were more rapids, and more, and more, until it was a very weary foursome who beached the canoe late in the afternoon on a bank under some large trees that would serve as a hotel for the night.

6

The Face on the Trail

It seemed an ideal place to make camp. A lovely pool a hundred yards across lay before it. Fish punctuated its smooth surface with darts and circles. Beyond the pool the jungle wall rose black but was topped by flowering trees that glowed yellow and crimson in the setting sun. Lazy white egrets drifted past.

Under the great ceibas where they proposed to make camp there was no undergrowth near the river bank, but it began a few yards back.

Where the clear space ended and the jungle began, John Hunt found a slight opening.

"Looks like a trail," he said, and he turned to Napo. "Indians?"

Napo looked doubtful. Then he examined the soft ground and pointed to footprints. But they were not made by human feet.

"Look, boys," Hunt said. "Here's your introduction to the animals of the Amazon. These stabs are made by the hooves of peccaries."

"Aren't they wild boars?" said Hal. "I was reading up about them. It seems that they go around in gangs and don't hesitate to attack men."

"You're right. When they come around, the safest place is up a tree. I knew one explorer who was treed for three days and three nights." He examined other tracks. "Looks to me as if the animals come down here to drink at night. These tracks were made by a capybara," pointing to tracks made by queerly splayed feet. "It's the world's biggest rat – as big as a sheep. And these are deer tracks."

"Yes," said Hal. "I'd recognize them anywhere," remembering the deer trails of Colorado, Canada, and the Maine woods.

"But there is something I never saw before."

318

The tracks he indicated were smooth and round as if they had been made by large saucers.

"*Tigre!*" exclaimed Napo. "This place no good."

"That's the *tigre* all right," Hunt admitted.

"What's a tee-gray?" Roger wanted to know, for that was how both his father and Napo had pronounced the word.

"It's the Spanish word for tiger. All through Mexico and South America they call this animal the *tigre* although it is not really a tiger. It wears spots, not stripes. When we get over the Brazilian border where Portuguese is spoken we'll hear it called the *onca*, meaning ounce. Our own name for it is jaguar. But call it what you like, it's the king of the forest."

"No good," wailed Napo. "We go back."

"He's got the we-go-backs again," Hal said in disgust. "What a chance to get some photographs tonight if they come down to drink!"

"And what a chance for them to get some nice little explorers," wondered Roger.

"Don't worry," Dad said. "They're not likely to attack us if we leave them alone. Besides, we'll be well up out of their way — in our hammocks."

The method of camp making was new to Hal and

Roger, accustomed to the tents, canvas flies and sleeping bags of the north. The jungle traveller cannot be burdened with heavy gear. He sleeps in the open. For him, no canvas house completely sealed in with canvas door and mosquito netting over the windows. The Minneapolis clerk who takes a run up into the Minnesota lake country for a few nights carries more elaborate gear for camping in this land where the most dangerous beast is the mosquito than the experienced explorer takes for a year's trek through the Amazon jungle.

In ten minutes camp was set up. It consisted merely of three hammocks strung between the trees.

The hammock is the bed of Amazonia. It was invented by the Amazon Indians and we owe our garden hammocks to their invention. Even in the town, the hammock is the only bed in most homes. All that one sees in the daytime is iron hooks in the wall – but at night the hammocks are strung up and the living room becomes a bedroom. Hotels, too, are furnished only with hooks in the wall. The guest is supposed to bring his own hammock.

But there are a few tribes in hammockland who do not subscribe to the custom, and the Jivaros are one of them. So Napo, instead of stringing up a hammock, made a hole in the ground. He was going to bury himself. The earth, superheated during the day, keeps the body warm during the night, which is sometimes surprisingly chilly.

After the beds, three aerial and one subterranean, had been made, Napo took up his bow and arrows. "Me get fish," he said.

Dad suggested that Roger would probably like to see how fishing was done with bow and arrows. Roger went along, but he seemed to have something else on his mind. He kept glancing back at the break in the jungle where animals came out at night, and where Indians, too, might emerge. Who could tell? Anybody watching him would have seen that he was up to no good. But nobody was watching.

He went with Napo along the river bank and stayed with him until Napo had spotted a trout swimming about a foot beneath the surface and had pierced him with an arrow. Napo took the fish back to camp to be baked in mud for supper – but Roger went to the boat, got something from it, and disappeared into the jungle. Presently he strolled back into camp and joined in building the fire.

It was now quite dark under the trees but a flickering yellow light began to radiate from the fire. Ghostly shadows leaped about. A scream or two came from the jungle as a preliminary to the nightly chorus.

Hal shivered slightly and glanced at the point where the trail entered the undergrowth. Then his eyes froze.

"Dad, look," he whispered. "An Indian."

His father looked. There was no doubt about it. An Indian face peered from the brush. The light was too poor to see it distinctly.

"Must be Napo," Hunt said. "He's getting wood."

"Yes, but he's getting it down near the river."

Napo came up the bank with a load of driftwood.

Hal reached for his gun but his father said, "Don't be hasty, they may be friendly. Let's try a present first." And he took a small mirror out of his pocket. Indians liked mirrors.

Napo, following the gaze of the others, was much puzzled at what he saw. In his astonishment he dropped his load of wood on his own toes. This brought a yell out of him that further startled Hal and his father, but did not seem to disturb the face on the trail. And Hal noticed that Roger, too, was strangely calm.

That kid has more nerve than I gave him credit for, he thought.

"Can't see him plainly," Dad complained, blinking. "But he looks pretty small. He may be just a boy. Perhaps only curious. Anyhow I'll try him with this present."

"But I'll back you up with the gun if there's any monkey business," Hal promised.

Dad walked forward gingerly. Hal held his gun and his breath. Roger made a sound something like a snicker, but it may have been just a gasp of terror. The face on the trail did not move.

Dad was within a few feet of it now. He stopped and began to laugh. Then he reached into the brush and pulled out the head. It was Charlie.

Roger exploded with merriment and rolled on the ground, kicking and roaring. Hal laid down his gun, took Roger up by the seat of his shorts, and started towards the river. Roger wriggled free and disappeared into the brush. He continued laughing like a hyena.

Hal began to laugh too, and only Napo remained serious, looking from one to another of his strange companions as if doubting their sanity. Then he gave up trying to understand them and went to take the fish out of the fire.

He took out a mud ball baked hard and dry, broke it on a stone, and there was the fish, cooked to a turn. With some potatoes baked in the same fire it made an appetizing meal.

Then the Hunts retreated into their hammocks, and

Napo into his hole. The blankets in the hammocks would be appreciated before morning. As for the mosquito nets, especially made with sleeves to fit over the hammock strings, they were not used for there seemed to be no mosquitoes around this camp site. To discourage ants and other small pests from crawling out from the trees into the hammocks, the hammock strings had been creosoted.

Roger squirmed and twisted, for he had never before tried sleeping in a hammock.

"Don't lie straight along it," his father advised him. "Lie on the diagonal. Then you won't be so likely to fall out."

But Roger was not one who could learn very much from being told. He had to learn from bitter experience.

Soon he and his father were sleeping soundly. Hal, clutching camera and flash bulbs, tried to keep awake but presently joined the others in slumberland.

Napo had buried himself well aside from the animal trail. His head projected oddly from the ground and moved this way and that as he looked about in the light of the dying fire, but before long it dropped and his eyes closed.

And, as the four slept, the forest awoke. "Awake for it is night," the animals seemed to say.

The cicadas began with a piercing chirp but managed to develop it into a screeching whistle. The tree frogs drummed, hoo-hooed, and croaked. The nightjar made a sound like the wail of a dying ghost, if ghosts ever die. Strange creatures that had not yet been given long Latin names by the zoologists added their contribution to the din.

Then there was a deep grumbling cough. Instantly all other noise was hushed. That was the honour accorded to the *tigre*, king of the forest.

7
Jungle Night

An ear-splitting yell broke the silence.

Dad woke with a start and turned on his flashlight. Again that wild yell. It seemed to be Roger's voice.

Both Dad and Hal beamed their lights on the trail. They fully expected to see Roger in the jaws of a *tigre*. But there was no sign of either animal or boy.

"Help! Help!" screeched Roger's voice. The lights swept around and focused on him.

He had gone stark, staring mad. He was doing a combination of the samba and the Highland fling, and splitting the welkin with his cries. He clawed himself furiously, tearing off his shirt and trousers and, quite naked, continued to leap and prance, slapping and grabbing at different parts of his anatomy.

"Hey, can't you do something?" he wailed.

John Hunt climbed out of his hammock, chuckling.

"I think you've found just the right thing to do," he said. "Dance boy, dance!"

He played his light along the ground.

"There they go. Get out of their line of march."

A black band was moving across the ground. It was about a foot wide. The procession seemed to have no end in either direction.

"What are they?" asked Hal.

"Army ants. Sometimes they make a procession a mile long. They eat everything that comes in their way – boys included. See the officers."

Along the edges of the column were ants that did not march steadily forward with the others, but kept running back and forth as if to keep the privates in line.

He went to the fireplace and got a stick that still glowed at one end.

"All right, Roger. Here comes the doctor. But I hope you won't think that the remedy is worse than the disease."

With difficulty Roger stood still as his father went over him, applying the hot coal to the rear ends of ants which had sunk their enormous pincers into his flesh. The ants thus attacked from behind relaxed their hold and dropped off.

Roger's wild antics had already broken off many of the bodies, leaving the heads and jaws firmly transfixed in the flesh. More drastic means had to be used to dislodge these. They must be picked out with the point of a knife. Then the wounds were spotted with merthiolate until Roger looked like a pink-and-white leopard, or perhaps an Indian in his war paint.

"But how did they get at you in the hammock?" his father asked.

Roger was sheepish. "Well, I wasn't in the hammock. I fell out. I was too sleepy to get back in, and anyhow the ground felt better than the old hammock. But I can't understand why they didn't go after Napo."

They hadn't thought of Napo. They played their lights on the spot where he should have been. There was a little mound of fresh earth and the ants streamed over it. The experienced Napo had gone completely underground.

Roger fingered his wounds. "How those fellows can bite!"

"Did you know that the Indians use an ant of that sort to stitch wounds? They make the ant bite the edges of the wound together. Then they cut off the ant's body. The jaws stay locked and keep the wound closed until it heals."

"An Indian village must have a merry time of it when one of these armies bears down upon it," Hal speculated.

"The best thing to do is to move out and leave the village to the ants. The Indians stay at a safe distance in the jungle until the army has passed. The ones whose houses were on the line of march are lucky. Their places are cleaned of vermin and insects."

The tail of the procession went by. Napo seemed to know when this happened and his head cautiously emerged from the ground. Roger, however, had had enough of Mother Earth – he put on his clothes, wrapped himself in his blanket, and climbed back into the hammock.

Again, darkness and silence. The forest, disturbed by the commotion in the camp, kept the peace for a while. Then one sound after another invaded the stillness until the boiler factory was going full blast once more.

Hal lay awake now, hoping that some of the denizens of the woods might get thirsty. But they had evidently been thrown off their routine by the strange doings in their forest. Only the most dull-witted of them would come tonight.

At last he arrived – the big half-wit of the woods. Hal heard a crackling of the underbrush as if some very heavy animal were approaching. He waited until he felt sure that it had left the brush and was crossing the camp site. Then he turned on his flash. The animal stopped and stood peering into the light. Hal's flash bulb flared, and he had a photograph of a tapir.

A good animal photographer takes his picture first and

then makes observations. If he should make his observations first the animal might be gone before the photograph could be taken. With the tapir safely tucked away in his camera, Hal proceeded to study the beast.

It was the first of its kind that he had ever seen, but he knew it from the pictures in the many natural-history books that he had studied. And yet, he could not help being astonished by the real thing.

Here was the largest wild animal in South America. This specimen must weigh twenty stone. It was some five feet high and six feet long. It seemed to have been put together with spare parts of other animals. It had the body of a huge pig, the mane of a horse and the trunk of an elephant.

Hal knew that some scientists contend that this is the elephant's American cousin. The beast's trunk was very short but it was evidently used in exactly the same way as the trunk of an elephant, to gather food and tuck it into the mouth beneath.

Fascinated by the light, the horse-pig-elephant stood quite still. The Cincinnati Zoo wanted just such a specimen. Hal was helpless. Even if they could catch the animal they could not transport it in a treacherous canoe down a boiling river. If only these beasts came in smaller, more portable editions.

As if in answer to his prayer, there was a rustling in the brush and out came the pocket edition. Well, it would not exactly fit into a pocket but it might be accommodated even in a crowded canoe.

It was a baby tapir, not a dull brown colour like its mother, but gaily marked with yellow stripes and white spots. It made a whimpering noise as it waddled to its mother and proceeded to help itself to some liquid refreshment.

Hal was about to prod his father awake with the butt end of his rifle when it occurred to him that it would be a great feather in his cap if he could capture this little specimen singlehanded. After all, it shouldn't be much of a problem. Surely the mother would not make too much trouble.

He tried to remember what he had read about the tapir – some authority had said that it was a very mild-mannered beast. And it was extremely nearsighted. Perhaps he could get almost up to it without its realizing what was going on.

He slid softly out of his hammock and crept forward, still keeping his light shining full into the tapir's weak eyes.

He tried to calculate his chances. If he frightened the tapir, which way would it probably run? He knew that tapirs habitually take refuge in rivers. Probably this animal, if alarmed, would make straight for the water. The little fellow could not move so fast and might be easily captured.

But the best-laid plans of mice and men and boy naturalists gang aft agley. A twig cracked underfoot. The tapir started, but not towards the river. Lowering its head, it plunged straight into the light. Hal was about to learn that even a mild-mannered mamma will defend its young.

The charging tapir gave voice, but it did not make the thunderous roar that one might expect from an animal of its size. It screamed like a mad horse, the scream ending in a shrill whistle.

The other campers awoke with a start. Dad and Roger tumbled out of their hammocks and Napo rooted up out of his burrow like a hedgehog at the first call of spring.

None of the them had time to act before the three-hundred-pound battery reached Hal.

Hal had the presence of mind to leap for a branch in order to let the brown torpedo pass beneath him — but the branch broke and he landed squarely on the tapir's back. Something else that he had read flashed painfully into his mind. The jaguar attacks the tapir by leaping onto its back; but the supposedly stupid tapir knows enough to tear its way through thorny underbrush or under half-fallen logs or low branches by which the jaguar is crushed and brushed off, a bleeding, mangled mass of pulp.

Horrified by this thought, Hal lost no time in tumbling from his mount. He breathed a sigh of relief as he lay on the quiet earth. But if he had thought that the tapir was done with him, he was mistaken. Even without the light, it knew where its enemy lay. A tapir's eyes may be poor, but its senses of smell and hearing are acute.

Hal heard it coming like an express train, its whistle wailing. He struggled to his knees and threw himself out of the way. As the lumbering beast hurtled past, two flashlights suddenly spotted it and then there was the roar of a gun.

Even the thick-hided combination of horse, boar and elephant with a touch of rhinoceros could not resist a 130-grain expanding bullet from Dad's .270 Winchester. The tapir turned a heavy somersault and lay still.

Hal hurried to the scene. He must find the youngster. That was not hard. The baby was already running to its mother. Reaching her, it settled down and began to take its last drink.

Hal had a tinge of regret. His companions looked on and nobody had anything to say for a moment. They let the little fellow drink his fill.

Hal stooped to stroke the smooth, colourful skin of the little orphan.

"Never mind," he said. "We'll make it up to you. We'll take you to a nice zoo where you can have the best of food and a swimming pool all to yourself. And no *tigres* to bother you. That's a promise."

8
Down the Dotted Line

Next morning there were more rapids, and then a great fall. They had to portage around it, first carrying the gear, and then the canoe. When the canoe was repacked at the base of the fall they all stepped aboard again – all except Napo.

He stood on the shore and looked stubborn.

"Me go back," he said.

Dad argued with him, but it was no use. This fall marked the end of the country that he knew. Beyond was the unknown, filled with mysterious terrors. He did not know the people. His only comment upon them was that they were very bad.

He would walk back home by a trail bordering the river. It would take him about two days to make his village.

Hunt paid him and Hal offered him a supply of provisions. Napo smiled his thanks but refused.

"Me eat," he said, tapping his bow. He could get what food he needed from river and forest.

After helping to push off the boat he lingered on the shore as if sorry to see his new friends go. As the canoe was swiftly borne downstream he called some sort of a goodbye in his own language and started to climb the steep, rocky slope beside the waterfall.

At the top of the fall he turned and waved, then was gone.

It seemed foolish for three men to feel lonely when one had gone. They still looked back at the edge of the waterfall. Napo was the only one of their party who had really known this jungle. Now they were starting into country from which no white man had ever come back.

Roger was the first one to snap out of it; he was not old enough to realize how much it meant. He had more confidence in his father and brother than they had in themselves.

"I think Nosey wants something to eat," he said. Because of its prominent proboscis and its way of poking its inquisitive trunk into everything and everybody, the little tapir had been nicknamed Nosey. "What does a tapir eat?"

"All sorts of leaves and shoots and juicy vegetable matter," Dad said. "But a baby tapir should have milk. Since there is no milk, you might try some very tender grass." They passed close enough to the bank for Roger to seize a handful of fresh young grass and he offered this dainty to Nosey.

Nosey turned up his nose at it, or would have, except that the nose was of the permanently turned-down variety.

"Now, you're not going to be a problem child," John Hunt said reprovingly. Nosey at once proceeded to be a problem child by attempting to jump overboard, but was drawn back by the harness that had been made for him out of lianas.

"Perhaps we'll just have to let him live on his own fat for a while until he decides to eat," said Dad, and he turned to something of more immediate importance. He took out pad, pencil and compass.

"Going to map the river?" Hal asked in some excitement.

"Yes. Would you like to help?"

"Let me do it and you help," Hal ventured. He could

338

think of nothing more thrilling than to chart the course of an unknown river.

John Hunt smiled indulgently. "Well, I'm sure you can do it," and he passed over the materials.

Hal's eyes sparkled. "Now, we begin with the fall — right? Has it a name?"

"Not that I know of."

"What shall we call it?" He thought of it as they had seen it, with Napo on its crest waving goodbye. "Napo Falls. How's that?"

"As good as anything."

Hal made a mark at the top of the pad and wrote "Napo Falls". Then he began to trace the river. The paper was blue lined in squares, each representing a square mile. Hal estimated the distance back to the waterfall and the distance forward to the next large bend. He consulted the compass to get the direction correct. He had often watched surveyors at work.

"I wish we had all the proper instruments," he said.

"They'd be too bulky to take on a trip like this. If we come out with a roughly accurate map, that will encourage surveying parties to come in and complete the job."

Every time a hill or mountain could be seen it went down on the map together with its estimated altitude.

Marginal notes recorded stands of trees, particularly those of commercial importance such as cinchona and rubber trees, or trees valuable because of their timber.

Dad continually contributed suggestions out of his former experience, but Hal made the map.

The changing width of the river was indicated, and the depth of it, and the character of the various rapids.

Hal realized what it felt like to be a real pioneer. All future travellers on this river would owe something to him for the work he was doing today. He felt his responsibility and did his job with all possible care.

So the day slid by without much thought of enemies who might be lurking behind this screen of jungle. Camp was made on a small island. It would be hard for any Indians to come to it without being detected.

Meat from the tapir shot the night before was the chief item on the dinner menu. It was very good, much like beef, but with just enough of a pork taste to give it a tang.

During the night they thought they heard drums, but were not sure, so great was the animal din of the forest.

Another day of canoeing and mapping followed and still there was no sign of Indians, and still Nosey refused to eat. Once in a while he whimpered like a baby or a pup. They began to worry about him. If he kept on this way he would never see a zoo.

The difficulty was solved, but in a way that nearly wrecked the expedition.

Rounding a bend, they saw two goats standing knee-deep in a natural meadow. One of them was a nanny and carried a full bag.

"Wild goats," cried Roger. "There's some milk for Nosey."

The goats stood quite still, eyeing the boat.

"They can't be wild," said Hal. "If they were they would run."

"But there's no village around."

"Perhaps it's farther back in the woods."

"Well, anyhow," suggested Roger, "on that beach would be a good place for lunch."

The suggestion seemed good and they ran the canoe ashore and took out a few provisions. From the beach they could not see the goats since a high bank came between.

After eating they lay half dozing on the beach. Hal and his father did not notice when Roger took a bottle from the kit and climbed the bank.

Some fifteen minutes later they were brought to their feet by a piercing yell and the whiz of an arrow. Roger came tumbling down the bank clutching a bottle of milk.

"Quick! They're shooting at me."

The three were in the canoe in a flash and paddling into midstream. The strong current came to their rescue. Another arrow whirred after them but fell short. In a moment they were around a bend and breathed more freely.

But their relief was short-lived. They saw a log canoe in a cove. They had not gone five hundred feet past it when three Indians ran to the boat, leaped in, and came in hot pursuit.

Mischievous Roger had some belated regrets. The three Hunts bent to their paddles as if their lives depended upon it — as they quite possibly did.

They were three against three. But the Indians were familiar with the river and knew the best channels. And they had had more experience in paddling a log canoe.

The Hunts held the lead for a mile, then were slowed up by a scraping over a hidden sand bar. The other canoe was fairly flying over the water. The Indians made a living thing out of it.

One of them laid down his paddle and took up a bow. It was seven feet long. He stood up in the boat to bend it and string the long, evil-looking arrow.

Twang — whiz. The arrow embedded itself in the

gunwale of the Hunt canoe and the feather on the end of it whirred like a rattlesnake's tail.

Dad was not one to forget his job as a collector, even at a bad moment like this. He pulled out the arrow and placed it safely inside the boat.

"Some museum will like that."

Dad tried a show of friendship. He lifted both hands and smiled. But Roger's theft had rather spoiled the friendship technique. The Indians responded with angry shouts and another arrow. This one caught John Hunt in his upraised right arm. A contortion of pain passed over his face.

That was enough for Hal. He lifted his Savage repeating rifle, loaded with high-power, flat-shooting .300 cartridges, famous for their "smashing power".

All right, now was the time for them to smash.

"Don't kill them," warned his father.

"I won't." He levelled his gun at the canoe to strike it just below the water line. The powerful rifle ripped the jungle silence with its roar. The canoe and its howling occupants were hidden by a shower of spray. When it cleared, the canoe was sinking and the Indians were splashing their way towards shore.

"Can I help you, Dad?"

"No. You and Roger keep paddling. But first pass the salt."

Hal gave his father a startled look. Had the old man gone crazy?

"Yes, I mean it, give me that can of salt."

Hunt had pulled out the arrow and laid it beside the other. He noticed that the tip was covered with a black gum. That was curare poison. He knew, because he carried some of it in his own kit – it was useful to the hunter.

He pulled up his sleeve. The arrow wound was slight. But the poison was enough to cause death in a few minutes. Animals and Indians who did not consume salt succumbed to it quickly. Salt-eating white men might succeed in throwing off its effect.

Hunt slashed the wound larger with the point of his hunting knife. Then he briskly rubbed salt into it. He filled his mouth with salt and washed it down with a little water.

"Sorry to leave all the work to you," he said as he stretched himself out in the bottom of the boat.

"Would you like to lie up on shore?"

"No, no. Keep going. I'll be all right."

Curare breaks the connection between the nerves and the muscles. It leaves the muscles limp. And that is why this deadly invention of the Amazon Indians is now being used to good purpose in European and American hospitals in cases where the tension of the muscles must be relaxed. But it is easy to go too far. Whether Hunt had taken in enough of the poison to relax him for ever, even he did not know.

The muscles in the head and neck were the first to be affected. He could not move his head. The numbness spread down over his chest to the between-rib muscles and the diaphragm, which take care of respiration. As they became faint, he had trouble in breathing. He would rather just stop. He kept manfully at it, knowing it was his only chance to hang onto life.

The boys did not realize the seriousness of the situation. It was just as well, since there was nothing they could do. Their best service was to put distance between them and an angry Indian village.

9
The Chase

Boom-boom-boom-boom, came an ominous sound through the forest.

"Drums!" Hal exclaimed. "Those Indians must really be annoyed."

He glanced back anxiously but there was no canoe in sight – as yet. He and Roger made the water churn with their paddles. The current helped, but unfortunately it would help their pursuers too.

Nosey made a whinnying sound like that of a pony.

"Just be patient, little river horse," Roger said. "No time for you now."

He pushed the bottle of fresh goat's milk into a shady spot, sopped his handkerchief in the river, and threw it over the bottle to keep it cool.

Hal did not forget his map, but no sketching and noting were ever done so swiftly. He begrudged every moment away from his paddle.

There was another sound now, the roar of a rapid. Ahead, green and white waves leaped in the sunlight. They were beautiful, but black rocks showed their sullen faces beneath them.

There was no time to get out and look the situation over. No time to pick and choose channels. The boat flew at the rapid as if it would conquer it by mere speed.

The current dipped and became a green toboggan. It hissed like a snake and there was something snakelike in the way it glided swiftly down and wound between the rocks.

There was a louder roar and Roger, in the bow froze as he saw what lay ahead. If Hal at stern paddle could manoeuvre the boat through this he was even better than Roger thought him.

The slope ended in a dive between two great boulders. If the flying arrow of a boat were steered just a trifle to the right or left there would be a resounding crash and nothing but splinters left on the Pastaza.

Roger poised his paddle to be ready to stave off if necessary. But would the paddle break if it struck the rock at this speed, or would it pull out of his hand or run into his chest and throw him out of the boat?

Luckily he did not have to find out. The canoe made a clean cut between the boulders and then smacked into the waves at the base of the incline. It was tossed up as lightly as if it had been a feather instead of a hollowed log, then came down to smash its way through the backlashers.

The noise of the torrent was like the thunder of a train going over a bridge and the spray was blinding. What looked like a white curtain blocked their path. They tore a hole in it and found themselves in small choppy waves like afterthoughts, and then in smooth, swift water fanning out into a quiet pool.

If ever there was a time when they would have liked to stop and rest and think, it was then. But they kept their paddles racing because, as the thunder of the rapids died away, they could once more hear the drums.

"Good work," said Dad weakly from the bottom of the boat.

Hal looked back. "I hope the Indians take time to carry around that." Then he made a sudden exclamation and dug in his paddle. "There they come."

A canoe was poised at the top of the slide. With a whoop that sounded painfully like a war whoop the Indians sent their craft down the chute, skilfully dodged the rocks, then disappeared in the churning foam.

The boys yelled with delight as they saw the boat come out of the lather upside down. Three dark bobbing objects marked the Indians. This was something to see, and Dad tried to raise his head, but it was no go.

Why had the Indians been capsized? Certainly they were skilful canoeists. Hal meditated that the cargo had helped to ballast his own boat through the rough water. And his father's weight low down along the bottom had contributed to success.

Another canoe now appeared at the top of the rapid. This one made the descent safely. Still another canoe followed. It rode on its beam for a tantalizing moment but righted itself in time.

It was some satisfaction that both canoes turned back to rescue the swimmers and their boat. Hal and Roger made full use of this intermission. The dugout slid around a curve into a long, straight stretch that seemed to end in a mountain. As they came closer a slit appeared. The river vanished between two vertical cliffs.

Here was a new problem. Hal was aware that a river usually narrows and speeds up in a gorge. There are not likely to be beaches or banks and the chances of making a landing in case of danger are very slim. Once in a gorge you can't get out of it except at the other end.

The right thing to do would be to stop and reconnoitre. He glanced back. The Indians had collected their forces and were charging down the river, three canoes abreast.

Hal steered for the mouth of the canyon. It was narrow and dark and the river slicked into it at high speed.

The Indians were only a hundred yards away now and coming full tilt. But there seemed to be confusion in their ranks. They were yelling in great excitement. They began to shoot but the arrows fell short. Just as the Hunts' boat entered the canyon's jaws, the pursuing canoes suddenly wheeled out of the current to the shelving shore.

Roger yelped with joy. "They're afraid to come on."

But an icy chill went down Hal's spine. It was not because of the cold shadow cast by the cliffs. If the Indians did not dare follow there must be something pretty bad ahead.

He strained his ears for the sounds of rapids. The stillness got on Hal's nerves. The river slid along rapidly without a ripple or a murmur. The cliffs were only thirty feet apart and rose sheer from the water. Their black forbidding faces were about two hundred feet high. Overhead was a narrow ribbon of blue sky that seemed very far away as if it belonged to another world.

"Ho-ho-ho!" yelled Roger, who wanted to hear the echoes. Hal jumped nervously. The sound was battered back and forth between the cliffs, rising and quickening until it became a devilish rattle and then wailed away in a mournful whine down the canyon.

"Shut up!" said Hal irritably.

The canyon twisted and squirmed. At each turn Hal looked for trouble but there was none. The river was free of rocks, deep and oily smooth and in a tremendous hurry. Another turn. Now a breath of sound drifted up the canyon, but before he could decide whether it was made by water or wind it was gone. He looked up to see if the trees that lined the canyon's edge were blowing. They were stone still. Far above, several dozen scarlet ibis in a great crimson V flew across the blue ribbon. Perhaps they had made the sound.

Looking up to that sunlit blue was like looking out through the bars of a jail into a free world. This gorge was like a prison. Hal instinctively dug in his paddle and hurried the canoe along towards whatever danger there might be ahead. He was impatient to get it done with.

He shivered. The equator was nearby and yet it was cold between these black, sunless walls. He felt strangely alone and helpless. His father appeared to be asleep. Roger had no feeling of responsibility. He was trying to feed Nosey from the bottle of goat's milk. The little tapir slobbered noisily and each slobber came back from the walls like a handclap. The youngster's whimper was turned by the cliffs into a faint, cackling laugh.

Hal admitted to himself that he was having a bad case of the jitters. He wished that they had stayed out of this hellhole. It would have been better to fight the Indians.

But he knew this was not true. If they had killed some Indians the only result would have been to bring hundreds more upon their necks.

Again a sound drifted up the canyon, and as the canoe swept around a curve Hal hoped to see the gorge open out. Instead, it seemed to be closing in. The crests of the cliffs came closer together and large trees locked their branches across the chasm. Presently the rock ceiling was complete overhead. They were in a tunnel. Roger could not see to feed Nosey and looked up, bewildered.

The darkness deepened. Now Hal could not see the paddle in his hand. The black water and black walls were all one. It was useless to steer; the current must do the steering. If there happened to be a great rock in the middle of the current – well, it was just too bad.

No wonder the Indians had not followed. Hal had read of streams that disappear underground to become subterranean rivers. He remembered a story under the title, *The River of No Return*. It was not a comforting thought.

"Holy smokes! What's that?" cried Roger.

"What?"

"Something flying around us."

The air was pulsating with the beat of wings. "Must be bats," Hal said. They were on every side. There must be hundreds of them. Hal pulled his head lower to avoid them although he knew that the radar-like equipment of the bat enables it to fly in pitch darkness without striking anything – unless it wants to.

Unless it wants to. Suppose these were some of the vampire bats that were so common in the American tropics and that liked nothing better than to pierce the skin of a warm-blooded animal, such as man, and lap up blood. But he tried to tell himself that they would not attack anything in swift motion.

Now the cavern was filled with the fine squeaking of the bats. But under their high soprano there was developing a deep baritone.

That was the sound of water. It grew into a thunder, but it was still distant. Could there be an underground waterfall? Would they be carried blindly over it and dashed to pieces on unseen rocks?

Hal had been taught to believe that he was master of his fate. But now he and his companions were being whirled along to an unknown destiny and there was not one thing he could do about it.

The river seemed to make a sudden turn and the canoe scraped against a wall. Hal clutched at the wall and his hand ploughed through bats clinging to its surface. The current pulled the boat away and it hurried on.

But now there was a faint gleam of light, enough to make out the wheeling and swooping of the bats. With the growing light, there grew also the thunder of water ahead.

Hal's spirits leaped. "We're getting out of it!" He did not mind the increasing thunder. Anything was better than that black rat-trap.

There were some cracks in the ceiling now. It was good to get a glimpse of blue sky – it seemed an age since he had seen it last.

Another curve, and both boys whooped as the roof burst asunder and the cliffs fell away into rocky slopes. The light was blinding. The fresh air smacked them hard in the face and it was full of a powdery spray. The river was churning up into white waves.

Roger peered ahead. "Where does it go?" The river seemed to meet the sky and end right there. The boat was only a few dozen yards from this end and running like a racehorse. There was no chance of making the shore.

"Waterfall!" shouted Hal, but the din was so great that he could not be heard. Roger glanced back to see that his brother was paddling furiously, and he did the same. Their only chance was to shoot the canoe over the brink so fast that it would come down on its keel rather than on its nose. Even so, they were in for a smashed canoe if there happened to be rocks below.

Roger yelled like a demon. This was fun, as long as it lasted. Hal thought only of the sleeping or unconscious form in the bottom of the boat. This was a mean spot for a sick man.

The canoe shot out into space. Hal, at the last moment, reversed his stroke and backed water strongly to hold the bow up. Then came a falling sensation. They seemed to fall and fall, and could hardly believe it later when they saw that the drop was only about ten feet. But that much of a fall is plenty in a canoe!

The prayer that the canoe would not split on a rock was answered – it soused into deep water, still right side up. Hal relaxed, Roger relaxed. That was their mistake. A strong side eddy with choppy waves upset the boat in a twinkling.

Even as it went over Hal leaped to get hold of his father. Gripping him, he went down and then came up to battle with the current, which was making a determined effort to smash them on the rocks.

Roger, swimming like an eel, struggled to right the boat and bring it to shore. The white tops of waves tumbled down upon his head time and again but he always came up to give a yell of defiance and to yank the boat closer to shore.

When he reached it he found Hal and his father laid out on the bank like corpses awaiting burial. Hal was done in. The nervous reaction from the weird ride through the tunnel and the plunge over the fall had left him cold and shaking. The impact of the water had roused John Hunt and his eyes were open but he was too weak to move.

The kit, lashed into the canoe, had made the trip safely. Roger unlashed it and put it out on the rocks to dry.

Then he suddenly thought of Nosey. Where was the little tapir? The end of its leash was still tied to the thwart. Roger followed the leash down to the river's edge and into a pool behind a big rock.

There was Nosey, having the time of his life. He rolled and dived and snorted like a baby sea lion. Roger let him enjoy himself.

Among the rocks were the battered hulks of two dugout canoes. There was nothing to show whether the canoeists had been Indians, or other adventurers whose attempt to explore the Pastaza had ended at this point.

John Hunt also saw the wrecks.

"Hal," he said weakly, "you took that fall like a veteran. And incidentally, thanks for pulling me out."

But Hal, in the warm comfort of the sun, was fast asleep.

10
Mystery of the Vampire Bat

There was not much sleep that night.

The camp had visitors. Not Jivaro Indians – though they were half expected. The visitors were of a much more strange and horrifying sort.

Roger, already covered with mementoes of his bout with the army ants, again proved to be an appetizing morsel. Some people are possessed of a chemical composition that attracts hungry creatures. Roger unfortunately belonged in this group.

They had not been in their hammocks more than an

hour when Roger woke. He could not tell what had wakened him. There was a slight pain in the big toe of his right foot. He put his hand on it and felt something wet.

He turned on his flashlight. His hand was smeared with blood, and so was the toe. The blood continued to pour out of a hole about an eighth of an inch in diameter that was as neatly bored as if it had been made with a gimlet.

"Hey! I'm being eaten alive," he yelled.

Hal woke from a dream that cannibals were making a meal of his younger brother. He was a little disgusted when he saw the small hole.

"You probably got your foot against a thorn."

"Don't be a dope. There are no thorns here. Besides, why does it keep on bleeding?"

Dad spoke from his hammock. "Listen!"

Somewhere above was a canopy of beating wings, hundreds of them.

Suddenly Hal remembered the bats of the caverns.

"Oh, no!" he exclaimed. "This is too good to be true."

"What's good about it?" retorted Roger, sopping blood with his handkerchief.

"They must be vampire bats. The London Zoo will pay two thousand dollars for one."

"I must see that," said Dad, struggling to get out of his hammock.

"Stay where you are. I'll bring it to you." And Hal took hold of the pedal specimen and nearly dragged Roger out of his hammock in order to show Dad the punctured foot.

"What am I, a guinea pig?" wailed Roger, but no one was paying much attention to his complaints.

"Think of it, Dad," Hal cried. "If we could only get one! You remember what Dr Ditmars told us – the one he got was the first ever exhibited in the Bronx Zoo. And it died after only a few months. And the London Zoo has never had one."

"Bandage his toe until it stops bleeding," Dad said. "Then put on iodine. You'll live," he assured Roger.

"But how are we going to catch one?" wondered Hal. "Of course we could wait until one bites Roger again and then grab it."

Roger glared at his brother. "Be your own guinea pig," he snapped. And when his toe was bandaged he covered himself completely with his blanket, face and feet included. "Now let the ugly little beasts try to get at me."

If it was a dare, it was soon taken up. The camp was quiet only a few minutes before there was another yelp from Roger.

The boy had forgotten to put the blanket under him as well as over. An exploring bat had discovered a slight rip in the seat of his trousers and had bitten him through the meshes of the hammock. But, again, the visitor had escaped.

Despairing of making a meal on Roger, the greedy little monsters were turning their attention to Dad and Hal. Dad had already had a caller. Before it could make an incision he grabbed at it, but it was off and away before his fingers closed.

Hal got a small hand net from the kit.

"Now I'm going to set a trap for them."

"What will you use for bait?"

"Me," laughed Hal, a little uneasily. "If William Beebe could do it, I can."

Beebe, the well-known naturalist, had deliberately exposed his arm and waited for a vampire to bite him. The creature landed lightly and began to make an opening. Beebe's imagination played tricks with him and he thought he felt blood flowing. He tried to seize the bat but it eluded him. Examining the arm, he found that he had interrupted the bat too soon – only a slight scratch had been made and there was no blood.

Hal determined that he was going to stick it out, no matter how it felt. The methods of the vampire bat had always been a dark mystery that was only now beginning to be cleared up by such men as Ditmars and Beebe.

The vampire had always been call a "bloodsucking bat". Ditmars had proved that it does not suck blood, but laps it up as a cat laps milk. There had been legends that the bat fans its victims to sleep with its wings. Others had it that the bat hovers over the body instead of alighting when it bites.

Hal would find out whether these stories were true. He stretched out his bare arm and lay very still. For a long time nothing happened.

Then the beat of wings seemed to come closer. Finally he felt a very light pressure on his chest, as if a bat had landed there. It was as light as a breath and if he had been asleep he would have never noticed it.

There was no sensation for a while. He could hardly bear the suspense. He wanted to leap up and beat the air to drive away the loathsome creature that wheeled around him.

Then he was aware of a slight tickling on his wrist. That was the the only sign that a landing had been made there. He was not even sure that he felt it.

But the tickling now seemed to be going up his arm to the elbow. Or it might be just the night breeze blowing over his arm. He couldn't be sure.

For a while there was nothing. Then his arm, near the elbow, had a slight tingling sensation as if it were going to sleep. This discovery excited Hal greatly. Scientists had often speculated as to how a bat could cut a hole without the victim feeling it. It was believed possible that the bat's saliva contained a local anaesthetic which numbed the spot where the bite was to be made. What Hal felt seemed to bear out this idea.

Like Beebe, Hal imagined that the hole was cut and the blood was flowing. He resolutely lay still. There was one thing sure – the actual cutting of the hole could not be felt, nor the lapping up of the blood. Or else the bat had flown away. He couldn't tell.

Perhaps he was just fancying the whole thing. But no, now he could really feel something – the very faint sensation of warm blood flowing down over the part of the arm that had not been drugged.

He felt he had learned enough for one lesson. He must capture the little blood drinker before it satisfied itself and flew away.

With all the force at his command he swung the net across his body and down upon his elbow, then twisted the handle smartly so that anything caught in the net could not escape.

He reached for his flashlight. Yes, he had not been just imagining things. His arm was a gory sight. He did not bother with it but looked at the net. A devilish-looking creature struggled in its meshes.

"I've got it!" he yelled. "I've got! Dad, look!"

An extraordinary face leered out of the net. Hal thought he had never seen a face more evil – except one, and his memory went back for an instant to the face of the man who had followed him that night in Quito.

The old legend that had given birth to the name of this creature came back to his mind. "Vampires" were supposed to be ghosts that came out of their graves at night to suck the blood of human beings. This superstition had been the basis of that terrible play, *Dracula*.

Certainly this bat embodied all the horror of the old legend. It was a thing of the night, dark, sinister, with beady eyes full of hate peering out through overhanging fur. The ears were pointed like those generally pictured on Satan himself. The nose was flat and the underjaw projected like a prize fighter's.

"Looks like a cross between the devil and a bulldog," John Hunt whispered, for the face seemed too dreadful to be spoken of aloud.

But they were yet to see the worst. The bat opened its

mouth in a vicious snarl. The long nimble tongue with which it had been lapping up its dinner was covered with blood. The beast seemed very short on teeth, but those it had were terribly efficient. There were two long canines, one on each side.

But the really amazing teeth, the ones that had given the vampire its fabulous reputation, were in the front of the upper jaw. They were twin incisors, slightly curved and as sharp as needles. It was with these lances that the bat made its deep but painless incisions.

Besides blood, there was a sort of watery mucus in the mouth. If he ever got this bat to a laboratory he would have that secretion analysed to see if it contained any narcotic agent that puts the flesh to sleep, or anything that prevents blood from clotting.

He looked at his arm. The blood was still running from the hole. His father staunched it by tying a handkerchief tightly around it.

That was what often caused death, especially to small animals – not the bite of the vampire, but the continued flow of blood after the bat had finished feeding. Blood ordinarily clots in a short time. Did the saliva of the bat contain a chemical that prevent clotting?

That was something to find out.

The bat beat its wings, but the net was strong. While no stories could have overstated the ugliness of this creature, its size had been exaggerated. It had been confused with the great fruit bat which may measure two or three feet between wing tips. The span of this bat was only twelve inches and its body was about four inches long.

"Little, but oh my!" came from Roger.

If they could ever get this thing home, how many thousands of people would look at it with the same wonder and awe with which they were gazing at it now! Here was a creature barely known to science – at least the Hunts did not know of a zoo or animal collection in the world that now possessed a specimen. But could they get it back alive?

Hal had a distressing thought.

"How are we going to feed it?"

"I was wondering about that myself," his father admitted. "It has to have about half a cup of fresh blood every day."

They looked at each other, puzzled. Then Hal turned his gaze upon Roger.

"Not me!" cried Roger. He was really ready to believe that he was about to be offered up, a living sacrifice, to science. With an iodined hole in his toe and another in his rear, he felt that he had done enough for the advancement of knowledge.

"We won't call upon you," his father assured him.

"Except in case of emergency," Hal qualified. "And if you don't want that to happen you'd better unlimber your .22 and get at least one warm-blooded animal per day for Vamp."

The idea cheered Roger considerably. He loved to use his gun and only wanted a good excuse. This was it. He could hardly wait until morning.

Vamp spent the rest of the night in the net. In the morning, she – for in spite of her lack of feminine beauty she was identified as a member of the fair sex – was transferred to a cage that Hal had made from strips of bamboo.

Roger, who usually could think of nothing in the morning except eating, was off before breakfast into the woods with his Mossberg. It was a 15-shot automatic equipped with a scope. It was loaded with high-speed Long Rifle cartridges. Although the gun was light and its calibre was only .22, he had killed a big puma with it in Colorado.

Now he secretly hoped to get a shot at a *tigre*. But after a half hour of stalking, all he came upon was a ratlike capybara, and a little one at that. The capybara, when full grown, is three feet long and the world's largest rodent.

This one was no bigger than a wharf rat. He almost scorned to bother with it. But, thinking of Vamp, and his own breakfast, he let fly.

The result was rather astonishing. The little capybara seemed to emit a roar that shook the forest as it fell over dead. Roger was paralysed with surprise. Then there was a flash of black and yellow in the bushes behind the capybara and the disappointed *tigre* that had been stalking it bounded away through the brush.

When Roger saw the size, power and grace of the big animal he changed his mind about wanting to meet it with a .22.

Thankful that he had not wounded it and brought it tumbling out upon him, he took up the little rodent and walked back to camp, with frequent glances behind him.

Breakfast was served to Vamp inside her cage, which was shrouded in cloth in order to make it as dark as the caverns that had been her home during daylight hours.

After a time Hal peeked in but the cautious Vamp was still hanging upside down to the top of her cage.

The three explorers had their own breakfast. Then Hal took another look. The bat was poised like a great spider over the rodent and was feeding greedily but, disturbed by the light, immediately retreated again to the top of the cage.

In that flash, Hal had seen enough. It was true. The vampire was not a bloodsucker as most scientists supposed it to be. Its mouth had not touched the wound. He had seen its long, bluish-pink tongue darting out and in at the rate of about four times a second. The movement was so rapid that a continuous column of fluid spanned the gap from wound to mouth. It was the technique of a cat or dog, but at high speed.

And to think that this operation could be carried on so gently that a sleeping victim was not wakened, and one wide awake scarcely knew what was going on!

Late in that day's journey another prize was added to the animal-collectors' bag. Like the vampire, it was small in size but large in value. But it was quite unlike the bat in appearance. It was as lovely as the other creature was ugly.

Camp was being made for the night when Hal spied the little creature in a branch of a tree. It was only two or three inches long, except for the tail, and could not weigh more than four ounces. It was covered with soft, golden hair except around the eyes and mouth. There the skin was white and the little fellow looked as if he had kissed a flour barrel and were wearing a large pair of white spectacles.

"It's a pigmy marmoset," Hal called to his father. John Hunt had already been made comfortable in his hammock. He was gradually recovering from the effect of the curare.

"Get it with the blowpipe," he advised Hal.

Roger ran to the boat and got a blowgun that had been presented to them by the Jivaro chief. He brought also a quiver full of darts and a small bottle of curare.

Hal dipped the point of a dart into the curare so that it picked up only the slightest touch of the poison. Then he fitted the dart in the near end of the seven-foot-long bamboo tube. The butt end of the dart was wrapped in the cotton from the kapok tree, making a ball just the right size to fit snugly in the bore of the gun.

Hal raised the blowpipe, put his lips to the mouthpiece, and blew hard.

Fortunately the pigmy, as curious as most monkeys, was sitting very still, taking a keen interest in the proceedings. It made a perfect target. Even so, Hal expected to miss, for he was not adept with the blowpipe – but the dart struck the little fellow in the side.

He chattered excitedly, pulled it out, and threw it away. He started to climb through the tree. But the poison acted fast. He paused, tottered a little, and then fell. He did not check himself with his tail, for the marmoset is not prehensile.

Hal picked him out of the grass. Roger knew his role in this little drama and had the salt ready. Some of it was rubbed into the wound.

"He's just numbed a little," Hal said.

The marmoset began to stir in Hal's hands. Its eyes opened. At first dull, they gradually brightened. The golden plume of a tail began to switch about and some tentative remarks came from the funny white lips under the white-ringed eyes.

Roger was delighted. "Feeling better, Specs?" And it was so that the little fellow got his name.

"I think we'll find Specs a very interesting companion," John Hunt said. "Perhaps sometimes a little too interesting. The marmoset is one of the liveliest, most alert, and most curious of all the monkeys. Of course most of the varieties are larger than this one. The pigmy marmoset is the smallest monkey in the world. That's a point of distinction that should make it interesting to any collector. Do you know, Hal, I wouldn't be surprised if this is a new variety of the pigmy. If he is, they may give him your name, added to his own. Then he'll be *Hapale pygmaeus hunti*."

"Well, to us," said Hal, "he'll just be Specs Hunt."

Specs Hunt came to realize very quickly that he was a member of the Hunt family, and demanded all the privileges pertaining thereto. He was a gentle little fellow, made chirps like a bird, but leaps like an acrobat, and was all over everything all the time. He did not seem to have a streak of the meanness that sometimes characterizes a monkey. He was mischievous in a merry way, but handled himself with such squirrel-like lightness that he rarely upset or broke anything.

His greatest delight was to play with Charlie's long black hair. He would leap out of it at Nosey, the tapir, and land upon his back. But when Nosey tumbled overboard for a bath, taking Specs with him, Specs was loud in disapproval and would clamber back into the boat and make straight for Roger, whom he had adopted as his special guardian.

He would climb inside Roger's shirt and lie there wet and cool against his skin until he dried.

It was going to be hard to part with Specs.

11
Noah's Ark on the Amazon

"The Amazon!" cried Hal, as the canoe swept around a curve and pointed its nose out into a far greater river, broad, swirling, and full of brown humps like lions' heads with manes flowing — mounds of water that hinted the power and speed of the current.

For five days they had followed the mysterious dotted line. When a new map was made that line would be solid. Hal completed his pencilled map by marking the juncture with the Amazon. Then he put the map carefully away in a waterproof bottle and placed the bottle in the waterproof medicine box. That map was one of the expedition's most cherished possessions.

The Amazon, greatest river on earth! Roger and his father were as excited as Hal. The other passengers seemed to share the excitement, or it may have been that they were only disturbed by the rolling and pitching of the little canoe.

The tapir whinnied, the marmoset chirped, and even the sleepy vampire in her dark cage squeaked in alarm. Only Charlie took the whole thing calmly. Hanging from

374

his thwart, the mummified hero did not even deign to open his eyes. He merely nodded gravely.

"Is this really the Amazon?" Roger wanted to know.

"Yes and no," said his father. "But mostly yes. Look on your American Geographical map. You'll notice that the entire river from here to the Atlantic is called the Amazon. But in addition to that, each part of the river has a special name. Some people call this section the Marañon, and the next section the Solimoes. But it's all the Amazon."

"How soon do we build the raft?" enquired Roger eagerly.

The canoe had been the best vessel for shooting the rapids of the Pastaza, but no animals of any size could be collected and carried in a canoe. Besides, on these great waters, a canoe was none too safe. It had been decided that upon reaching the Amazon they would build a raft to transport their animals and themselves downstream.

Roger had even suggested the name for it. *Noah's Ark*.

"The sooner the better," Hunt said. "But we can't land here — the current is too strong. Let's watch for a cove."

The wind blew fresh from the far shore, a mile away. If it had not been for the current, they might have imagined themselves on a lake instead of a river. On the port side the near shore was a riot of flowering trees. Near the bank, waterfowl bobbed up and down in the ripples and went up in a cloud as the boat approached.

Roger reached for the shotgun. But the careening of the boat reminded him to be prudent.

Birds of all kinds, colours and calls adorned the forest. This was evidently a bird paradise. But the most astonishing bird was the jabiru stork, as tall as a man, which walked along the shore with the stately step of a king.

They rounded a point where the wild lashing of water sent the marmoset scurrying into Roger's shirt; then they slid into a calm bay. There was no current here except a lazy eddy that circled backwards around the curved shore. There was a gentle beach of pure sand, again reminding them of a lake shore. Behind this a gigantic ceiba tree threw its branches out to cover almost an acre of ground and beneath its shade nothing else dared to grow except light grass, forming a broad level park.

It was an ideal camping place for raft building. Nothing could be better for building purposes than the trunks of giant bamboo that grew in clumps near the shore, and lianas that would serve as cables to bind the craft together. It took them two days to build the raft. On both days they saw other rafts pass far out in the river and felt assured that they were on the right track. The Indians had found the raft to be the most practicable vessel for this particular stretch of the Amazon.

"But every raft has a house on it," exclaimed Roger. "Let's put a house on ours."

Accordingly a thatch hut with bamboo frame, reed walls and roof of palm leaves was constructed on the raft. Home sweet home afloat!

Now that there was a vessel large enough to accommodate them, two big animals joined the floating menagerie. One was a giant iguana, six feet long.

The huge tropical lizard was lying on a low branch when Roger discovered it. For once, Roger had been walking quietly, because he had been stalking a bird. Therefore, although he was only a dozen feet from the iguana, it was not disturbed.

In fact Roger was the more amazed of the two. He was used to seeing lizards a few inches or even a foot long, but this was unbelievable. It looked exactly like some pictures he had seen of prehistoric monsters.

It was green with brown stripes around its tail. It had a row of spikes down its back and another row of spikes under its chin. Its feet were like hands with long, thin, clawing fingers.

Roger slipped back to camp. "I think I saw something," he whispered.

"You *think* you saw it?"

"Well, I may be crazy," admitted Roger, "but it looked like an alligator up a tree."

"Alligators don't climb trees," his brother said scornfully.

"All right, come and see for yourself."

The three Hunts crept cautiously through the brush. The creature was still there, apparently half asleep.

"An iguana!" exclaimed Hunt. "Remember, you had an iguana steak at the Jivaro village. It's much prized by the Indians as food. They have an odd way of catching it. Let's try it. Get some noosing cord."

"I have some in my pocket," said Hal.

"Good. Make a noose and have it ready to slip over his head."

"But we can't just walk up to him and noose him, can we?"

"No. We have to sing to him first. And pet him."

The boys looked at their father suspiciously. He must be joking.

"That's the way the Indians do it," insisted Hunt. "The iguana is very susceptible to music, and likes to be stroked."

He picked up a stick. "Here, Hal, stroke him with the end of this. And you sing, Roger."

Roger was no singer and he began to make a sound that it was hard to believe would charm either man or beast. Hal stroked the rough skin, standing as far away as possible.

The iguana moved slightly, opened its eyes wider, and turned its head to examine the visitors. Its jaws opened in what was perhaps just a lazy yawn but Roger was so startled by the array of sharp teeth that he stopped singing.

"They can give you a mean bite," Hunt said. "But he won't bite if we handle him gently. Sing, Roger, sing." So Roger sang and Hal stroked.

"Gently, gently," warned their father. "No zoo will take him without a tail. If you startle him, he'll lose it."

Roger stared. "Lose his tail? Just the way those little lizards do up home?"

"Just the same. All right, Hal, I think he's ready for the noose. Let me tie it to the end of your stick."

Hunt fastened the noose to the stick, then very warily lowered it before the iguana's nose. Every time there was the slightest movement he stopped and waited. Then, as softly as a caress, the noose was passed over the animal's head and slowly drawn tight.

"Got him!" yelled Roger.

"Quiet. Remember the tail."

Very gently Hunt began to pull. At first there was no response. Then the iguana slowly got under way, let itself sluggishly down to the ground, and allowed its captor to lead it into camp. Once it made a rush at Hal's heels, champing its jaws in terrifying fashion. It was half led, half lifted onto the raft.

"Now I suppose I have to get food for it," guessed Roger. "What does it eat?"

"Almost anything. Tender leaves and fruits, small birds, little animals."

And Roger went foraging.

The other new passenger was no less unique. It also was six feet long – but up and down rather than horizontally. A jabiru stork like the one they had seen upon approaching the camp site was attracted by some freshly caught fish that Hal had left in a pail on the beach. From the shadow of the big tree Hal watched quietly.

The great bird, high up on its thin legs like tall stilts, looked down gravely into the pail. Jabirus always look as if they are meditating deeply in spite of the fact that they have nothing on their minds but fish. Their shoulders are hunched and their heads bowed.

This solemn visitor seemed to think it all over and to decide that scooping up fish out of a pail was easier than hunting them in the river.

He was truly a majestic bird. His great body was covered with pure white feathers. His head was a glossy black, and there was a handsome red ring around his throat. He raised his wings slightly and Hal estimated that when they were fully spread they would measure seven feet from tip to tip. He could already see this greatest of all the world's storks walking through some zoological garden to the wonder and admiration of thousands of visitors.

Solemnly the great body teetered on its two slender supports and the foot-long bill darted into the pail. It was odd to see a bird that looked so wise and old make such a sudden movement. The fish disposed of, the stork resumed its air of great wisdom and stalked slowly down the beach.

Hal was helpless. He thought of lassoing the bird but despaired of getting close enough before the great feathered aeroplane would take to flight. He would have to let it go.

But he believed the tall visitor would come back, having learned how easy it is to get dinner out of a pail.

He replenished the pail with more live fish and left it exactly where it had been. He drove in four stakes and to the tops of them fastened the four corners of a net so that it spread like a roof about eight feet above the pail. He triggered the net with a slip cord that ran along the ground back to his retreat under the tree.

He had almost given up hope that day when, in the long light of the setting sun, the not-so-wise old stork came slowly stalking along the beach. He stopped twenty feet away to examine the pail and the net above it. This required thought. He stood on one leg – miraculously keeping his balance – tucked the end of the beak into the feathers on his breast, and meditated.

Finally reassured by the fact that neither the pail nor the net moved, he walked slowly under the canopy, eyed the contents of the pail for a moment, and then plunged.

At the same instant Hal jerked the slip cord and the net fell. Alarmed, the bird flew up. This action was not a bit wise for it only served to entangle him more securely in the net. In its meshes his toes, wing tips, and beak were all caught. He continued to thrash about. White feathers flew like snowflakes.

Before long those powerful wings would break the net. Roger and Dad were also witnesses to this experiment, and John Hunt now suggested, "Better get in there fast with the foot rope."

Hal ran up with the rope. Roger was not one to be left out of a game like this and he succeeded in getting in a spot where he was given a hard clout in the stomach by one of the bird's feet.

But during the instant while the foot was extended, Hal succeeded in getting a noose over it.

"The net is tearing! Hang on!" he yelled, as the stork burst through the net and soared up into the air. For a moment it looked as if both Hal and Roger would be carried away in the fashion of Sinbad the Sailor borne aloft by the roc. But their combined weight was too much even for the great aviator. They managed to get their end of the rope to the raft and tie it to a log.

The bird rose fifty feet until it was checked by the taut rope. Then it flew round and round in tight circles. The boys retreated from sight in order to give their captive a chance to recover from his surprise and fright.

But a jabiru stork has too much dignity to remain frightened long. Gradually the bird circled lower and finally lit on the raft. After wagging his great bill from side to side as if to say, "Well, I never!" he seemed to reflect, "I must remember that I am a philosopher and little things like this can't disturb me."

He collected himself, preened his ruffled feathers, shifted

his weight to one foot and tucked the other away, hunched his shoulders, poked his beak into his beard, and mused on the silly ways of men.

The banks of the Amazon would have been lined with astonished people if there had been any people to line them, as *Noah's Ark* sailed seawards with its extraordinary passenger list: tapir, vampire, marmoset, iguana, jabiru, three specimens of homo sapiens and a mummy. But this was only a beginning.

John Hunt was captain, Hal was first mate, and Roger was steward. It was Roger's business to feed the menagerie. That would have been simpler if they had all been willing to eat the same things. But he had a lot of fussy diners. Nosey preferred milk, but was beginning to accept leaves and shoots, Vamp wanted fresh blood, Specs was not content to eat vegetable matter like other monkeys but demanded insects, the giant iguana loved bulbs and blossoms, and for fish-eating Stilts every day was Friday.

The crew usually spent the night on board, moored to some island. The hut made a good bedroom. The hammocks were strung diagonally from corner to corner. They criss-crossed. Roger's was nearest to the roof, Hal's just below it, and their father's near the floor.

When Roger wished to descend, he stepped upon his brother and then his father. This amused him and he found reason for coming down frequently during the night with the excuse that he heard something strange and wanted to investigate.

Hal grew weary of being a stepping-stone, and plotted revenge. One night when his brother was sound asleep Hal unhooked one end of the boy's hammock, carried it out the side of the hut which had been left open, and lashed it to a tree on the bank. Roger was suspended over the water. In due time Roger awoke and prepared to torment his companions as usual. But this time he thought he would pretend to fall out of his hammock. He would come down on Hal with a terrific plop and scare the wits out of him. Hal would think that a jaguar had landed on him.

He eased himself to the edge of his hammock, balanced a moment, then let himself go.

There was a terrific plop, but not on Hal's chest. And the yell that rent the night was not Hal's but Roger's. It was muffled by a bubbling sound as he went below the surface of the Amazon.

Hal lay chuckling. Dad, awakened by the yell, leaped out of his hammock.

"Roger, is that you? Hal, I thought I heard Roger."

"Yes, I heard him too," said Hal, choking. "I think he went out."

Another burbling yell informed them of Roger's position and Dad was out in a flash to help him.

"A crocodile's got me," wailed Roger.

Hal stopped chuckling and tumbled out in a hurry. It was his turn to be scared. What fool thing had he done? This river was full of crocodiles as well as razor-toothed cannibal fish which could strip off all the flesh from a bather in a few moments. You might go in fifty times and not be attacked — but there was always the chance.

He pulled his hunting knife from its sheath as he ran outside. "I'll show that croc what's what!" He remembered what he had been told to do in case of a hand-to-hand encounter with a crocodile — gouge out its eyes.

He could dimly make out Roger in the water. He dived in and clutched Roger's legs, expecting to find them in the jaws of the crocodile. He found no monster but only a half-submerged log.

Roger had never really thought it was a crocodile. But now that he felt his legs gripped he was sure that a crocodile or perhaps even an anaconda had him in its toils. His terrified yells brought his father diving to the rescue and the three Hunts grappled madly with each other while the marmoset chirped, the bat squeaked, but the great stork was too far gone in wisdom and slumber even to open one eye or to put down his tucked-up foot.

To warm chilled bodies, a fire had to be built on the six-inch-deep bed of dirt that served as a fireplace in one corner of the hut. Then the crew retired once more, each grumbling that the whole business was the fault of the others.

Even solemn Stilts was disturbed the next day as the raft went in wild career down a series of rapids. Probably if a prize were given to the worst vessel in which to shoot rapids it would be awarded to the raft.

Noah's Ark was a bedlam of animal and human noises as it plunged into terrifying white waves among black rocks. It was impossible for three men to watch all four corners and every few seconds one corner or another was stuck on a boulder. Then the raft spun around as if a giant hand were twirling it. Somebody had to jump overboard to lift the logs free.

"Rock dead ahead!" cried Roger. There was no chance of avoiding it since there was another rock to the left and one to the right. The Hunts tried to delay their rush with poles and paddles, but it was no use. Hal's pole snapped in two.

The raft seemed doomed. It would surely be broken to pieces. The animals would be scattered and lost.

The rock struck the raft square in the middle of the forward deck. It was fortunate that the raft builders had not had nails or bolts with which to make a rigid vessel. The bamboo logs were only lashed together with lianas. The centre logs yielded, slid up over the rock, and something like a camel's hump passed along the raft and came out at the stern end.

For once, the stork had to put both feet down to keep his balance. The raft hung together but the strain on the hut was too much, and the thatch roof parted. No one minded that. None of the valuable animals had been lost.

Then the raft was teetered wildly this way and that until the disgusted stork took to flight. Forward he flew to the full length of his fifty-foot line and it looked exactly as if the great bird that is supposed to bring babies had decided that all the other passengers on the raft were innocents whom he must guide to safety.

When still water was reached he returned to the raft, looked from one to another of his companions, and made sarcastic little remarks deep in his throat.

Only one or two rafts were seen each day and there were rarely any Indian villages along the banks.

And then, one morning, a city!

After they had been seeing nothing but jungle for days, it seemed as big and as lively as New York. It was Iquitos (pronounced ee-kee-tose).

It was their last outpost before plunging into the deeper jungle of the Amazon. They tied the raft up to a pier. Hundreds of river boats were loading or unloading rubber, tobacco, cotton, timber, ivory nuts and Brazil nuts.

John Hunt stayed on board to guard their property while Hal and Roger eagerly set out to explore the streets. It was a frontier town with sawmills, shipyards, cotton gins, machine shops, and distilleries that produced rum from sugar cane juice. They passed a custom house, municipal palace, and a motion picture theatre showing pictures that they had seen years before on Long Island.

Following their father's instructions, they went in to call on the United States Consul. He had a cablegram for John Hunt.

Hal took it with a sense of foreboding. They almost ran back to the raft.

Dad opened the envelope and unfolded the message.

390

Hal thought of the cablegram received in Quito – would this also be a threat from some mysterious enemy?

When Dad looked up, Hal knew that something was seriously wrong.

"Boys," Dad said, "we've got to go home!"

12

Disaster

Hal took the radiogram. He saw that it was from his mother.

ALL BUILDINGS EXCEPT HOUSE DESTROYED BY FIRE
ANIMALS BURNED TO DEATH ENTIRE COLLECTION LOST
MUST BE WORK OF INCENDIARIES POLICE BAFFLED
ANONYMOUS THREAT TO BURN HOUSE ALSO WHAT
SHALL I DO

So this was the sequel to the warning in the first
message:

AFFAIRS AT HOME WILL REQUIRE YOUR ATTENTION

"There's nothing we can do but get back there as fast as we can," said Dad.

He looked beaten. Nearly everything he owned had been wiped out. His animal collection was his livelihood. And to a man who loved animals, it was painful to think of them trapped in flaming buildings and burned to death. And now, this menace to their own home – perhaps to his wife as well.

Hal's thoughts were following a slightly different line.

"Who could have done it?" he wondered, and his thoughts went back to a face illuminated by a flashlight. "Dad, I told you about the man who followed me in Quito. You didn't take it very seriously – neither did I, then. But . . . do you think . . . ?"

"It's hard to see any connection between a tourist in Quito and a fire in Long Island."

"Yes, I guess you're right. But who could have it in for us?" Hal's analytical brain was working hard. "It can't be a personal grudge. You get along with everybody. You haven't any personal enemies. It can't be political – you don't mix in politics. There are lots of revolutionaries in these Latin American countries with axes to grind, but you've never had anything to do with that sort of thing. So it must be economic."

"What do you mean, economic?" Roger wanted to know.

"Someone stood to gain if Dad lost. Now, the only ones who could possibly gain if our business suffered would be our competitors – the other animal collectors. Most of the zoos and circuses and museums turn to us first. With us out of the market they will have to turn to somebody else."

"You're talking nonsense, Hal. None of the collectors would do this to me. I'm on the best terms with them."

"How about the biggest collector of all, except you?"

"You mean Griffis? Why, Griffis is an old friend. Besides, he sold out his business."

"Exactly," said Hal tensely.

"What are you driving at?"

"He sold it to a man named Sands. Do you know him?"

"Only by reputation," admitted John Hunt. "I think they call him Shark Sands – because he used to do some sharking in the South Seas. He seems to be a general roustabout. They say he ran a pearl-diving business and then got into gold mining in Australia. There was something about his working a mine that didn't belong to him and he got out just ahead of the law. He got into more trouble in the Philippines and skipped just in time to escape a murder charge. Oh, there are plenty of stories about Shark Sands. But he's no animal man. He wouldn't know a kangaroo from an elephant. He hasn't either the knowledge or the honesty to make a success of this business."

"Right," said Hal. "And that's exactly why he has to win by foul means."

John Hunt brushed away the suggestion impatiently. "You have a healthy imagination, Hal. But the important thing right now is to get home. A plane leaves here Tuesday, Thursday and Saturday. That means there's one tomorrow morning. We'll be on it."

And he strode uptown to make reservations.

Hal lay awake most of the night, thinking. In the morning over coffee he said, "Dad, you can cancel one of those reservations."

"What do you mean?"

"I mean I'm going to stay on the job here. Don't you see that what this – whoever it is – wants most is to make us call off this expedition? There's nothing he'd like better than to see us all come trotting home. He destroyed our animals – the last thing he'd like to see would be a new Amazon collection in the market. We can't let him beat us. Of course you have to go. I can handle this thing alone. I'll hire some men to help me."

"I wouldn't think of it," said John Hunt. "You're only a boy."

"But I'll stay with him. And I'll help him," said Roger.

John Hunt smiled at Roger's notion that his services would be valuable. "No, you are both too young to wrestle with this jungle."

"Listen, Dad," said Hal earnestly. "Your collection is gone. What are you going to do for money? The only way you can get back into business is to get a new collection. You've already invested a lot in this trip. If that fails, you are broke. Am I right?"

John Hunt reflected moodily. "I'm afraid you are."

"Think of Mom, think of all of us. The best thing you can do for us is to let Roger and me go through with this job."

"You don't seem to realize, Hal, that this is dangerous country. It's not Colorado."

Hal resorted to sarcasm. "So you think you have to take care of your little boys, don't you? I hate to rub it in, Dad, but I've got to remind you that you've been on the sick list half the time so far. Roger and I have done the work. If we could do it then we could keep on doing it."

"I couldn't let Roger. He's too scatterbrained."

Roger looked crestfallen. "I won't be scatterbrained. I'll promise to be as sensible as a judge."

"He'll mind what I say," said Hal, "won't you, Roger?"

Roger shot his brother a venomous look. But he swallowed the bitter pill. "Yes, I'll even take orders from Hal if you'll let me stay."

"All right," said John Hunt reluctantly. "But remember . . ." And he launched into detailed instructions to Hal. "And you," he said to Roger sternly, "no mischief!"

"Cross my heart!"

Dad flew on the morning plane.

397

13
Escape

The boys watched the plane until it was a mere speck in the sky.

Then they turned to each other with a solemn look. Suddenly they felt very much alone. They were two boys against the jungle. Hal's brave words of a little while ago seemed rather silly.

"We've got the easy end of it," Hal said, trying to reassure both himself and Roger. "We're only up against animals. He's up against an enemy who will stop at nothing."

"Well, if he'll stop at nothing," said Roger uneasily, "perhaps he'll even get at us down here."

"How could he?" scoffed Hal. "If Dad had thought that, he wouldn't have left us here. No, the danger spot right now is Long Island. Well, come on, we have a job to do." And they struck off towards the piers.

Hal was relieved to see that the raft was still there. He had somehow had a crazy notion that it would be stolen.

As they approached the raft the native policeman who had been asked to keep an eye on it came running up waving his arms and talking excitedly. Hal had studied

Spanish for two years and Portuguese for one in preparation for this trip. But he was not prepared for the weird hodge-podge of the two languages hurled at him by the policeman. He made out that during their absence a boat had arrived and the crew had set about untying the raft's cable from the pier and making it fast to the stern of the boat as if to take the raft in tow.

When the policeman objected, a man came out of the boat onto the pier and claimed that he was one of the owners of the raft. He just wanted to move it to a safer position. The policeman was polite, but suspicious and asked the stranger to wait until the others returned. There was quite an argument. Finally the stranger said he wouldn't wait, but would come back later, and off he went in his boat.

Hal tried to get a description of the stranger, but all that he could make out was that he was big, bad looking, and "no gentleman". And he spoke Spanish with an English accent.

Hal rewarded the faithful policeman with an extra coin and then went with him to the police station to lodge a complaint. Roger, armed to the teeth, and feeling very important, stayed to guard the raft.

The police were inclined to dismiss the matter as of no significance.

"Just somebody who made a mistake," said the chief, and added languidly, "However, we'll keep on the lookout for him."

It was quite evident that if anything was to be learned about the mysterious stranger, Hal would have to find it out for himself.

He went to the consul and told him the whole story.

"No one answering to that description has been here," the consul said. "Of course he might make a point of staying away. I don't know how you could find him or what good it would do you if you did. After all, you have nothing against him. He has done nothing actionable, nothing that could put him in jail. If the police arrested him they would have to free him and then he would be more determined than ever to do you down."

"What do you advise me to do?"

"Frankly, I'd advise you to follow your father's example. Hop on a plane and go home. Evidently there's a pretty sinister plot hatched up against you. We might protect you while you are in Iquitos, but as soon as you start down river there's nothing but jungle law. It's every man for himself – and you're only a boy."

The last words stung Hal. He was taller than the consul,

and stronger. Perhaps he didn't know as much but he would learn, and he would learn by taking any hard knocks the jungle had to give him.

"Thanks a lot," he said, "but we have a job to do and we're not going to let Shark Sands or any gunman of his stop us."

The consul looked up at him with a smile and put out his hand. "Well, you have plenty of spirit. Good luck!"

Hal returned to the pier to find Roger with his .22 in one hand, their father's Colt .45 in the other, and a bare hunting knife thrust through his belt. He stood on the pier with his feet braced apart and his lower jaw protruding, and he looked for all the world like Horatio defending the bridge.

The truth was the kid was scared to death. He was mightily relieved to see Hal.

"Did you find him?" he asked.

"No. But leave him alone long enough and I think he will find us."

"That's what I'm afraid of!"

They proceeded to carry out their father's instructions. The homemade raft had served well on the upper river, but for the wide and often stormy waters that they were about to enter, well-constructed boats were necessary.

More room would be needed if they were to take on more animals, especially if they happened to be large ones such as the jaguar and the anaconda. And to propel such boats, they would have to have a crew.

Leaving the friendly policeman on guard over the already valuable animal cargo, they explored the shipyards.

"Here it is," cried Hal at last. "Just what we're looking for."

"This really *does* look like Noah's Ark," laughed Roger.

It was the sort of craft that the Amazon people call a batalao. Fifty feet long, it had a deep cockpit, and was clinker-built – that is, the planks along its sides overlapped like the clapboards of a house. The whole afterpart of the vessel was covered with a roof that certainly looked as if Noah or some other early man had made it. The barrel-shaped thatch house called a toldo gave the whole thing the appearance of a gipsy van or a covered wagon. The vessel had a generously wide beam of about ten feet.

For the pilot who must manipulate the rudder there was at the stern a little platform perched so high that by standing on it he could look over the top of the house and see what was ahead. On the gunwales near the bow were oarlocks where four men might stand to the oars.

There was a sort of sidewalk the full length of each gunwale so that in shallow water the men might pole the boat by starting at the bow, digging their poles into the sand, and pushing while walking down the boat's edge all the way to the stern.

Hal purchased the batalao that was to be their new Ark. He bought also a lighter boat about twenty-five feet long called a montaria. He and Roger preferred to call it a skiff. It was almost as light as a skiff and capable of considerable speed. It also was fitted with a toldo but smaller than the house on the Ark.

With the help of the shipyard proprietor Hal engaged his crew. To man the two boats and to help him and Roger in trapping animals he worked out that he needed six men. Five of his recruits were Indians and the other, whose name was Banco, was a "caboclo" or mixture of Indian and Portuguese.

There would be a third boat, the dugout in which they had descended the Pastaza, but it would simply be towed like a dinghy behind the Ark.

All were highly excited over the prospect of the long jungle voyage as they rowed the Ark and the skiff alongside the raft and proceeded to transfer the animals and the kit from the raft to the boats. It was already getting dark. Hal was anxious to get the work done while the light lasted so that they could sail at dawn.

A crowd collected on the pier to watch and give advice. They were much entertained by the process of hoisting the awkward iguana into the Ark. The great stork, worried by so much company, flew up to the length of his fifty-foot line and circled in the sky. In the meantime the other end of the line was transferred to the Ark and, as the bird descended, it was drawn down gently into its new quarters.

The work was about done when a figure that stood head and shoulders above the rest of the crowd pushed through and came down on the raft.

Hal at once recognized the man. To make sure, he turned on his flashlight. There could be no doubt about it. It was the same brutal face that had leered out of the night at him in Quito.

"Hello," said Hal. "I believe we've met before."

"Oh, that so? Oh yes – for a minute up in Quito. Believe I was trying to find a church."

"I hope you lit your candles and made your prayer."

"All right, buddy, enough of that. I been wanting to see you."

"You took the words right out of my mouth. I've been

wanting to see *you*. I believe you took an interest in this raft when I wasn't around."

"Oh that! Just a case of mistaken identity, mister. We took it for another raft."

"Of course," said Hal. "By the way, I didn't quite get your name."

The stranger laughed. "I ain't much on names. Just call me the boy's best friend." Again he opened his snarling mouth in a laugh, and his teeth were snaggled and discoloured like a crocodile's. Hal at once had a name for him – the name of the big treacherous brute of these waters.

"All right, I'll call you Croc, just to have a handle for you. Now what can I do for you? Besides dumping you overboard."

"Now listen, buddy, I don't want no trouble," said the man christened Croc. "I just want to make a deal with you."

"For Shark Sands?"

The man started with surprise. "I don't know what you're talking about. Now I just wanted to see if you'd like to sell your collection."

"What'll you give for it?"

"A thousand dollars cash."

"It's worth five times that."

"Perhaps," said Croc, a crueller glint coming into his eyes, "but that's what I offer and you'd better take it. If you don't, you'll be kinda sorry. You'd better take it and you'd better do something else. Buy tickets for home."

"And you'd better get off this raft before I throw you off."

Croc's eyes went bloodshot. "You snivelling little rat," he said. "I see I've been too easy with you. All right, if you won't take it the easy way, take it the hard way. I'll be seein' you, buddy."

And he climbed the pier and pushed his way angrily through the crowd.

Roger looked at his brother, wide-eyed. "I have a feeling we're going to see Sunny Boy again before morning."

"It would be just like him to do something during the night to prevent us from leaving," admitted Hal. "Or, if he doesn't do that, at least he will have all night to get ready to chase us down river."

"I know the answer to that one."

"Yes – get a head start. As soon as these people go away we can slip out of here. We can travel all night. Before he can get started we'll be half a day's distance ahead of him."

"But while we're trapping animals, he'll catch up."

"Perhaps so, but there's a chance that we can lose ourselves so that he can't find us."

"What do you mean, 'lose ourselves'?"

"The river is miles wide and full of islands . . . there are dozens of channels between the islands. How will he know which one we have taken?"

"I hope you're right," said Roger devoutly.

Hal called Banco and told him to have the men ready to embark within an hour.

"No, no, *senhor*," said Banco in Portuguese. "We cannot go before morning."

"We are sailing at ten o'clock tonight," said Hal firmly.

"It is dangerous to sail the river at night. No, no, we cannot go."

Hal understood that it was hard for Banco, an older man and well-acquainted with the river, to take orders from a boy. But it was necessary for Banco to learn at the start who was to be boss of this expedition.

Hal took out his wallet. "I'll pay you for this evening's work and we'll go without you."

Banco was thunderstruck. "You can't go without me. You don't know the river."

"I don't know why you think you are so necessary,

Banco," Hal said. "We've come this far without you – we can go on without you."

Banco refused the money. "We'll be ready to sail at ten, *senhor*," he said, a little sullenly.

The animal show being over, the onlookers drifted away to the cafés and plazas. Within an hour the waterfront was deserted. Then a flotilla of three boats slid silently out into the rolling current of the Amazon. The raft was left behind.

"Sunny Boy wanted it," Roger said. "He can have it now."

Banco stood at the helm on the little platform in the stern of the Ark. Up forward, four men stood at the oars. Hal was one of them. The men would have to get used to the idea that the master was going to work right along with them. The dugout was towed behind. Roger was in the montaria with two oarsmen.

The animals were on the Ark inside the toldo, where they would not be worried by the presence of so many strangers on board. Vamp hung upside down in her cage suspended from the roof. The pigmy marmoset clambered from one rafter to another, making nervous chirps. Nosey put his trunk out of the door once in a while, but always retreated, whinnying like a frightened horse. The giant iguana lay on the floor sound asleep, and Stilts maintained his dignity on one foot in a corner.

Charlie, the Jivaro mummy, was the only one allowed to enjoy the fresh air. He was far aloft at the masthead, his black hair waving against the stars.

A tired old last-quarter moon hung in the sky. It was not a bright and cheerful moon, but a moon of mystery and dread. Roger did not like to look at it. Hal was too busy rowing to notice it.

But his blood ran chill as he heard the forest gnashing its teeth. Savage cries from the mouths of hundreds of wild animals combined into one great roar that seemed to be the savage voice of the jungle itself. Most bloodcurdling of all were the ear-splitting howls that one could imagine as coming from a hundred packs of ravenous wolves, or from an army of man-eating lions – but Hal knew that they were merely the night songs of howler monkeys. Although no bigger than a dog, the howler can make more noise than a jaguar. The sound is a deep rumbling roar that would naturally come only from an animal many times as big. A single howler can easily make himself heard at a distance of three miles. The sound is hard for human nerves to endure. It is as if all the agony in the world were being let loose at once. Hal remembered the comment of a naturalist who said that the first time he heard the howler he was so startled he thought all the *tigres* on the Amazon were "engaged in a death struggle".

He could well believe that this was one of the most sullen, morose and savage of the monkeys. If cornered, it would attack viciously and could inflict a severe bite. Its jaws were amazingly powerful. The naturalist Up de Graff had tried to keep one off with the muzzle of his gun – the infuriated creature clamped with his jaws upon the muzzle and bit so hard that he closed the bore.

Hardly less hair-raising were the voices of millions of frogs and toads, booming, moaning, thundering and screeching. They nearly drowned the hoarse croaking of crocodiles, which were evidently numerous along the bank, the whinnying of tapirs, the wild cry of a bird called the horned screamer, the sharp little grunts of peccaries, and many other sounds that were unknown to Hal.

But he had come to know well one sound, the coughing roar of the jaguar. Although it was not very loud, it had the effect of stilling the jungle as if it had been suddenly struck dumb. "Uh-uh-uh-uh-uh!" it went.

The wind freshened. Both boats had been stepped with masts and Hal now ordered up the sails.

Again Banco protested – it was not safe to race down the river in the dark when rocks, sandbars, or half-sunken logs could not be seen. Hal knew that he was quite right, but the desire to put a long distance between him and his pursuer induced him to take the chance.

With both sails and oars at work, the boats flew downstream like scared cats, dodging islands sometimes by only a few feet. Twice the Ark struck a sand bar but managed to struggle across into deep water. Once it struck a log a resounding plunk and the log gave a deep croak and swam away.

The exhausted moon did not give as much light as the stars. The Southern Cross looked frosty in the chill night air. The jungle tumult died down during the middle of the night, then grew again towards dawn. The noise was as good as a clock. When it was at its height, you knew that there was only half an hour left before morning. When the rising sun lit the flowering tops of the trees there was no sound left but the gurgle of the Amazon under the keel and the far cries of a gorgeously coloured flock of roseate spoonbills flying north.

After the sun had risen high enough to reach to the bottom of the leafy gorge the boats were following between two wooded islands, everybody relaxed in its welcome warmth and let the vessels drift while enjoying a breakfast of coffee, mandioca cakes and dried meat.

But the animals, too, were hungry. The island on the

right seemed to be about a mile long. It would be a good place to forage for food for the animal passengers. Hal ordered the flotilla into a quiet cove fringed by majestic Brazil nut trees.

As the boats touched the beach a huge crocodile moved over a few feet to make room, but was too sleepy to swim away. Only its nose and its eyes that bulged like electric bulbs showed above the surface. Its chin rested on the bottom just off the bank.

After a hard night, everyone was glad to rest a while. Most of the men lay on the shore, but Banco and three Indians, afraid of ants and ticks, stretched themselves out in the bottom of the small canoe.

Everyone took a nap. Everyone but Roger.

14
Bucking Bronco Crocodile

Roger forgot that he had sworn off mischief.

The opportunity was too inviting. The crocodile's nose would suit his purpose nicely. It was sharp and pointed, very different from the blunt nose of an alligator. And the crocodile, when it takes off, is as unlike an alligator as a speed boat in comparison with a log raft.

Roger edged over to the painter of the dugout. One end of the line was attached to the bow of the canoe and the other to a log on the shore.

Roger quietly unfastened the line from the log. He made a slip noose in the end of the line. Then he squirmed ever so gently over to the sleepy saurian.

Suddenly leaping into action, he slapped the noose over the crocodile's nose and jumped back out of the way.

The crocodile came to life with a vengeance. It made a lunge at Roger but, missing him, wheeled with a mighty thrash of its powerful tail and plunged out into the bay.

The line came taut with a jerk that shook the sleep out of all four men and set them to yelling like demons. The enraged crocodile yanked the boat this way and that, nearly upsetting it every time he changed his course.

For a time he gave them a free ride, shooting across the bay like a meteor.

Then he turned and rushed at the boat with his great jaws open. They closed with a crunching noise on the gunwale just where Banco's arm had rested an instant before. Splinters flew as the big teeth ground the edge of the boat.

The crocodile changed his tactics. He removed his jaws but brought his heavy tail into action. He swung it like a pile driver against the boat, making it shiver from stem to stern.

Roger by this time had quit laughing. As usual he was having his regrets a little late. Hal and the others had been awakened by the yells. They jumped into the montaria, Roger with them. They set out for the canoe but it shot here and there in such crazy movements that they found themselves going around in circles.

It was still a little funny, Roger thought. How could the men in the canoe be hurt? Banco was reaching over with a knife to cut the line. Then the crocodile would swim away and everyone would think it was a good joke.

Comforting himself with these thoughts, he was horrified to see something happen that he had not thought of. The crocodile dived. Straight down he went in deep water and the canoe followed. The bow dipped and disappeared, the stern rose high in the air. All four men spilled out, the legs and arms going like flails and their yells frightening the birds and monkeys so that the forest broke into a sympathetic din.

Plop! – the four disappeared beneath the surface. Four men in bed with an angry crocodile!

Roger reached for a gun.

"That won't do," Hal cried. "One shot wouldn't kill him. It would only make him worse."

"What'll we do?"

"Cut the painter. He's just frightened. If we can cut that painter perhaps he'll make off."

Hal was about to go overboard but Roger was ahead of him. He knew that this was his job. He dived into the boiling water that was already beginning to show blood. He found the bow of the canoe. With his hunting knife he slashed the line that held the thrashing monster. The crocodile suddenly leaped out of the water like a bucking horse, then dived.

The men righted the canoe and climbed back in. Roger regained the montaria. He had seen the blood in the water and with a heavy heart he looked across at the canoe, expecting to see one of the men badly wounded.

But they appeared to be all right. One of them held a bloody knife. So it was the crocodile that was wounded.

Suddenly there was a new commotion in the bay. Again the crocodile was thrashing about, but this time because it had been attacked by the cannibals of the

Amazon – the ravenous and savage fish called piranhas.

Let a bather, either animal or human, have so much as a scratch on him, and the piranhas, attracted by the blood, are upon him at once. They are only a foot long. With their mouths closed they look as innocent as a perch. When they open their mouths, two semicircles of razor-edged teeth are revealed.

The piranhas are the most feared of all creatures that swim in the Amazon, crocodiles included. They come in shoals, a hundred or a thousand or more at a time. Following up a blood trail, they attack ravenously, stripping all the flesh from the bones in a matter of minutes.

Nor do they always require blood to set them off. More than one canoeist has had his fingers nipped off neatly as he dragged them in the water. A single bite is enough for this operation. The strength of the piranha's jaws is incredible.

A National Geographic Society expedition had found that in catching them it was necessary to use copper wire between the line and the hook. And two strands of the size of wire used for locking turnbuckles on an aeroplane were not enough; three were needed.

The water was churned white by the furious fish. Streaks of deep red appeared in the white.

The Indians in the canoe were jabbering excitedly. They paddled to the scene of conflict. One had a fish spear and proceeded to spear enough food to supply a bountiful fish dinner for everybody. When he had done, more than twenty fish lay in the bottom of the boat. The men kept well out of their way for even a piranha out of water does not become any better tempered.

Close by was a sand bar on which the canoe beached. The fish were spread out on the sand and their heads were chopped off. Roger picked up a head that had been severed from the body for almost a minute and studied the open jaws. He was startled when they snapped shut like a steel spring. He decided to wait until the fish were good and dead before studying them.

An Indian smiled at Roger's surprise. He put the blade of his hunting knife in the mouth of a head that had no body. The jaws snapped shut with such force that the points of the teeth were broken. The Indian took out the knife — on each side the hard steel was nicked in a semicircle by the piranha's teeth.

"At the New York Aquarium," Hal recalled, "a

piranha bit a pair of surgical tweezers made of the very best steel and left nicks in it. They even eat each other. At the aquarium they can't keep more than one in a tank. If they do, the bigger one makes a dinner of the other."

Some of the piranhas had neat slices of meat cut out of their backs. Banco explained that as soon as a piranha is caught on a spear and is helpless to defend himself, all his companions rush upon him. If he isn't drawn out quickly nothing comes up but a skeleton.

"And speaking of skeletons, look at that," Hal said, pointing in the water. The fish had departed, the turmoil had died down, and a long white skeleton like that of a prehistoric monster lay on the bottom.

"That's what they do to our cattle," Banco said. "The cattle are bled by vampire bats during the night; then when they wade into the river the piranhas smell the blood and go at them."

Roger spent the rest of the morning collecting food for his wards. When the noon meal was served all the piranha's sins were forgiven, and Roger's also for the piranha is excellent eating.

Hal even deigned to say, "I don't care if you get into

mischief every day, you young rascal, if it brings us a meal like this!"

But Roger decided within himself that he would get no more fish dinners by tying a canoe to a crocodile.

15
Great Snakes!

Hal kept looking up river for any sign of Croc and the gang of ruffians that he would bring with him.

There was nothing to be seen but an occasional Indian canoe.

Perhaps Croc had not as yet come this far, or perhaps he had already gone by, hidden from view by islands. If he had passed, there was no certainty that he might not return to make a more careful investigation.

Hal was willing to have a fight if necessary, but hoped to avoid it. His business was to make a collection and get out with it, not to fight. The odds would probably be heavily against him. Croc's gang would be made up of armed thugs; Hal's crew were simple boatmen. They had bows and arrows for fishing, and a few blowpipes for catching birds – but no guns.

Besides, Hal did not want any blood on his hands, either his own or that of others. Any killings might lead to arrest, a long stay in jail awaiting trial, and then an ordeal in some Brazilian court. Such affairs sometimes ran on for a year or more. The expedition would be a failure and his father's ruin would be complete.

So Hal resolved to keep out of Croc's way as long as possible. If a gory showdown must come, at least he would not invite it. He would lie low in this cove until dark — then travel again by night.

His men lay on the ground asleep, full of man-eating fish. Hal and Roger followed their example.

So there was no reception committee to welcome the lady who came to call. It was a pity that no one saw her, for she was really a beautiful sight. Her smooth skin was a delicate pale brown ornamented with dark brown spots with light centres. She had a handsome dog-shaped head. She used it to stand on. She was twice as tall as a tall man — in fact the branch around which her handsome red-black-and-yellow tail curled was twelve feet above the ground.

Although tall, she was slender, with a waist measure of no more than twelve inches. Her slim body undulated gracefully as if she were doing a slow dance.

Resting her chin on the ground, she uncoiled her tail from the branch. There she stood for an instant, a muscular column of serpent twelve feet high. Then her body descended to join her head. It did not fall but came down with a smooth balance and poise that an acrobat would have envied.

She raised her head and studied the sleeping forms. How would one of these do for dinner? The boa constrictor, second largest snake in the Americas, is famous for the ability to swallow something three times as big as itself. But the lady in question merely slid over the first Indian, so softly that he felt nothing, then over another and another. Now she had reached Roger. She contemplated him long and thoughtfully. Possibly she decided against him because, although he was not so large as the others, even he would take six weeks to digest.

A sound on the Ark attracted her. Specs, the marmoset, was at the top of the mast playing in Charlie's hair.

The boa slid past Hal's head, crossed the beach, and glided up the gangplank to the deck of the Ark. She stopped to consider the great stork. Now there would be a good meal — but those long bony legs were a nuisance, and there was no nourishment in that big horny beak. Besides, it was sharp and might punch a hole in her skin from the inside — if indeed she could get it inside before it could peck a hole from the outside. The jabiru stork was no mean antagonist. Stilts was eyeing the intruder with stern disapproval and making throaty threats.

The boa turned her attention once more to the juicy little morsel at the masthead. Specs had clambered up the halyards. The boa preferred to use the mast itself as her escalator. It was smooth and slippery but she did not need any projections to climb by. She was not a constrictor for nothing. She could hug her way up.

She spiralled up the mast as swiftly as if it had been lying on the level. Specs did not notice her until her jaws were opening to receive him. He made a wild leap into space and landed on the roof of the toldo.

The boa was confronted by Charlie, who was shaking his head gravely in the afternoon breeze. The movement made him seem very much alive and the boa investigated him with evident curiosity. But she was too fastidious a diner to be satisfied with this shrivelled scrap of human leather. Without nibbling even so much as an ear, she turned and went down, using her own body as a staircase.

She had nearly reached the deck when a little whinny stopped her cold. The young tapir in his gay, yellow-striped coat thrust his enquiring nose from the toldo and then trotted out on deck.

The descending boa, her body still coiled around the mast for half its height, stopped and projected her head. She remained so still that she might have been a bronze statue of herself instead of her living self. Nosey, the little nitwit, wandered straight into the face of danger. His feeble eyes were bent upon the deck on the lookout for food.

When he had come within two feet of her, the boa struck. Her soft, silky neck snapped out as stiff and straight as a ramrod. Her jaws opened and the sharp, incurved teeth closed like a vice on Nosey's nose.

He whinnied to high heaven, at once arousing the sleepers on the beach.

Hal came running, gun in hand. But when he saw the beautiful boa he knew he could not use that gun. He must have this creature for his collection. And yet he could not afford to lose his tapir.

The boa's first act was to lock her jaws upon her prey. Her second was to let her coils come slithering down from the mast and to whip them around the body of the tapir. Her third, if Hal could not act in time, would be to apply the killing pressure, crushing the bones, reducing the flesh to a pulp, and stopping the heart. Then would come the long pull, the animal being slowly drawn down the boa's swollen throat.

Hal fired his gun close to the boa's head, hoping to startle her into releasing her hold.

"I can do better than that," shouted Roger, thinking

his brother had missed. And Banco came tumbling up with a knife.

"Don't hurt the snake," Hal warned. "We want it alive." He jumped into the toldo for some noosing cord.

When he reappeared the situation had changed. A new actor had taken part in the drama. The giant iguana, annoyed by a crack from the whipping tail of the serpent, had sunk its teeth into it. Instantly the deck became a circus for a whirling ball of reptile fury with the innocent little tapir at the centre of it.

Hal and the men stood back. They might as well have tried to stop a tornado. The iguana, looking like a monster of the days before the dawn of civilization, the spines on its back and chin standing out like the hackles of an angry rooster, gripped the snake with its long, sharp claws and held on with its alligator-like teeth. The teeth of the boa had now been transferred from the tapir to her new enemy. But Nosey was so entangled in the coils that he revolved with them, screaming with terror.

Hal looked on in dismay. The two demons would kill each other. The ugly iguana and the lovely boa were both valuable. It was the battle of beauty and the beast. He must not let either win at the expense of the other. But what to do? He had caught snakes before, but never a boa

428

constrictor. What could one do with noosing cord in a mêlée like this?

Another idea came to him and he dropped the cord. He noticed that every time the iguana came out to the full length of the leash that tied him to a log of the craft, the whirling dervishes came to a momentary halt. If he could be there just at that instant and get his fingers on a certain nerve in the snake's neck . . . Every snake had such a nerve centre, and it was its tenderest spot, its Achilles' heel.

The next time the line snapped taut Hal's hand flew to the boa's throat, the fingers sinking deeply into the undersurface. He was pulled violently about by the thrashing reptile, but he held on. The Indians were dancing about him, trying to seize some other part of the boa's whirling body.

Then Hal saw that the boa's jaws had relaxed their hold on the iguana. He felt a surge of triumph. He was Tarzan after all.

The feeling changed to one of horror as the boa transferred her full attention to him. Her coils whipped around his body. Roger seized the end of the tail and manfully tried to pull it loose.

"Stand clear!" yelled Hal. One Hunt in trouble was enough. But Roger stuck to his apparently hopeless job.

Hal ground the fingers of both hands into the throat at the back of the snake's head. The open jaws with their gleaming teeth reached back towards his hands. A grip just behind a snake's head is supposed to be safe, but some snakes can almost turn in their skins to get at their captor. Hal was thankful that the boa has no poison, but he was aware that its bite can be painful and sometimes fatal.

"Me kill! Me kill!" screeched Banco, brandishing his knife. But Hal shook his head. He felt he had already won two points, for the iguana and tapir had retreated to safety.

The snake in its violent convulsions got close enough to catch her teeth upon his shirt and tore it from his shoulder. Blood trickled from a scratch.

More serious was the tightening of the coils. He was beginning to lose his breath. With all his strength he tightened his own grip. Then there was a shout of joy from Roger. He was beginning to have some success. The tail came free but whipped about so savagely that Roger, still hanging onto it, danced a fandango. He kept pulling and walked around Hal, unwinding the serpent. The Indians laid hold and helped him. The jaws and the head drooped. Hal relaxed his grip, hoping fervently that he had not gone too far and killed this superb representative of the world of snakes.

430

The boa went limp and six men had no difficulty in holding her, stretching out her lustrous brown body to full length. The men stood there in a sort of daze.

"Now we've got her, what do we do with her?" came from Roger.

Hal felt bruised and weak. It was as if the wits had been squeezed out of him. Yes, what would they do with the boa now that they had her?

One of the Indians came up with the answer. He pointed to the cabin, or toldo, on the montaria. Sure enough, thought Hal, the Indians were quite accustomed to making a pet of the boa constrictor. In the Indian villages it was common practice to have a boa in the house to keep the place free of rats and mice. This snake had been fighting for its life and had shown its savage nature. But if it were kindly treated it would become tame and even affectionate.

"Just the place for it," said Hal.

Together they carried the weakly squirming boa off the Ark and onto the skiff. They put her into the toldo and closed the door. There she would be apart from the other animals. Perhaps later she would learn to get along with them. If she were kept well-supplied with food, she would have no incentive to gobble up the other passengers. Her first meal was a young peccary brought in by one of the crew. The pig squealed loudly as it was tossed into the toldo. A moment later it still squealed but with a muffled tone, for the squeal was halfway down the boa's throat.

The men opened the door to watch the proceeding. The boa was too fully occupied to pay attention to them. Her head seemed twice as big as before and her throat bulged.

"How can she make her head so large?" puzzled Roger.

"That's because her jaws are not locked together at the back like ours," said Hal. "They're only attached to her skull by a sort of elastic. She can pull her lower jaw away from her upper far enough to take in something a lot bigger than the usual size of her own head. But that's not the most wonderful thing about her. Watch her 'jaw-walking'!"

The boa was inching the peccary in by a curious movement of her lower jaw – or jaws, for there were actually two of them. They worked separately. The right jaw would grip and pull, and the left one would then do the same, the one on the right would release its grip and move forward to grip again, and so on. Thus the victim was "walked" into the mouth and down the throat.

"I see where my job is cut out for me," said Roger ruefully, "getting food every day for that big girl."

"I don't think she'll be much trouble," Hal assured him.

"That meal will last her a week — perhaps two. She'll just lie in a corner and sleep it off. I don't think we even need to keep the door closed. She won't think about escaping until she gets hungry again — and by that time we'll have some more food ready for her."

Roger admired his brother's book knowledge. And it was all to work out exactly as he said except for one unexpected development — something that would provide the expedition with sixty boa constrictors instead of one!

All the rest of day the boa lay asleep in the corner of the toldo. It was possible now to examine her freely. The head could be picked up, the jaws opened, and she could even be turned over on her side.

"Look!" exclaimed Roger. "Feet! She has feet."

Sure enough, just where legs would naturally be if it was natural for a snake to have legs, there were two claws.

"It just shows," Hal said, "that somewhere away back in the ancient history of the boas, they had feet like lizards and other vertebrates. These are the remains of them."

"Why did they lose them, I wonder?"

"Because they became clever enough to walk on their stomachs," Hal guessed. "Think what an advantage it is in the jungle not to have arms and legs to get tangled in the underbrush. A snake can slip through a tangle of vines that would stop anything with legs."

"But none of the snakes we used to catch had these leftover legs."

"No – but I understand all the boa family has them."

"What's the boa family?"

"Oh, there are about forty kinds of boa. The python is one. You'd have to go to Asia to find it. But the biggest of them all, in fact the largest snake in the whole world, you are likely to run into any day here in the Amazon."

"The anaconda?"

Hal nodded. Roger's eyes sparkled. "Are we going to try to get one of them?"

"Yes. But we won't have as easy a time as we had today. Our boa is as gentle as a kitten compared with the anaconda."

"Gentle!" exclaimed Roger, looking at the twelve feet of powerful muscle. "There was a while this afternoon when I thought the kitten was going to swallow a mouse, and you were it."

That night the miracle happened, and one snake became sixty, or perhaps even seventy, no one ever knew exactly how many because it was impossible to tell just how many the big stork swallowed when no one was looking.

The flotilla was sliding down river under a moon even more forlorn than the one the night before. Suddenly, above the bedlam raised by the howler monkeys, frogs and big cats of the forest, came a whoop from Roger. He was in the skiff with two of the Indians. He clutched at his knee, where something was squirming up inside his trousers. Then something dropped from a halyard onto his shoulder and wriggled around his neck.

The two Indians stopped rowing and started yelling. They danced about as if shaking things from their bare feet. Then they scrambled up onto the bow and stood perched there on all fours, chattering like monkeys and looking down with dread into the hold of the boat.

Roger shinned up the mast and looked down. Were his eyes deceived by the weird moonlight, or was the whole inside of the boat crawling?

"What's the matter?" It was Hal's voice. The Ark had pulled alongside and the gunwales of the two boats rubbed. Instantly there could be seen something like little waves or ripples running over the gunwales from the smaller boat to the larger. Then the crew of the Ark joined in the dance.

"Snakes!" yelled Hal. "Are you all right, Roger?"

"They're all over me."

"Have you been bitten?"

"No. They don't seem to bite. But how those little beggars can climb!"

And he slid back to the deck, for he had found that snakes could go up a mast as readily as he.

Hal turned on his flashlight. Snakes everywhere! They were little fellows about a foot long and as thick as a pencil. Hal took one up and pressed its jaws open. He was thankful that there was no sign of poison fangs.

Then it dawned upon him. The big boa had become a mother.

"Whoopee!" he cried. "Now we have enough boas to supply all the zoos in the world."

The other members of the crew were not so happy about it. It was difficult to step anywhere or put a hand to anything without contacting a slithering little form. The youngsters seemed especially fond of pockets. Perhaps they liked the warmth. Hal pulled them out until he was tired and resigned himself to carrying a baby serpent in each pocket.

The Indians were reassured by the evidence of the flashlight. They knew that the little boas were quite harmless – in fact the girls in the villages allowed them to twine through their hair.

Roger was already beginning to worry about having to feed the multitude.

"Perhaps they'll all swim away," he said hopefully.

"No chance," said Hal. "If they were anacondas – yes. But boas don't like the water. They'll probably stay near their mother."

The only other individual on board who was as happy about the snakes as Hal was the big stork. Tonight, tethered out on deck, he thrust his great bill like a shaft of lightning in this direction and that, each time engulfing a snake. His long neck wriggled as they went down. When Hal noticed these goings-on, he quickly put a stop to them by trying the stork's beak shut with a piece of cord.

"That's a job for you," he said to Roger, "to keep Stilts so full of fish that he won't want our babies."

The boats went on their way, raising their sails when a breeze came up shortly after midnight. The jungle was now still. The passage was narrow, between an island and the mainland.

A canoe shot out from the shore into the dim path ahead, and there were shouts in Portuguese. Someone seemed to be calling for help. Hal, though suspicious, could not pass anyone who really needed assistance. He ordered down the sails. The Ark slid up alongside the canoe.

"Is this the Hunt outfit?" a voice came from the canoe.

"Yes," said Hal, more suspicious than ever. But what had he to fear from two men in a canoe?

"It's them!" one of the men shouted. And there was an answering shout from the shore and a clattering of oars being made ready in a boat.

"Sails!" called Hal, but before they could be hoisted one of the strangers stood up in the canoe, grasped the gunwale of the Ark with one hand and levelled a revolver with the other.

"The first man who moves will get plugged," he warned.

The men froze in their places as if struck by a sudden paralysis. Roger had been collecting snakes on the deck of the Ark and putting them into a covered basket. He stood with the basket in his arms by the gunwale just above the canoe.

Judging by the sounds from shore there were quite a number of men boarding a boat considerably larger than the canoe in which the two sentinels had been stationed. It was painful to Hal to have to stand helpless while his enemies prepared to attack, but the levelled revolver was very persuasive. It was pointed straight at him.

Roger made a slight movement. The man standing immediately swung the gun to cover him.

438

"Never mind him," said his companion. "He's only a kid."

The muzzle went back to Hal. Roger felt heartily insulted. So he was only a kid! Not even worth covering with a gun!

He took advantage of the fact that he was not closely watched. He quietly uncovered the basket. A large boat could now be seen putting out from shore, well loaded with men. The oarsmen were being urged on by a ragged-edged voice that was certainly Croc's. Croc's voice reminded you of a stone wall with broken glass on top.

Roger swung the basket and threw the contents upon the two men in the canoe.

16
Bullets at Midnight

A bath of snakes slithered down over the heads of the unwelcome visitors. Bang went the revolver, let off by a nervous trigger finger. The bullet pinged into a tree on the island. The men roared with rage and terror, thrashing about violently, trying to free themselves of the uncanny little crawlers. Who was to know that they were not deadly?

The man standing let go of the gunwale of the Ark in order to have both hands free for his battle with the serpents. He had no sooner done so that he lost his balance and went overboard, capsizing the canoe.

"Hey, I can't swim," blubbered one of the men, but Hal did not tarry to rescue him. The sails were up in a flash and the men bent to the oars. The pursuing boat also ran up a sail.

Hal noticed that the shouted words of the men following were only rarely in Spanish or Portuguese, but mostly in a wharfside English. Croc might have brought the thugs to South America with him or, more likely, he had picked them up in Iquitos. Along the wharves of Iquitos, where ocean liners dock after a voyage of 2,300 miles up the Amazon from the Atlantic, there were always plenty of rough characters from North America or Europe who were quite willing to engage in crime for a consideration. Along with such a gang of willing murderers, Croc doubtless had one or two Indians or caboclos who knew the river. Perhaps one of them was sheeting home the sail, for it seemed to be making the best use of every puff of air.

But the men at the oars could not be river men. Perhaps they were more accustomed to the deck of a cargo steamer than to the rower's post in a montaria. There seemed to be a bank of four oars on each side. Of course they had to work in unison to be successful, but they were continually tangling with each other to the accompaniment of curses that echoed back from the forest wall.

Croc had been forced to pause long enough to pick up the two men dumped from the canoe, right the canoe, and attach the painter to the stern of the larger boat.

"Good boy, Roger!" said Hal, seeing the fruit of his brother's endeavours. Every moment gained might mean the difference between success and failure, life and death.

He felt less cheerful when bullets began to come from the pursuing boat. They zinged by in such a savage hurry that Hal knew they must be coming from powerful rifles of a long enough range to reach them even if they were half a mile away instead of a poor 500 feet.

One struck the stern, one crashed through the toldo, and one crumpled a leg of the helmsman's platform so that it tipped precariously. Banco abandoned the rudder and came tumbling down to safety. The Ark swung off course.

"Get back to the helm," Hal ordered.

Banco replied with a torrent of excited gibberings and huddled down in the shelter of the toldo.

Hal leaped to the platform, grasped the tiller, and brought the Ark back on her course. But a precious moment had been lost.

Bullets smashed around him. What a fool target I must make! he thought. High on the platform, he must be plainly silhouetted against the stars. It could only be a matter of time before he would be hit – unless he could do something to delay Croc's boat.

"Roger!" he called, and Roger came running. "Cut the painter of the dugout."

"What for?"

"Quick! Cut the canoe loose and swing it broadside."

Roger caught the idea. Lay this heavy, hollowed log across the path of Croc's boat. The canoe would be lost, but in a good cause.

He drew in the line until he had his hand on the bow of the canoe. Then he cut the line and gave the log boat a strong push backwards and sidewards. Its forward progress checked, it floated with its port beam towards the oncoming boat.

"That'll stop them for a minute," said Hal jubilantly.

As if in answer a bullet ripped through his trousers barely escaping his hip, and disturbing a boa in his pocket. The snake wriggled, then became quiet again as it snuggled against his warm leg.

The black dugout, he hoped, would blend in with the black of the Ark so that Croc and his men would not be able to see it until it was too late to avoid it.

His guess was nearly correct, but not quite. Croc's boat

was only some ten feet from the floating canoe when it was observed and a hoarsely barked order shifted the course far enough to the right so that the big boat merely grazed the dugout's stern.

A yell of derision came from the boatload of thugs. The yell drowned out a shouted warning in Portuguese. Someone who knew the channel was trying to make himself heard. With all their might, the men at the oars shot their boat straight up onto a sand bar. The keel ground and gritted with a screech, and the sail, still pulling, instantly upset the craft. Some of the occupants rolled out on the bar, some into the water.

Hal's men slackened a little to enjoy the situation.

"Pull!" Hal shouted. "Keep going! If we just keep going, we've got them licked!"

The two boats, with the skiff in the lead and Banco once more at the tiller of the Ark, sped down the dark, winding passage. One or two more shots came from the men on the sand bar, but they went wild. The sound of angry voices died in the distance. Hal breathed again.

But he knew that he could hardly hold his lead. There seemed to be eight or ten men in Croc's gang. Even if they were not very good oarsmen they should be able, with the help of the sail, to propel their light montaria faster than Hal's eight, including himself and Roger, could row two boats, one of them a heavy batalao.

He could not depend upon the sail. The one on the Ark was large and pulled powerfully when the wind was from behind. But both sails were squares and so were useless except with a following wind.

Besides, his job was collecting, and that meant making frequent stops. No, a straight getaway was impossible. The game of hide-and-seek must continue. But it was not easy to hide two large boats made conspicuous by their masts and toldos.

The flotilla swept out of the passage into an expanse of river perhaps five miles wide. It kept getting broader and there was no other island in sight. If dawn found them here they would be as conspicuous as a fly on a windowpane.

The jungle animals were already beginning to announce morning. Gradually the stars dimmed in the east, a cold, grey light crept over the water, small clouds in the sky began to blaze pink, and then up bounced the tropical sun.

Everybody peered back along the course. A speck in the distance was probably Croc's boat. If they could see it, certainly Croc could see the Ark. Unluckily the river was becoming wider and wider. It was now ten miles from shore to shore, and more than ever like a sheet of glass on which it would be impossible to hide.

Hal looked at his map. Ahead there should be a cluster of islands – but beyond them there was another embarrassingly open stretch.

Then he noticed a blue line indicating a passage between what appeared to be the mainland and what really was the mainland. He thanked his stars for a highly detailed map. He looked towards the north shore and could see no passage – but he knew it was there and he changed the course of his little fleet.

"There is nothing there," said Banco. Used to following the main channels, he knew of no such passage.

But it was there, and they found it. The boats were now temporarily cut off from Croc's view by a screen of islands concealing the entrance to the passage. Croc, Hal hoped, would waste time looking for them among the islands and would not discover the little waterway through the jungle.

The passage was narrow and the trees met overhead. Their great white trunks went up two hundred feet before they branched to form a roof. It was like going down the nave of a cathedral – except that no cathedral would be alive with brilliant birds and chattering monkeys. The sails were of no use here, for the breeze was cut off by the forest. However, the surface was glassy smooth, and rowing was easy.

Crocodiles grunted as the waves from the boats struck them. Stilts exchanged remarks with two stately jabirus standing one-legged on the bank.

"Look! A lizard walking on the water!" cried Roger.

Everyone stopped rowing to witness the remarkable sight. The lizard, tail and all, was about three feet long. Its stood on its hind feet and balanced itself with its tail which touched the surface of the water. Its clawed front feet were raised in the air like hands.

"It's a basilisk!" cried Hal.

"It looks savage," Roger said.

"But it isn't. The men who named it thought it must be the ferocious creature of the old stories – you know, a basilisk was supposed to be able to kill a person just by breathing upon him or merely by looking at him. And the way it stands up like man, or a ghost, must have made it seem more weird."

"It must be a ghost," said Roger, beginning to think that his mind was being addled by the mysterious gloom. "How could anything real run on the water?"

447

The basilisk, in quest of food, ran from one shore to the other, and upstream and downstream, paying no attention to the boats. It went with amazing speed. Whenever it stopped for an instant it began to sink.

"It's body is very light," Hal said. "And see how large and flat its feet are – as broad as lily pads. As long as it keeps going it can stay up. What a sight it would be in a zoo!"

And he set about capturing it. He contrived to get his boats one on either side of the nimble animal. The basilisk was beginning to get worried. An angry red crest rose up on its head, another on its back, and still another on its tail. It looked something like a turkey gobbler with three red banners waving instead of one.

Suddenly leaving the water, it skittered up some twigs which touched the surface, and took refuge on a low branch. Hal made a pass at it with his net on the end of a long pole. But it leaped into the water, disappeared entirely for an instant, then bobbed up like a jack-in-the-box and began to run again.

One of the Indians, a young fellow named Aqua, who was always willing to do more than he was asked to do, made a mighty leap out of the montaria and landed squarely upon the basilisk. They both vanished under the surface. When Aqua came up his arms were empty. The lizard had wriggled free and presently it shot up into the air, reminding one of those reverse motion pictures in which a diver dives out of the water instead of into it.

But now it was really annoyed. With its three crests flaming mad, its jaws open, and sharp claws extended, it lunged straight at Aqua. Even a leaf-eating lizard can be provoked to anger. Aqua made ready to defend himself, but it was Hal who saved him from being badly scratched.

Down came the net, arriving just in time to trap not only the lizard but the head of the Indian. The basilisk, surprised by this new attack, clawed at the net instead of Aqua. The Indian struggled free, and Hal drew the net with its lively contents to the boat.

He lifted the new passenger on board. It was remarkably light for so large an animal. Hal exclaimed over its beautiful colouration – green and brown with dark crossbars and red crests. And what talent! The creature could run equally well on land or on water, was a good swimmer, and could climb trees almost as nimbly as a monkey. Any big zoo would be happy to pay from £100 to £150 for it.

If he could just get it to a zoo! And he gritted his teeth

as he thought of the man who was apparently determined either to steal his collection or destroy it.

The basilisk tried to run off with the net. Two men held the net while Hal ventured to put an arm inside and slip a noose over the animal's head. It was hard to avoid the snapping jaws. Finally the line slipped into place just behind the head crest and forward of the front legs. Hal tied another knot in it to make it fit snugly. No amount of squirming or clawing could dislodge it.

Then he removed the net. The basilisk was now like a dog on a leash, but the leash was thirty feet long. The other end of it was tied to a post of the toldo.

"Why no cage?" Banco asked.

"Would you like to be in a cage? As long as I can, I like to give the animals as much freedom as possible. Besides, if they're not caged, they can help feed themselves."

The basilisk's only idea at the moment was not to feed itself, but to get away. It scooted across the deck and then across ten feet of water to the nearby bank and climbed a tree. Since the boat was moving along, the line at once became well tangled in the brush. The Ark had to be backed up to the shore; Hal untangled the line and drew the protesting lizard on board.

Banco grinned at Hal's embarrassment. "Better let me make a cage," he said.

But Hal stuck to his theories. "When we get a *tigre* you can make a cage for him, but not for a harmless lizard."

He had seen too many animals die in cages. Even in the zoos the trend nowadays was towards providing animals with open parks as similar as possible to their native habitat.

So he tolerated Banco's scorn as his four leashed animals, the tapir, the stork, the iguana and the basilisk, proceeded to wind themselves up with each other. He patiently unwound them as often as necessary.

The woodland waterway was eight miles long. It came out, according to the map, at the junction of the Napo and Amazon rivers.

Whether they were being followed down the passage, Hal could not tell. But he had a new plan for eluding his pursuer. When the end of the channel was reached, he directed his little fleet not out into the great waters of the Amazon, where it would again be clearly visible, but to the left, up the Napo.

Soon the bends in this river concealed the boats from any voyagers on the Amazon. Hal selected a quiet cove and made ready to spend the rest of the day there.

This time no gangplanks were run out. The baby boas would have used them to escape to shore. The boats were moored some twenty feet out and the men waded to the beach.

Roger was the first ashore, and therefore the first to stumble into trouble.

17
Wrestling Match

Roger gaped. He rubbed his eyes. This couldn't be true. There just couldn't be any such animal.

It stood up like a bear on its hind legs. It looked like a bear as far up as its neck. From there on it looked like nothing else in heaven or on earth. Its head was all snout. There was no mouth, no jaws, nothing but a small hole at the end of the snout. And out of this hole came chain lightning.

The creature had huge muscular forearms like a gorilla's and great curved claws four inches long. With these it was tearing open a huge anthill that stood as high as a man. As the ants swarmed out, a red, fiery, lightning-like tongue nearly two feet long darted in and out so fast that it was impossible to follow it.

Hal arrived on the scene. "A giant ant bear!" he shouted. "We must get that."

Roger marvelled. "I didn't know an anteater grew that big."

"There are different varieties. This is the largest. What a find!"

"Well, if it's only an anteater," said Roger scornfully, "I can grab it for you. You got the last thing – the basilisk. Let me nab this one." And he started forward.

"Look out! It's dangerous."

"Dangerous? How could it be, with only a tongue? It hasn't a tooth in its head."

"But its claws—"

"I'll grab it from behind."

The ant bear, in spite of very poor eyesight, realized that something was wrong. It brought its front paws down to the ground and lumbered off, slowly and awkwardly, with its front feet turned in. Behind it came the most fantastic tail Roger had ever seen – an immense brush two feet thick and several feet long. The entire weird outfit from snout tip to tail tip easily measured seven feet.

Roger came down with a flying tackle on the ant bear's back and locked his arms around its chest. He expected now to carry it out to the Ark, and that would be that.

He was more than a little surprised when the supposedly timid anteater reared up on its hind feet and scratched his hands so badly with its claws that he had to let go. He jumped out of the way of the slashing claws.

The anteater, still on its hind feet, sparred like a pugilist, advancing upon Roger and striking out with one arm and then the other. The red tongue darted like the tongue of a snake.

Hal was worried, but he knew that Roger would not thank him for interfering. He was ready to give the bear a smashing blow on the head with the stock of his gun if the situation became too critical.

"Lay off," Roger panted. "This is my bear."

Retreating, he stumbled against a log, and went over backwards. Instantly the hairy giant was upon him. The embrace that Roger had given it was now returned with interest. Like the bear of northern climes, this one knew how to hug. Hal remembered that it was said to be able to crush the life out a puma in this fashion.

But Roger was not done. He struggled to his feet, bringing the bear erect with him. No stranger wrestling match had ever been seen. Roger got hold of the long snout and made as if he were trying to unscrew it. The gigantic tail switched and thrashed about, whipping him on one side of the face and then on the other, or getting in front of his eyes so that he could not see what he was doing. But he could always feel that tremendous and increasing pressure.

He tripped the beast and sent it hurtling on its back, but it did not relax its hold. The wrestlers were up again in a flash. Roger tried lifting his opponent clear of the ground, but it hung on just the same. The sticky red tongue slapped into Roger's face. It seemed to be covered with mucilage. Roger let the bear take full honours in that kind of attack. His own tongue was dry and tight against the roof of his mouth.

He could not stand this hugging much longer. He violently twisted the snout – that was the easiest thing to get hold of. If a boxer didn't like to get punched in the nose, why shouldn't an ant bear's nose be sensitive too?

Suddenly the bushes parted and a new gladiator entered the arena. Another big ant bear came to the aid of its companion.

Two against one. It wasn't fair. Hal levelled his gun at the newcomer. But it was so close to Roger that he did not dare shoot.

Aqua leaped in with a knife – if one could call his thirty-inch–long machete a mere knife. It was practically a sword, and a murderous-looking one at that.

Up came the ant bear on to its hind feet. It stood fully six feet high. Aqua was five inches shorter.

The other bear had chosen to wrestle with Roger. This

one preferred to fight a duel with deadly weapons. Its great gorilla-arms flailed out at the Indian. Each arm ended in three sabres, four inches long, and razor-sharp. They were keen enough and powerful enough to tear open anthills made of baked clay almost as hard as cement. So firm were these hills that the downpours of the rainy season had no effect upon them, and it was difficult to dent them with a hammer or a hatchet. Yet an anteater sometimes kept slashing at a ten or twelve-foot-high hill until it had brought it completely to the ground. It would attack a log so firm on the outside that an axe would raise clean chips – and would hack its way through to the rotten heart filled with termites.

It was quite capable of making ribbons out of Aqua, if it could just get at him. But Aqua fenced skilfully. He parried every thrust with his machete. Whenever there was a chance he lunged at the creature's body. He could seldom reach it. His knife was long but the bear's arms were longer. Once when he came too close he received a deep slash on his chest. The blood welled out and Hal started to his rescue, but Aqua waved him back. He, like Roger, wanted to win his fight alone.

Aqua had one advantage over his opponent. The bear was fast with his arms, but slow on his feet. Aqua was fast all over. But, on the other hand, the bear fought with six blades, Aqua with one.

Aqua feinted a jump to the right, but, as the bear was turning, he leaped to the left and closed in on the animal's flank. Before it could turn, he swung his machete with all his strength and cut cleanly through the neck. The long pointed head dropped off. The body dropped to the ground, but the muscles still jerked. Blood poured out. One of the men came running with a bottle – the blood would make a most acceptable dinner for Vamp.

But Roger and his giant had not suspended operations to watch the duel.

"Hold tight!" yelled Hal. "Don't let him slash you."

Roger clung close so that the bear could not swing at him with those vicious daggers. But he felt the claws sinking into his back. And the embrace of the beast was crushing him. He could not stand this sort of thing much longer.

Then he had an idea. He wrestled the bear out to the water's edge. Perhaps anteaters hated water. He was wrong in that – the anteater is an excellent swimmer. Nevertheless, Roger was on the right track. The bear did not mind being dragged out into the bay – but when Roger dipped its pointed nose under the surface and held it there, it showed signs of discouragement.

Now it fought to free itself, but Roger hung on. In its struggles it pulled Roger from his footing and he suddenly found himself on the bottom of the bay with the bear on top of him. He was now getting a dose of the medicine that he had prescribed for his antagonist. The question was simple: Which one of them could last longer without breathing?

The bear gave in first and rose to take breath. He did not get it, for Roger took care that the long proboscis he was still clutching should not come above the surface of the water. The bear's muscles relaxed.

"Don't drown it," came Hal's warning.

Roger dragged the now inert body of the anteater out of the water and dropped it on the deck of the Ark.

The captive opened its weak eyes, flicked its red tongue, and made a few feeble passes with its claws. Hal noosed a heavy line about its body to make a sort of harness before and behind the front legs, and made fast the other end. The bear now had the liberty of a very short leash.

"If he behaves himself, we'll give him more rope later," Hal said.

The wounds of the gladiators were treated. Roger felt like a collapsed balloon and stretched himself out on the beach.

"Guess you'll have to do the foraging today," he said to Hal. "And I don't envy you the job of getting enough ants for that bear!"

Hal was poring over one of his manuals. "It says here that they live for years in the zoos on chopped meat and raw eggs. They don't have to have ants." His brow knitted as he read on. "Gosh, if I'd known this I wouldn't have let you play with that bear. They really *are* bad. They've killed plenty of Indians. Here's an account of one that even killed a jaguar – sank its claws into the heart. And a hunting dog is apt to be ripped open from stem to stern before it can get near enough to bite."

"Then perhaps it will get tough with our other animals?"

"No. They say it's very peaceable – provided it's let alone."

"Well, believe me, I'll let it alone from now on," moaned Roger.

The Indians carved up the dead beast and ant bear steaks were featured on the luncheon menu.

The meat was tough, wiry, and as sour as vinegar. Roger took one bite and no more. Hal made a brave business of finishing his portion, but his face was screwed up into a knot with distaste.

"Believe I'd almost rather have plain ant without bear," he said.

461

18
Go West, Young Man

"Fire!" exclaimed Hal.

His fleet was once more sailing down the Amazon.

As it rounded a point, a red reflection came across the water from a blaze on shore.

"An Indian village burning up," Roger guessed.

"No Indian village," Banco said. "Young man from Rio. He made a farm here. Perhaps attacked by Indians."

"Steer for the shore," Hal ordered.

Banco did not move the tiller. "Indians may be there still. We would all be killed."

"We could help him put out the fire," Hal insisted. "Make for shore."

Banco stubbornly held his course. Hal mounted the platform and forced over the tiller. The caboclo went down to the deck, muttering.

Both boats were moored a few feet from shore, for Hal was ever mindful of his cargo of little boas that would escape if the vessels were allowed to touch the bank. The men leaped ashore.

Hal and Roger each took the precaution to carry a rifle, and the Indians were armed with bows and arrows and spears.

Banco made a show of trying the edge of his long knife but he lagged behind when the men climbed the bank. He had no stomach for a fight. When no one seemed to be noticing, he turned back towards the boats.

But Hal had been watching him. He was not quite ready to believe that Banco would cut loose and sail away, leaving them to whatever fate was awaiting them. But he was taking no chances.

"Up in front!" he ordered sharply. "Quick, get up in front. You are going to lead us."

Banco grumbled and growled, but he went forward with the willing Aqua and stayed there for a while at least.

As soon as they topped the bank they could see the fire plainly. A frame farmhouse was ablaze. There were no Indians to be seen. A lone man was vainly trying to douse the flames with buckets of water from the well.

Hal broke into a run. He took care to see that Banco ran also, encouraging him by pressing the muzzle of his revolver between his shoulders. So stimulated, Banco developed remarkable speed.

The man looked round and, seeing armed men rushing at him, he had every reason to think that he was about to be attacked. He clapped his hand to where his revolver should have been – but there was no revolver.

"Have you got some more buckets," cried Hal, not thinking to try to say it in Portuguese.

The man looked mightily relieved. "Over in the shed," he answered in English.

Hal and his crew dashed to the shed and found an assortment of buckets, pails, and cans.

Then to the well. It was equipped with an endless chain to which were attached six tubs. As the windlass was turned they came up full and each man in turn filled his vessel, ran to toss the water on the fire, and came back for more.

The roof of the little house was of corrugated iron. That may not be beautiful, especially when it has been rusted by Amazon rains, but it has the advantage of being fireproof. The blaze in the walls was quickly put out by the relay of fire fighters. The young farmer went inside the somewhat blackened interior and lit a lamp. Then he slumped to the floor.

Hal and Roger carried him to his bunk. He lay there as limp as a rag, with eyes closed. Hal went over him to see if he was wounded. Aqua took a towel from the wall, ran out to soak it in water, and returned to put it over the prostrate man's forehead.

Hal admired the strong, clean-cut, and intelligent features of the young farmer. Then the eyes fluttered and opened. A wan smile passed over the pale face. The lips moved and he spoke just one word: "Thanks."

Roger came with a glass of water and they held the man's head as he drank. The eyes of their patient roved about the room and they followed his gaze. Everything was at sixes and sevens, empty boxes on the floor, cupboards open and stripped of their contents. It was plain that the man had been robbed. The place had been thoroughly looted. Nothing of value remained, only scraps and fragments. Blood was spattered over papers and floor. Hal picked up a purse. It was empty.

"You must have had a real fight," Hal said, looking at the smashed chairs and the bloodstains.

The farmer nodded. "A real fight," he said faintly.

"Do you live here all alone?"

Another nod.

"Isn't that dangerous — in Indian country?"

"They weren't Indians."

"Not Indians! Then who . . . ?" He guessed the truth. Croc's gang. "What language did they speak?"

"English, mostly. They asked me if I had seen boats with animals go by. I said no. They wanted food. There were eight or ten of them to feed, and I gave them all I could spare. Still they demanded more. They helped themselves, took all my supplies, put them in their boats. When I objected, the big fellow knocked me down."

"The one with a face like a vampire bat's?"

"That's right. How did you know?"

"I've met him. In fact, he's chasing us down river. We're the ones with the animals. I hope that's his blood."

"I'm afraid not. I went for my guns but they had already stolen them. I got a knife. When the big fellow saw it he slipped behind the others and let one of them take it. The fellow I cut swore he'd get revenge. He fired the house. They took me out and held me off until the fire was too strong for me to stop it. Then they let me go and went off to their boats. By the way they laughed, they must have thought it was very funny."

"How does it happen that you speak English? You're not English?"

"No, Brazilian. My name is Pero Sousa. I learned English in school in Rio."

"I've heard it's the most beautiful city in the world," said Hal. "Why did you ever leave it?"

The young pioneer smiled and lay quiet a moment before he answered. "There were posters on the walls in Rio. They said just what used to be said in North America – 'Go West, Young Man'. Only they said it in Portuguese. Our government wanted us to develop this back country. So I came. Perhaps I was foolish." He lay quiet again, eyes closed.

Then he opened his eyes and a light burned in them. "No, I wasn't foolish," he said fiercely. "Not unless Columbus was foolish when he went west to discover the New World. Not unless the Pilgrims were foolish when they went west to land on Plymouth Rock. Not unless Americans were foolish when they went west to build the United States." He raised himself on his elbow and fixed his eyes intently upon Hal. "Think what a chance there is here for young fellows like you and me. This is the world's last great frontier. A lot of it hasn't even been explored. It's rich in minerals. It has the biggest forests of fine woods on earth. It has the world's greatest river to carry all of its products to the sea. This Amazon valley could feed the world. But not unless it has men – plenty of men. Now there's less than one man to the square mile. Think of that! In the United States there are forty-three to the square mile, and nobody considers that country crowded. We need men – not just Brazilians, but men from your country and everywhere. There are fortunes waiting here for men who are willing to work."

"You had better rest just now," Hal advised.

"Fortunes!" Pero repeated. "But the most important thing is not the money we can make here. The most important thing is peace in the world. And why don't we have peace? Because there is too much suffering and hunger. If the Amazon is brought into production it can relieve that suffering and hunger."

"I know," said Hal. "But don't you think you'd better relax now and get some sleep?"

Pero smiled and settled back on his pillow. "This must all sound like hot air to you. But tomorrow morning I'll take you around the farm. You won't believe it until you see it – what this soil will do."

Hal looked about at the fire-ruined walls, the smashed furniture, the gun racks without guns, the looted drawers and boxes, the empty purse.

"Don't you realize that you have been wiped out?" he said. "You have no guns, no clothes, no supplies, no money to buy seeds or farm machinery. I can see you have a good education. You would do well in the city. Why don't you go back to Rio? We'll take you down-river. If this happened once it will happen again. There are plenty of other gangs like that one. Besides, there are always the Indians. One man can't do anything against the jungle. Go with us tomorrow morning."

But Pero only smiled that gentle, tired smile of his. "Thank you, my friend. But I'll stay here. In the morning I'll show you why."

And, in the morning, Hal understood why. Pero could not show him the pigs, for they had been stolen; nor the cattle, for they had been slaughtered and the meat taken away to feed Croc's gang. But the thieves had not been able to take away the vegetable gardens in which beans, rice, corn, lettuce, cucumbers, radishes, and carrots flourished. Hal was astonished.

"But I understood that the soil was so leached by the rains that nothing much would grow."

"That's the story," laughed Pero. "But you can judge for yourself whether it is true. The only trouble we have is that things grow *too* fast. We have to be all the time fighting back the jungle, and fighting down the weeds. Things grow as if by magic. A bamboo shoot will grow a foot in a night. I'm not joking. Seed corn that would take two or three weeks to bud in the United States, buds here in three days. And look at the size of those oranges."

Hal gazed at a young tree loaded with fruit as big as footballs.

"They can't be oranges! No oranges ever grew to that size."

"They are oranges. In California they call it the Washington navel, but they got it from Brazil. It grows only one-third as large in California."

There were young mango trees, avocado trees, cocoa trees, breadfruit trees, banana plants, all heavily loaded with fruit. There was a tract of good pasture land covered with fresh green elephant grass. In the woods within the borders of Pero's property were fine hardwoods, mahogany, cedar, rubber, towering skyscrapers of trees loaded with Brazil nuts and cream nuts, and huge, wide-spreading fig and garlic trees. There were trees valuable for their oils, much in demand in the industrial north. Pero was right. The world needed Amazonia. Men who dared to bring its riches to mankind were performing a great service.

"Just to show you how important all this is," Pero said, "the United Nations is taking a hand in it now. They've raised millions of dollars from all the nations that are interested in what the Amazon has to give them. They've organized what they call the Amazon Institute – and they're sending dozens of experts in mining, forestry, agriculture, and everything else, down into this country to map out its possibilities. Some of them were here. They liked my farm."

Hal put out his hand and gripped Pero's.

"I don't blame you for sticking. Good luck!"

But when Hal and his crew sailed away they were short one revolver and the precious .270 Winchester rifle. They hung on the gun racks in Pero's cabin. He would discover them there in due time. He would also find a box of ammunition for the guns, some clothing, and, in one of the pockets, his own purse, not empty.

471

But Pero had given Hal more than Hal had given him – a new determination to win in spite of both man and jungle.

19
Tiger Comes to Call

Days passed with no sign of Croc. He continued pursuing, not knowing that what he pursued was behind him. Sooner or later he would realize the truth and would lie in ambush for the arrival of the Ark. Hal kept a constant lookout.

He kept taking on new passengers, most of them small: a gorgeous scarlet ibis, a roseate spoonbill, a golden conure, a cock of the rock, and a curassow that soon became a pet.

But Hal was dissatisfied.

"These small things are all right. But we've just got to get an anaconda. And a tiger."

He took his problem to Aqua. He had come to rely more and more upon the faithful young Indian. During the long hours on deck Aqua had been teaching the two boys the *lingua geral*, which means general language. Each Amazon tribe has its own language, but there is also a general language known to Indians throughout the great Amazon basin. Any explorer should be acquainted with it, since many Indians did not speak Portuguese, and almost none of them knew English.

"I think you will get *el tigre* soon," Aqua said. "We are coming now into tiger country."

"I can never get this quite straight," complained Roger. "Is it a tiger or a jaguar?"

"Jaguar is the literary name for it," Hal admitted. "But you won't find anybody down here calling it that. South Americans call it a tiger and since it's a South American beast I suppose they have a right to name it. I'll call it a tiger too. No matter what we call it, I want one."

"You say it's South American," Roger objected. "But we heard of one in Arizona."

"Yes, and there are plenty of them in Mexico. But they're different. They're small. They seldom weigh over fifteen stone – these run up to thirty. The Mexican animals are dark coloured – these are a bright yellow with black marks. Of course the mark isn't a stripe; it's a sort of broken ring. The Mexican variety will run away from trouble if it can. These down here don't hesitate to charge. And they're very fierce and strong. I've just been reading here what Sasha Siemel says about them. He says that a South American tiger can kill an African lion."

"Isn't he the fellow they call the 'Tiger Man'?"

"Yes. The big cattle ranches employ him. The tigers are hard on cattle. One ranch loses three thousand cattle a year to the tigers. Siemel fights with a spear. He thinks it's more reliable than a gun — because it takes a lot of shots to kill a tiger. Even when you shoot a tiger through the heart it may continue its charge and kill you before it dies."

"I'll enjoy seeing you tackle a tiger with a spear," Roger grinned.

"I'm afraid you won't have that pleasure. That's an old Indian custom — I'll leave that to Aqua. But I hope it won't be necessary; we want to capture one alive, not dead."

Tigers were certainly becoming more common. Their roars at night were more frequent. The terrifying thing about the roar of a tiger was that it seemed to be very close at hand even if the animal were two or three miles away. The roar began with a series of coughs that came faster and faster and louder and louder until they turned into a thunder that seemed to shake the woods — certainly it shook the nerves of anybody listening. Then the cry died away and ended in a few grunting growls. When it was all finished the air seemed to be still vibrating.

You could tell, roughly, how near the animal was by the grunts at the end of its roar.

"If you cannot hear those grunts, he is far away," Aqua

said. "If you can hear them, watch out – he is close!"

The roar, with its rise and fall, had the eerie effect of a siren. It was hard to sleep through it. Travelling was now done mostly by day and hammocks were slung on shore at night. A camp fire was kept burning all night. Hal was never quite sure of this fire – did it keep animals off, or attract them? Perhaps it frightened the more timid ones. But one night he looked from his hammock to see a great yellow-and-black head not twenty feet from him. The tiger did not see him but was gazing with evident curiosity at the fire, its big yellow eyes gleaming in the light. Presently the animal lay down full length, for all the world like a cat by the hearth. Its enormous jaws opened in a gigantic cat yawn.

Hal was quite unprepared for this visit. He had no cage ready, no net, and his men were asleep, some on shore and some on the montaria. Those who did not mind having baby boas crawling over them were on the boat.

If he called to the men, the animal would be alarmed. His gun lay beside him but he could not bring himself to use it. He did not want to kill the superb beast. On the other hand, he did not care to go to sleep within twenty feet of a tiger – and the tiger seemed to have no notion of leaving.

One of the Indians rose to put more wood on the fire. The tiger sat up on its haunches and watched the proceeding with interest. Hal hardly dared breathe. Softly he took up his Savage and aimed, but did not fire. One bullet would only change a placid cat into a raging devil.

At least he hoped the cat was placid. He told himself that animals, even the most savage ones, rarely attack man unless they are cornered or wounded. But he knew that this did not quite hold true of the jaguar. There were too many cases of man-eating on record. Lumber-jacks and rubber gatherers were frequently killed by tigers. A sailor escaped but left an arm behind him. Three padres were caught in a church; two were killed and the other got away. In the Buenos Aires zoo was a tiger that had taken three lives. Then there was the Argentine scientist whose camp was visited every night by a tiger that had taken a fancy to the dried beef; when it was hung out of reach the disappointed tiger attacked the man himself, smashing his skull with one crunch of his jaw.

There were dozens of other cases Hal had read of, but he could not remember them now. He did recall only too clearly one reported by the naturalist Azara: six men went to sleep around a camp fire; in the morning four of them awoke and found the bodies of the other two that had

478

been dragged some distance into the jungle and half devoured.

The Indian came around between the fire and the tiger. Hal's finger fondled the trigger. He could feel the cold sweat on his forehead. The tiger stretched out its nose, as if sniffing. Would this brown, two-legged creature make a good meal or not? But it did not move.

Suddenly, back in the brush, there came the high whinny of a tapir. Instantly the tiger's great head swung around in that direction. It rose and padded off without a sound.

Presently out of the jungle came a terrific noise – the shrill screeching of the tapir and the thundering roar of the forest king.

Everyone in camp woke up with a start.

Roger said with an unsteady voice, "Gee, I'm glad we have a fire. That really does keep them off."

Hal did not choose to worry his brother by telling him what he had seen. In five minutes Roger was asleep again. But Hal kept watch the rest of the night.

In the morning he found the tracks. Each footprint was as big as a soup plate. It was almost perfectly round. The spaces between the toes were even and there was no sign of claws – the jaguar keeps them drawn well back as he walks.

There was nothing about the print to suggest that it had been made by a savage beast. It was as soft and smooth as if someone had pressed a velvet pad into the dirt. Hal remarked about this to Aqua.

"The *tigre's* paw *is* soft," Aqua said, "but strong! Just one blow from it will kill an ox."

With Aqua's help, Hal and Roger followed the trail back into the jungle. They came at last to the spot where the struggle between the tapir and tiger had evidently taken place. The grass was trampled, earth torn up, and underbrush broken. But there was no carcass of a dead tapir.

Hal was disappointed. He had hoped to capture the tiger here. When the big cat kills a large animal it usually eats what it can, leaves the carcass for some hours, and returns to eat again. The wily hunter will be there with his gun or his cage at the time of the second visit.

But this time the tiger had been more wily than the hunter.

"Look at the path," cried Roger. "There must be Indians."

"No Indians," said Aqua. "The tiger made this path."

"But it's as wide as three tigers."

"He was dragging the tapir."

Hal stared. It was hard to believe. Out of the trampled arena led what was almost a road, three or four feet wide, with every bit of underbrush flattened as if a steam roller had passed over it.

"How could a jaguar drag a tapir?" he marvelled. "It's as heavy as a cow."

There was no doubt about it. The largest of South American wild animals had been dragged through virgin forest that even a man with a machete and no burden would have had trouble in penetrating.

They followed the trail. In some places it was more of a tunnel than a path since the tiger did not stand more than three feet high. They stooped and scrambled through.

At any moment they expected to come upon the carcass, and perhaps the tiger. But the trail went on for more than a mile. Then it came out on the bank of the Amazon. It continued to the water's edge. And that was all.

Hal looked across the river. It was several miles wide. His respect for the jaguar grew.

"I didn't know it could swim," said Roger.

"Better than you can. The jaguar loves the water. Perhaps his wife and kids live on the other side and he wanted them to share his meal. But think of swimming all that distance pulling something twice as heavy as himself!" But

Hal remembered the account in one of his manuals of a jaguar that killed a horse and swam with it across the river; and the report by the famous Brazilian, General Rondon, of a horse that was dragged a mile through heavy brush to a water hole where the jaguar might enjoy drinks with his meal.

The cleverness of the animal was almost equal to its strength. It could have gone straight to the river past the camp – but it took a roundabout route to avoid any risk of losing its prize.

On the way back to camp, Aqua showed the boys a strange sight – a tigers' manicure parlour. It was a large tree. At a height of about six or seven feet above the ground were deep scars and scratches made by the claws of jaguars.

This was the way, Aqua explained, that they sharpened their claws. They behaved just like house cats. Standing on their hind feet up against the tree, they dragged their claws repeatedly through the bark. Where their breasts rubbed the tree, it was worn smooth.

20
Tigers Take No Nonsense

Tiger country it was. That became clear during the day's voyage.

Roger was up ahead in the skiff. Suddenly he signalled his two men to stop rowing. He pointed to a cove. Hal stopped his oarsmen and the Ark drifted up alongside the skiff.

On the log projecting out over the cove was a large jaguar. His great head was turned the other way and he did not see the silent boats. He was busy fishing.

He was using his tail as bait – or, rather, as a lure. He would tap the surface of the water lightly with his tail. Insects or fruit dropping upon the surface would make a similar sound. The fish would come up to investigate.

Suddenly the tiger made a quick thrust into the water with his paw and came up with a fish in his claws. He popped it into his mouth and ate it with relish. He looked lazily about and saw the boats. He got up slowly, too dignified to run, and walked solemnly into the forest.

Aqua was grinning. "Very smart tiger," he said proudly, as if he owned it.

Roger was not willing to believe what he had seen. "Do you think he was really using his tail to attract the fish? What does your book say, professor?"

Hal was, as usual, deep in a manual. "Well, here's something pretty wonderful. And it's by a naturalist you can trust – Wallace. Listen to this:

"'The jaguar, say the Indians, is the most cunning animal in the forest: he can imitate the voice of almost every bird and animal so exactly as to draw them towards him: he fishes in the rivers, lashing the water with his tail to imitate falling fruit, and, when the fish approach, hooks them up with his claws. He catches and eats turtles, and I have myself found the unbroken shells which he has completely cleaned out with his paws: he even attacks the cowfish in its own element, and an eye-witness assured me that he had watched one dragging out of the water this bulky animal, weighing as much as a large ox.'"

"Wow!" commented Roger. "And you think you're going to catch anything as strong and as smart as that! You're crazy."

Banco became interested. "Does the *senhor* wish to catch a *tigre*?"

"That's what I'm aiming to do," said Hal. He hoped

that Banco, who had been a pretty sour customer during the trip so far, was now going to offer to help him. It was a vain hope.

"You cannot capture a *tigre*," said Banco.

"Why not?"

"It needs twenty or thirty men. We are only seven men, and a boy."

"But the 'tiger man' kills a tiger single-handed."

"He kills it. He doesn't take it alive. That's different."

Hal had to admit the truth of this. But he was all the more determined to take home a tiger.

He cut short the day's journey at noon and ordered a landing. After eating, the men were set at work building a cage. When Banco objected, Hal said, "Banco, we're going to stay right here until we get a tiger — no matter if it takes a month."

To make the cage not only strong but light, stout bamboos were lashed together with green, wiry lianas. A door was built at one end. The cage was kept small enough so that the animal could not get leverage to break it. It was about four feet wide, four feet deep, and ten feet long.

Nearby Hal found a trail to the shore where animals were accustomed to come down to drink. He looked eagerly for tiger tracks, but had to call Aqua. The Indian found them, and they were big enough to satisfy the most ambitious collector.

Hal and his men began to dig a pit. The Indians were willing to work, but Banco sat on the sidelines muttering to himself. The pit was made six feet deep and about as wide. It was squarely in the middle of the trail.

Then the men, under Hal's direction, cut some poles and laid them across the hole. Hal laid the heavy loop of a lasso on the poles. Then he climbed the great fig tree that overhung the pit and tied the other end of the lasso to a branch, making the rope between the branch and the loop fairly taut.

Then the poles and the loop were covered with leaves and dirt so that the pit was no longer visible.

The cage was brought up and placed nearby, but out of sight among the bushes.

The idea was that the tiger should fall through the loop which would tighten around him as he dropped into the pit. Then he would be drawn out and dragged into the cage. Banco snorted sarcastically.

"This you cannot do," he said.

They retired to camp and waited. It was just getting dark when Hal heard a commotion in the direction of the trail. He stole through the woods to the pit.

486

But he was due for disappointment. The pit was occupied, but not by a tiger. The great blunderbuss of the woods, the tapir, had fallen into it. Hal already had a tapir and did not want to take on another. Space in the boats was too precious.

It was a two-hour job to haul out the heavy beast, cut it free, repair the pit, cover it, and reset the lasso.

Then back to camp for another wait. But Hal was less hopeful than before.

"Aqua," he said, "we don't want all the animals in the jungle falling into that pit. We want a tiger."

"Then let us call one," said Aqua.

He went to his pack of belongings and brought out a steer horn. Hal followed him to the trail at the point where it came out on the riverbank.

Aqua put his lips to the horn and a sound that certainly did not sound like Aqua's voice came from it. It was exactly the voice of a tiger, beginning with a few deep coughs, rising to a fiendish roar, and dying down to low, slow grunts. It was so that moose were called in the north woods – but how different the call!

They listened. The small animals of the forest had been paralysed into silence by the roar. But there was no answering tiger call.

"Guess we're in for a night of it," Hal said.

All night, at intervals, Aqua made his call. It was not until just before dawn that there was a distant coughing answer. A faint grey was lightening the black river, but the darkness inside the jungle was still complete.

Aqua called again. Again the answer. Each time it was closer. Now they could hear the low grunts at the end of the call. That meant that the animal was not more than a mile away.

Closer and closer it came until it seemed that the beast must be just beside them in the bushes. Then a roar was cut off in the middle – and when it came again it had a new note. It was not the voice of one coming to meet a friend, but of one who had been tricked and trapped by an enemy. There was so much savage rage in it that the icicles prickled up and down Hal's back.

"He's in the pit!" he said.

They ran to the pit, where they were joined by the others from the camp. The pit was like a huge pot furiously boiling with something that showed yellow and black in the dawn. Everyone shouted with joy except Banco, and even he seemed sourly impressed.

The rope hung straight and taut from the tree, and the branch to which it was fastened was shaking violently. Evidently the tiger was well caught in the noose.

Now the little matter of getting him into the cage! Hal looked at the wildly churning mass of muscle with dismay and the ear-splitting roars of the beast unsteadied his nerves. This whirling demon was certainly in no mood to walk into a cage.

Hal had the cage brought up to the edge of the pit, and the door opened. He climbed the tree and untied the end of the line. He came down, passed the rope in through the door and out at the back between the slats. Now, if everybody would pull, the tiger might be drawn up out of the pit and into the cage.

It was an excellent theory. Tigers had been caught that way. But he reckoned without Banco. That gentleman, instead of pulling with the rest, sat under the tree and made sneering remarks.

The tiger, furiously trying to climb out of the pit, was helped by the men pulling on the rope. Now he was up to the door of the cage. He could not see the men back in the bushes, but Banco was plainly visible.

The big cat's eyes blazed, and with a terrific roar he lunged at Banco. The rope scorched through the men's hands and was pulled free. Banco let out the most piercing yell of his life and scrambled up the tree.

If he had had time to think he might have acted

differently. It was the worst thing he could do. The jaguar, expert tree climber, came up after him.

"Shoot him! Shoot him!" screamed Banco. Hal's Savage was in his hand but he did not raise it.

Higher and higher went Banco. Perhaps he thought that if he got up into branches that were weak enough, the heavy jaguar could not follow. This might have worked if he had not run into a wasps' nest.

An angry buzzing stopped him. His fingers had broken the nest and the residents came out a hundred strong to see who their visitor was. The welkin rang with his cries of distress as he was stung in dozens of places at once, on face, hands, legs, and through his thin shirt. The tiger was coming on, sinking his claws deep into the bark, and moving with the terrifying grace and beauty of a great snake.

Not that Banco saw any grace and beauty in it! He looked down into two eyes like headlights and open jaws lined with sharp teeth. The tiger was no longer tearing the sky apart with his roar. He was growling softly and deeply as if enjoying the prospect of such an easy meal.

Hal was ashamed of himself for viewing this spectacle with so much satisfaction. But he could not idly leave

Banco to the wasps and the tiger. He caught the end of the rope and lashed it around a branch so that the animal could not go any higher.

Banco did not know that this had been done and expected to be seized and devoured at any instant. Hal was content to let him live in terror a moment longer. Perhaps it would be good for him. Banco thrashed furiously at the wasps, only exciting them to more stinging. Slapping and striking, he lost his grip and slipped down towards the waiting jaws. He caught himself just in time.

Hal's heart popped into his mouth. Perhaps he was carrying this game just a little too far.

He called the men, loosened the rope, and they all laid to and began to draw the beast down the tree. The cage was brought to the foot of the tree and the rope was once more passed in through the door and out the back.

"All together!" cried Hal. "Pull!"

They pulled with a will, and the rope broke.

Instantly Hal was shinning up the tree. He had dropped his rifle, but his revolver was in its holster. He knew what he had to do. Kill the tiger before it killed Banco. Banco was screaming hysterically. The tiger was inching steadily upwards. They were so close together that Hal had not dare to fire from the ground for fear of hitting the man instead of the beast.

The tiger, with a savage growl, made a lunge at one of Banco's feet, missing it by inches. Banco pulled it out of reach, retreated farther into the wasps' nest, and shrieked to high heaven.

The tiger was making ready for another lunge when Hal brought the butt of his revolver cracking down on one of the animal's hind feet. It had the desired effect. The beast forgot Banco and turned to face his new tormentor. His head was now out of line with the cringing form above and Hal fired.

He didn't wait to see if the bullet had found its mark. The earsplitting roar told him that it had. He slid down the tree so fast that he ruined a pair of shorts. He was certain the tiger would follow – and it did.

He had no sooner reached the ground than the tiger leaped from a branch fifteen feet up and came whizzing down to land on the spot where his enemy had just been. But Hal had made a quick jump to one side. He fired again. He missed. His hand shook, the revolver wobbled. He fired again and again. He realized now that Roger was firing with the Savage. The tiger rolled over, got up, wheezed blood, bellowed hoarsely, and came on again.

Hal felt sick and numb. Everything was a blur, the tiger, the men, the woods, all whirling madly. He tried to get hold of himself. He fired straight into open jaws that were spewing blood over him.

Then he was conscious that someone else was in the fight. Aqua was there with his spear. It was the famous old Indian way of fighting, the way that had been adopted also by the "tiger man". But the spear had two blades instead of one. It was something like a two-tined fork.

The tiger was already shot through and through. Yet he charged again with a coughing roar that filled the air with red spray. No man could have stopped that express train. Aqua did not try to stop it with his own strength. He let the earth beneath him do the work. As the weapon pierced the tiger's chest, Aqua pressed the other end of the spear into the earth, thus letting it take the force of the blow.

The tiger was stopped dead in his tracks. Aqua lunged forward with the spear, trying to push the animal over onto its back. But the tiger swerved, shook itself loose from the spear, and came on again with a roar, making a leap at Aqua's throat.

Hal and Roger kept firing. The king of the jungle was being steadily shredded to bits but he fought on. Again Aqua plunged the spear into his chest and the other end into the ground. The spear bent like a bow but it stopped the charge. The tiger staggered weakly. While it was off balance, Aqua heaved with all his might.

Over went the animal onto its back. But all its four paws were towards Aqua, clawing the air. The Indian sidestepped to get behind the beast's head, still pinning the body firmly to the ground.

Once behind the head, he could work more safely. He was out of reach of the powerful legs which shot out in all directions as the animal furiously tried to wrench loose.

Aqua see-sawed the spear back and forth, pressing it farther and farther in, piercing the heart. Hal emptied the rest of his revolver into the great head. There was a wild struggle that tore up the earth and brush for yards around. But the roars were becoming weaker. The big feet swiped the air with less force. The powerful beast went limp and lay still, blood flowing from the heart.

The two boys and Aqua had no sense of victory. This was a battle they had lost, not won. They still had to take a tiger alive.

21
Tiger by the Tail

The crew ate the dead jaguar, in spite of the fact that the taste of it was not very agreeable. Indians believe that eating a brave animal makes you brave. Hal waited a day and a night for another jaguar to come along the trail, but none came.

"All right," he said, "if they won't come to us, we'll go to them."

He and Roger and three of the Indians struck back up the trail into the jungle following tiger tracks. The spoor, marked plainly in the soft ground, led them finally to a low ridge in the side of which was a cave. The tracks disappeared within the cave.

Hal approached the entrance cautiously. He drew his revolver but hoped fervently that he would not have to use it. One death struggle with a tiger was enough.

He peered into the darkness. He could see nothing and could hear no growling, nor even breathing. But there was a strong animal smell. Perhaps the cave was deep and the tigers were far back.

The men carried a net of strong manila rope, and this Hal place over the mouth of the cave. It completely covered the opening. The four corners were staked to the face of the bank – but very lightly, so that the plunging of the tiger into the net would tear them loose. Hal made fast a heavy line to each corner. At a distance of ten feet these four lines were joined and braided to form a single heavy cable which went up over a branch of a tree and down again within reach.

If a tiger ran out into the net the four corners would come loose and close in on the animal. Then everybody would haul on the rope which passed over the branch and down to the net. Shut inside the net, the tiger would be lifted clear of the ground. There the beast would be quite helpless. After it had spent its fury, it might be manoeuvred into the cage, net and all. The door would be locked. Then the net could be eased off and pulled out through the slats.

Hal had read all about it in a book.

Four men were placed on duty at the end of the rope. Every four hours they were relieved by another squad. The two times when something was most likely to happen were sunset and sunrise. It is then that the jaguar prefers to go out to drink at the river or a waterhole.

All day Hal and his men were on watch and after the sun had gone down the suspense was hard to bear. Nothing happened. The net flapped idly in the evening breeze. The jungle animals started their evening chorus, but there was no sound from the cave. Hal was disgusted.

"I will show you another way to get *el tigre*," Aqua said. "Come down to the river."

Hal was glad of a change. He left four men on duty at the cave and went with Aqua. They waded out to the skiff. Taking up the anchor, they rowed the boat well away from the camp. Aqua rummaged in the toldo and brought out another net.

Then he produced his steer horn and put it to his mouth. Hal thought that no tiger could have made a better tiger call.

"On nights like this when the river is smooth," Aqua said, "*el tigre* likes to go swimming. A *tigre* in the water is easier to catch. He is too busy swimming to fight."

Again and again he called. Hours passed. Hal was cold and sleepy. He had always supposed that hunting a tiger would be the most exciting sport in the world. He was bored. He longed for his hammock and a heavy blanket.

"I think he is coming," whispered Aqua, and Hal shook off his drowsiness. Somewhere between the boat and shore, grunts sounded of a sort that could not come from a crocodile. Aqua called again. There were more grunts or coughs, half-smothered by water.

Then Hal could see something swimming. He kept perfectly still. Now he could make out a tiger's head, but it was small. His hands tightened on the net as he made ready to throw it.

The swimmer paused, as if uncertain. Aqua called again, very softly. It must have been good tiger language, for the tiger came on.

Hal was not sleepy now. He tingled all over with excitement. He realized too late that he had not given enough thought to his plan of campaign. He had placed too much confidence in Aqua.

Suppose they caught the tiger in the net – then what?

He had no time to figure this out, for the tiger was now beside the boat. The top of its head showed above the water, also the tip of its tail. By reaching out, Hal could grab that tail.

He had a sudden inspiration. His arm shot out and he seized the tail.

"Row, Aqua, row!" He heaved upwards on the tail, sinking the tiger's head in the water. "Row like mad!"

Aqua leaped to the oars and pulled. Hal braced himself and held on. A gurgling roar sounded from somewhere under the surface. The tiger was dragged along by its tail. It thrashed about savagely but could not get its head forward nor its front paws up. Much of the time the head was under water. The animal was, in fact, rapidly being drowned. It stopped struggling. Now it was a dead weight. Hal called to Aqua and they lifted it into the boat. This was not too hard, for it was a small animal – weighing not more than eleven stone.

They laid it on the net. Even in the dim light they could see that it was a beautiful animal, a real prize. Hal hoped they had not thoroughly drowned it. He cautiously felt for the heart – it was still beating.

He wondered if he should apply first aid. It wasn't necessary to decide this question, for the tiger stirred.

Hal jumped to his feet. "Quick! Close the net!"

They brought up the edges of the net and lashed them together. It was none too soon. The tiger was growling now and striking out feebly. She would spend the next few hours trying to get out of that net, but she was as safe as a kitten in a bag. They fastened the net to the mast.

"That'll do until morning. Then we'll make a cage for her."

Hal was not satisfied. The little tiger was valuable, but he still wondered what was in that cave.

When nothing came out at dawn, he decided to go in and investigate.

He held a revolver in one hand and a pole in the other. Near the end of the pole, but not at the very end, was strapped a flashlight.

If he found a tiger he hoped to confuse it with the light, prod it with the pole, and make it run out into the net.

He walked slowly back into the cave, playing the light before him. The cave was deep and twisted off to the left. As he came to the turn he heard a low growl in the darkness. He began to wish he had stayed out in the sun.

He moved the light beam here and there but could see nothing, nothing but two bright spots. Then he realized that the two spots were eyes. Another growl made him feel cold.

In vain he tried to pick up the rest of the body with his light. Surely he could see a brilliant yellow skin with black marks. But there seemed to be nothing but those two burning eyes. Again came a challenging growl.

Hal reminded himself that a wild animal usually does not attack unless it is cornered. He must be careful not to corner this one.

He went far over to the right wall so that the beast might escape along the left side. The cave was wide and there was plenty of room for it to get by without coming near him. Then it would rush out and they would have a big tiger in the net.

He knew it must be big by the deepness of the growl and the distance between the eyes. But he was greatly puzzled because he could not see the rest of the animal. There appeared to be nothing around those eyes but black cave.

He waited, but the tiger did not move. Hal crept forward, close to the wall. He still hoped the beast would not insist upon being prodded.

It was no use. The closer he came the louder the growls, but the beast did not stir.

Or was it stirring? Yes, the eyes moved now. They were moving towards Hal. This would not do. Hal shouted, but the eyes came on.

He fired into the wall to alarm the beast. He could have fired between those eyes but he was still resolved to get this one alive. He crowded against the wall. Why didn't the animal run past him and out into the net?

The end of the pole struck something hard between the two eyes. Hal could see it now – it was the face of a black jaguar. His heart leaped. This was the greatest animal treasure of the Amazon jungle. Black jaguars were as rare as hen's teeth. He could not think of a zoo that had one – or of a zoo that did not want one and would not pay handsomely for it.

No matter what happened he would not use his revolver. He slipped it into the holster. He put both hands to the pole and gave the tiger a manful jab on the left cheek, hoping to divert the beast to the other side of the cave and out into the net.

He might as well have jabbed a rock. The tiger took two more prods without seeming to notice them. Then he swiped the pole with one big paw. The pole was smashed into splinters against the wall and the light went out. A deafening roar filled the cave. Hal turned and fled.

Around the turn he went with the vengeful beast close behind. No Olympic runner could have beat Hal Hunt then. With a flying leap he plunged into the middle of the net. He prayed that he would hit it with enough force so that it would break loose and not bounce him back into the savage jaws.

The net did break loose. Then men at the rope had heard the roar and they were ready. As something, they did not know what, struck the net they hauled.

Up went the net like a bag with Hal inside. The astonishment of the crew who had bagged a man instead of a tiger can be imagined. They were speechless with surprise, and then they laughed. How they laughed! The tiger halted at the mouth of the cave and then retreated into the darkness.

Hal would have given anything to be on the other side of the globe at that moment. The men's hilarious laughter made him feel pretty small. It didn't help much that his own brother, Roger, laughed more loudly than anyone else. He rolled on the ground, kicking the dust, and screaming with joy. When he could speak again he said, "Oh boy! Won't this be a good one to tell when we get home!"

Dangling from his branch, Hal said gruffly, "Let me down."

The men were too merry to be careful. Paying out the rope, they neglected to hold tight – it slipped through their hands and down Hal came, in a heap. This did not help to soothe his pride. He pushed the net away from him and got up. He stepped out of the net with great dignity.

"Ho, ho! The great tiger man!" chortled Roger.

Hal looked about at the laughing faces. His nerves had been badly shaken but he was getting control of them now. After all, it must have been pretty funny. He grinned.

"Too bad you didn't have a camera, Roger," he said. "That was sure one for the book."

But his thoughts were grimly fixed upon the magnificent creature in the cave. He was going to get that tiger!

505

22
Black Beauty

It was a council of war.

Hal, Roger and Aqua were trying to decide how to capture the black beauty. They were not getting very far.

"We've got to nab it," Hal said. "It's the last word in tigers. Even a Bengal tiger isn't worth as much. But the net idea won't work with this big fellow. He's too wise."

Aqua was stirring up some bird-lime. He had made it from the juice of the breadfruit tree. It was more sticky than thick paste or flypaper.

The Indians used it to catch birds. They would smear some of it on the limb of a tree where birds were in the habit of alighting. A bird that came in contact with it could not get away. When it beat its wings, they too would be caught. It stayed there until the hunter came for it.

Aqua had been using the method to catch birds for some of the hungry animal passengers.

Suddenly he paused and stared at Hal. An idea was breaking in the Indian's head. He pointed at the bird-lime.

"This will catch the tiger," he said.

Hal laughed incredulously. "It's good for birds — and perhaps monkeys — but you might as well try to stop a tiger with a bottle of mucilage."

"This will catch the tiger," Aqua repeated. "All our people use it."

He called in some of the other Indians as witnesses. They nodded when he explained his idea and told stories of how they or their friends had captured the big cats with bird-lime.

Hal thought he was being kidded. Perhaps the men had not forgotten what a ridiculous figure he had cut hanging from a branch in a bag. They thought they could make a fool of him. And yet Aqua had always been respectful before this.

Well, if it was a bluff, he would call their bluff.

"Okay," he said. "You and the boys can go ahead and catch Black Beauty with bird-lime."

Aqua leaped up and talked excitedly with the other Indians. They went to gather more of the sticky substance. They took it to the tiger trail at a point a few hundred feet from the cave.

They took the net that had trapped Hal and laid it on the trail. They covered it carefully with leaves so that it was not visible. They spread great quantities of bird-lime on the leaves. Then they scattered more leaves on top.

"Now all we have to do is to wait," said Aqua.

Wait, wait! Animal collecting was nine-tenths waiting. Hal hung his hammock in the woods within easy earshot of the trail. Aqua slept nearby. They alternated watches through the night. They heard no tiger.

In the morning they crept to the trail and found an agouti caught in the lime. The agouti is a two-foot-long rodent.

Hal was disgusted. He was about to tear the animal loose when Aqua said, "Leave it there. It will draw *el tigre*."

A low growl made them wheel about.

At the mouth of the cave stood the most splendid of jaguars. He was black as night, sleek, long and powerful. His yellow eyes blazed. His savage black face parted in a snarl that showed gleaming white teeth. He looked quite capable of carrying out the reputation that the black jaguar has among the Indians of being the most ferocious of the cat tribe.

He had been cooped up in the cave long enough. He was about to go to the river for a drink of water and anyone who got in his way would be unlucky.

Hal was about to take to the woods, but Aqua said, "No. He might come after us. That would take him away from the lime."

Instead of going into the woods, Aqua ran down the trail, Hal following. Now the snare was between them and the tiger. They were, like the agouti, tiger bait.

The huge black beast came padding down the trail. It was wonderful that an animal so heavy could move with such smooth grace. Within that glossy pelt there must be nearly thirty stone of bone and muscle.

Hal, remembering his encounter with the black monster in the cave, did not welcome another interview. He was distinctly uncomfortable. What if Aqua's plan did not work? Suppose the beast merely walked through the bird-lime and came on? Was this powerful brute going to be stopped by a little stickum?

The tiger's pace quickened. He broke from a walk into a well-oiled run, his glossy shoulders moving like pistons. If Hal had not been scared to death he would have admitted that it was the loveliest movement of muscle he had ever seen.

Why didn't the beast pay attention to the agouti? He seemed to look straight past it at the two men. Hal felt very foolish, standing in plain view, waiting for a tiger to

509

pounce upon him. And he hated that low, vicious growl. He would rather hear the beast roar. But the tiger was not wasting his breath on roars.

He was now almost up to the snare. Suddenly the agouti caught his eye and he stopped dead. He crouched to the ground. For a full minute he lay there, little black ripples moving along his muscles as he tensed them.

Then he sprang.

What a leap it was, all of a dozen feet. In mid air he roared, and his roar shook the forest. He came down like a black avalanche upon the helpless agouti and seized it by the neck.

But instantly he let it go. His attention was attracted by the stuff under his feet.

Now, thought Hal, we shall see if bird-lime can hold a tiger. No, Aqua was wrong. The tiger was now lifting one foot. It was covered with white. Then he raised another paw and looked at it with surprise.

Hal had had enough of this. "See!" he cried. "It isn't holding him. Come on. Let's get out of here."

But Aqua put a hand on his arm. "Wait. You do not understand. Watch."

The tiger was trying to lick the stuff off his paw. It did not come off. He bit at it savagely. He got it smeared over his face. He tried to rub it from his face. He only succeeded in plastering it over his eyes. He lay down in order to get the use of his four paws. Now the strange stuff was all over one flank. He tried to get it off and only succeeded in making matters worse.

Now Hal understood. His grandmother had told him of the old custom of putting butter on a cat's paws to keep it busy until it became used to a new home. The cat was so fully occupied that it had no time to worry about anything else.

And so the tiger was not worrying now about the agouti or the two men. He was a cat with only one idea – to get rid of that gum. Cats of all kinds like to be clean.

Roger and some of the Indians arrived in time to see the strange spectacle. The tiger saw them out of smeared eyes and gave them a few growls; then went back to licking and biting at his fur. He sat up on his haunches and began washing his face with his paws, exactly like a house cat.

"I think we can take him now," Aqua said.

He had the Indians bring up the cage. He passed the net rope through the front door and out between the slats. Then he drew gently on the rope, making tension on the four lines that went to the four corners of the net. The other men laid hold to help him.

"Slowly, slowly," he said.

The far edge of the net draped itself lightly over the tiger. The beast was drawn inch by inch into the cage. His own struggles helped. Every time he moved any part of his body in the right direction the net was tightened so that he could not move back. At last both the net and its sticky contents were inside the cage. The door was locked. The prisoner took his mind off his work long enough to make a few thrusts at the bars, then went back to his task.

"He'll be doing that for a week," Aqua said. "He won't stop until he gets every bit of it off his fur."

The tiger paid no heed to anything but bird-lime as the cage, set on two long poles, was carried down to the river. The Ark was brought up and the cage was hoisted on the deck and set in the toldo. The agouti, which one of the Indians had cut loose from the net, was served for dinner.

Hal beamed with delight and went around congratulating everybody, even Banco. He owed a special debt of gratitude to Aqua. This exploit had crowned the expedition with success.

Well, almost. He still wanted an anaconda. And he still had to escape Croc, get the collection down river, and on board a steamer for home.

But he was so happy that nothing seemed very difficult now.

23
Giant Anaconda

You can't strike a match on an anaconda. It was Hal who made this remarkable scientific discovery.

He had voyaged two hundred miles further down the Amazon. His collection had been increased by one upside-down sloth, one well-plated armadillo, and one small, graceful Amazon deer.

They were moored in a little bay where they had spent the night. It was not a clean-cut bay with sand beaches, but marshy, the sort of place, Aqua said, where anacondas might abound.

In the morning Hal went aboard the Ark to see how the animals were faring.

He found the wood ibis gone. Only a few feathers remained. Its cage had been smashed. The bird could not have done that. Only something heavy and powerful could have accomplished it.

He looked about at his other animals to see if any of them had a guilty look in its eye. The giant iguana had its eyes closed and lay basking in the morning sun. It was quite capable of such a deed, but its leash was too short.

The basilisk was a strict vegetarian. It was out at the end of its line for a morning run on the water. The great stork had only one eye open and it didn't look guilty. The jabiru stork enjoys mice, frogs and fish, but is not enough of a cannibal to consume other birds and would certainly draw the line at eating its own cousin, the wood ibis.

The way the cage was smashed suggested that the boa constrictor had done it, but this was impossible since the boa was in the other boat, sound asleep, still digesting her pig.

Hal gave it up. The vampire bat was chirping her call for breakfast.

Hal set about preparing Vamp's meal. He got out a bottle of defibrinated blood – that is, blood from which the fibrin had been removed by whipping. The fibrin is what makes blood clot. Vamp would not accept clotted blood. But it was too much of a job to obtain a fresh animal for her daily. The blood of a single capybara would feed her for three days – if it could be kept fresh. The blood in the bottle was three days old, but still liquid thin.

But it was cold. Hal poured a cupful of it into a pan which he placed in the fireplace in the corner of the toldo. He arranged some shavings and sticks under the pan. Now to start a fire.

He had the habit of striking his matches on a post of the toldo. But this time the first match failed to light. He tried it again and again, then threw it away. He tried more matches, but they did no better.

In the half-dark of the toldo he thought the post looked peculiar, but his eyes were still blinded by the outside sunlight and he could not see very well. He tried another post. His match lit at once.

When the fire was blazing he looked up at the post that had failed him. Then he backed off from it, his nerves doing a dance. A huge snake was coiled around the post. He had been trying to light matches on its scales.

He thought at first that it was his boa, escaped from the montaria — but then he saw that it had none of the boa's colour and grace, and it was three times as big.

He realized with a jolt that he was looking at the anaconda, the world's largest snake. The royal python of India was sometimes longer, but more slender and lighter in weight.

He could not estimate the length of this serpent because of the way it was coiled around the post, but he could see that it was more than a foot thick. At one place there was a special bulge — perhaps that was Hal's wood ibis!

The body was an evil-looking dark green and the head

was black. The eyes were fixed upon Hal, who could not move, he was so fascinated. He thought of the stories told by Indians of how the anaconda is supposed to be able to hypnotize man or beast with those terrible eyes. Hal did not believe such tales. But he felt numb and it was only with an effort that he walked out of the toldo. He glanced back uneasily but the snake had not moved.

Hal tried to shout to his friends on shore. His voice would not come. It was not until he got ashore that he could command himself.

"An anaconda!" he said breathlessly. "There's an anaconda in the toldo."

The men were greatly excited by the news. "Let's catch it," Roger said.

"All right, but how? You don't just go up and throw your arms around an anaconda."

Hal sat down on a log and tried to think. If they noosed the snake in the toldo it would thrash about, tear the toldo to bits, kill the other animals, and quite possibly sink the Ark.

Aqua had helped him before. Hal turned to Aqua now. But the Indian had no suggestion.

"We never take it," he said. "The Indians all fear it."

"But you make a pet of the boa constrictor."

518

Aqua smiled. "The boa is our friend; the anaconda is our worst enemy. The 'deer swallower' is full of devils."

Hal noticed that Aqua had used one of the Indian names for the anaconda – the deer swallower. It gave him an idea.

"Perhaps we can use the deer to attract the snake to the shore. Once we get it ashore we might be able to make it fast with lines."

The idea was passed on to the men. Not one of them was willing, not even Aqua, to go aboard the vessel of which the anaconda was now master and try to use the deer as snake bait. Each man was afraid that he might prove to be more attractive bait than the deer.

The plan bounced back upon Hal.

"All right, I'll go," he said, and gingerly walked out the gang-plank which had been laid from the Ark to the bank – for there was no danger now of the baby boas swimming ashore since they had become too large to roam freely and had been confined in a cage.

Before leading forth the little deer to its fate he would make sure that his prize was still there. He glanced inside the toldo. The fire was sputtering weakly and a few rays of sunshine came in through the holes in the thatch roof.

But the post was no longer draped with serpent. The

anaconda was gone. It would be hard to say whether Hal was disappointed or relieved. There was a large hole low down in the reed wall. The snake must have gone that way, then slid over the gunwale into the water.

As Hal stood, wondering what to do next, something like an earthquake seemed to shake the heavy boat. Hal staggered out of the toldo expecting to see that some large waves were running in from the Amazon. There were no waves. He looked ashore and could see no sign of earthquake. Anyhow, this was not a land of earthquakes.

While he stood there puzzling over the mystery, suddenly the two tons of boat beneath him heaved up bodily and rolled against the bank. Hal lost his footing and went sprawling on the slanting deck. He crawled ashore into a circle of excited men. The boat was on an even keel once more but the water boiled around it.

"It is the anaconda!" Aqua exclaimed. "There must be a nest of them here."

Banco was ordering up the men. "We will leave here at once. The anacondas are very bad snakes. They are evil spirits." He played on the superstitions of the Indians. All sorts of devils were supposed to make their home within this malevolent serpent.

Hal stopped Banco with "We will not leave here without

trying to get an anaconda. But first we'd better get a cage ready for him. It really ought to be a bath-tub." And he told Roger the story of a New York artist who borrowed a fifteen-foot anaconda for the purpose of painting a picture of it. Seeking advice from the great snake man, Raymond L. Ditmars of the New York Zoo, he constructed in his Greenwich Village apartment a pen about twelve feet long containing a wooden bathtub five feet long, thirty inches high, and a yard wide. This worked very well – until a leak from the tub soaked through to the apartment below and the tenants there complained to the landlord. That worthy objected to having a serpent as a tenant and both the snake and the artist had to move.

So a bathtub was constructed for the hoped-for prize. But a bathtub could not be made out of sticks, and there were no boards to be had.

Aqua solved the problem.

"We will make a woodskin," he said.

"Good," said Hal. "Take over the men and do it."

Hal had seen many woodskins on the river. A "woodskin" is a boat made out of the skin of a tree, that is, the bark. A boat would do nicely as a bathtub. And a woodskin could be made far more quickly than a dugout.

The men located a large purpleheart tree. They cut a

line through the bark around the base and, erecting a scaffolding of poles, cut another line twenty feet up. Then they made a vertical cut, and began to pry the bark off with wedges. When it was free, they had a sheet of bark twenty feet long and about ten feet wide.

The ends were laced shut with lianas and "cocked up" with tough vines and "bush ropes", and the crack was made watertight with latex from the rubber tree.

Now it would keep water out like any good boat; or keep water in like any good bathtub.

It was necessary to construct a bathroom – that is, a cage to contain the bathtub and its occupant.

The men worked rapidly but it was the next day before the curious tub-in-a-cage was finished and set in the last available space on the deck of the Ark and Hal could begin to think of getting a tenant for it. Hal was determined that this time no anaconda should find him unprepared. He planned his campaign carefully. He strung a line from the mast of the Ark to a tree some forty feet within the beach. He tethered the deer to this line near the water's edge.

Then he prepared three nooses, one for the anaconda's head and the other two for its tail. The cage was placed in readiness.

Now all that was needed was the anaconda.

The men hid in the bushes and watched. It was the old game of waiting once more. The day wore on. The deer nibbled at the grasses that fringed the beach. It was a beautiful animal, small compared with its Canadian cousin, with a glossy tan coat, large brown eyes and fine antlers. Hal hoped he would not have to sacrifice it.

After three hours of watchful waiting, Hal's desire for action got the better of him. Were there really any anacondas in the bay? Was there actually an anaconda nest as Aqua had supposed? And what did an anaconda nest look like? That was something that he as a scientific observer ought to know.

He slipped out of the bushes, across the beach, and into the water. The bottom dropped off steeply. With a few powerful strokes he was under the surface, looking for trouble. It was hard to see because of the cloudiness of the water. He first made sure that there were none of the man-eating piranhas about. Then he looked for anything that might be described as an anaconda nest.

It was something like going through the jungle, because long reeds grew up from the bottom. They were slimy and disagreeable to the touch. Sunken logs lay about in crisscross fashion and under them there might be a refuge for small animals but certainly not for a family of the largest snakes in the world.

He came to the top to breathe and went down again. Now he studied the steep bank that fell off from the beach. Suddenly he found himself at the mouth of a submarine cave running back into the bank.

If he wanted any proof that this was the nest he got it at once. Two small snakes not more than five feet long came out of the cave and swam off through the reeds. Then the large terrible-looking head of an adult anaconda protruded from the cave. It moved towards Hal.

Hal lost his appetite for investigation and rose to the surface. He could already imagine those great jaws closing on one of his legs. Then he would be drawn down inside that black cave and devoured at leisure. He went through agonies of fear during the instant that it took him to scramble up on the beach.

"What did you see?" whispered Roger.

"Anacondas at home," said Hall. "You're sitting right on top of their house. There's a big cave running back beneath you."

"But how could they live in a cave under water? Don't they have to breathe air?"

"Perhaps the roof of the cave is above the water line," guessed Hal.

Another long wait. Roger dropped off to sleep.

Hal grew tired of watching the ripples that lapped near the feet of the deer, so at first he did not notice something that had broken the surface of the bay. Then he saw it, and it was moving. It was something like the periscope of a submarine. He realized that it was the nose of an anaconda. This snake has adapted itself to life in the water by developing a nose, not in the usual place, but high up on its head so that it may breathe while keeping the head submerged.

Now and then a ripple gave a glimpse of the eyes. They were placed well out so that they could look not only up and forward, but down, a feat of which land snakes were not capable. They were placed so far apart that it was plain the head that carried them must be very large.

And the great head was coming straight towards the deer. Behind the head the water was disturbed far back, showing that under the surface there must be a huge propeller at work – a propeller perhaps twenty or thirty feet long, who could say? The longer the better, thought Hal.

Hastily he slipped through the bushes to the tree and

laid hold of the line. He was glad to see that an Indian who had been posted on the Ark at the other end of the line was awake.

The moving head arrived at the beach. It slid out of the water with the chin resting on the sand. The deer saw it and would have taken to its heels if the line had not held it. The terrified animal struggled violently, its hooves tearing up the sand and flinging pebbles into the snake's jaws.

Hal began to pull on the line and the Indian at the other end paid out accordingly. The deer was drawn slowly towards the tree. The snake followed. Every time the anaconda seemed about to strike, Hal drew the deer out of its reach. Hal himself was concealed behind the tree. The other men were hidden in the bushes.

When the deer reached the tree the anaconda was six feet behind and coming fast.

"All right, boys, go to it!" shouted Hal.

He leaped out with the head noose. The men closed in on both sides with the tail ropes.

When the snake saw Hal it did not retreat but raised its head menacingly. The slightest mistake now would be serious. The snake was about to strike. Before it could do so it must be noosed by the head and the tail.

Hal shot forward straight for the villainous head and the jaws that were already parting to make a meal of him. He slapped the noose over the bulging head and drew it tight on the slender neck.

The other end of the noose rope ran into and through the cage in the usual fashion. The end of it had been made fast to a tree. With the tail held firm, so that it would not lash about, it should be possible to draw the snake inch by inch into the cage.

But it was not to be so easy. The men with the tail ropes became excited and confused. They managed to get only one of the nooses in place. As the snake plunged forward towards Hal, whipping its tail, this rope was jerked out of the Indian's hands.

Banco and two Indians were knocked flat by the thrashing tail. Aqua boldly leaped in with the other noose. The tail suddenly whirled forward and encircled him. He fought wildly to free himself. The loop of serpent holding him moved up the snake's body so that the tail was again free. It continued to flail about.

Roger, trying to catch the flying tail rope, was given a swinging swipe on the side of the head that knocked him unconscious.

Not held by the tail as it should have been, the snake

was advancing upon Hal. Backing up, he tripped and fell. In the second or two that he lay there he lived a lifetime. All the tales he had heard of anacondas devouring cattle, of a horse found in an anaconda's stomach, of men who had lost their lives to this fearless serpent, flashed through his mind. His time had come.

But while his brain was taking the long way around, his body was working like chain lightning. He jerked himself out of the way of the striking head and leaped to his feet.

He saw with horror that Aqua was already lifeless, blood spouting from his mouth and ears, his body tossing limply about. Hal's hand went for his revolver but it had been thrown out of its holster when he fell.

The snake was turning its jaws towards Aqua. Hal leaped for the snake's head and buried his thumbs in its eyes. He held on grimly as the anaconda's body writhed and whipped. The coil relaxed and Aqua was thrown out into the brush.

Hal went to the body of his friend and felt the heart. It was still.

He returned to the battle with the greatest of snakes. He was determined that Aqua should not have died in vain.

The head rope, passing through the cage and tied to a tree, was holding firm although it allowed far too much play. The tail rope had been caught now and lashed to another tree.

In vain the snake tried to capture more of its tormentors with its teeth or its tail. Hal got two Indians to help him haul in on the head rope. Every time the thrashing snake came nearer to the cage, it was held there until the next gyration brought it still nearer. Finally its head was in the door of the crate.

Its body was now almost straight, held taut by the tail rope. Hal ordered that this rope be slackened gradually as the head was drawn into the cage. The men worked with more confidence and courage as they saw that their enemy was being beaten. One of them even ventured to tie a rope to the snake's middle, and was knocked down twice in the process. By this rope the heavy body of the snake was drawn forward.

Finally the snake was in up to the full length of the cage. But there were still ten feet of snake outside!

The tail rope was now passed in through the cage and by means of it the tail was drawn in. The door was closed. The capture was complete.

Hal took no pleasure in it. It had cost too much. He took off his torn shirt, soaked it in the bay, and wiped the blood from Aqua's face. He had grown to be very fond of the able, intelligent and good-hearted young Indian. He felt that he and Roger had lost their most loyal friend.

Somehow the future seemed dark and dangerous, now that Aqua was gone.

The men carried the cage and its captive on board and half-filled the tub with water.

At dusk they buried Aqua under the tree where he had given his life.

24
Nine Headless Men

On down the river. It was no fun now. Hal could think only of reaching Manaos, getting his collection on board a steamer, and sailing home.

The jungle had become a place of death and terror. He had a sinking feeling that there was more trouble ahead.

To make matters worse, Roger had come down with fever. He had been too careless about taking his daily dose of malaria-preventing atebrin and keeping his mosquito net closely drawn around his hammock at night.

He lay in the toldo of the montaria with the boa constrictor and a few other animals to keep him company.

Hal had begun to hope that they were rid of Croc; but one day he heard war drums beating and, as his fleet rounded a point, he saw an Indian village on fire. That looked like Croc's work. He felt sure of it when he saw Croc's boat drawn up on the beach.

Hal did not feel able to interfere. With Roger sick and Aqua gone he could not fight Croc's gang. He hoped only that he could get by without being seen.

Some five miles farther downstream he pulled in for the night to a sheltered landing place behind a point.

As the men made camp, they stopped every few moments to listen. The drums of the burned village could still be heard. The rhythm was taken up by other drums behind the camp and downstream, and then in unseen villages on the other side of the river. The whole forest seemed to throb with the threat of the drums.

Hal's men were very nervous. They huddled together and whispered. Banco seemed to be stirring them up. Hal walked over to the group.

"What's the matter, Banco?"

"The drums, *senhor*. The men are afraid of the drums."

"Why are they afraid? Indians would not hurt Indians."

"They are not of the same tribe. The Indians in this forest are very savage. They hate the white man. Perhaps white men have attacked them today. They seek revenge. If they find you they will kill you, and all who serve you."

Hal laughed. "I don't think it's as bad as you make out, Banco." Many times on the trip he had noticed that Banco's liver was pretty white.

The men had gone out on the cape and were jabbering excitedly and pointing upstream. Hal joined them.

Against a red sunset the smoke of the destroyed village rose into the sky. But it was not this that attracted the attention of the men. A boat was coming downstream. Hal could count nine men in it, but not one of them was paddling.

In fact, they did not move at all. They might as well have been sacks of meal. No sound of conversation came across the water.

A chill began to creep through Hal's veins. He noticed that a strange terror had gripped his own men.

Again he studied the men in the boat. They were much closer now. Still they did not move. Hal strained his eyes in the failing light. He could see no heads on the men. Of course he would see them in a moment. Every man had to have a head.

The current carried the boat within fifty feet of the point. Banco screamed like a woman. Hal had to believe it now. Nine headless men sat in the boat. Their size and their bloodstained shirts made it plain that they were not Indians.

They must be Croc's cut-throats, their own throats now cut by the vengeful Indians whose goods they had tried to steal and whose village they had fired. Then the Indians had arranged this gruesome exhibit and sent it downstream as a warning to all and sundry.

Along with his horror, Hal felt a vague sense of relief. This must mean that he no longer needed to fear Croc. As for the Indians, he had never yet found any reason to fear them if they were treated fairly.

He went back to the camp site and strung up his hammock and Roger's. There was no camp fire that night.

The men usually slept on shore but tonight they preferred to lie in the montaria. To make more room for themselves they transferred what few animals it contained to the Ark.

Roger was always dead to the world when asleep and Hal, thoroughly tired, slept soundly in spite of the drums. Once, half awake, he thought there was a slight commotion on the montaria — then he slept again.

25
Deserted

Hal was awakened by the sun in his face. He stretched lazily, put his arm over his eyes, and rested.

He always enjoyed these few moments in the morning – lying at ease, listening to other men work. The Indians would be gathering fuel for the fire. It would be a little difficult, for there had been rain during the night. The water still dripped from the strip of canvas stretched above Hal's hammock.

There would be the chatter of Indian voices, the clatter

of pans, the smell of woodsmoke, and then the smell of coffee.

But all this ought to be already going on. The men usually turned out just before sunrise. He could hear nothing – nothing but the ordinary forest sounds and the continued angry mutter of Indian drums.

He uncovered his eyes and looked out into the camp site where a breakfast of turtle's eggs, baked curassow, and coffee ought to be on the fire.

There was no one in the camp site.

This would not do. The men were getting lazy. He would soon fix that. Hal climbed from his hammock and pushed out into the clearing. He started for the montaria which had been moored close to the beach.

Then he stopped, puzzled. The montaria was gone.

The fear of the future that had come to him when Aqua was killed flooded back upon him. But perhaps the men had just gone fishing.

He knew he was fooling himself. They would not all have gone – some would have stayed to attend to the morning fire.

He went out on the point. He could see far downstream and up. There was no boat.

There was no use kidding himself. His crew, fearing the

wrath of the local tribes, had set out for home. He could thank Banco for this. Only Banco could have persuaded them to abandon two boys in the jungle.

They had taken his boat. He had to admit that this was fair enough, for he owed them money. But probably they had also stolen everything else they could lay their hands on.

He went back to the bay and boarded the Ark. At least they had not made off with that. The animals had not been touched and they joined in demanding breakfast. Hal examined the supplies, nets, fishing gear, canned foods, valuable papers, medicines, guns, and ammunition. Not a thing had been touched.

That was to the credit of his crew. But it did not change the fact that he and Roger were now alone against the jungle – and Roger lay helpless in his hammock. The Indians were on the warpath. Hal thought of the gruesome sight of the evening before. It was not hard to imagine that soon two more headless bodies might be floating down the Amazon.

He heard a faint call from Roger. He took the boy a drink of water and his morning dose of quinine. Roger's forehead was very hot. Hal told him what had happened.

Roger was too sick to care. His mind wandered a little

and he did not quite grasp what Hal told him.

"Why can't you let me sleep?" he said peevishly.

Hal let him sleep while he went to get something together for breakfast. He found himself making all his movements to the rhythm of the drums. Would those drums never stop?

He gave Roger a spoon–fed meal of eggs and coffee. Then he took his rifle and went out to find food for some of his animals – especially the anaconda, which was too restless for the good of its cage. It had whipped all the water out of its tank. There was no use putting in more until the snake was satisfied. Then it might lie still.

Hal followed the shore downstream, hoping to find an animal coming to the river to drink.

Suddenly he saw, to his great astonishment, what he took to be an Indian standing waist deep in the water and, beside him, an Indian woman with a child in her arms. Another look, and he realized that these were not Indians. As he came closer he could make out their tiny slits of eyes, blunt noses, and thick lips.

Sailors in tropical seas had often been fooled just as Hal had been. Many a sea-going man had sworn that he had seen a creature with the body of a woman and the tail of a fish sitting on a rock combing her hair or suckling her child. Possibly it was in this way that the legend of the mermaid had begun.

But at close range Hal saw that this madonna of the Amazon had none of the beauty we like to think of as belonging to the mermaid. Her face and that of her gentleman friend were as homely as the face of a cow. And Hal knew that he was looking at the sea cow, the manatee, or, as the Brazilians call it, the fish ox.

There they sat on their tails among the weeds, the female feeding her baby, the male nibbling at water lilies, their erect bodies swaying slightly in the swell that came in from the Amazon.

What mammoths they were! If the parts concealed by the water were in proportion to the parts he could see, each of the animals must be at least ten feet long and weigh a ton. He could not undertake to deliver one of these to the anaconda.

Then a splashing of flippers drew his attention to another member of the family. It was a youngster perhaps five feet long and probably weighing not more than fifteen stone — just a fair snack for the big reptile. It was floundering about in a few inches of water, feeding on the grasses that grew along the bank.

Hal fired. At the sound, the two large heads immediately

sank out of sight. But the young manatee began to beat clumsily with flippers and tail in the shallow water. Hal came closer and fired again. He was thankful that he had a .300 in his hands, for he knew that the hide of a manatee is so tough that the Indians make shields of it.

The sea cow slowly bumbled itself around, but before it could get started towards deep water Hal had it by the tail. He did not attempt to carry it overland. Letting the water support its weight, he pulled it through the shallows until he got it alongside the Ark. Then he heaved the head up until it rested upon the gunwale and teetered it there, inching the body higher until it flopped over into the boat.

The hide was slippery enough so that he could drag the big animal to the door of the snake's cage. Now came the ticklish part of the performance.

How was he going to get the heavy "fish ox" into the cage without letting the anaconda out?

The snake was very active this morning. It kept striking its big head against the door of the cage. It lay with its thirty feet of length doubled so that the end of the tail was also near the door. Both the head and the tail were dangerous.

Hal had no fear of snakes, ordinarily. He had handled many kinds, from water moccasins to big Rocky Mountain rattlers. But he could never look at this giant of the snake world without a quivering of his nerves.

It was not just that the serpent was so huge. It was mean. No one had ever been able to make friends with an anaconda. In this respect it was quite different from the sweet-tempered boa constrictor, which might be made a household pet and become as affectionate as a dog or cat. The anaconda was the gangster of snakedom. He was on bad terms with everything and everybody.

And Hal knew that the moment he opened that door, jaws like a steel trap would close on his leg and that anxious tail would whip around his body.

The baby tapir came up to nuzzle its long nose against him. The big snake glared at it hungrily, then drew back its head and shot it forward with terrific strength against the door of the cage.

Hal picked up the tapir and carried it down the side of the cage to the other end. The anaconda's head followed. Hal tethered the little animal within a few feet of the bars. The evil eyes that seemed so hypnotic were fixed upon it. But the tapir, thanks to being very near-sighted, was not disturbed.

Hal went back to the cage door. He still did not dare to take the time to ease the manatee through the door, for the snake might wheel about before he was half done. He studied the manatee. Its flat, paddlelike tail gave him an idea.

He tied a stout rope around the door and the door jamb so that the door would open only two inches. Then he pushed the flat tail of the manatee through this crack.

He went and got the tapir and brought it back near the door. The snake followed and discovered the appetizing tail of the sea cow. The serpent's jaws immediately locked themselves upon it and began to draw it in.

Once a snake has begun a meal it thinks of nothing but to finish it. Hal eased the rope so that the door opened wider and wider to admit more and more of the great walrus-like mammal as the snake sucked it down. When the whole manatee was within the cage, and half of it within the reptile as well, Hal could close and lock the door.

"There," he said with satisfaction. "Digesting that will keep you out of mischief for a few weeks at least."

He was sorry in a way to see so strange a mammal that would have attracted so much attention in a zoo disappear down a snake's throat. But he knew that no aquarium outside of the tropics has been able to keep a manatee alive for more than a few months. Probably it would not even have lived until he could get it home.

He went foraging again for his other animals. Just keeping this menagerie fed was a full-time job. He missed Roger's able help. And a burden seemed to settle upon him as he thought of undertaking singlehanded to sail his floating zoo down river.

There was just one silver lining – he no longer had to worry about Croc and his gang. Or did he? Were they all dead? He had never known exactly how many men there were in Croc's party. On the night of the attack he had estimated the number at eight or ten. There had been nine headless men in the boat – surely that was the entire band. And yet he was haunted by the uneasy feeling that Croc might still be alive. It was a daytime nightmare that kept nagging him. He tried to laugh it off, but it was not easy to laugh, alone and deserted, in a dark and sinister jungle. Men had been known to go mad in the terrible loneliness of this black forest.

And so he was quite willing to believe that he was touched in the head when he saw Croc stumbling towards him through the gloom. There was no mistaking him – the only other face like that was a vampire bat's. And even that was an insult to the vampire. The man's shirt and trousers were bloody and torn. His hair was unkempt, his face scratched by underbrush and haggard with sleeplessness and terror.

544

He stopped and stared at Hal. Then he came on with a rush. Hal raised his gun. He lowered it again when he saw that Croc was not armed. Croc collapsed at his feet.

"Buddy, am I glad to see you!" he whined. "Don't let them, buddy. Don't let them get me." He threw his arms around Hal's leg and sobbed, "They'll kill me, buddy. That's what they'll do. They'll kill me."

"And a good job too," said Hal, kicking the man off. "Don't you think it's a little strange to come to me for help?"

"Listen, buddy, listen," wailed Croc. "We're white men, ain't we? We white men have got to stick together. You won't let those dagoes get me?"

"Did you fire that village?"

"Oh that – that was a mistake."

"Did you kill any Indians?"

"Not many. What's a few Indians?" He slowly got up and looked behind him, still trembling. "They're after me. Where's your camp, buddy?"

Hal looked him over for a long minute. How he would enjoy filling this skunk with lead! He ought to give the cringing cur a kick and send him out into the jungle to die or be captured by Indians.

He turned and led the way to the camp. Croc, as big

and shambling as a giant anteater, shuffled along beside him. "God'll bless you for this, buddy," he croaked. "I knew you couldn't leave a white man in this beastly jungle. You and me is going to be friends, eh buddy? Best of friends. Everything forgotten and forgiven, ain't that right? That's the spirit."

He pulled up short as they came out into the camp site. "Where's your men?"

"Gone up river."

"Cripes! That's the way with them Indians. Never can trust them. Did you lose your animals too?"

"No. They're in the batalao, just around the bend."

"Fine!" Croc said with enthusiasm. "Buddy, you're in luck. Just when you lose your men I come along. You can depend upon me. I'll help you get that boat down river. Least I can do. Got anything to eat, buddy? I ain't eaten for twenty-four hours."

Hal fed the man.

"Where's your brother?" asked Croc. "Out gunning for game?"

"No. Back there in his hammock. Fever."

"Ain't that just too bad. You really *are* alone, aren't you?"

Hal glanced at him sharply. "I'm alone, but that doesn't mean that you can try any tricks. You're alone too. We saw your friends go by last night. How did you escape? I'll bet you were hiding in the bushes while they were fighting."

"What's the use of having men if you don't make 'em fight for you? Now, let's not get to arguing. Let's be done with feudin'. Sort of thing I been through sobers a man up. I made up my mind back there in the jungle that if the good Lord would just bring me out safe I'd never touch a hair of any man's head again. I'd be as gentle as a lamb. That's the way I says it to myself — gentle as a lamb. I wouldn't hurt nobody, no matter what I was paid to do it. I tell you, when you get to where any minute may be your last, you change your mind about a lot of things. And when I saw you — I couldn't 'a' been gladder to see my own brother." He helped himself to another large piece of dried meat. "Yes, sir, that's what we'll be, brothers."

"Like Abel and Cain," said Hal, but Croc did not catch his meaning.

"Just like brothers," he repeated. He looked out across the Amazon. Hal followed his gaze. The water was higher than the day before and the current past the point was more swift. An uprooted tree drifted by. Floating islands, always to be seen in the Amazon, were more frequent now. They were signs of the coming of the great annual flood.

"Must be heavy rains up river," Croc said. "A week from now right here where we're sitting will be under water. Chunks of dirt big enough to build a house on will be floating down. And them drifting trees can stave in a boat without trying. But don't you worry – we'll put your craft safe into Manaos before things get too bad. Lucky I came along. Leave it to me, buddy." He stood up, grinned his ugly grin and thumped himself bravely on the chest.

An arrow whizzed past him and struck a tree. Croc was in the bushes in a trice. Hal could hear him running heavily through the underbrush.

Roger called weakly from his hammock, "What's up?"

"Lie low," Hal warned. "Indians."

He advanced in the direction from which the arrow had come. "We are friends!" he shouted in the *lingua geral*, the general language of the Indians.

The answer he got was another arrow, barely missing his shoulder.

He thought of the nine headless men and of Roger lying helpless in his hammock. The best way to defend Roger would be to carry the fight away from him, up into the woods. He ran forward. His gun was ready. If they would not accept friendship they would have to take bullets.

As he broke into the jungle another arrow sang by. He thought it strange that the arrows always came singly.

Then he saw the reason — there was just one Indian. Upon seeing that he was pursued by a man with a gun, he turned and fled. Hal followed him for about half a mile. The Indian was too fleet for him and finally disappeared in the direction of the burned village.

He was doubtless a scout. He would come back with all the warriors of the village. Hal ran back to camp. There was no time to be lost. He and Roger and their unwelcome guest must board the Ark at once and be off.

He stripped down the hammocks and carried them and Roger's heavy, half-conscious form through the underbrush to the shore of the bay. He had not had time to think of Croc. Now he felt a cold dread of what he might discover when he came out on the beach.

He burst from the thick screen of leaves into the sunshine, and halted. It was true then. A man really could be capable of sailing off and leaving two boys at the mercy of the jungle, and of hostile Indians. The Ark did not lie moored near the beach.

Far out in the river the Ark sped downstream under full sail aided by a powerful current. Croc had nothing to do but steer. He stood on the steering platform at the stern with his hand on the tiller. He waved his other hand and his harsh voice came distantly across the water.

"So long, buddy. See you in hell!"

26
The Floating Island

Hal raised his gun. He lowered it again – the range was too great. Besides he remembered that he had only one cartridge left. That one had Croc's name on it. Somehow he would catch up with that devil and bore a hole clear through his evil carcass.

As he calmed down he realized that his chances of ever seeing Croc again were slim.

He laid Roger on the sand and began to take stock of the situation. He had no boat. He had no tools to make one. He had his hunting knife and, given a week, he might whittle out a raft. He was given not a week, but only minutes, an hour or so at the most. The scout might not have had to go all the way back to his village to contact his band. The Indians had been hunting Croc and might be very near by.

He and Roger might hide in the jungle. But they had none of the things they would need. He had stowed everything on the Ark in preparation for sailing. Even the pans he had used to get breakfast were on board.

He took an inventory. Between them they had two

shirts, two pairs of trousers, two pairs of alpargata sandals, two hammocks, one knife, one gun with one bullet — and that one bullet reserved.

Nor was the jungle a good hiding place. From white men perhaps. But not from Indians. The enraged Indians scouring the forest in search of Croc would find them sooner or later.

And the greatest objection to hiding out in the woods was that it would not bring him any closer to Croc. As he watched the black speck of the Ark disappearing down river it seemed futile to hope to bring Croc to a reckoning, or to recover his collection.

That was the worst of it — losing the animals. That meant failure for his father's business and victory for Shark Sands and his henchmen. It meant, too, that Hal would not get the chance to go to the South Seas — the reward that had been offered by his father for success in the Amazon enterprise. But he was not ready to give up yet.

His roving eye lit upon a floating island passing the mouth of the bay. A wild thought came to him. He did not to stop to analyse it — there was no time to weigh chances. He lifted Roger and made his way out to the end of the point.

The river was browner, more turbid, and more rapid

than usual. The main current boiled past close to the point. Something colossal must be going on in the headwaters on the flanks of the Andes. The swollen river was dotted with moving islands. They were of different kinds, although all due to the same cause − flood.

One that passed very close was a kind that he did not care to trust − a bed of water hyacinths torn loose from some marsh. Only the leaves and flowers showed above the surface. Below, the bulbs must be tangled together in a tightly-knit mass. But the whole mat was not more than a foot thick and might not support two husky boys. Even if it did, one of those great floating trees with branches milling around like paddle wheels, and roots projecting like the tentacles of an octopus, might roll over the islet, destroying it and everyone who happened to be on it. Many boats, even large steamers, had been stove in by those crazily thrashing trees.

Then there were islands made up of brush. In some rapids a bush had caught on a rock. Other bushes, sticks and logs had joined it, and the whole had been matted firmly in one solid mass and had finally broken loose to sail downstream as an island − an island without soil.

But more amazing were the islands that had soil, plants, even trees − everything an island should have except the ability to stay in one place. A strong current had undercut a piece of land and carried it off entire. Some of these islands were two hundred feet across. He had heard that they were at times twenty feet thick.

But Hal could not wait for the ideal island – he must take the first reasonable chance that came along. He explained his purpose to Roger who only half-understood what it was all about. Something that looked like a large pasture came floating down and when it grazed the point Hal stepped aboard with his burden. He was thankful that he did not immediately sink through into the river.

In a moment the point was left behind and the two boys were embarked upon as strange a voyage as anyone had ever made.

Perhaps it had been a crazy idea. But anything was better, Hal told himself, than sitting on shore waiting to be beheaded. Now they were leaving behind those eternally thumping, nerve-wearing drums. And he was on the trail of Croc.

True, Croc could go faster with a sail than he could on a floating island. But suppose the wind dropped, or veered to blow upstream. Suppose Croc got caught on a sandbar or on a sunken log. Lots of things might happen to delay him. Hal considered that he had a fighting chance.

He surveyed his floating kingdom. He laid Roger down in the grass and walked about, frequently testing the ground to be sure that it was strong enough to hold him. His island was a good half acre in size. Much of it was in grass but there were also many small trees, especially cecropias, rubber trees and bamboos. The fast-growing bamboo was tall but all the other trees were not more than a few feet high.

Hal's active mind went to work on this curious fact and he came out with what he believed to be the answer. His island was quite evidently only a year old. The flood of a year ago had deposited a half acre of silt somewhere and, when the water subsided, there was a new island. Seeds sprouted and trees attained a year's growth. And now comes this year's flood to undercut the island, lift it from its firm base, and carry it off bodily down river.

The only trouble with his theory was the fact that on the downstream side of the island lay an enormous tree that must have taken a hundred years to grow. He walked over to examine it. It was a great silk-cotton, or kapok tree. Its trunk lay in the water and its huge branches rose some fifty feet into the air. At the base of the trunk was a tangle of big roots.

No, his theory still held water. This tree was not a part

of the island. The two had merely become jammed together while floating down river.

But he could use the fallen giant to good advantage. He strung up the hammocks between the branches, then brought Roger and laid him in his hammock where he would not be in danger from snakes or army ants or any other wild life there might be on this little floating world.

Which reminded him that he must feed his patient and himself. That was a sobering thought. Many an adventurer in the Amazon forests had died of hunger even though he had the entire jungle to draw upon. Hal had only the resources of a half acre. Robinson Crusoe had had much more to work with.

Hal spent the rest of the day having bright ideas that didn't work out. He looked among the bamboos for shoots, but there were none small enough to be edible. He tried the berries on a bush, only to make himself sick. He saw a little tree which he believed to be the famous cow tree which, when slashed, gives forth a very good substitute for cow's milk. He slashed this one but it was too small – only a few white drops exuded.

This was proving more of a job than he had expected. Once he had read the Fighting Forces Handbook, *Survival*, and had derived from it the idea that survival whether in the jungle, in the Arctic, in the desert or at sea, was really a simple matter. It did not appear so simple now.

But there must be plenty of fish in the river. He had no line — but he would catch them as the Indians did. He spent two hours fashioning a wooden spear with a barbed point. Then he went to the edge and looked down into the swirling current.

He soon realized that he had wasted his time. The current was so full of silt that he could not see one inch into its depths.

A heavy squall came up and Hal was promptly drenched to the skin. He didn't mind that. But after the rain came a strong wind, with nothing to stop its sweep across the great river, here eight or nine miles wide. Hal began to shake in his wet clothes and long for the shelter of the forest. It was hard to believe that he was within four degrees of the equator.

He continued his vain quest for food until dark. As night closed in, he made his brother as comfortable as possible. Fortunately Roger had been protected from the rain by the canvas over his hammock.

Hal would have liked the cheer and warmth of a camp fire. But there were two good reasons for not making a fire: (1) the Indians might see it; (2) the matches were on the Ark.

So Hal, quite forlorn and miserable, and humiliated by his failure to find food, crawled into his hammock. He was discovering how grim the Amazon can be to those who meet it unprepared.

There was something a little terrifying about barging through the darkness at the mercy of a strong current. What if his hurrying half acre should crash into a point, or a fixed island? He tried to tell himself that it was not very likely. His craft was carried by the current, and the current goes around things, not into them. A lone Indian who wanted to travel night and day, but must get some sleep, would tie his canoe to a floating island and wake up in the morning to find himself some thirty miles further downstream.

It suddenly struck Hal that night travel gave him one great advantage over Croc. Croc would doubtless stop and camp every night. Knowing so little of the river, he would hardly sail it in the dark.

Hal listened to the jungle roar. Sometimes it was far away and he knew that they were miles from shore. Then it would grow louder and louder as they approached a cape or a large island, and die away as they left it behind.

Once as they brushed the shore, the thundering voice of a jaguar not fifty feet away raised the hair on his scalp. He prayed fervently that the beast had not stepped out upon the floating island.

The biggest scare of the night came when the island scraped over a sandbar and the tree, with its lower branches rubbing on the bottom, began to revolve like a millwheel. Hal had visions of being neatly drowned if the branches to which the hammocks were fastened rolled under. Before this could happen the tree was in deep water and righted itself.

Hal gave up the idea of getting any sleep. He had no sooner done so than he slept, and did not wake until the sun looked in on him.

He scanned the horizon for the Ark, but there was no sign of it.

A faint call came from Roger. Hal climbed through the tree to his brother's hammock. Roger, half asleep, was calling for a drink of water. Hal put his hand on the boy's forehead. The patient seemed a little better.

Roger opened his eyes. He looked about him dully for a moment – then his eyes popped as he saw the swift river and flying shoreline.

"Hey, what's going on? How did we get here? Where's the Ark?"

"I'm glad you're well enough to ask questions," Hal said, and told him all that had happened.

Roger tried to rise but gave it up. "I'm as weak as a cat. Say, how about some breakfast?"

"You really *are* better," said Hal with satisfaction. "But as for breakfast — I'm afraid there will be a slight delay. I'll see what I can do."

He went out into his half acre, determined to make it yield up food and water.

One dare not drink water straight from the river except at the risk of typhoid and dysentery. It must be boiled. But how to boil water without any pan or teakettle, and without any fire?

Then he saw his tea-kettle. A joint of bamboo would do the trick. He went to the clump of bamboos and selected one that would not be too hard to cut with his hunting knife. He cut just below one ring and about eight inches above it. At each ring was a partition closing off the hollow interior. So Hal now had a pot three inches in diameter and eight inches deep. If what he had read was true, this pot would not burn when filled with water and placed over a fire.

But how about the fire? The first thing to do was to gather together something that would burn. Everything he touched was wet with last night's rain and this morning's dew.

Then he thought of the tree in which they spent the night. He took off some of the seed pods, each about twice as large as a walnut. He broke open the shells and found plenty of dry, fluffy cotton, the kapok used for mattresses. This would do nicely as tinder.

Then he cut through the wet bark of the tree. Sure enough the inside layers were dry. There was a plentiful supply of this material, and he piled all he could use upon the tinder.

Now he needed only flint and steel and he could make a fire. The blade of his knife was steel — but he had no flint. A stone might do. He searched his half acre but found not a single stone. The truth is that stones are almost non-existent in the Amazon flood plain. So the flint-and-steel idea was no good.

Well, he would use the fire-thong method. Primitive man had made fire that way — so could he. He found a piece of dry rattan that would do as a thong. He planted a stick slantwise in the ground, slit the end of it, put a little tinder into the slit, and then set to work drawing the thong rapidly back and forth in contact with the tinder.

The friction should make the tinder break into flame. It didn't.

In the South Seas, where he hoped to go, the islanders used the "fire plough". A groove was made in a piece of dry wood and a stick was moved back and forth in the groove so fast that the wood dust broke into flame. Hal rubbed vigorously for half an hour. Nothing broke, except his patience.

He stood with his hands in his pockets, puzzling over the problem. His right hand toyed with something round and flat. He drew it out absent-mindedly and looked at it. It was a lens that he had removed from his camera when he had substituted a telephoto.

"That will do it!" he exulted, and held the lens so that the rays of the sun passed through it and came to a point upon the tinder. In two minutes he had a fire.

Roger smelled the smoke. "Lucky you had matches," he said.

"I didn't have any matches."

"Gee whiz, don't tell me you made a fire without matches! You're getting pretty smart. What did you do, use a fire drill?"

"No," admitted Hal. "A Bausch and Lomb Tessar f 4.5. Afraid I'm not such a hot woodsman."

"Never mind," said Roger. "I'm betting on you."

Hal boiled the water, cooled it, and he and Roger drank.

But they were both hungry. Hal tried plaiting a fishline from grasses, but they broke. Then he discovered a rough piece of driftwood caught on the fringe of the island. Fibres like coarse hair clung to it. It must be the trunk of a piassava tree. This fibre was sold to North America and Europe to be made into brooms and brushes, ropes and cables. If it was good enough for that, surely it would do for a fishline.

While Hal was at work on the line he heard a chattering sound and looked up. A monkey looked down at him from a branch of the tree. Hal seized the weapon that had proved so useless in spearing fish and threw it in approved Indian fashion. It speared the monkey, which fell into Hal's hands. This was luck.

He postponed completing the fishline and immediately skinned the monkey. He laid aside some bones that would make good fish-hooks. He kept also a number of sinews. They could be used as leaders to fasten the hooks to the line. Then he roasted the monkey over the fire and breakfast was served. The fact that the time was nearly noon made the breakfast only more delicious.

Hal finished his line, attached a monkey-bone hook by a monkey sinew, fastened on monkey's knuckle bones as weights, baited the hook with monkey meat, and began to fish.

Presently he felt a strong tug on the line and he had immediately prospects of a fish dinner. He pulled up the fish and was astonished to find that it was only a few inches long. He was still more surprised when, upon grasping it to take it off the hook, it began to grow within his hand. It became too big for his hand, too big for both hands, and reached the size of a football.

He showed the curiosity to Roger. Roger tossed it against a branch and it bounced back like any well-behaved ball. Hal pierced it with the point of his hunting knife and it collapsed like a toy balloon.

"What's the idea of blowing itself up?"

"To frighten its enemies. Just the way a bird in a fight will fluff out its feathers, spread its wings, and raise its crest. Lots of animals act that way. It's animal nature and human nature. Plenty of men pretend to be bigger and more formidable than they really are."

He tossed the fish back into the water, knowing it to be poisonous.

His next catch put up a strong fight before he could get it out.

"It's a snake!" Roger exclaimed, as six feet of writhing fury rose into the air at the end of the line.

"An eel," Hal corrected.

But even Hal did not know that it was an eel of the electric variety until he took hold of it. He promptly let go again and slumped down in the grass, a violent pain coursing through every joint. The island faded out. When he came to, Roger was kneeling beside him.

"You scared me half to death," Roger said. "What struck you?"

Hal could not speak at once. He saw the eel lying in the grass. Roger was too close to it for safety. Hal tried to warn him, but the words would not come.

Roger, squatting on his heels, presently got his rear in contact with the eel. He brushed it only lightly and his trousers protected him, but nevertheless he went up into the air with a yell of pain. He didn't need to ask again what had struck Hal.

The paralysis disappeared gradually, but Hal's joints ached all the rest of the day.

With the true zeal of the collector, he resolved to take home this living storage battery. In the ground he dug a pit which filled with water. Using dry sticks, he pushed the eel into the pit.

"That will take care of it for the time being," he said.

He got Roger back into his hammock. The electric shock had not helped the convalescent.

"Too bad it isn't a cure for malaria," Hal said. "The Indians use it as treatment for rheumatism. And two of the big hospitals in North America send planes down here to collect electric eels for use in medical experiments."

"How much of a shock do you think you got from that thing?"

"I don't know. But they've measured the voltage and find that the average eel packs a wallop of three hundred volts."

"The bigger the eel, the bigger the wallop, I suppose."

"Not always. They tell of one eel only forty inches long that had an electromotive force of five hundred volts."

"Is that enough to kill you?"

"Well, perhaps not. But if you were in the water it would be enough to paralyse you so that you would drown. A good many cattle and horses have died that way. Humans too."

"If we ever get to the Ark, how are you going to carry this thing on board?"

"I've been wondering about that myself," Hal said thoughtfully. "Of course an electric eel doesn't have to shoot the works if he doesn't want to. The discharge is entirely voluntary. It's set off by a little trigger in his brain. It's just possible that if he were handled very, very gently he wouldn't turn on his dynamo."

"You'd be taking an awful chance."

"You're right." Hal's forehead kinked. "If I could just remember – I saw an electric eel taken apart one time in the Rockefeller laboratory. The thing that sets off the discharge is a nerve that runs all the way from the brain to the tip of the tail. If you cut that nerve anywhere, then only the part of the eel between that point and the head can shock you. You can take hold of the tail."

"And when you try this little experiment," said Roger, "be sure to give me a seat with a good view. That's something I want to see."

"No time like the present," said Hal, and he promptly staged the act. Taking his knife, which fortunately had a nonconductive wooden handle, he made a quick, light slash on the eel's back six inches forward of the tail. Then he touched the tail, and felt nothing. He took hold of it, lifted the eel into the air, and dropped it back into the pit.

"Operation successful."

Hal returned to his fishing and in due course pulled out a paiche. When he opened its mouth, several dozen tiny fish spilled out – for the paiche is the extraordinary fish that carries its young in its mouth. A very good precaution, thought Hal, in a river as full of voracious creatures as the Amazon. Particularly the dogfish loves to feed upon paiche small fry – and as soon as the dog-faced brute comes into the neighbourhood the little fellows make a dash for mother, who opens her capacious mouth to receive them. The big paiche made a very satisfactory evening meal.

The next day Hal saw a distant canoe and waved and shouted and even considered firing Croc's cartridge as a signal. The men in the canoe did not see the figure on the floating island.

Far more distressing was the event of the day following, when the Ark itself was sighted, moored to the shore. The island serenely sailed by it at a distance of a mile. Hal might possibly have swum to it in spite of a river full of teeth, but Roger certainly could not. There was nothing to do but sail on.

Croc was not visible – possibly he was in the woods foraging for the menagerie. How would he know what to feed the animals? If Hal did not get back to them soon, half of them would be dead. Or suppose Croc did know how to take care of them? Suppose he got them safely to Manaos and on board a steamer and away? Suppose Hal had to go home empty-handed?

Once you started supposing it was hard to stop. Suppose

he, too, came down with fever, by turns delirious and unconscious, and they both lay helpless in their hammocks until one of the terrific squalls for which the rainy season was famous broke up their island or rolled the tree over and fed them to the fishes.

The next morning Hal awoke to find that his island home was no longer travelling. At least, it was not travelling downstream. It had washed into a bay, and a back eddy was slowly carrying it round and round.

This was maddening. The Ark under full sail would speed by and be lost to him while he doddered around this bay. Every time the floating island came to the mouth of the bay he tried to pole or paddle it out into the main stream, but it was far too big a ship for one sailor to manage. The wind was upstream this morning and exerted just enough pressure on the high branches of the tree to push the mass back into the bay for another round.

Then Hal, looking up river, saw the Ark. It was not under sail. That surprised him – then the reason occurred to him. The same upriver wind that had pushed the island into the bay was making it impossible for Croc to use his sail. The Ark merely drifted with the current.

Hal had a sudden hope. If the wind had eased the drifting island out of the main current and into the bay, why shouldn't it have the same effect upon the drifting boat? Perhaps Croc would be joining him in a few minutes.

He prepared to receive him. He examined his Savage with a grim smile. Then he climbed into the tree and coached Roger.

"Lie still," he said, "and keep quiet."

Roger promptly climbed out of his hammock. "I'm sick of that thing anyhow," he said, wobbling a little as he hung onto a branch. "If there's a fight, I'm going to be in it."

"What can you do?"

Roger's eyes flashed. "I don't know, but I can do something. That fellow is as big as two of you. You'll need me."

"All right, but keep out of sight among the branches. He might see these hammocks," and Hal took them down.

Current and wind were carrying the Ark straight into the mouth of the bay. Hal patted his Savage. He scanned the deck in search of Croc. Finally he saw him, lying on the deck, sound asleep.

The animals called in vain for breakfast. Hal could hear the little tapir's whinny, the deep grumble of the jaguars, the chittering of the tiny marmoset, and the voices of the several birds.

How good everything looked, including Charlie, the mummified head, swinging by his hair from the masthead.

The big stork was as wise and one-legged as ever. The little deer was beautiful. Hal even had affection to spare for the evil anaconda.

The Ark entered the bay and followed the circling island. Hal feared that they would go around indefinitely, a few rods apart. But the island did not float as swiftly as the Ark. The heavy half acre scraped now and then on the bottom or against the shore. The Ark gained upon it and presently was wedged against it.

"Here we go," whispered Hal. Roger carried the hammocks. Hal slipped to the pool and very gently lifted out the eel by the tail. The boys sneaked on board the Ark behind the toldo. Hal laid the eel on the deck. It lay there quietly, never being very active out of water.

With the deck of his boat once more under his feet, the world looked good to Hal. He looked with surprise at the gun in his hand. The lust to kill had gone out of him. His fists felt as if they could do all that was necessary. He laid the gun down.

He stepped around the corner of the toldo. He beamed upon Black Beauty, who returned his advances with a cold stare. He beamed upon the anaconda, which did not trouble to open an eye, being still occupied in digesting the manatee.

More cordial was the pet boa constrictor. She wriggled across the deck to Hal, who leaned to caress her upraised head.

Nosey, the tapir, nosed his leg, and Specs, the marmoset, scrambled up and inside his shirt. Hal took him out, petted him a moment, and put him aside. Inside his shirt might not be a safe place for a marmoset a few seconds from now.

Hal looked down at Croc. The giant lay on his back, his face twisted and ugly even in sleep. He wore one of Hal's holsters and in it was Hal's own revolver. Hal stooped, gently extracted the revolver, and laid it on the anaconda cage.

Then he gave Croc a smart kick in the ribs.

"Uh-uh!" Croc grunted like an annoyed jaguar. His face squirmed as if snakes moved under the skin. His eyes opened by just a crack – then snapped wide as he saw Hal.

He rolled over and came up on his feet all in one motion, slapping his hand to his holster. He found no gun.

He charged into Hal like a wild bull. Hal, although tall and heavy for his age, weighed a good six stone less than his opponent. He stepped aside and let the big fellow go crashing into the toldo. The yellow tiger snarled and the black one roared. The birds squawked.

Croc turned, but before he could throw his weight

forward he got the full impact of Hal's fist in his face. Every shred of muscle the boy could command was put into that blow. He expected to see Croc crumple up.

Croc hardly seemed to notice the blow and came on again. This time his big ham of a fist contacted Hal's forehead and sent him spinning across the deck. His hurtling body knocked the single prop from under the giant stork, which went screaming into the air to the full length of his fifty-foot line.

Before the boy could rise, Croc seized one of the long, heavy oars of the batalao and brought it down with a crash – but not upon Hal, who had rolled out of the way and was now between Croc's legs, trying to upset the monster. He might as well have tried to throw an elephant.

Croc kicked the wind out of him. But Hal rose unsteadily to his feet and came back into the fight. He threw himself upon Croc and backed him against the anaconda cage. Croc flailed out with his heavy right fist. Hal went flat on the deck.

A roar of savage laughter came from Croc. Then he saw the revolver on the cage roof. He seized it and stepped forward to end Hal's troubles.

Then a scream escaped him as he saw a sight so horrible that he would remember it the rest of his life. A great greenish serpent was whirling in the air and coming straight towards him.

Roger, gripping the electric eel by the tail, swung it around his head like a lasso. David with his slingshot never approached Goliath more boldly. The terrified Croc fired, he did not know where or at what.

Now the green-black coils were going around his neck, round and round. An excruciating pain shot through him. His big hulk dropped unconscious to the deck.

27

The Caged Man

Hal and Roger stood looking down at the fallen giant. Hal was badly shaken up and his convalescent brother was puffing after his bout of eel swinging.

"What do we do with him now?" panted Roger. "We've got to do something quick before he comes to."

The electric eel, its good work nobly done, was ambling slowly across the deck towards the water. Hal seized it by the tail, opened the anaconda cage, and managed to get the eel inside.

"It can't hurt the big snake, nor vice versa. And that tub of water is just made to order for an eel."

"But what do we do with Croc? Tie him up?"

"He deserves something worse than that," Hal said. "It would give me great pleasure to scare the liver out of him. He has it coming to him."

Roger's mischief mill began to work. He looked back and forth from Croc to the cage.

"I wonder how he would like the world's scariest snake for a travelling companion!"

Hal chortled. "Fever has made you brilliant, my boy."

They heaved and hoisted until they got the one big giant into the cage of the other. They closed and locked the door. Croc lay not in the water but on the cage floor beside the tub where it narrowed at the end. A foot away from his face was the head of the sleeping anaconda, its body in the tub. Around it swam languidly the hero of the recent encounter, the electric eel.

The colour had drained out of Croc's usually beef-red face. Hal could see no sign that the man still breathed. He began to wonder how he would explain Croc's death to the police at Manaos. If he and Roger sailed into that port with a corpse on board they would most certainly be held for murder. He prayed silently that his worst enemy would come to.

A shiver ran through Croc's big frame. He began to pant.

Then his big eyes opened and he saw within a foot of him a head bigger than his own and almost as ugly. In terror he jerked his own head back and brought it with a resounding crack against the wall of the cage.

He looked about him frantically, found that he was trapped, saw the two boys regarding him with interest. He clawed at the door. He bellowed to high heaven.

"Let me out! Open the door!"

"Better pipe down," Hal advised. "You'll wake your friend and then he'll swallow you."

Croc compressed his voice into a harsh whisper. "If I ever get out of here I'll murder you."

"I know it. That's why you're going to stay in."

Croc arched his body against the tub and tried to break out the wall. But the cage had been made strong enough to withstand all the lashings of the most powerful of serpents. Its three-inch-thick bamboo pillars creaked a little but held fast.

The anaconda's head moved slightly. Croc flattened

himself against the wall and his eyes bulged. Ignorant of snake ways, he could not know that an anaconda, no matter whether asleep or awake, is hardly dangerous when full of dinner. He burst into hysterical curses.

When he saw that he could not frighten his captors into releasing him, he changed his tune.

"Listen, boys, this joke has gone far enough. I know you're good boys. You wouldn't really leave me here to die."

"You left us to die," Hal reminded him.

"Now, buddy, you've got me all wrong. I just wanted to save your collection and your boat, see. Hasn't it all worked out good? The jungle is no place for a coupla boys. I had to take care of you, see."

"We'll take care of *you* now," was Hal's unfeeling reply. "Come on, Roger. We have work to do."

And leaving their prisoner to rage or blubber as he pleased, they went ashore to gather meat, blood, insects and leaves to suit the various tastes of their animals.

"This ought to be the last feeding before we get to Manaos," Hal said.

"Are we that close?"

"We should get there tomorrow, if we have a good wind."

Returning to the shore they found that the floating island had left the bay. That must mean that the contrary wind had died down. They fed the animals, then hauled in the anchor. The Ark also circled out of the bay and into the main stream of the Amazon. A slight breeze was drifting down river. Hal ran up the sail and took his place at the tiller. Roger, still weak from his bout with fever, stretched out on deck close to the cage containing the three devils.

Roger kept watch to see that none of them escaped. The noisiest of the three was Croc. He was mad with fear when the anaconda sleepily opened its eyes and regarded him, stretched its jaws apart in a great yawn, and went to sleep again.

Camp was made for the night on a grassy point, but Croc stayed in his cage. Dried meat was passed to him between the slats. The killer, now in dread of a greater killer than himself, spent an uneasy night. Which was quite unnecessary, for the serpent he so frantically feared slept profoundly.

In the middle of the next morning the water suddenly changed from brown to black. That meant that the Rio Negro, Black River, had joined the Amazon.

The course of the Ark was changed and they sailed ten

miles up the black stream to the great jungle city of Manaos.

At Manaos the Rio Negro is four miles wide. At other points it is fifteen miles wide. And yet it is merely a tributary to the Amazon.

Manaos, where men made fortunes during the great rubber boom, is a thousand miles from the Atlantic Ocean. And yet it is an ocean port, and the boys found its docks full of cargo steamers that had sailed from North America, England or Europe down the Atlantic and a thousand miles up the Amazon to reach this, the greatest city of the Amazon basin.

The Ark, which had seemed so large, looked small in comparison with these ocean liners. The boys made it fast to a pier under the towering stern of a ship from Glasgow. The animals and the savage human in the anaconda cage immediately attracted a curious crowd. Roger undertook to keep guard while Hal went into town to police headquarters.

He asked for and got an interview with the chief of police. He quaked inwardly lest the chief should refuse to believe his story. He was greatly relieved when that dignitary said, "We owe you a great debt, *senhor*. We have word of all this from up river. We have a charge of robbery and incendiarism against this man by one under the name

581

of Pero Sousa, and also complaints from the Cocamas, who charge him with murder of twelve of their people. My officers will accompany you to your boat."

Croc was removed from his cage and taken into custody.

Hal then visited the steamship offices. The result was a contract to transport his collection home on the good ship *Sea Gull*, Captain Brig Harris, master.

And then to the cable office to report to their father the successful outcome of their venture.

The following morning they received his reply:

YOUR MOTHER AND I MUCH RELIEVED TO KNOW YOU ARE WELL CONGRATULATIONS ON A FINE JOB YOU WIN THE TRIP TO THE SOUTH SEAS WILL MEET YOU WHEN YOUR SHIP DOCKS

The next few days were busy ones. Crates had to be made for the animals that had not already been caged. The collection had to be insured – Hal estimated its value at £10,000. The cages had to be hoisted on board the *Sea Gull*. The good old Ark had to be sold. Food had to be stored for the collection during the voyage home.

But it all got done. And there were no happier boys in Brazil, or possibly in creation, than the two who stood at the rail as the *Sea Gull* pulled away from the piers of Manaos into the glossy black current of the Rio Negro. Behind them, in cages occupying half the fore-deck, squawked, growled and chattered their precious menagerie. The removal of Croc from the picture lifted a great weight from their shoulders. Six days down the Amazon and twelve up the Atlantic and they would have their collection safe home.

"And next year the South Seas!" exulted Roger.

"Where I want to capture an octopus," said Hal.

"And I want to go whaling."

"And I want to dive for pearls."

"And I want to get shipwrecked on a desert island!"

ARCTIC & SAFARI
⌇⌐ ADVENTURE DOUBLE ⌐⌇

Hal and Roger Hunt face danger from all sides among the
ice floes of Greenland in *Arctic Adventure*. But is it the killer
whales, the grizzly bears or an evil human who will be
the biggest threat?

And in *Safari Adventure* the boys fly straight into the jaws of
death when they find themselves hot on the blood-stained
trail of a gang of poachers in Africa.

ISBN 0 099 48772 1

SOUTH SEA & VOLCANO
⌇⌐ ADVENTURE DOUBLE ⌐⌇

In *Volcano Adventure* Hal and Roger Hunt's research
into the volatile volcanoes of the Pacific erupts into an
awesome adventure when they join forces with a
world-famous volcanologist.

And they sink even deeper into danger on a top-secret
mission in *South Sea Adventure*, where they're not the only
ones looking for the treasure of Pearl Lagoon ...

ISBN 0 099 48774 8